THE GARDEN OF
LOST SECRETS

ALSO BY KELLY BOWEN

The Paris Apartment

THE GARDEN OF LOST SECRETS

KELLY BOWEN

FOREVER

New York Boston

Copyright © 2023 by Kelly Bowen

Reading group guide copyright © 2023 by Kelly Bowen and Hachette Book Group, Inc.

Cover copyright © 2023 by Hachette Book Group, Inc.

Forever
Hachette Book Group
1290 Avenue of the Americas, New York, NY 10104
read-forever.com
twitter.com/readforeverpub

First Edition: May 2023

Forever is an imprint of Grand Central Publishing. The Forever name and logo are trademarks of Hachette Book Group, Inc.

The publisher is not responsible for websites (or their content) that are not owned by the publisher.

The Hachette Speakers Bureau provides a wide range of authors for speaking events. To find out more, go to www.hachettespeakersbureau.com or call (866) 376-6591.

Library of Congress Cataloging-in-Publication Data

Names: Bowen, Kelly (Romance fiction writer), author.
Title: The garden of lost secrets / Kelly Bowen.
Description: First edition. | New York : Forever, 2023. | Includes
    bibliographical references.
Identifiers: LCCN 2022057892 | ISBN 9781538722145 (trade paperback) |
    ISBN 9781538722169 (ebook)
Subjects: LCSH: World War, 1939-1945--Fiction. | LCGFT: Historical fiction. |
    Novels.
Classification: LCC PR9199.4.B68523 G37 2023 | DDC 813/.6--dc23/eng/
    20221213
LC record available at https://lccn.loc.gov/2022057892

ISBNs: 978-1-5387-2214-5 (trade paperback), 978-1-5387-2216-9 (ebook)

Printed in the United States of America

LSC-C

Printing 2, 2024

"Parents can only give good advice or put them on the right paths, but the final forming of a person's character lies in their own hands."

—Anne Frank

To my mom and dad, who offered wisdom and unconditional support down each path I chose, but more importantly, held me accountable for each one of those choices. For that, I will always be grateful.

THE GARDEN OF
LOST SECRETS

CHAPTER

1

Stasia

The dead man had no boots.

It was the sight of his bare, filthy toes pointed up into the shadows of the narrow alley that made Stasia Neimic stop where she was, her hand frozen on the bars of her bicycle. She had seen dead people before, of course, but those had been as cherished in death as they had been in life and treated accordingly. This man was not cherished. He had been discarded, and Stasia found that realization unbearably sad.

The man had died propped up crookedly against a crumbling brick wall, surrounded by refuse and broken glass. It was difficult to tell how old he was, but the grey in his matted beard and stringy hair suggested that he had been at least her father's age. He was dressed in the remnants of a soldier's uniform from two decades ago, the blue greatcoat almost unrecognizable as anything beyond a buttonless, dull grey tatter.

A knot of pedestrians, their arms laden with baskets and bags from the market, hurried by Stasia, their steps quickening even farther past the mouth of the alley as they either deliberately ignored the dead man or simply chose not to see. Stasia opened her mouth to call after them but then closed it, not sure what she would say. What she would ask for. The dead were beyond anybody's help. But she couldn't just walk away.

Stasia left her bicycle at the top of the narrow lane and picked her way to the body, ignoring the stench of rotting garbage and urine. She crouched down, taking in the claw-like fingers that, even in death, still clutched the neck of a bottle of gin. The ravages of the contents of that bottle, and undoubtably hundreds before it, were written across his sunken and gaunt face, pale and still beneath the beard.

She should at least cover him with something. His coat, perhaps, until she could find someone to collect him. Or maybe there was something in the alley that she could use to—

"Back away. Don't touch him."

The order was snarled, and Stasia shot to her feet, stumbling back.

A boy who couldn't have been much older than Stasia's fifteen years shouldered past her and replaced her in a crouch in front of the body. He was tall and lean, wiry muscle cording his forearms, where his threadbare shirt was pushed up over his elbows. His hair was pale blond and cut very short, his face an arrangement of bitter angles and angry planes.

"Did you touch him?" Cold grey eyes pinned her where she stood.

Stasia found her tongue. "No, I was just—"

"Did you take anything?"

Stasia stared at the boy. "I was going to cover him. You think I would steal something from a dead man?"

He looked away from her and was now rummaging in a worn satchel he had slung across his body. He had pulled out a small paper-wrapped bundle. "He's not dead," he mumbled.

"What?"

The boy placed the bundle in the man's lap and reached for the empty bottle clasped in his lifeless hand. "He's not—"

The man that Stasia had believed dead jerked to life, his eyes snapping open in blind panic, his mouth open in a soundless scream. The arm that held the gin bottle swung wildly, the bottle catching the boy on the side of the head with a hollow thud before shattering. The boy crumpled to the side, and the man in the coat lurched to his feet, only to stagger two steps to the side and collapse again.

Stasia remained frozen where she was for a heartbeat, her breath caught in her throat, too startled to react. The man was now curled in a ball on the ground, his hands over his head, whimpering. The boy had managed to push himself to his hands and knees, a deep gash above his left eye bleeding copiously and leaving bright, scarlet inkblots on the collar and shoulder of his shirt in the dramatic way that scalp lacerations are prone to do. His eyes were squeezed shut, his hands clenched into fists, and he was muttering curses under his breath.

Stasia ignored the man and went to the boy first. "Look at me."

The boy put a hand to his temple and opened his eyes to inspect his bloody fingers as he drew them away. "Shit," he groaned.

She put a hand on his shoulder. "Look at me," she said again in the voice that her grandfather always used when dealing with difficult patients. Direct, firm, but not harsh.

The boy looked up. His eyes were clear and furious as he met her gaze directly. "Don't touch me," he snapped, wrenching away from her.

Satisfied that his faculties seemed to be in order, Stasia stood and retreated, eyeing the gash above his eye. "You're going to need that stitched," she told him. And that was the truth. She'd stitched less grievous wounds on her grandparents' ornery gelding.

He ignored her and slowly pushed himself to his feet, pressing the sleeve of his shirt to his wound.

"Did you hear me? You're going to need that st—"

"I don't need anything, certainly not from you. This is your fault."

"I was just trying to help—"

"I don't need any more of your help," he spat. "You've done more than enough." He pulled his shirt sleeve away and grimaced at the bloodstain. "Shit," he muttered again.

Stasia turned her attention to the man still curled on the ground. Very slowly, she crouched beside him, speaking softly to him the way she might with a terrified child. Gently, she took the broken neck of the bottle from his fingers and set it aside before he could do any more damage, to himself or someone else.

"Can you sit up?" she asked the man in the same voice she had used with the boy.

At the sound of her voice, the man stopped whimpering and dragged himself up and away from her. He was trembling, and he clutched his hands over his ears. "I can hear them," he mumbled. "Always hear them. Always, always. They're comin' back. The planes."

"There are no planes," Stasia told him.

"I told you not to touch him." The boy was back, pushing his body between them. He turned, forcing her back another step. "Go away and leave us alone."

Stasia shook her head, confused at the boy's reaction. She had expected anger directed toward the man who had struck him. At the very least, she might have expected the boy to disappear, but instead he stayed, ignoring his injury and putting himself between the man and Stasia as though she was the threat. "I didn't mean to—"

"Leave." The word was desperate, and it made her pause.

And then retreat.

Stasia stopped where she had left her bicycle but went no farther. She would respect his wishes for the moment but she was not abandoning him. Not until she could assure herself that he was all right. And that he would have his wound tended. Because he hadn't been entirely wrong when he had said that it was her fault.

She watched as the boy helped the man sit back up against the wall, speaking to him in low tones. Seemingly oblivious to the blood that was still sheeting the side of his face, the boy cast about for the paper bundle that had rolled away in the scuffle. Finding it, he unwrapped it and pressed it into the man's hands, his voice rising in argument when the man batted it away. It looked like a piece of cake, Stasia thought. Or maybe part of a loaf, though it was hard to tell from where she stood.

She bit her lip. This man hadn't been discarded after all. She wasn't sure what or who he was to the boy, and she wasn't sure of the circumstances that had brought him to this time and this place, but he still had someone who cared, despite his actions. Somehow, this knowledge made her even sadder.

The exchange went on for a while, the conversation or argument rising and falling in volume, the boy's shoulders slumping and straightening with it. Eventually, he stood and threw up his hands. The man on the ground shouted something unintelligible at him and twisted his face away, his body slouching even farther down the wall. The boy turned, his expression blank, his posture rigid, his eyes firmly on the ground. He stalked toward Stasia, stopping only when he became aware of her presence. The bleeding above his eye had slowed but the skin was already starting to purple and swell.

"Couldn't help yourself, could you?" he sneered. "Had to stay for the show?"

Stasia blinked. "I don't understand—"

"I told you to leave us alone."

"You need to have that cut tended."

The boy made a rude noise and continued walking. She let him get ahead of her before pulling her bicycle from the wall, pushing it as she followed him at a distance. He was headed west, away from the shops and cafés, across Boulevard des Belges, toward the Hôtel-Dieu. Good. Someone at the hospital would tend to his laceration.

Except he didn't seem to be heading to the hospital to find a doctor. Instead, he hurried past the gates of the hospital, head down, wiping at the blood on the side of his face with the sleeve of his shirt again. Two women, dressed smartly in summer frocks and heels, deliberately veered away across the cobbled pavement to avoid him, both tucking their handbags more securely beneath their arms, though if he noticed, he gave no indication. Stasia frowned in disbelief, feeling resentful toward the women for their callousness. Surely they had to see that he was injured? Surely someone cared?

The boy turned and continued down the northwest side of the hospital, pausing only when he reached a pair of battered, utilitarian doors set into the long building. Outside these doors, gathered against the building's stone walls, were stacks of discarded detritus that looked like broken equipment, and it was through this abandoned collection that the boy seemed to be searching for something. From across the street, Stasia watched with bewilderment as he pulled a length of wire from the top of a tangled mess, wound it neatly, and slid it into his bag.

From another pile, he picked an assortment of small parts and pieces, most of which Stasia couldn't identify, and all of which vanished into his satchel with the same practiced efficiency. When he reached the last stack, he paused before he extracted a small tin wedged between the pile and the building. He tipped it over in his hands and grinned, though it almost immediately turned into a grimace as he touched the side of his face.

One of the doors banged open without warning, and the boy whirled, nimbly jumping to the side. A portly man stumbled out, yelling and waving his fist. Stasia couldn't hear what he was saying but his fury was obvious and clearly aimed at the bleeding boy, who now had his bag tucked firmly at his side as he sprinted away from the lane. Without looking back, the boy darted behind a news seller and his stacks of papers and then bolted around him, easily outpacing the puffing hospital employee who was attempting to give chase.

Stasia mounted her bicycle and continued to follow him until he finally slowed and, free from any pursuit, started walking south along the lazy curve of the Seine. For a fleeting moment, she wondered if she should simply leave him be. He'd made it more than clear that her help and her presence were not welcome. In the next moment, she knew that she could not—would not—abandon him. He was hurt, partly due to her actions, and he was even heading in the same direction as her grandparents' farm. Satisfied she had given herself all the justification she needed, Stasia angled her bicycle toward the road.

It wasn't hard to follow him, though she was glad for the bicycle because she didn't think she would have been able to keep up with his long-legged strides otherwise. She drew even with him past the port, where to her left, the river's surface sparkled like diamonds under the bright June sunshine. As he left the city behind, his steps made little puffs of dust that rose and scattered in the breeze, giving a faint chalky scent to the air that was already heavily laced with the pungency of the thick, earthy vegetation lining the river's edge. Stasia slowed enough to keep pace with him, waiting for him to acknowledge her presence.

He didn't.

Up close, Stasia could see that the wound was bleeding again. The swelling was worse, enough so that she doubted he was able to see much out of his eye any longer. Dried blood had crusted in his pale hair and above his ear. If the wound pained him, he didn't show it, but Stasia knew it had to be throbbing with every step he took.

"You really need stitches," she finally said.

The boy said nothing, merely increasing his pace.

"It wouldn't take long," Stasia tried. "And it will heal faster."

"Go away." He kicked at a rock in the road. "Leave me alone."

"No," she replied pleasantly.

"You're just going to follow me then?" He still hadn't looked at her.

"Yes. Until you agree to have your wound tended."

A humourless bark of laughter escaped. "Tended by whom? You?"

"Yes."

That seemed to get his attention. He turned his icy grey eyes on her, though the effect was rather tarnished by the fact that one of those eyes was almost completely swollen shut. "Right. Because you're a doctor." It was a statement loaded with mocking incredulity.

Stasia was used to that. "Not yet."

"What does that mean?"

"It means my mother died of polio when I was six. And as soon as I am old enough to attend university, I will apply to the faculty of medicine and become a doctor and figure out how to keep anyone else's mother or sister or father or son from dying of the same."

His mouth snapped shut, and he looked away from her.

Stasia was used to that response too. Over the years, she had learned that it was better to tell people things like that up front. They always wondered anyway, and at the very least, it prevented the predictable array of snide comments about her ambitions that she would have received otherwise.

"In the meantime, I have learned some basic skills. Stitching cuts that would otherwise leave nasty scars being one of them." She steered her bicycle around a divot in the road, trying to keep the wrapped packages in the basket balanced.

Alongside her own satchel was a packet of wooden buttons, new clothespins, rolling paper and two tins of tobacco, a two-pound canister of sugar, and three bricks of lavender-scented soap. All of which had been on the shopping list her grandparents had furnished her with and all of which now sat in her basket. And all of which would be delivered back to them a great deal faster if this obstinate boy would be a little more agreeable.

"My name is Stasia," she said. "What is yours?"

"You don't know who I am." It was a statement and a question all at once, loaded with suspicion.

"Should I? Are you a prince or something?" She kept her voice light but images of the two women who had hastily avoided him and the hospital man chasing him away sprung to her mind.

"You're clearly not from here."

She snorted. "You've come to that conclusion because I don't know who you are? That is awfully arrogant, no? You really must be a prince." She dropped her voice to a conspiratorial whisper. "Or perhaps a politician."

The boy was staring out at the river. "Maybe I've just come to that conclusion because your French is not good enough to fool me."

"I wasn't trying to fool anyone." Stasia was working hard at perfecting her French, because just good enough at anything had never been good enough for Stasia, but she didn't appreciate the reminder that she hadn't entirely mastered the language. "I live in Rotterdam. I stay with my grandparents for the summers. The Moreaus. Do you know them?"

"No." He tore his gaze from the river and focused on her again. Stasia tried not to wince. The swelling around his eye really was getting worse with each passing moment.

"Where?" he asked.

Stasia waved her hand in the general direction of the thick wood where the river continued to loop south that was a darkened blur from this distance. "The other side of the forest. They have a farm. Wheat and vegetables. Rabbits. Some milk cows and two dozen hogs."

"Why are you staying with them?"

"My father designs and manages ports. He lives in Rotterdam but he often visits ports all over the world for work. Sometimes I go with him, but in the summers, I come here. My grandparents need the help." She paused. "This really isn't fair, you know. I've told you an awful lot about me, and you've still yet to tell me your name."

He sent another stone flying with a vicious kick and said nothing.

"Who was the man you tried to help?" she asked abruptly. "The one I thought was dead?"

He remained silent.

"You were kind. Even after he struck you."

The boy made a strangled noise but didn't answer.

Stasia counted to twenty before she sighed in exasperation. "Fine. I guess I'll just call you Thomas."

"What?"

Stasia pointed at the small tin from behind the hospital that he still held in his hand. It was a blue-and-gold tobacco tin with *Usines Thomas Phillipe, Culdessarts* emblazoned across the front.

The boy she was calling Thomas only grunted.

They continued on in silence for another two miles or so, Thomas studiously ignoring her, and Stasia coasting along on her bicycle studying him. She wondered if perhaps they would go all the way to Le Havre like this, Thomas too stubborn to acknowledge her and Stasia too stubborn to leave him—

Without warning, he abruptly sprinted off the road down a weed-strewn path, vanishing on a trail crowded on both sides by a riot of trees and shrubs all in desperate need of a pruning. Stasia followed him, wondering how she had never noticed the path before, though her musings were cut short as she was forced to dismount or lose her head to the low, overhanging branches. She hurriedly pushed her bicycle, branches and vines clutching at her calves and catching on the hem of her skirt. Other trails forked away into shadowy footpaths, none of them giving any indication of which one Thomas may have taken. She muttered under her breath, certain that by the time she navigated this overgrown gauntlet, Thomas would be long gone. Which was no doubt the idea.

She picked up her pace, as much as that was possible, choosing the route that accommodated her bicycle, and finally stumbled out of the dense canopy of shade, blinking in the abrupt, brilliant sunshine.

And found she had come face-to-face with an angel.

Forever frozen in time, the angel was caught in flight above a jutting stone pillar, her wings unfurled behind her graceful body toward the heavens. A face sculpted in sorrow gazed down, stone hands extended as if reaching for something she'd never grasp. The carving was haunting and beautiful all at once, and Stasia was certain that she had never seen something so poignant. Especially given the extraordinary garden in which the angel resided.

This was nothing like her grandmother's neatly ordered kitchen garden. This garden had crumbling stone walls the color of cream that enclosed the space and were covered with bright amethyst flowers bursting from a curtain of emerald. Tall hedges soared around a riotous rainbow of blooms, shading a myriad of mysterious stone paths and opening into small islands of brilliant sunshine like the one she was standing in. Some of the blooms Stasia recognized—the bold crimson-and-tangerine helenium and the lacy blue-and-violet salvia—because her grandmother grew them too, but there were many she didn't know. Tucked away in the corner was a tiny stone building the same color as the garden walls, squeezed between the umbrella canopies of two dwarf beeches. Rust from the heavy iron handle streaked the lower part of the faded door, while stubborn spots of ancient cobalt paint still clung to the edges of the wood.

Stasia abandoned her bicycle once again, leaning it against the rough bark of a tree, and withdrew her satchel from the basket, slipping it over her shoulder. Captivated, she ventured deeper into the garden. She skirted two massive stone urns, cracked and chipped but still overflowing with greenery as if to make up for it. Trees rose up beyond the far wall of the garden, a dense backdrop of forest filled with cool shadows.

She drew closer to the angel, spinning in a slow circle as she went. It was the sort of place where Stasia couldn't help imagining beautiful princesses in flowing silver gowns walking beside magical unicorns with flowing silver manes. She could envision fairies and elves flitting about in this hidden, sun-kissed world, and if Stasia listened hard enough, she fancied she could hear the twinkle of their wings under the drone of the bees tending the flowers and the songs of the larks in the branches. Her fingers were itching to pull her pencils from her bag and start drawing the visions that danced in her head—

A low curse jarred her out of her fantasy. As enraptured as she was, Stasia had missed Thomas sitting in the shadow of the stone angel, almost invisible in the tall grass at its base. He cursed again, breaking her enchantment altogether, and she watched as he bent his head in renewed concentration.

Silently, Stasia observed him and, after a moment, realized that he was bent over the stolen tobacco tin, attempting to roll a cigarette. After another moment of covert observation, it became clear that he had never rolled a cigarette before.

"I can show you how to do that if you like," she offered.

Thomas jerked to his feet, the paper fluttering away and tobacco scattering to the ground like crooked brown snowflakes. "Jesus Christ," he growled.

"No, just me."

"What did I do to deserve this? What will it take to get rid of you?"

"Let me tend your cut, and then I'll leave."

"I told you I don't need or want your help. With *anything*." He edged farther away from her.

"I don't really care what you think you don't need," Stasia replied, withdrawing a small pouch from her bag.

"What the hell is that?"

"A medical kit. I can clean and suture your wound right here."

"You're completely daft, you know that?"

Stasia ignored his hostility. "My grandfather was a stretcher-bearer in the war," she told him. "The first aid he rendered in the field before he got the soldiers to the ambulances often meant the difference between life and death."

"I'm not dying," he snapped.

Stasia ignored that too. "Now he keeps little kits like this with him wherever he goes, just in case. He taught me to do the same. You'd be surprised how often *daft* turns into *helpful*." She took a step toward him.

"You're not fucking touching me," he snarled. He took another step back, looking like an injured animal about to bolt.

Stasia stilled. Then, very slowly, she slid the little medical pouch back into her bag. "Fine. I won't touch you." She moved away from him. "And I will leave. But not until I draw the angel."

"Till you do what?"

She pointed above his head. "Draw the angel."

"Why?"

"I like drawing. And writing stories," she said easily. That he was still talking to her meant that he hadn't fled. She was determined to keep it that way.

"About stone angels?"

"About all sorts of things. And this angel looks sad."

"It's a piece of rock," he grated. "Rocks don't have feelings."

Stasia wandered around the other side of the sculpture, looking for the best vantage point. She paused as a slate roof and upper row of faceless, rectangular windows became visible over the riot of vibrant greenery. "Oh," she blurted, "we're behind Château de Montessaire."

"Thank God you're planning to be a doctor and not a detective," Thomas sniped, and Stasia laughed, which seemed to surprise them both.

She'd seen the same roofline and top floor windows from the road many times before but she'd been distracted and had failed to realize that they were already this close to home. Her grandparents' farm was on the other side of the forest that bordered the back of this garden. In truth, Château de Montessaire was their closest neighbour, though she had never been on the vast property.

The château had been built at the top of a rolling hill by an early Comte de Cossé in the middle of the eighteenth century, purportedly for his beloved bride, who had died before the château was ever finished. Or at least that was the story Stasia had been told. Château de Montessaire, still in the hands of what remained of the de Cossé family, stood now overlooking the river and the surrounding area, presiding like a sad, lonely, once grand queen over her subjects. But if Stasia had known that this garden existed, she would have visited long before.

She settled down on a patch of grass where the sun's rays hit the sculpture at the perfect angle. She opened her bag, aware that Thomas was still watching her, and took out her sketch pad.

"You're serious. You're still not leaving."

"After I finish my drawing," Stasia assured him. "I promise."

He was silent for a handful of heartbeats, and then he asked, "What else do you have in your bag?"

"My pencils. Receipts for my grandmother. My canteen."

"Got any food?"

"A biscuit."

"That's it?"

"Yes."

He sighed loudly, as if this were an unforgivable oversight on Stasia's part.

"Would you like it?" Stasia pulled out the kerchief-wrapped biscuit and offered it to him, thinking of the piece of cake he had left with the man in the alley. "I'm not really hungry."

Thomas hesitated and then took it from her warily, as if half expecting her to snatch it back. He retreated and shoved the biscuit in his mouth. "It's a grave," he said abruptly.

"What is?"

"The angel you're drawing. Pull back the vines and you'll see the dates underneath. The dead girl was about your age." He paused. "Died about sixty years ago and was buried right here," he added around a mouthful of crumbs.

"Oh?" She reached for her pencil.

"And there's another one."

"Another what?"

"Grave. Right beside the angel one. It has a little flat marker but you can't see it because of all the grass. That one is for an old lady."

"Mmm." Her pencil was poised over the paper, yet the first lines that would shape the beautiful sculpture didn't come. Instead, her gaze dropped from the angel, and now her pencil flew in swift, sure strokes.

"And it's haunted. This garden."

"Ghosts are things people make up to keep other people away and out of their business," she told him.

"Clearly it's not working very well," he muttered.

Stasia laughed again.

Thomas threw up his hands and bent to retrieve the cigarette paper from the long blades of grass. "You're trespassing, you know," he said.

The image on her page took shape. "So are you."

"No, I'm not."

"Of course you are—" Stasia's pencil froze.

Slowly, she looked up to find that Thomas had resumed his seat under the angel. A new cigarette was being rolled, with even less success than the first.

"You're not a prince," she said into the silence.

He made a rude noise but otherwise ignored her.

"You're not a prince," she repeated. "You're the Comte de Cossé."

CHAPTER

2

Nicolas

8 JUNE 1935
ROUEN, FRANCE

The Comte de Cossé was long dead.

Everyone knew this, of course, except for this girl from Rotterdam. And the idea that she actually believed that he was the comte of anything was enough to startle a laugh from somewhere deep inside of him. And once that first sound had escaped, another followed, more bubbling and spilling out of him until he was doubled over, gasping for breath, his good eye watering with tears.

It was only the stabbing throb of his face that slowed his laughter. That, and the warm trickle of blood as it slid down the side of his face where his cut had opened again and now splattered onto the edge of the cigarette paper still clutched in his fingers.

"Shit," he muttered, wiping the edge of the paper, the laughter draining as quickly as it had come, leaving him with a wretched emptiness inside. He closed his good eye and rubbed his temple with the heel of his hand.

"Here." Long fingers plucked the paper from his, and Nicolas started, unaware that the girl with the eyes the color of expensive brandy, hair the color of dark cinnamon, and wearing a simple blouse and skirt the color of a summer sky, had settled herself beside him on the grass. "You're wasting your tobacco."

"Never asked you, did I?" he mumbled but his response lacked any real animosity because he was too distracted watching those quick, capable fingers smooth and then crease the paper with effortless efficiency.

She held out her hand. "Pass me the tin."

Wordlessly, Nicolas obeyed.

She set the paper in her palm and then pinched a new measure of tobacco, placing it carefully along the paper's crease. "The trick is to roll it to tighten the tobacco before you try to tuck the paper," she said, grasping the new cigarette between her thumbs and forefingers and doing just that. "And the gum has to face you along the top." She slipped the lower edge of the paper beneath the top, rolled it deftly, licked the gummed edge, and ran her thumb along the seal. "All done." She held out the cigarette.

"How'd you learn to do that?" He took it from her slowly.

"I roll my grandfather's cigarettes for him. He taught me."

"He can't do it on his own?" He regretted the scornful words as soon as he uttered them.

"He lost his fingers on his left hand in the war. It's easier for me."

"Oh." He was holding the cigarette awkwardly.

Nicolas didn't miss the way her eyes went to the side of his face, though there was no pity there. Only consideration. And a steady kindness that had yet to waver since she had appeared unwanted in that alley. Yet she said no more about tending to his wound.

Instead, she asked, "Are you going to smoke that?"

"Maybe."

Stasia slipped a hand into a pocket sewn into her skirt and withdrew a lighter. She flipped it open, and the flame jumped. So did Nicolas.

"May I?" she asked, holding out the flame.

"Your grandfather give you that too?" He tried and failed to keep the envy from his voice.

"My grandmother." Stasia lit the end of his cigarette. "She too believes that it's necessary for a woman to always be prepared."

"You're not a woman." Nicolas instantly regretted that too because that was untrue. And her age had nothing to do with it.

Stasia only tucked the lighter back in her pocket without comment and sat back, resting easily against the base of the stone pillar, the angel hovering above their heads. Her face was tipped toward the sun, her eyes closed and her dark lashes making long, curved shadows across cheeks dusted with a faint constellation of freckles. A smile tugged at her lips.

Did nothing offend her?

"I'm not a comte," Nicolas muttered. "And certainly not the Comte de Cossé. I am nothing." He took a tentative puff on his cigarette and immediately coughed. And kept coughing.

"Takes awhile to get used to it," Stasia said, sounding amused.

"I beg your pardon?" Nicolas wheezed as he stubbed out the cigarette, not willing to embarrass himself further.

"I near coughed up a lung the first time I smoked." Her eyes were still closed, and she was grinning now, a dimple appearing on her left cheek that he hadn't noticed before. "So please don't stop on my account, Thomas."

"Nicolas," he said suddenly. "My name is Nicolas Navarre."

"Oh." She opened her eyes and sat up. "It's nice to meet

you then, Nicolas Navarre. I might have called you Thomas forever."

He waited but the distaste and derision that usually came with mention of the Navarre name was absent. Instead, the silence stretched on, broken only by the sharp song of a bird somewhere in the garden. "My father is Etienne Navarre."

Stasia gave him a curious look. "I'm not sure what you're trying to tell me."

"That was the man you met in the alley. The one who gave me this." He touched his swollen eye and waited for her reaction.

"Oh" was all she said. "I wondered."

"Your grandfather may have lost his fingers in the war but my father lost his mind. When I was a kid, he'd have these headaches. Wouldn't sleep for days. Couldn't remember even the simplest of things. And as I got older, it only got worse. Now, in the intervals when he's not in prison, he roams the streets of Rouen with whatever imaginary demons that dance in his head, destroying everything he touches." He had no idea why he'd said all that.

The girl sitting beside him said nothing.

"My mother tried to fix him but died trying. I can't fix him either."

Still, she said nothing.

"He's a weak and immoral man." The words kept tumbling out, and he seemed unable to stop them. "At least that is what they say. Because everyone else who fought in those trenches and survived came home and was strong enough to get on with their lives. Even those with horrible injuries. My father came out of that war without a scratch." He stopped to take a breath. "I don't know why I'm telling you this other than someone will tell you anyway—"

"And this is why you are determined to make me leave?" she interrupted, sounding merely . . . thoughtful.

"There is a German proverb that says the apple does not fall far from the stem." Nicolas repeated the phrase he'd heard over and over.

"Ah." Stasia stared at him for a moment before she crawled across the grass and retrieved her bag, paper, and pencil, then returned to sit across from him. She started drawing again, occasionally glancing up.

Nicolas ground his teeth in frustration. It was as if she hadn't heard a word he'd said. This girl from Rotterdam, who had pedalled herself into his life in a blinding ray of breathtaking beauty and misplaced compassion, who couldn't possibly know anything about him because she came from a world that was nothing like his and would return to go places where he could never follow, wasn't understanding what he was trying to—

"My grandfather," she said, breaking into his muddled thoughts, "still wakes up screaming some nights, and the only thing my grandmother can do is sing quietly until he sobs himself back to sleep. We never speak of it in the mornings. Twice a week, he has me load, fire, and clean his pistols, and the urgency and rigour with which he expects me to complete those tasks is not part of a simple firearms lesson. And then there are the medical kits." She paused. "I'm fairly sure that some small part of him believes the Germans will come back, though he's never admitted that to me. We never speak of the Germans either." She frowned at the page and bent to make a correction. "So by your logic, he too is weak and immoral. As am I, for I share the same familial branch from your proverb."

"You're not weak. Or immoral." The fierceness of his words caught him off guard.

"You don't know that. You don't really know me."

"I know that you are kind."

"Perhaps I am kind and weak and immoral."

"That's ridiculous."

"It is, isn't it?" Her pencil resumed its travails.

Nicolas opened his mouth and then closed it again. "I know what you're trying to do. But you don't really know me either," he finally stammered.

"True," she allowed. "But an immoral man doesn't try to protect a veritable stranger with noble, if idiotic, logic. Nor does a weak man sit in a garden and tell a veritable stranger difficult truths about himself like you did."

"Maybe it's because you are a stranger that I can."

"Perhaps you're right." She narrowed her eyes. "But what happens when we become friends? Will you still tell me truths? Or is that when we should start lying to each other?"

When we become friends. Nicolas rolled that statement around in his head, feeling as though he had been set adrift and uncertain how to proceed upon this sea of brutal, plainspoken honesty that he hadn't expected and wasn't sure he wanted. "I don't have friends."

"You may never be able to fix him, you know," she said, as if he hadn't even spoken. "Your father. He is broken in ways that you and I can't see or even imagine. But I do know he's not the only one, only less skilled at hiding it. All you can do is love him, even if that seems impossible sometimes."

"Mostly I hate him." The admission slipped out.

"If you truly hated him, you wouldn't care." She put her pencil down on the grass beside her. "Here." She tore the paper from her pad and held it out to him.

Nicolas took the drawing from her hand, turning it slowly, unable to take his eyes from it. Looking at the image was a little unsettling. It was like looking in a mirror, yet the person on the page was not him. She had drawn his torso and head in profile, and the swollen, raw mess that was undoubtably the other side of his face was invisible. His bloodstained shirt had been replaced by a swirling cloak, and the stolen cigarette in his hand had been exchanged for a gleaming sword.

He touched the corner of the page with his finger. "I don't understand."

"I made you a prince."

"Why?"

"Because you are not nothing, Nicolas Navarre."

Nicolas wasn't able to answer through the peculiar emotion that was tightening his chest and throat.

She slid her pencil and paper back into her satchel and pushed herself to her feet. "And drawing you was much more satisfying than drawing a rock." She slid her bag over her shoulder. "*Bonne chance*, Prince Nicolas."

"Where are you going?" he managed roughly.

"I promised you I'd leave when I finished my drawing. I can't imagine breaking promises is a good way to start a friendship." She started toward her bicycle.

"Stay." He didn't care that that single word might have sounded desperate.

She stopped in her tracks and slowly turned. "If you let me tend to your face, I will."

"All right." Dimly, he was aware that he had probably just been manipulated. But somehow he no longer cared. As long as she stayed.

"Good."

They stared at each other across the sun-soaked clearing.

She was the first to look away. "Do you have a chair? Or a bench? It would be best if you were sitting and I could stand."

He rose, careful not to crease the drawing. "In the shed. I'll fetch it." He hurried toward the tiny stone building, put his weight behind the ancient wood door, and stepped inside. There was a potting stool that would—

"Do you live here?"

He spun. Stasia had followed him and had wandered to the long counter that ran the length of one side, opposite the wall with a ragged cot jammed between cluttered collections of old shovels and rakes and shears and hoes, the tools draped in silvery spider webs.

"Maybe," he mumbled, carefully putting the drawing up on a crude shelf where it wouldn't get damaged. He reached for the small stool.

"Does no one from the château care if you're here?"

"No one lives there. So no, no one cares."

"Why not just live in the château then?" she asked. "If it's empty?"

He picked the stool up with a jerk. "A hired man from the city comes to check it every week. Last year, there were workers here for a month fixing the roof because someone was supposed to move in. They never did but I don't want to be caught. It's easier to stay here. No one ever comes into the garden."

"Have you ever been inside the château?"

"Yes."

"Will you show it to me?"

"No."

"Oh." She didn't seem offended. "What happened to the people who used to live in the château?"

"They're all dead. I heard some relative owns it now."

"And they don't want it?" She sounded incredulous.

"Dunno. But they haven't sold it, so even if they don't really want it, I guess they don't want anyone else to have it either."

"That's so sad that no one loves it anymore." She tipped her head. "It deserves better."

"It's just a building," he muttered. "At any rate, I can keep my things here, and no one bothers me." He nodded at his workbench.

"Your things?" Stasia repeated, distracted. She picked up a ragged book from the top of a pile near the edge of the bench and ran her fingers over the title. "*Electricité, A.L Guyot, Applications Domestiques et Industrielles, Conseils Pratiques, Formules, Plans et Devis*," she read. "That sounds complicated."

Nicolas abandoned the stool and snatched the book from her hands. "Not really." He placed the book reverently back on the pile, torn between equal parts of relief that they were no longer speaking of family and of trepidation that she was handling his things.

Unfazed, she turned her attention to a polished wooden box, the corner of it shattered and scarred, the disembowelled insides hanging out the back. "A radio," she said, turning it over.

"Yes." He took that from her hands too. "It's not fixed yet." He put it aside.

"You can fix them?"

"Yes."

She was running her fingers over the top of a toaster, one hinged door missing. "What else do you fix?"

"Toasters. Irons. Percolators. Fans. Whatever I can find."

"Where do you get all of the pieces and parts?"

"Places." He knew he sounded defensive.

"You mean you steal them?"

"Sometimes." It was better that he reminded her exactly what kind of person he was.

"Does that make you feel bad?"

"What kind of question is that?"

She shrugged but didn't answer.

"I don't have the luxury of feeling bad," he sneered.

"What do you do with all these things when you fix them?" Now she sounded merely curious.

He frowned at her apparent disregard for his admitted thievery. "Survive. Sell them. Trade them for food or clothes."

"How did you learn how to do that? Fix these things?"

"I took some apart. Figured it out. And there are books that tell you how the electricity works and drawings that show where pieces go. It's not hard."

She gave him a long look. "If it wasn't hard, everyone would do it. You underestimate yourself."

Nicolas shrugged uncomfortably, unwilling to argue and well aware that this conversation had once again veered into unfamiliar territory. .

She spun in a slow circle, examining the rest of the shed's interior. "It must be very dark in here at night."

He shrugged again. "I don't mind the dark."

"Here." She dug in her pocket and her lighter appeared in her hand. She held it out to him. "You should have this."

"Why?"

"In case it gets too dark and you need a light." She pressed it into his hand and only let go when his fingers curled around it.

He looked down at the dull pewter gleam in his palm. "I don't want your charity."

"It's not charity. It's just good sense." Cheerfully, she snatched up the stool and marched out of the shed. "Hurry up," she called over her shoulder.

Nicolas followed her, the lighter clutched in his hand. He

would never have given something so valuable away, especially to someone he didn't know. "Why are you being so nice to me?"

"I'm not being nice. I'm being useful. Now sit." She pointed to the stool and set her bag on the ground.

Nicolas sat. "Are you this nice to everyone?" It came out far more harshly than he had intended but she was making him feel . . . vulnerable. Exposed. And he didn't know what to do about it.

She bent to rummage in her bag. "I don't know. I never really thought about it."

"How can you live like that? Isn't it exhausting? Always happy all the time? Always thinking the best of everyone?" He was still being unnecessarily harsh but he couldn't help himself.

She was still bent over her bag. "My grandmother says that your soul is like an empty pail, and that you get to choose what you fill it with. You could fill it with happiness and kindness, which are light, or anger and sadness, which are heavy. Now, no one can be happy all the time because sad things happen to everyone, but a light pail can always accommodate a little sadness without dragging you down."

"That's the stupidest thing I ever heard."

Stasia looked up at him and grinned briefly before continuing her search. "You asked me a question, and that is my answer. I don't need your approval."

Nicolas reflected that, in that moment, he had never felt smaller.

"I think I'll write a story about you," she said, her words somewhat muffled.

He almost fell off his stool. "What?"

"Hold this." She straightened and thrust the little pouch she had brandished earlier into his lap.

"I don't—" he started but never got any further because her hands were sliding over his scalp, gentle and sure all at once, tipping his head back.

"Close your eyes," she instructed, "and don't move."

He closed his eyes, or at least the one that wasn't already swollen tightly shut. He felt her take something from the kit on his lap and then something soft and damp was being dabbed around his cut, a sharp, acrid scent assailing his nose.

"Yes," she murmured as she continued, "I think you shall make a very fine prince in my story."

"I don't want to be in a story," he said. "And I thought you were going to be a doctor."

"Writers and doctors aren't exclusive." She laughed. "I write and illustrate lots of stories because I like doing it. Mostly fairy tales. I'll write you into one that will be something like Little Briar Rose. It's my favourite."

"I don't even know what that is."

The dabbing stopped. "What?"

"This Briar Rose story. And aren't you a little old for fairy tales?"

The dabbing resumed. "Fairy tales are crafted to remind us of our humanity. Of our principles and moralities."

Nicolas scoffed.

"Little Briar Rose is a story about a princess cursed by an evil fairy to sleep for a hundred years, until a prince wakens her with a kiss and they fall deeply in love and live happily ever after," Stasia told him. "I always liked that part best. And no one is too old for happy-ever-afters. Isn't that what everyone wants? Happiness?"

"If you say so."

The cloth lifted from his skin, and once again, she delved into the pouch on his lap.

"This part might sting a bit," she said, and he felt her warmth at his shoulder. Her fingers probed carefully around his cut, and he stiffened.

Stasia didn't seem to notice. "At any rate, that's the Grimm brothers' version of the story," she said as she worked. "The older version of the story is longer. And a little more macabre. I suspect you'll like it better."

A sharp sting over his eye, followed by a tug as she put the first stitch in, made him swallow. His fingers tightened around the edges of the lighter he still held in his hand.

"After the prince wakes the princess with a kiss," Stasia went on easily, as if she were sitting in a fancy parlour drinking cognac and not in an abandoned garden stitching a wound, "they fall madly in love, and they marry in secret and have two children. Eventually, the prince becomes king, and he brings his family to his castle. When the prince's mother, who is actually an ogre, discovers this, she orders her cook to kill the children and serve them with sauce."

Despite himself, Nicolas's lip curled. "That's disgusting."

"Oh, but it gets better. The cook, being a kind woman, substitutes livestock to trick the queen mother. But then the evil queen orders the death of the princess." She gently tipped his head farther to the side.

Nicolas resisted the sudden, insane urge to simply lean into her steady warmth. When was the last time someone had touched him with such care? When was the last time someone had simply cared?

"The cook once again deceives the queen mother and saves the princess, but not for long. The queen mother discovers the cook's trick and prepares a giant tub of vipers and other deadly creatures in the hope that she can finally get the job done and rid herself of the beautiful princess once and for all."

Another sharp prick tugged at his brow but he ignored it. "That sounds rather extreme, no?"

"Maybe." Her breath tickled his cheek, and she shifted.

He heard the snick of scissors but Stasia remained silent.

"Well, then what happened?" he demanded.

She chuckled under her breath. "The prince arrives in the nick of time to see the queen mother's true nature. The ogre, now exposed, throws herself into the tub and justly meets the grim fate that she had intended for the princess."

"I'm supposed to believe that the prince had no idea that she was an ogre? For his entire life?"

"Don't frown," Stasia admonished him. "You're wrinkling my stitch."

Nicolas forced himself to relax his expression, unaware until then that he had been frowning. "I don't want to be a prince in any story if princes are all that stupid."

"Fair point. I'll write a different story with a clever prince," she assured him. "But you could consider that maybe the prince's mother was just very good at hiding who she really was."

He felt her step away from him. "No one is that good."

"Mmm. Maybe. At any rate, I'm done."

"What?" He opened his good eye to find her studying his brow critically.

"I'm done. It only needed five stitches. It will heal quickly, I think."

"Five?" He lifted his hand to the wound but she swatted it away.

"Don't touch it."

"You told me that story to distract me."

"Did it work?" She was smirking.

"Maybe."

"So you do like fairy tales." She sounded positively smug.

Nicolas tried to hide a smile, a strange, foreign feeling. "Maybe."

"I'll tell you another one if you come back to the farm with me and let me put ice on the swelling," she said. "Yes?"

His smile faded.

Stasia's face fell but she only shrugged. "It was worth asking." She scooped up the pouch and closed it then fetched her bag from the grass. She wandered back toward her bicycle.

Nicolas sat frozen on the stool beneath the angel, unable to utter anything, words trapped and bouncing around his mind, careening into unfamiliar emotion.

"Perhaps I will see you again?" she asked, as she pulled her bicycle from the tree where it leaned. "Perhaps I might come back here in a few days? At least to look at your stitches?"

Still he couldn't find the right words.

"Well, it was nice to meet you, Prince Nicolas." Stasia tucked her bag into the basket and started toward the path that would take her back out to the road. "Thank you," she said suddenly, stopping to look back at him.

Which made no sense at all because she had given him her food, her lighter, her drawing, her care, and her kindness while he had given her nothing. Worse than nothing.

"Thank you," she repeated. "For your trust."

Nicolas's heart missed a beat, and he finally found the right word. "Yes," he said.

"Yes?" She looked at him quizzically.

"I'll come with you."

And the girl from Rotterdam smiled.

CHAPTER

3

Isabelle

8 NOVEMBER 2021
ROUEN, FRANCE

Isabelle Lange's heart missed a beat as she stared at the château. Or rather, as she stared at the sign being hammered into the overgrown grass that lined the long drive in front of the château. Yanking the wheel of her truck to the side, she pulled off the road and brought her vehicle to a shuddering stop. She turned off the ignition and hopped out, turning her hood up against the bite of the November wind and the low clouds that still threatened more drizzle.

For Sale was emblazoned in a bright red flourish across the white sign, above the stylized proclamation of *Luxury Estates and Exceptional Properties*. A number and the name of a Paris agency she didn't recognize was written in fancy lettering just beneath. The man who stepped back to cast a critical eye on his handiwork, however, she did recognize.

"Luc?" Isabelle asked with delighted disbelief as her boots crunched on the weed-strewn gravel.

Luc Legassé looked up from the sign, and the familiar, instant grin that hadn't changed since he was five years old spread across his tanned face. "Izz," he said, dropping the hammer into the toolbox at his feet, and in two steps, he had enveloped her in a crushing hug.

Isabelle allowed herself the indulgence of leaning into his strength for a brief moment, inhaling the scent of woodsmoke, wool, and the faint undertones of soap.

Abruptly, he pulled back to gaze at her, brown eyes shining, his grin still firmly in place. "I was hoping to run into you soon. You look wonderful."

Isabelle felt her cheeks flush as the object of such unapologetic warmth. "I don't look wonderful, I look a mess," she said, glancing down at her clothes covered with streaks of grease and plaster dust from her last job. "And filthy."

Luc shrugged. "Still wonderful." He ran a hand through unruly, coffee-colored hair, dark above the collar of his rough canvas work jacket and accessorized by the pencil he had stuck behind his ear. "How have you been?"

"Busy," she told him. That wasn't a lie. "I didn't know you were back."

"Got back last weekend," he told her.

"Where were you working this time? You're still tanned."

"Couple of resorts in Bali and one in Bora-Bora. Moved a boat for a client to Palau."

"And you came back to this?" Isabelle glanced up at the leaden, moody sky and the wet, naked branches of the trees. "Voluntarily?"

He shrugged. "Cyclone season. Most tourists head back up north, and the work goes with them." He shoved his hands in his jacket pockets. "And I didn't want Dad to be left alone over the holidays." His dark eyes settled on her. "I was sorry to hear about your father."

Isabelle nodded, knowing the movement probably looked as stiff as it felt. "Thanks. But he's doing much better now. It will take more than a stroke to fell Richard Lange."

"That's good to hear. How's your mom holding up?"

"Fine." On some days.

"And your sis—"

"What are you doing now?" Isabelle blurted before he could finish his question. She really did not want to stand here talking about her family.

He shrugged again. "What needs to be done. Wherever it needs."

Which, for all the years that Isabelle had known him, completely summarized the itchy-footed, free-spirited life of Luc Legassé. "How long are you here for this time?"

"Planning on sticking around for a bit."

"Oh?" She didn't bother hiding her pleasure. "I'm glad."

"Don't suppose you need an extra carpenter on any of your jobsites?" he asked.

"So this is why you were hoping to see me. You need me to give you a job."

"No." A horrified look crossed his face. "God, no. That's not at all—"

Isabelle laughed. "I'm teasing you, Legassé."

"I knew that."

"Mmm-hmm." She was still smiling, and it felt good. It had been a long time since she had laughed with such ease. "So you're not selling luxury estates and exceptional properties?" she asked, gesturing at the sign.

It was Luc's turn to laugh, his eyes crinkling in the corners.

"Hardly. A friend of a friend knows the listing agent and suggested that I help him out. I've been hired to put up signage and get the grounds into some sort of order to be more attractive for potential buyers." From his toolbox, he pulled out a clipboard with a sheaf of papers, all with the same agency logo across the top. "The agent knows that this place is, ah, less than move-in ready. The price will reflect it, I've been told, but at the very least, the hope is that cutting the grass and clearing the front will make it look less of a wreck. It might appeal to an overseas buyer."

Isabelle barely heard him. "Show me."

"What?"

"Show me the château."

"What, you're going to buy it?" He sounded amused.

"Yes." Not a whole truth. Once upon a time, she and her sister had promised each other that if this building ever came up for sale, they would buy it together. Once upon a time, she and her sister had made grand plans for the abandoned château. Emilie, head of her own award-winning architectural firm, and Isabelle with her small but sought-after restoration company.

The perfect team to make the château whole again. Once upon a time.

"It's a listed property," she prompted. "Which means it will be eligible for grants and tax incentives."

"You're serious." Luc was staring at her.

"Yes. Provided the financing is doable."

"You'd restore it?"

"Yes."

"And do what with it?"

"Make it a destination. A place where visitors from all over the world would come to stay and experience Château de

Montessaire and all the history that surrounds it. Every incredible thing that is Normandy—" She stopped. "You're looking at me like I've lost my mind."

"I think you might have." He glanced down at the clipboard. "Built in 1730. Extensive damage in 1789." He tapped his pencil on the paper. "Let them eat cake and all that."

"I'm aware," Isabelle answered drily. "Revolutions are messy."

He continued reading from the clipboard. "Repairs done in 1791. Remodelling work recorded in 1840 and again in 1874, and who knows what that means, though probably nothing good. Roof repair in 1934, and again in 1970. Fire damage to the northwest ground floor in 1944, and that remains unrepaired. Unoccupied and empty since then." He looked up at her. "Do you know how much work a place like this will be?"

"I don't know, Luc. I've spent my entire career here in Normandy, restoring historic buildings, while you've been puttering around the Mediterranean and Caribbean and Pacific and who knows where else, banging together docks and tiki huts and umbrella bars for tourists. But please, tell me. How much work would a project like this be?"

"Touché." He held up his hands.

Isabelle bit her lip and sighed. "I'm sorry. That was rude." Luc came and went like the seasons but he worked harder than anyone she knew save, perhaps, herself. Her words made her sound like a shrew, jealous of Luc and his freedom.

Then again, she was still living in the same family farmhouse she had grown up in. Perhaps she was jealous.

"No." He sounded amused again. "That was deserving. An appropriate answer for a stupid question."

"Not a stupid question at all. A reasonable one." Isabelle

dropped her gaze, still feeling foolish and not a little ashamed. "I would give anything to see the places you've been. Are they all as magical as they look in ads and movies?"

"Movies don't even begin to do them justice. I'd show them all to you. In any order you like. You just have to say the word." He sounded earnest, and Isabelle felt foolish all over again. As if she could ever simply drop everything to explore beaches halfway around the world.

"Maybe," she mumbled, knowing maybe was an unlikely stretch. "In the meantime, will you show me the château?" she asked. "Please?"

"Of course." Luc bent down and picked up his toolbox, tucking the clipboard under his arm. "I don't have the key. The firm is sending an appraisal team this week before they officially list it and make it available for viewing. The agent will want to show you the interior of the property himself. But we can take a look at the outside for now if you like."

"Very much."

"Have you ever been inside?"

"No. Never. But I've imagined a million times what it might look like from the details in the stories my great-gran wrote about this place." Isabelle felt excitement crackle through her as she fell into step beside Luc and headed up the drive.

"I'm supposed to take photos and document existing exterior damage. Probably best that you're here," he continued. "You'll likely know more than me what needs to be fixed and how much it will cost. I can't imagine that there are too many umbrella bars on the grounds. I'll be out of my element."

She deserved that. She swiped at the ends of an overgrown bush crowding the edge of the drive. "Very funny."

"I thought so."

"Do you know who's selling?" she asked, hustling to keep up with his long stride.

"Think so." He grasped the clipboard from beneath his arm and consulted the top corner of the page. "Jacques Neville Brodeur. With a current address in... Tokyo. Ever heard of him?"

Isabelle shook her head. "No."

"Probably the last stop in the de Cossé family when the inheritance train ran out of track. Either way, he doesn't want it." He paused as they reached the top of the drive, the château looming up in front of them out of a ragged, grasping sea of unkempt shrubs, bushes, and vines. The wind gusted, sending a storm of dead leaves swirling.

They both stared up at the building.

The château wasn't large, certainly nothing compared to Chambord or Chantilly, and had been built for function rather than folly, though was no less beautiful for it. Perhaps more so, because it was a place that one could envision more as a home and less as a monument. It was devoid of the common clutter of competing architecture—no dramatic turrets, pilasters, or parapets, and it had escaped the abrupt, contrasting stone-work that Isabelle often found dizzying in its geometry. Isabelle had always thought the long, rectangular building, with its two stories of tall, balanced windows, five on each side of center both up and down, had been designed and built by a soul with an appreciation for the subtle. The details, both natural and man-made, spoke for themselves.

The stone façade, the color of cream, exuded a dignified warmth, even in the November gloom. The wide, carved ma-sonry that framed the pair of arched wooden doors centered on the ground floor was sleek and refined and was repeated around each window. Two massive chimneys bookended the château, jutting up above the dark, slate-tiled roof with smaller chimneys interspersed in between. A pair of dormers were set into both the north and south slopes of the roof, gazing out at centuries' worth of sunrises and sunsets come and gone.

From the front, the château was a picturesque homage to history, marred only by the wide weathered boards covering the last two northwest ground-floor windows and the faintly discoloured stone around them. At least someone had cared enough to seal the wound to keep the elements at bay, and the exterior damage did not appear grievous. The inside might be a different story.

"Fire damage, unrepaired, 1944." Isabelle wasn't aware that she had spoken aloud until Luc answered her.

"From when the Nazis commandeered the château in 1940. Made themselves quite comfortable here during the occupation," he said. "And then tried to burn it all down to destroy documents and evidence as they panicked and scrambled to retreat after D-Day. With noble, brave Resistance fighters in pursuit, of course."

"Right." Isabelle made a face. "I think I've heard every version of that story that there is to hear."

"I think we all have," Luc agreed wryly. "It's funny how it changes depending on who is doing the telling and how often it gets repeated."

"And how much alcohol was part of the retelling." She put a hand on her hip. "I dislike it."

"Which part?"

"The . . . romanticized myth, perpetuated by movies and books that, from the beginning of the war, France was overrun with handsome, valiant partisans, skulking about in the woods with sniper rifles and guns and explosives. This idea that all of

France was united in hostility and resistance toward the Nazi occupiers."

"Oh, I'm with you. Ninety percent of the population collaborated with the Nazis and the Vichy government, either by choice or because they were too exhausted or terrified not to. The tiny rival Resistance factions, at least in the beginning, were often unorganized, ill-equipped, and vulnerable to the far superior intelligence capabilities of the SS and certainly the Gestapo. At least until the SOE got involved. And of course, the Vichy's adoption of the Service du Travail Obligatoire requiring forced labour of Frenchmen certainly bolstered the Resistance's ranks, but not until 1943."

Isabelle stared at him.

"Did you know that the Resistance claimed it had killed over six thousand soldiers of the Second SS Panzer Division on their way to Caen after D-Day, though historians now believe that number was closer to just thirty-five?"

"I . . . didn't," Isabelle said slowly. "I'm impressed."

"A hobby of mine. Always been interested in it. The occupation of Normandy, that is." He grinned at her. "I read on the beach, you know. Between drinks in tiki huts."

"You're never going to let that one go, are you?"

"Not soon." He was still grinning.

"Fair enough." Isabelle paused thoughtfully. "Every once in a while, on a job, I get to work on a building or with people whose family histories were tied into actual Resistance activities. There are occasionally scraps of evidence left behind, but only that. Scraps. Because the real Resistance fighters—the ones who risked capture and torture and imprisonment and execution—didn't talk or brag about their exploits. They never spoke of them. At all. Even decades later."

"So I guess you don't have plans to use the legend of Briar Rose, femme fatale and fearless Resistance fighter who skulked about these very woods with guns and explosives, as a draw when you open the château?"

"No." Isabelle scoffed. "Not a chance. Because the legend of Briar Rose is just that. A legend. And I won't be a part of furthering romanticized myths. Such exaggerated legends are the product of one of two things, either people's desperation to find hope at a time when there was little or people's desperation to assuage their own sense of guilt that they themselves did nothing."

"Harsh."

"Maybe." She raised a shoulder. "The Resistance was active here before and after D-Day, to be sure. But there is no actual evidence that exists that proves Briar Rose was ever real. So I'll stick to facts and leave the legends and storytelling to the moviemakers."

"But it's such a great legend, no?" Luc nudged her. "And don't they say legends are born somewhere in truth? I mean, who wouldn't embrace an avenging angel who suddenly appeared to lead her troops when they needed her the most to drive the evil forces from their home?"

"I think you have her confused with the Maid of Orleans."

"I do not have anything confused. I wrote a history paper on her in high school even. Briar Rose, not Jeanne d'Arc."

"Citing tavern sources?"

Luc pretended to look offended. "Maybe. The sober ones, anyway. Do you remember Monsieur Dubois? Who used to own the Briar Rose tavern in Val-de-la-Haye?"

"He still does."

Luc came up short. "What? He's still alive?"

"Alive and refusing to relinquish his spot behind the bar."
Isabelle laughed. "Though his shift ends after dinner now and
not in the wee hours of the morning. He's been known to fall
asleep at his post from time to time."

"He must be over ninety."

"Probably. I helped him with a window in his tavern last year."

"No kidding." Luc shook his head. "Well, if you ask him—
and I did when I wrote that paper—he'll tell you that he was
a kid when the château was occupied by the Nazis. My actual
assignment was to write about the Jedburgh teams dropped into
Normandy but I got derailed by his stories. He told me that
he tagged along with his older brothers when the Resistance
organized here before June of '44 and acted as a gofer and look-
out. And he says he met Briar Rose in person."

Isabelle rolled her eyes. "He also says he met Arletty."

"He named his tavern after her," Luc persisted. "Briar Rose,
not Arletty."

"And there are restaurants and bars named after Jeanne d'Arc
yet no one claims to have met her."

"Aren't you the cynic."

"I struggle to believe that Monsieur Dubois really met a person
who left behind no trace of her existence, but I'll play along here.
What did he have to say about the legendary Briar Rose?"

"That she was cold. And ruthless and cunning. Scared him a
little, he said. But she was also beautiful."

"Oh, for pity's sake, why is every legendary heroine beautiful?" Isabelle grumbled. "Ruthless and cunning isn't enough?
It's like beauty is a prerequisite or something."

"Maybe you should ask him about Briar Rose yourself."

Isabelle blew out an exasperated breath. "No. I will not
encourage him."

"But—"

"No."

"Fine." He held up his hands in defeat. "So when you buy this place, restore it, and then market it, we'll skip advertising mythical Resistance fighters. Maybe we could find something from the Revolution? Surely there is a badass hero or heroine somewhere just waiting to be made into a brochure."

Isabelle looked heavenward, shaking her head. "Do us all a favour and don't quit carpentry to go into marketing. Please."

"Oh ye of little faith." He was still grinning as he put his toolbox down on the wide, shallow steps leading up to the door, tucking it out of the damp, beneath the arched overhang. "On that cheery note, since we can't see the inside of the château, where would you like to start on the exterior?"

"Let's start with the west end where the damage is," Isabelle said, and there was a peculiar relief that came with her words that gave her pause. Assessing the outside was what she did for any other project that she took on—a careful appraisal of the outer structure and grounds. An evaluation of windows and eaves and downspouts, of foundation and masonry and tile.

But despite her desire to see the interior of the château, there was something that made her relieved that it would not be today. Something that made her want to prolong her first steps into the château, as if she did not want to relinquish the anticipation and eagerness. As if she were not yet ready to lose the magic from within the walls of her imagination to the reality that she would likely find within the walls of the château.

"Sure." Luc shrugged in his affable Luc-like way and pulled the pencil from behind his ear. "You make comments, and I'll make notes."

Isabelle stepped from the weed-strewn gravel and waded into

the overgrown yard. She ignored the droplets that clung to the branches and dead vegetation that left dark splotches on her jeans, her attention riveted on the château. Along the way, she examined the bottom sill of the first ground floor window, squinting up at the lintels and corners, pleased with what she saw. "Manage the water, and manage ninety percent of your problems," she murmured. "The masons of old knew what they were doing. This sort of skill saves more structures than you can imagine. Thank the gods it saved this one."

"This place must really mean something to you."

"My great-gran loved this château. She wrote so many stories about it. Emilie and I grew up on them. I think she definitely passed that love on to us."

"What kind of stories? Luc asked drily, eyeing the abandoned building. "Murder mysteries?"

"Fairy tales." Isabelle crushed a stand of drooping, brown weeds beneath her boot, picking her way along the building carefully. "It was like a magical castle to her, I think, where brave knights and warrior princesses battled fire-breathing dragons and wicked warlocks. And always her heroes and heroines found their happy-ever-afters. She illustrated each of her stories too." She reached out to run a finger over a discolored streak on the stone, imagining the fire that had left it.

Flames not from a fire-breathing dragon but from something far more evil.

Luc's gaze had followed her motion. "Did your great-gran write anything about the fire? Or the occupation? It must have been difficult to have watched a place you loved stolen and damaged like this."

Isabelle frowned. "She never wrote or said anything about it. She spent her summers at the farm with her grandparents—my great-great-grandparents—but she was Dutch. She wasn't here during the war. She came back to France after."

"So I guess she never met the elusive Briar Rose? Even though she was a writer of fairy tales? Maybe they collaborated."

"Stop." Isabelle made a face. "No, she didn't meet a woman who never existed. And even if she had, they would have had nothing in common. Great-Gran was the exact opposite of cold, cunning, and ruthless. She was the sweetest, most gentle, kindest person I have ever met in my life." She snatched the pencil from his fingers and poked it into the front of his jacket. "And if you mention Briar Rose again, I will be forced to find another carpenter who has a much better grip on reality."

His lips twitched. "Sorry. Just the mention of fairy tales and all . . ."

She threw the pencil at him in exasperation.

He deftly snagged it out of the air. "Well, she must have had some stories to tell. About the war, that is." His tone had sobered.

Isabelle opened her mouth to answer and then hesitated. "No," she finally said. "I mean, I asked her about it when she was still alive. A few times. But she'd get this . . . I don't know, *hard* expression across her face and say 'eyes forward' and then change the subject. I never pressed. Maybe I should have."

Luc tapped the edge of the clipboard against his thigh. "Or maybe you did the right thing by respecting her wishes."

"Maybe." Isabelle scuffed the toe of her boot into the litter of leaves beneath her feet. "She was special, you know? The one I went to for advice or to talk through the hard things that I struggled with. I just . . . I wish I could have been her confidant too. The person she could have shared her hard things with."

"Perhaps she did not wish to burden you."

"She would never have been a burden. She was my hero."

"Well, if she were here, and her great-granddaughter were standing in front of her magical castle considering making it magical once again, I suspect she would say 'eyes forward,' no?"

Isabelle smiled ruefully, glancing up at Luc. "When did you get so wise?"

"Under the shade of tiki huts, I'm sure."

Isabelle shook her head, still smiling.

"So tell me, if Emilie is as captivated by this château as you, would restoring it be a joint venture?"

Her smile slipped at the mention of her sister. "That has always been the plan." Isabelle tried to keep her answer neutral, unsure if that statement was still true.

"But she's still in Paris, right? Would she come back to work on this—"

"She didn't come back when Dad had his stroke so who knows what she might come back for—" Isabelle clamped her mouth shut. Luc did not deserve to be the recipient of her bitterness and anger. She cleared her throat and stepped back, casting a critical eye over the damaged corner of the château. "Aside from the custom window replacement, there are some areas here that will need repointing."

She could feel Luc's gaze on her but ignored it.

After a moment he bent his head and made a notation on the clipboard. "Repointing," he repeated.

"With proper excavation by a proper mason," she continued, "who can match the mortar both in color and historically accurate content to stabilize and maintain the integrity of the stone."

"You?"

"I'm not a mason."

"But you know a good one."

"Two, in fact. And they are as necessary as they are expensive." She glanced at Luc. "That should be considered in the purchase price."

"Duly noted." Luc made another notation on the clipboard and pulled out his phone, snapping a series of photos of the damaged joints. "Shall we continue?"

Isabelle nodded, and they moved on, circling the château, occasionally stopping to confer and take photos. At the back, they both paused in front of a weed-infested area that separated the château from the formal garden that existed behind. Two crumbling stone columns, covered in the twisted carcasses of dead vines, marked the entrance to the garden. A narrow stone path wove away from the château and between the two columns, disappearing into a tangle of overgrown bushes shadowed by the spindly branches of ancient trees.

"Did you want a tour of the gardens?" Luc asked dubiously.

"I've been many times," Isabelle murmured. "Long ago."

In their younger years, she and Emilie would sneak through the forest between the properties and spend clandestine hours in these gardens, plotting their restoration of the magical landscape that featured even more prominently than the château itself in Great-Gran's fairy tales. In the garden, surrounded by the ignorance of youth and by color and sunshine and dreams, Isabelle had once believed that the happy-ever-afters so lovingly crafted were possible.

"It's supposed to be haunted, you know," Luc said. "The garden, I mean. Since you've rejected my suggestions of the legend of Briar Rose, maybe the ghost of the de Montessaire gardens would appeal."

"Ghosts are things people invent to keep other people out of their business," Isabelle murmured. "Or at least that was what Great-Gran always used to say."

"Well, it certainly looks like it worked," he said, eyeing the wall of seemingly impenetrable, overgrown vegetation. "We could try to take a quick look. There is—"

"Let's move on," Isabelle said, probably too brightly. "I'd rather see the rest of the exterior before we lose our light or the sky decides to open up again." As if in answer, the wind gusted, sending droplets of rain and leaves pelting against her back.

Again she could feel Luc's gaze on her but he only said, "As you wish."

She glanced sharply at him but he was already making his way along the back of the château. She followed, continuing their assessment, Luc taking multiple photos along the way. The back of the château was a mirror image of the front, with a wide entrance that led out toward the garden and a smaller, narrow entrance farther down that would have been used for servants and deliveries.

At the east corner, they both stopped. A jumble of twisted, rusted metal sat just outside the walled garden, visible beneath the naked stems of vines. Directly behind it, the stone wall was streaked with blackened discoloration.

"What do you think that used to be?" Isabelle asked.

Luc shrugged. "I have no idea. There's not much left." He craned his neck. "It looks like it burned."

"Maybe something else that the Nazis destroyed when they retreated?"

"Possibly."

"Hmm." Isabelle turned to look at the château opposite. "It looks like the windows here need replacing as well." The two windows here were boarded up, similar to the northwest windows, but unlike those windows, there were no telltale streaks that suggested fire damage.

Luc made another note.

"The exterior is in remarkably decent shape, all things considered," Isabelle said. She found herself working to focus against the surge of exhilaration that danced through her limbs. Because this was more than a chapel or a cottage or a tavern. This was Château de Montessaire.

Luc tucked his clipboard back under his arm and returned his pencil to its perch behind his ear. He took another photo of the eaves above their heads before slipping his phone back into his pocket. "It deserves you, you know."

"I'm sorry?" Isabelle looked up at him.

He was gazing at her intently. "It deserves a second chance."

"I haven't seen the inside of the place yet," Isabelle replied lightly, unsettled by his expression. "I might run screaming in the other direction four steps in."

Luc scoffed. "For as long as I've known you, you've never run from anything."

That was true, she supposed. She had never run anywhere. Ever. She had no idea where she would go. "There is a first time for everything."

"Hmph." Luc was pushing his way through the overgrown vegetation, glancing up at the sky that had darkened and threatened more rain.

She followed as they returned to the front.

"Are you going to call Emilie?" he asked over his shoulder. "If the two of you are seriously thinking of restoring this place, she'd probably want to do a walk-through with you, no?"

Isabelle was glad she was behind him because the discontent

that immediately dimmed her excitement was no doubt written across her face. And she hated it. "Yes. I should."

"Should?" He had reached the steps where they had started and where he had left his toolbox.

"I will." Because the truth of the matter was that Isabelle could not take this project on by herself. Financially or logistically. "I will," she repeated. "Call my sister, that is." She sighed and stared down at the toes of her battered boots. "And see if Château de Montessaire is enough to bring her home."

CHAPTER

4

Stasia

8 JUNE 1938
ROUEN, FRANCE

S he saw him the moment she stepped off the train and onto
the platform.

Stasia stopped in her tracks, ignoring the sounds of annoyance
as passengers bumped and jostled around her. The man waiting
for her was Nicolas, yet he wasn't. He seemed a little taller
and maybe a little broader, but that wasn't what had changed.
His hair was longer, his clothes newer, but that wasn't it either.
Maybe it was the quiet confidence he seemed to effortlessly
exude. Maybe it was just the way he was standing, leaning easily
against a post, his hands in his pockets. The perfect picture of
casual composure if it weren't for his eyes, which anxiously swept
the knots of passengers as they disembarked from the train.

It took a moment for his ice-grey gaze to land on her. He
straightened abruptly, his hands falling from his pockets and his
lips curling into a tentative smile. Stasia felt her stomach do a
delicious, dizzying somersault.

She hurried forward, her cheeks aching from the ridiculous grin she knew was plastered on her face, and dropped her bag at his feet before embracing him in an impulsive hug. Nicolas's arms went around her, squeezing her tight, and Stasia closed her eyes, wanting this moment, this sensation of joy and rightness and home, to last forever.

"I didn't know you'd be here," she murmured into his chest. "I thought my grandfather would have fetched us. I didn't know you'd been promoted to chauffeur."

"I haven't been promoted." A laugh rumbled through his chest against her ear. "But I made a bet with your grandfather to see who would come for you."

"And did you win or lose?"

He didn't answer right away.

Stasia pulled back with no little reluctance to look up at him, though he caught her hand in his, as if he, too, was unwilling to let her go.

His eyes held hers, intense and direct. "I won."

Stasia felt her cheeks heat, and she was sure she was blushing down to her toes. "What was the, ah, bet?" She was having a hard time thinking when he was looking at her like that.

He smiled. "You'll see."

Stasia nodded, words failing her. What she wanted was her sketchbook. To capture this Nicolas and his devastating smile that was hers and hers alone so that during the long months when she was a country away from him, she'd still have it with her.

"So this must be the famous Nicolas Navarre?" The slow, accented drawl came from behind her.

Stasia spun, a twinge of shame and mortification pricking. In her haste to see Nicolas, she'd all but abandoned her friend behind her. "I'm so sorry. Margot, may I introduce Nicolas Navarre? Nicolas, this is my very dear friend Margot Kaufmann."

Margot, with her honey-blonde hair, sea-blue eyes, and willowy height that turned heads wherever she went, stepped closer to Nicolas, and stuck out her hand, giving him a frank, assessing look. "It is a pleasure to finally meet you. If not for the profusion of letters that continually arrive from France, I would have suspected Stasia had made you up."

"Made me up?" Nicolas clasped Margot's hand.

"An imaginary French lover is an effective way to keep the Dutch boys at bay, you know," Margot told him with a grin.

"He's not my lover." Stasia almost choked on the word, her face burning. Margot was only a year older than Stasia but sometimes Margot's worldliness made it feel like more. "And that's rather cynical," she muttered.

Margot threw back her head and laughed. "It is, isn't it?" She released Nicolas's hand. "I have enough cynicism for the both of us," she told him in a mock whisper. "Which is for the best, I think. This brilliant girl of yours, with all of her kindness and happiness and goodness, should not be so afflicted."

Stasia's face heated all over again. "I'm not—"

"I'm quite real," Nicolas replied easily before Stasia could sputter some sort of defence. "And guilty of excessive correspondence." He turned a smile on Stasia that made her toes curl. "And I agree: This girl is quite brilliant." He glanced back at Margot. "Welcome to Rouen, Miss Kaufmann."

"And a gentleman too," Margot murmured, elbowing Stasia. "I now understand why you are utterly besotted."

"I'm not besotted," she protested weakly.

Margot snorted. "You are a terrible liar." She patted Stasia's arm fondly. "It's one of the very best things about you."

Stasia glanced at Nicolas, wondering how much he had over-heard, but he had turned his attention to a small girl standing behind Margot. She had the same blue-green eyes and the same honey-blonde hair, though her delicate features were pinched with worry. "You must be Minna." He crouched down so that they were level. "I heard that you moved to Rotterdam from Berlin to live with Miss Neimic and her father. And that this will be your first holiday in France with your sister."

Minna looked up at Margot, who repeated Nicolas's words in German. She nodded shyly at him.

"How old are you?" he asked.

Again Margot translated.

"*Funf.*" Minna held up five fingers, studied him intently, and then asked Margot a question.

"She wants to know if you're really a prince," Margot trans-lated, sounding amused.

Nicolas blinked. "A what?"

"A prince. Stasia has read her all the stories she's written about you. And showed her the pictures she drew of you." Margot's eyes crinkled with smug mirth as she mouthed the word *besotted* at Stasia over Nicolas's head.

Stasia looked up at the sky and wished the ground would swallow her whole.

"Oh, she did, did she?" Nicolas had the gall to sound just as amused as Margot.

Stasia dared to steal a glance at him but he wasn't looking at her. Instead, he was leaning closer to the little girl.

"Yes," he said in a low voice, nodding. Minna's eyes went wide at his confirmation that needed no interpretation. "But you can't tell anyone," he whispered and put a finger to his lips.

Minna didn't need a translation for that either and nodded

her understanding back. She put a tiny finger to her own lips. "*Geheime.*"

"Yes. *Geheime.*"

Stasia's heart squeezed with an emotion so intense it hurt.

Minna was pulling something from the pocket sewn into her skirt to show Nicolas. It was a folded square of paper, the edges ragged and curled, and it wasn't until she opened it that Stasia recognized it. It was a drawing she had done for the little girl, hoping to distract her, one afternoon not long after they had fled Berlin, when Minna had been inconsolable. Stasia had drawn Minna as a fairy princess, with an intricate crown and delicate wings, and she had perched the fairy princess on the back of an agile hummingbird poised in flight above a sea of lilies.

She hadn't realized the girl had kept it. She certainly hadn't realized that Minna carried it with her.

Nicolas was studying the drawing quite seriously. "Ask her how she learned how to tame the hummingbird," he said to Margot, waiting for her to translate.

Minna listened to her sister and then giggled.

"Ask her if she could teach me," he said, pointing to the drawing and then himself.

Minna giggled again at Margot's translation and nodded enthusiastically, tucking the drawing back into her pocket.

"Excellent. We royals need to stick together." Nicolas stood and reached for both Stasia's and Margot's travelling bags and then bowed with a flourish to Minna, who squealed in delight. "Until then, Your Majesty."

For no good reason, Stasia found herself fighting something perilously close to tears.

Nicolas started walking, and it took a gentle push from Margot for Stasia to follow. Her friend caught Minna's hand and fell into step behind Stasia and Nicolas as he steered them across the platform and into the grand station with its soaring roof.

When Stasia had brought Nicolas home to her grandparents' farm that day, it had never been with the expectation that he would stay. Yet he did stay, permanently, and her grandparents had come to rely on his strong hands and clever mind about the farm. Stasia and Nicolas's friendship had blossomed that summer and those that followed, the long hours they spent together replaced with long letters in the months they spent apart.

She'd been holding his hand last July when his father, finally succumbing to his demons that he couldn't drown with drink, had been buried, with only Stasia and Nicolas and her grandparents standing in the cemetery at the edge of his grave. Nicolas had been right beside her when her grandfather had suffered a bout of pneumonia shortly after, keeping her company at his bedside in the evenings and taking on the responsibilities of the farm singlehandedly until her grandfather had recovered.

She'd spent hours telling Nicolas about all the places in the world that she had visited with her father, and he'd listened raptly. He'd spent hours showing Stasia how to fix simple things around the farm, and she'd learned quickly. She'd taught him basic first aid. He'd taught her basic electrical theory. He'd been her partner, her companion, her confidant, the honesty in which they'd started their friendship never wavering.

But everything had felt different from the moment she had stepped onto that platform where he waited. And then Margot had branded Nicolas with the word *lover*—in jest, of course—but now that word couldn't be unsaid or unimagined. And everything that idea suggested and evoked had wedged itself in Stasia's mind, where it smouldered and writhed and did scandalous things to the rest of her body every time she looked at him.

She'd lied to herself, for a while now, if she was being completely honest. Up until now, she'd done a reasonably good job of refusing to admit to herself or anyone else that she felt anything but friendship for Nicolas. But friendship did not turn her insides upside down. Friendship did not overwhelm her awareness, or consume her in a peculiar, aching longing that was as novel as it was terrifying. Somewhere along the way, at a juncture that she couldn't really pinpoint, friendship with Nicolas Navarre had given way to something else entirely.

Stasia swallowed with difficulty around a mouth that had gone dry. She cast about for something casual and clever to say. "Thank you," she managed, wincing. That wasn't clever at all. But she meant it.

"For what?"

"For what you said to Minna. I think that's the first time I've heard her laugh."

"Being a prince has its benefits from time to time." He looked like he was fighting a smile. "Your drawing was beautiful."

"It was nothing."

"It was not nothing, Stasia. And I speak from experience."

"Um. Well." Stasia cleared her throat. "It's been hard for her. For their whole family." She stole a look over her shoulder at the child, who was clutching her sister's hand and staring wide-eyed up at the station's walls of long windows and cathedral-like arches. "I know I've talked about it a little in my letters but what's happening in Germany is not right. Or fair."

Nicolas nodded. "Your grandparents have spoken of it as well. And news comes over the radio all the time."

"The Kaufmanns stayed as long as they could. But they were too afraid to stay any longer. Berlin is no longer safe for any Jewish families." She glanced behind her again but Margot had fallen back, pointing out something high above in the windows of the station to Minna.

"It is a good thing that they could come to you, then," he said.

"Yes." Stasia quickened her steps. "Rotterdam is not Berlin, thank goodness. They'll be safe there. And I've always wanted a sister. Now I have two."

"What's the connection between your families?"

"Our fathers went to university together. They're both engineers, though Mr. Kaufmann designs buildings and not ports."

"And there wasn't anyone in Germany who could help them?"

"It wasn't a faceless mob who harassed and threatened them, Nicolas. It was their neighbours, people they've known for years, who decided that their religion makes them the enemy because a small man with a big voice has told them so. They couldn't trust anyone. An entire country has lost their minds."

"It sounds terrifying."

"They were forced to leave their business, their friends, their entire lives behind. Which is why I think Margot harbours more fury than fear."

Nicolas released a heavy breath. "I can certainly understand that. Being angry is far easier than being afraid. What will they do now?"

"Stay with us as long as they need to. Minna will go back to school in the fall. And Margot is already registered to attend university in Amsterdam with me. We'll be university colleagues, just like our fathers were, which pleases us all, I think. She wants to study international law and one day work at the League of Nations."

Nicolas adjusted his grip on the bags as they exited the station out into the slanted light of early evening. "Impressive."

"She really is," Stasia answered, refusing to acknowledge a

twinge of what felt horribly like jealousy. "She's confident. And clever and outspoken, though you probably already figured that out. She will make a formidable lawyer."

"But can she stitch a bleeding cut?" he asked, nudging Stasia with his elbow as they navigated the thinning crowd on the pavement outside. "Find a way to heal an angry patient who didn't think he wanted to be healed?"

"She hates blood."

"Well then, it's a good thing I had you." He stopped abruptly and dropped the bags. "Your carriage, my lady."

Stasia stumbled into him, one hand on his chest, the other on his arm. "I'm sorry." Yet she made no move to pull away.

"Don't be." He was looking at her with an intensity and heat that scattered her thoughts all over again.

Stasia's gaze shifted to his mouth. A faint shadow of blond stubble dusted his chin and the skin above his lip; tiny laugh lines bracketed his mouth. Sluggishly, Stasia wondered what it might be like to kiss this man. What it would feel like to slide her fingers up his neck and across his jaw, threading them into the short hair at the nape of his neck—

A long, low whistle snapped her out of her imaginings with a jolt. She tore her eyes and hands away from Nicolas. He still hadn't moved.

"Sure you have a farm and not a castle?" Margot crowed with delight. "Now I really might believe you are an actual prince."

Stasia forced herself to focus. Margot was walking alongside a magnificent Renault coupé, letting her fingers trail over the swooping curve of the front fenders. The boxy midnight-blue car gleamed in the light, with the chrome on the grille and the round headlights polished to a blinding sheen.

Stasia felt her mouth drop open. "Is this my grandfather's Reinastella?"

"Yes." Nicolas looked smug.

"How...When...Why..." She stopped, trying to put her thoughts into order. "This vehicle doesn't run. I mean, it's never worked. And not for his lack of trying." She stepped toward the vehicle and touched the straight, smooth lines of the roof. "The only place I've ever seen this is under a tarp in the barn."

"It runs just fine now."

Stasia peered into the gleaming interior. "I've never even been allowed to touch it. How did you—" She straightened. "This was the bet."

Nicolas opened the passenger-side door and carefully stowed the bags into a corner of the backseat. "He told me that if I could get it running, I could drive it." His voice was muffled inside the car. He backed out and leaned an elbow against the frame. "And that I could use it to pick you up at the station. So I fixed it."

"You make it sound like it was easy."

He pushed the hair from his eyes, almost silver in the light. "Believe me, it most certainly was not. But I was sufficiently motivated."

Out of the corner of her eye, Stasia could see Margot was smirking gleefully at her.

"My grandfather saved the life of a lieutenant colonel in the war," she told Margot with as much nonchalance as she could muster and deliberately looking away from Nicolas. "Six years ago, the officer passed away and quite unexpectedly willed his Reinastella to my grandfather. It has never run properly but my grandfather couldn't bring himself to sell it."

"Ah." Margot was still smirking. "I suppose it just needed the right...touch."

Stasia willed herself not to blush again and failed miserably. "We should get going," she said, way too loudly. "I'm sure my grandparents are anxious to welcome you."

Nicolas came around the driver's side and opened the door for Margot and Minna, seemingly oblivious to Margot's shameless insinuations. "Two weeks. That's how long it took me to make this beauty give up her secrets. Now she purrs."

Margot helped Minna into the coupé and gave Stasia an arch look. "Oh, I just bet she does," she said before sliding into the backseat.

★ ★ ★

The night was still, not a breath of wind to disturb the songs and scurries of the creatures that inhabited the darkness. The musky scent of wisteria perfumed the air, still thick with the day's humidity. Stasia looked up at the blanket of stars overhead, the sky almost silver in places where there were so many. The moon was full and bright and bathed everything in a pale, ethereal glow. She should be tired. The train ride had been lengthy, the welcome her grandparents had given lovingly effusive and prolonged, and she had made sure to see both Margot and Minna settled comfortably in their own room before she had retired to hers. Yet her mind would not settle, and sleep had eluded her. Restless, she had slipped silently from the house, through the thick ridge of trees, and past crumbling stone walls until the silent form of the stone angel appeared, her wings blotting out the stars above.

Stasia rested her palm on the stone edifice, still warm from the day's sun. She pulled aside the tangle of vines that had twisted themselves across the engraving, the pads of her fingers tracing the letters and numbers.

"Couldn't sleep?" The question came from behind her.

Her fingers stilled but she did not startle. Perhaps she had expected him.

"No." She shivered though she wasn't cold. "How did you know I was here?"

Nicolas stepped into the moonlight beside the angel. "Because I know you." He paused. "And I couldn't sleep either."

Stasia let her fingers drop from the stone.

"I missed you, Stasia."

The air seemed to thicken around her, something that she could not name crackling over her skin. "And I you." It was not a little frightening, this moment, though mixed in with the fear was a precarious anticipation. She felt as though she were on a runaway train, hurtling toward the edge of a cliff, unable to stop, the safety of friendship and familiarity passing by in a blur.

"She was sixteen when she died." Stasia gestured at the stone marker. She needed to slow this runaway train, even for a moment, before she reached a point of no return. Give her a chance to breathe. A chance to think.

She hadn't looked at him yet. "I've always wondered what regrets she took with her. Things she never got to do. Parts of life she never got to live."

Nicolas moved, coming to stand beside her, not touching her but close enough that she could feel the heat of his body. "Maybe none."

"Maybe."

"And you?"

Stasia turned then. "And me what?"

"What regrets would you have?" He was looking down at her, his eyes shadowed in the moonlight. "If today was your last day?"

Stasia tried to form words but found she couldn't. Hazily, she understood that she could leave this garden now, stop herself, stop the both of them, from careening over the edge of the cliff. All she had to do was walk away. She remained motionless.

"Should I tell you mine?" he asked.

Stasia nodded.

He shifted so that they were facing each other. His hand came up, and he brushed a stray tendril of hair from the side of her face. Yet his fingers did not leave her skin and instead travelled lightly along her jaw, his thumb grazing her bottom lip. He dipped his head and brushed his lips against hers, his kiss gentle and unhurried. "I would regret not doing that," he breathed against her skin.

Stasia closed her eyes, her breath coming in shallow sips, every nerve ending in her body on fire. "What are we doing, Nicolas?" she managed.

"You tell me."

"I don't know."

"Yes, you do."

She opened her eyes.

"Is this the part when we start lying to each other?"

"No. We will never lie to each other." And nor could she lie to herself.

"Then tell me the truth," Nicolas repeated, but now his voice sounded strained.

Stasia caught his hand in hers and pressed it over her breast against her heart. She raised her other hand and rested her palm against his chest, his skin hot under the thin linen of his shirt. Beneath both of her hands, she could feel the pounding of his heart matching hers.

"Once upon a time," she whispered, "there was a girl from

Rotterdam who met a boy from Rouen in a secret garden. This boy from Rouen was very honest and very smart so she took him home to meet her grandparents, who welcomed him into their family."

She slid her hand higher, skimming the edge of his jaw the way he had done. Stroking the outline of his bottom lip the way he had done. He sucked in a sharp breath and shuddered, and for the first time, Stasia understood that she possessed power too. That she affected him as much as he did her.

"The boy from Rouen lived on her grandparents' farm for many years," she continued. "And the girl from Rotterdam visited him every summer, and she watched as the boy grew into a man who remained honest and smart. One day, the girl from Rotterdam brought a friend home, and her friend accused her of being besotted with this man. Only her friend was wrong. The girl was not besotted."

"Stasia—"

"Shhh." She stilled his lips with her fingers before sliding them up the side of his cheek, tracing the outline of the scar over his left eye. "She wasn't besotted," she breathed. "She was in love with him."

He made a muffled sound and kissed her again, and she kissed him back, only there was nothing gentle about this kiss. It was a searing kiss, desire and desperation, love and longing finally acknowledged.

Stasia wasn't sure how long they stood under the moonlight, lost in each other, before he pulled back, breathing hard.

"I want to show you something," he whispered against her ear.

"What?" She rested her head beneath his chin, trying to get her bearings and catch her breath.

"Follow me." He caught her hand in his and pulled her across the garden and toward the shed. He let go just long enough to push the door open.

"Are you going to tell me you built a car in here?" she teased as he closed the door, plunging them into darkness. "Or maybe an airplane?"

"Not quite." The sound of a lighter snapping open was followed by the bright flare of a flame.

"You still have it," Stasia marveled. "The lighter I gave you."

"Of course I have it." The flame morphed into a soft glow as he lit a kerosene lamp resting on the table. He slid the lighter back into his pocket, picked up the lamp, and held his free hand out. "Come with me."

"Where?" Stasia was bewildered.

"Just trust me."

She put her hand in his and let him lead her to the very rear of the shed. Where once there had been a cot jammed up against the wall, there was instead a gaping hole in the floor, narrow stone stairs descending into blackness. A trap door, similar to the ones that covered coal chutes, was propped open against the wall.

"What is this?" Stasia looked up at him.

His fingers tightened around hers. "I'll show you."

He led her down the stairs, both of them ducking before they could straighten at the bottom. It was a tunnel, Stasia realized, that curled away into darkness somewhere beneath the garden. She followed Nicolas and his light, squeezing through where it narrowed and ducking in the places it became low. Finally, they arrived at a short wooden door, fresh scrape marks on the earthen floor of the tunnel betraying that it had been opened recently.

"Where are we?" Stasia asked, but Nicolas only smiled at her.

He slid a heavy bolt, pulled the door inward, and beckoned her forward.

Stasia stepped into a cool chamber, three of its walls constructed of large stone blocks. Above her head, thick wooden beams were studded with rows of hanging hooks and wire baskets. An assortment of ancient wooden shelves and cupboards lined two of the walls, while more free-standing shelves were in the center. Across from her, another set of stone steps rose out of sight.

"A cellar?" she asked. She eyed the stairs. "Are we under the château?"

"Its kitchens, to be exact." Nicolas closed the door behind them, and Stasia watched with some wonder as it seemingly vanished. On either side, the wall it was set in was covered with identical wood panels of equal size and shape.

"How did you know this was here?"

"Found it years ago."

"Should we be here? I mean, we're trespassing—"

"No one's here. No one's been here for a long time. I just want to show you something."

"What—"

Nicolas kissed her, stopping whatever she was going to say. "Just come with me."

Stasia nodded. Together, they climbed the stairs, and Nicolas whisked her through the kitchens. In the pool of swaying lantern light, Stasia got the impression of long counters surrounding a massive butcher block, ghostly forms of pots and pans gleaming dully from pegs above. From there, Nicolas ushered her into a long, wide passage, the eyes from a dozen portraits lining the walls watching them pass as the light bounced by. They crossed a grand entrance hall, the dark green of the papered walls making the massive stone staircase to her left seem like a pale, ethereal expanse leading heavenward.

Stasia would have stopped to stare but Nicolas was pulling her onward, her hand still wrapped tightly in his. He led them through another set of tall, rounded doors into another hallway, and finally, at the second door on their right, he stopped. With care, he pushed the door inward, its hinges protesting faintly, and led her inside.

The glow from the lantern was not bright enough to light the far corners of the room but it didn't matter. Stasia gasped, craning her neck as she gawked at the expanses of books that covered the walls. The shelves reached all the way to the lofty ceilings, and the still, stuffy air was redolent with the fragrance of dust, wood, leather, and the unmistakable and slightly musty scent of ink melded with paper that she always associated with old books. She let go of Nicolas's hand and shuffled forward, reaching out to touch the rows of spines. He followed her with the light, the silhouette of her shadow dancing ahead.

She turned away from the books to gape at the rest of the room. In the center of the space, a wide desk loomed, its ebony surface like a swath of midnight in the soft light. It was bare save for a typewriter and a small cup that bristled with abandoned pens, as if their owner had simply walked away from their task and forgotten to return. She wandered over to the desk, wistfully tracing the outline of the rounded typewriter keys dulled by dust.

"I think I could live in this room forever," Stasia murmured. "I would write a million stories at that desk on that typewriter."

Nicolas didn't say anything, merely kept her company as she continued exploring. She stopped abruptly when she reached a yawning, empty hearth on the far side. Two sculpted griffins strained forward, caught forever in time with their wings spread, raptor beaks open, and glittering amber eyes fixed on their prey.

Stasia pressed her hands together in delight. "How extraordinary."

"I thought you'd like them," Nicolas said, coming to stand beside her. "Though I always thought that they seemed rather out of place in such a . . . proper, dignified library."

"On the contrary," Stasia murmured. "Since ancient times, griffins have been guardians of priceless possessions. I can't think of a better place for them than a library."

"Maybe there is a hidden fortune stuffed up the chimney."

"Maybe." Stasia laughed. "I wish I had my drawing things here. They definitely belong in a story." She leaned her head against Nicolas's shoulder. "Thank you for bringing me here. I wish someone lived here to enjoy it. It's a beautiful room."

Nicolas didn't answer but slowly put the lantern up on the top of the mantel and turned to face her. "I have to tell you something," he said.

"Tell me what?" Stasia slipped her arms around his waist, resting her head in the crook between his shoulder and chin. She closed her eyes, refusing to think about the precious window of time that still existed before she would have to board a train to Amsterdam and school. Without him.

"I love you," he said.

Stasia smiled into his chest. "I know."

"And I've joined the navy."

Stasia's head came up so fast that she clipped Nicolas's chin. The breath was punched from her lungs, and her blood chilled to ice.

"It didn't seem like something I should say in a letter." He was rubbing his jaw.

There were questions she needed to ask, things she needed to say, except she couldn't force her throat to work.

He was looking at her, his forehead creased into furrows. "Say something."

Stasia could only stare, her thoughts impossible to put into order.

Nicolas reached out to touch her face but she pulled away from him. She stumbled back, stopping only when the backs of her thighs collided with the edge of the ebony desk.

"Why?" It was the only syllable that Stasia was able to blurt.

He approached her warily, stopping only a breath away but not touching her. "It's my ticket to somewhere," he said quietly.

"What's wrong with here?" Her throat loosened, and her voice rose.

"There is nothing for me here."

"That's not true. The farm is here. My grandparents are here." *I'm here.* She didn't say the last part because her throat closed up again, and she found herself teetering dangerously close to tears.

He yanked a thread from the cuff of his sleeve and twisted it between his fingers. "I know. And I will never be able to repay their kindness to me. But I can't take advantage of them forever—"

"You're not taking advantage of them. They adore you. If they were sitting right here, they'd tell you the exact same thing."

"Maybe. But Stasia, I need to find my own way. Like you've found yours."

She blinked, hating the way the backs of her eyes burned. *Selfish shrew*, the rational part of her mind accused her, *wanting to keep Nicolas here. Wanting him here with her.* And until a minute ago, she would have blithely told anyone who asked that she was neither selfish nor shrewish. Now she wasn't so sure.

He looked away from her. "There was a recruiter in town who said the navy is looking for men like me."

"Like you?"

"Who like engines and things. He said I might even get training and work on a battleship or a carrier. And he also said they've built the fastest class of destroyers anywhere in the world."

It's his job to tell you what you want to hear, she wanted to shriek, but she kept her mouth shut, trying to remain logical and not give in to debilitating emotion.

"This is my chance. My chance to see the world. To become something that one day my children might be proud of."

"I'm sure your father said the same thing," Stasia mumbled despite herself, a sinking sensation in the pit of her stomach yawning wider and deeper with every word out of his mouth.

He jerked like she'd struck him, and the thread snapped in his fingers.

"I'm sorry," she said. "That was unfair."

"I know what you're suggesting. But my father was in the army. In the trenches on the front lines in the mud and the shit and the blood. The navy will be different."

Stasia squeezed her eyes shut before opening them again. "Will it?"

"I thought you of all people would be proud of me."

"I am." She despised how wooden that sounded, even in her own ears. "I am proud of you," she repeated with more force.

"You don't sound like it." Nicolas tossed the broken thread to the side. "You promised me we'd never lie to each other."

"You're right." Stasia met his gaze, the glow from the lantern shaping shadows across his face. "I'm not proud. I'm scared. I'm terrified about what might happen to you. The navy, however impressive you might believe it, fights *wars*, Nicolas. People die fighting those wars. Spain is at war and threatens to drag the rest of the continent in with her. And right now Germany is devolving into something incredibly dangerous, and it's only a matter of time before they—"

"No matter what Germany tries, they can't touch our navy," Nicolas told her. "France has one of the most powerful navies in the world to defend our coasts. And on our borders, we have the Maginot Line and troops at the ready. We have not been sitting idly by these last years. We're ready for anything."

"Did the recruiter tell you that too?"

Nicolas frowned.

"I'm sorry." Stasia shook her head.

"I'm doing this," he said tersely. "In fact, it's already done. I don't have the means or the schooling to go to a university, not like you. I don't have any real training, only what I've taught myself. This is my chance. I can't stay here forever, watching life pass me by. You haven't. You can't expect me to."

Stasia was silent. He was right. Everything he said was accurate. He had never once asked her to sacrifice her dreams for him. If she truly loved him, she had to do the same.

"When do you leave?" she asked quietly.

"At the end of the week."

"Have you told my grandparents?"

"Yes."

"They didn't say anything."

"I asked them not to. I wanted to tell you. I just want to be . . ." He trailed off, his voice sounding strange.

"To be what?"

"I want to be good enough for you."

"What?" The question slipped out on an almost inaudible breath as she froze.

"You are the most extraordinary person I know. You're generous. Compassionate. Beautiful. Smart, smarter than anyone—"

"Stop." Stasia put a hand on his chest, trying to find the right words to express the emotion that was threatening to steal her voice again.

"No. I won't stop." He reached for her, cradling her face gently between his hands.

Stasia couldn't move.

"You met me at my worst, at my lowest, and when I was my most awful to you, and all you offered me in return for that was kindness. Kindness and friendship and everything that I did not earn and did not deserve. Not then." He paused, his hands dropping from her face to find her fingers and holding them tight. "But I want to earn it. All of it. All of you. Forever." His words were rushing out. "When I come back here, to Rouen, to this place, to you, I will be somebody. I will be something that you will be proud of. I will have wages in my pocket and a skill that will keep them there. I'll be able to build us a house, anywhere in the world you want to live. I'll build a room like this of your own where you can write a million stories, at a desk like this, on a typewriter like this. I want to give this all to you."

He stopped to take a breath, both of them staring at each other in an abandoned château with only a pair of silent griffins as witnesses.

"I don't need you to give me anything. I don't need you to prove yourself to me," she said, and a tear slipped down her cheek despite her best intentions. "I just need you to love me."

He reached up to wipe it away with his thumb. "Marry me."

"What?" Her breath hitched.

"Marry me," he said again. "Not now, but . . . after. When

you've found your place and I've found mine, and we will build a future together. Come back to me."

Stasia felt another tear slide down her cheek, and she ignored it, a tumult of thoughts and words in her mind as she once again fought for the right thing to say. The right words so that Nicolas might understand what she felt.

He let go of her hands and dug in his trouser pockets and pulled out something small that gleamed dully in the low light. "I made this for you," he said, catching her right hand.

It was a ring, Stasia realized. A simple, unadorned band of pewter, or maybe hammered steel. It was impossible to tell in the dimness. Or through her tears.

He slipped it on to her finger. "This is my promise to you. That I will wait for as long as it takes for you to find your dream. That I will be behind you every step of the way, even if we are apart. That I will find you no matter how far our worlds take us. That I will love you always." He looked up at her, the truth of his words shining across his face.

Stasia finally found the right word. "Yes."

And the boy from Rouen smiled.

CHAPTER

5

Nicolas

Holy Mary, Mother of God. Look at them guns." The words came from the man beside Nicolas and were breathed with reverence under the weight of shock and awe.

Nicolas could only nod as he gaped at the massive battleship with her towering turrets looming out in the harbour. Twenty-three thousand nine hundred tonnes. One hundred sixty-six meters long. Parsons steam turbines capable of pushing her twenty knots. An arsenal of guns bristling from her decks that could tackle any enemy from land, water, or the skies. The flagship of the French navy. All of this he knew from studying the ship on paper but none of that prepared him for the reality of the *Bretagne*.

His first glimpse of the battleship anchored in the water sent chills racing over his skin. Around him, the entire harbour was a hive of activity, as were the ships docked within. Aboard the *Bretagne*, men swarmed over her decks and dangled from ropes along the hull. Everyone, it seemed, moved with an orchestrated purpose and efficiency that left Nicolas more than a little intimidated.

The coxswain charged with transporting the new recruits to the ship lounged on the pier and laughed. "You all look like you just saw Jesus," he said, though not unkindly.

"Kinda did," the man beside Nicolas agreed readily, taking no offense. "That is the most beautiful thing I ever seen in my life. What are they doing to her?"

"Upgrading her rangefinder in the DC tower," the coxswain told them. "Among other things. Helps when your guns hit what you're aiming at." He grinned before turning to address a sailor who had approached.

"Goddamn, but I'm glad to be behind those guns and not somewhere in front." Nicolas's companion whistled, smoothing his meager moustache with his fingers in what Nicolas guessed was an attempt to make himself seem older than he was. In truth, it had the opposite effect. Nicolas wondered if he was even eighteen.

A wiry hand appeared in front of Nicolas. "Oscar Fontaine. Messman."

"Nicolas Navarre. Engineer's apprentice." He shook his hand.

"Well, hell, you're one of them smart ones, then," he chortled.

Nicolas cast another eye at the overwhelming complexity of the towers and structures of the battleship, knowing that the guts of the ship would be just as overwhelming and just as complex. "That remains to be seen," he said. "I've got a lot to learn." He had no idea what his duties would actually be but this was as far away from a cantankerous Reinastella as one could get.

He wished Stasia were here to see this ship. Wished so badly that she could share this moment with him because, whether she truly believed it or not, she was the reason he was standing here. She had changed the course of his life just as profoundly as the magnificent battleship waiting for him in the harbour would do. There had been moments in the last months when Nicolas was certain he'd made a terrible mistake. That he had reached too high and that he should have been content with what he'd had in Rouen. But then he'd looked at this ship and his doubts had vanished. This was where he belonged.

Beside him, the slight man was almost dancing on the balls of his feet with eagerness as more recruits joined them on the pier. "Where you from?"

"Rouen," Nicolas answered. "You?"

"Paris." His dark eyes flashed. "Why'd you join?"

Nicolas cleared his throat. "I like to fix things. Wanted to see the world." Those were his standard, easy answers. "Why did you?" He turned the attention back to Fontaine.

"Navy feeds you rations three times a day. Hell, I'd 'a taken twice. And I was already used to living jammed into tiny spaces with a mess of bodies, so I figured what the hell? Seemed like a step up. Or at least a step off the streets to somewhere."

Nicolas was a little taken aback by the bluntness. "I understand."

"No offense meant here, but I doubt it. You look like a farm boy."

"You're not wrong, I suppose. Though I lived in a garden shed for two years."

"Huh." Fontaine tipped his head, surprise flitting over his narrow features. "Was it a nice garden at least?"

Nicolas found himself laughing. "Yes. It was a beautiful garden. The winters were awful, though."

"They always are." Fontaine rubbed his chin thoughtfully. "You gotta go underground in the winter—"

"Attention!" The coxswain had straightened and snapped out a salute.

The recruits standing on the pier did the same.

An officer, built like an outhouse, had stepped onto the pier in front of the recruits. He had the stripes that labelled him as an ensign but he did not introduce himself as he paced back and forth. Occasionally, he stopped to stare at a recruit, a frown and a sneer alternating at regular intervals. "Look at the man standing beside you," he barked. "And then look at the one behind you and the one in front of you."

Nicolas did as he was ordered, as did each recruit, who stood silent in the midst of the chaos of the port.

"Now listen carefully!" the officer shouted.

As if any recruit who had made it to this pier had done anything other than listen carefully, Nicolas thought. Not listening to your commanding officers meant punishment. Push-ups. Latrine duty. Never-ending runs. Scrubbing mess hall floors until their knees and hands progressed from agonizing to numb. Moving heavy sandbags from one pile to another and back again for no discernible purpose other than torture.

The ensign had stopped, his hands were tucked behind his back, and his body now remained perfectly still. "At the beginning, there were more of you," he railed. "Children who arrived at training camp with lunches packed by their mamas and thinking that it would be fun to sail on a boat and play with big guns. Children who were not prepared to do what it takes to represent the finest in France. They quit. Ran back home with their tails between their legs, and I say good riddance, because that is not the sort of man I want beside me or in front of me or behind me in a fight." He paused to draw a breath. "But what's left here today are the men I want standing with me if the world goes all to hell. You can believe that." He released his hands and started walking along the front of the line again.

Nicolas stole a glance at the officer as he approached.

"If your recruit commander has done his job, you have all run enough damn miles that you could have been to Siberia and back by now," he shouted. "You have climbed and crawled and forced your way through things that are impolite to speak of in civilized society. Your lives have been made a living hell on land and on the water because I can damn well guarantee you that the enemy will do nothing less." He stopped in front of Nicolas.

Nicolas kept his eyes glued straight ahead.

"You are the men who have been assigned to the greatest battleship in our entire goddamn fleet, and I expect you all to treat that like the privilege it is. I don't know what the immediate future holds in store for us. We go where the admiralty points us to do the job they require. The Germans are getting unruly again, and someone will have to put a leash on them sooner or later. Spain still seems determined to drag us all into a war. We may be needed in the Mediterranean or the Atlantic. We might expect to move anywhere between North America and North Africa, to places you boys can't even spell much less imagine." The officer stopped to draw a breath.

Nicolas kept his face blank, even as excitement thrummed through him. He wanted to see those places so badly he could taste it.

"Everything you've done since you signed your name over to the navy has been a test," the ensign continued, still standing directly in front of Nicolas. "No matter your assignment on this ship, all of you will start at the bottom. And you will take pride in that, and you will take pride in working your way up." He poked a finger into Nicolas's chest before moving on.

"The navy is not the army, gentlemen. While those boys are running around in trenches looking for things to shoot at and feeling good about the rifles they operate, you, men, will be operating a war machine on the open seas that can obliterate entire cities. You are part of a fleet of the most deadly weapons in the world, and we are still building more." He stopped to glance at the coxswain still standing at attention. "Welcome to the *Bretagne*, men. Good luck and Godspeed." He pivoted and stalked away.

Nicolas relaxed, though he was still wound tight with a mixture of excitement and apprehension. He was equal parts thrilled at the opportunity that sat anchored in the harbour waiting for him and terrified that he would find himself falling short of the task.

"Whooee, looks like trouble comin' this way, Navarre," Fontaine said quietly, picking up the duffel at his feet.

The ensign, the one who had walked away only a moment ago, was returning with a second man, this one wearing the stripes of a first-class officer. Both men stopped in front of Nicolas.

"This is him? Navarre, Nicolas?" The officer read his name from the clipboard he carried, his eyes shadowed by the brim of his hat. He was perhaps ten years Nicolas's senior, with close-cropped brown hair and ramrod straight posture.

"Sir." Nicolas stepped forward, baffled and not a little alarmed by whatever irregularity this was. If his training had taught him anything, it was that irregular was never a good thing.

The ensign fixed Fontaine with a steely stare. "Find a different post, sailor."

Oscar didn't need to be asked twice. He skittered away with haste.

"Is something wrong, sir?" Nicolas asked.

The ensign ignored him. "This is Chief Petty Officer Durant. He would like a word with you."

"Sir?" Nicolas had no idea what was happening. Petty Officer who? And from where?

The officer with the clipboard tucked it under his arm and considered Nicolas with a detached, silent intensity. Nicolas began to feel like he was a bug pinned to a board.

"Your test scores suggest that you are very good at math," he said abruptly.

"Yes, sir?"

"Is that a question, sailor?" the officer demanded.

"No, sir."

"What university did you study at? It is missing from your paperwork."

Nicolas blinked. "I didn't. Go to university. Sir," he added hastily.

Something that looked like annoyance crossed the officer's face. "I see. I am told you are also very clever at repairing engines and mechanical systems and the like."

"Yes, sir." He could at least reply to that with some confidence.

"You repaired a boiler on the training vessel the *Léopard* five weeks ago?"

Nicolas shifted uneasily. "I wouldn't say repaired, exactly, sir. The engineers and the crew did the repairs. I only made a suggestion based on—"

"Did you or did you not evaluate the malfunctioning boiler and offer instruction to the crew on how to repair that particular malfunction, after which time, the boiler, which had been out of service for six days, was put back into working order?" The officer sounded furious.

Nicolas clasped his hands behind his back, his fingers digging

painfully into his palms. He did not look away. "I'm sure the engineers would have discovered the problem in due course—"

"Yes or no!" the officer roared.

"Yes, sir."

"Very good." The clipboard reappeared, and the officer pulled
a thick envelope from beneath the clip. "Report to the chief
engineer upon boarding the *Bretagne*. You will most likely find
him below decks in the engine rooms."

"I'm afraid I don't understand." Nicolas took the proffered
envelope gingerly.

"There is very little to understand." It was the ensign who
answered him. "Among the engineer's apprentices, the navy
always likes to find those with exceptional skills and talent. It is
in our best interests to ensure that those individuals are placed in
positions where they might be most beneficial."

"But do not consider this an accolade, sailor," the officer snapped.
"It's not. Merely an acknowledgement that you might actually
manage to do something worthwhile. Eventually. You'll still need
to prove to your commanding officers that you can do more than
change a lightbulb aboard the *Bretagne*, do you understand?"

"Yes, sir." Nicolas was at a loss for what else to say.

Both officers stalked back the way they had come, leaving
Nicolas standing on the pier, aware of the curious looks he was
getting from his fellow recruits. He stared down at the envelope
in his hands, the weight of what he held making itself known for
the first time. The boy who once fixed toasters and percolators
with stolen parts now held orders that would open the doors
of an engine room of one of the most powerful battleships in
the world.

He slid his hand into his pocket, feeling the reassuring
weight of the lighter wrapped in a worn square of folded paper.

He pulled it out and rested it on top of the stiff envelope. Gently, he pulled open the corner of the paper to reveal his own countenance in profile, set above a swirling cloak and a brandished sword. *You are not nothing, Nicolas Navarre,* Stasia had said when she had given him this drawing once upon a time in a forgotten garden.

He would prove her right or die trying.

"Holy Jesus," Fontaine had sidled back, standing on his tiptoes to watch the departing officers over Nicolas's shoulder. "You must be a wizard or somethin' for the fancy men to take notice of you 'afore you even get onto the ship. I'm stickin' with you." His eyes narrowed as his gaze transferred to the paper Nicolas held. "That a letter from your girl?"

Nicolas quickly refolded the drawing and slipped it and the lighter back into his pocket. "Why would you say that?"

"'Cause no man gets that kind o' expression on his face unless he's thinking of a girl."

Nicolas ducked his head and grinned. "Maybe."

"What's her name?"

"Stasia."

"She waiting at home for you?"

"She's from Rotterdam. But she's in Amsterdam now. Becoming a doctor."

"No shit." Oscar seemed delighted at this revelation. "A real doctor?"

"A real doctor," Nicolas confirmed with no little pride.

"Huh." He rubbed his hands together. "Jus' think how smart your babies will be with a wife like that."

Nicolas laughed. "We're not married."

"What?" Oscar looked appalled. "Why not? Is she mean or ugly or somethin'?"

"She's the kindest, most beautiful girl in the world. We're just waiting."

"Huh." He punched Nicolas lightly on the shoulder. "Maybe you're not near as smart as I thought."

Nicolas's grip tightened on the envelope containing his orders as longing pierced through him. "Maybe you're right." He cleared his throat. "What about you? You got a girl?"

Oscar found this funny. "Nah. Gotta see the world and all its beautiful women before I settle on one."

The coxswain was shouting orders for the recruits to board the tenders that would take them across the harbour. Nicolas moved forward, hefting his own duffel over his shoulder, and he and Oscar joined the queue of men.

"You really fix the *Léopard*?" Oscar shuffled forward.

"You really eavesdrop on private conversations?" Nicolas asked drily.

"Of course," Fontaine scoffed. "I can listen in my sleep for the bastard who's come to stab me for the heel of bread in my pocket."

"I don't think anyone on board the *Bretagne* will stab you for a piece of bread."

"You know, I think that may be my favourite thing about the French navy," Fontaine grinned.

"That everyone has their own bread?"

The scrappy Parisian shook his head. "That your friends an' allies don't try an' kill you."

CHAPTER

6

Stasia

14 MAY 1940
ROTTERDAM, THE NETHERLANDS

The German tanks came yesterday.

They had rumbled through the streets on the southern side of the Nieuwe Maas with a growl, terrifying in its constancy, that was heard clearly across the ribbon of river. There was something about the guttural snarl of the armoured vehicles that Stasia had found more chilling than the rest of the fighting that had gone on in the days before—the rattling of machine guns, the whine and thump of mortars, or the groaning of the antiquated navy boats sent up the river in a desperate attempt to stanch the German attack. Even the shriek of the Dutch bombers intent on destroying the city's bridges in an effort to keep the invaders out of the north had not been as unsettling as the creeping advance of the Panzers.

Perhaps it was that the arrival of the tanks lacked the chaos that the first three days of fighting had been marked by. For in chaos, there was still hope that victory might be salvaged. That

Rotterdam, though it might be burning and crippled, could yet be saved and would not fall to an enemy that still forced its way forward.

"Why have they stopped?" Helen Kaufmann's panicked question bounced off the walls of the flat as she paced incessantly. "What are they waiting for? Why aren't they coming across the river?"

"Stop it, Mother," Margot whispered harshly from where she was sitting at the tiny kitchen table. "You're not helping. And you'll wake Minna."

Stasia kept her eyes glued out the window in the direction of the river. She didn't know why the tanks had stopped or why the guns had quieted. She didn't know why the armoured vehicles hadn't rolled across the desperately and inadequately defended bridges and infested the north the same as they had the south. Why German troops weren't right now flooding over the bodies and wreckage that littered the banks and bridgeheads.

The radio broadcast news but often it was conflicting, the rough, tinny voices offering little in the way of reassurance or direction. It seemed no one had any real answers, and the two people who might—her father and Margot's father—were somewhere just to the east of their Kralingen neighbourhood, working frantically with those who were still trying to find ways to reinforce and defend the bridges and ports. Stasia and the others had gotten a brief message two days ago assuring them that both men were fine, but nothing since. Stasia was sick with worry.

"We can't stay here." Helen was wringing her hands. "I need to find Behtram, and we need to leave."

"And go where?" Margot demanded, pushing her chair back with a scrape. "There is nowhere to go. It's too dangerous."

"We left everything behind and ran once," Frau Kaufmann cried. "And now the Nazis are here. We have to run again."

Stasia turned from the window, wondering if there was anywhere left to go, even if they could simply flee. Wondering if the same thing that was happening to Rotterdam was happening across the country.

At the beginning of the week, both their fathers had insisted Stasia and Margot leave university, at least temporarily, and return to Rotterdam. Both men had heard rumours, they said, that after the invasion of Poland and Denmark and Norway, Germany would next turn its eyes west. Both decided that their daughters would be safer away from the coast, from the rich prizes that would be Amsterdam and The Hague.

"I'm going." Helen had stopped abruptly in the middle of the flat. "I'm taking Minna and going down to the port to find Behtram and getting out."

"My father said that we'd be safe here," Stasia said quietly. "That the military is negotiating."

"Negotiating?" Helen's voice was shrill. "Negotiating what? Terms of our surrender? How many people have to die before the Nazis take what they want anyway?"

"I don't know," Stasia mumbled, feeling faintly nauseous at the thought of surrender. What would that mean? "But I don't think that we should—"

"No," Helen snapped. "I'm not listening to you or anyone else. You know nothing. So I'm going to do what's best for myself and my family. We're getting out of this city." Helen was already striding down the narrow hall toward the bedroom where Minna was napping.

"Wait," Margot hurried after her, catching her elbow. "Stasia and I will find out what is happening."

Helen spun. "How? How are you going to do that?"

Margot looked at Stasia helplessly.

"Mama?" Minna had appeared in the doorway of the bedroom. Her eyes were wide and fearful, and her hair was still rumpled from sleep.

Helen crouched by her daughter and smoothed a hand over her head. She spoke in rapid, soothing German to her daughter, worry creased across her face.

"I'll go," Stasia volunteered. "I'll go to the port. Someone will know what is happening, even if I can't find my father."

Margot was already shaking her head. "No. That's—"

"Better than having Minna out on the streets," Stasia finished for her. "I grew up here. I know these neighbourhoods. I know how to get to the port. It's not far at all, and I'll be quick and careful. I'll find out what's happening."

"Then I'm coming with you." Margot crossed her arms over her chest.

Helen was looking back and forth between Stasia and Margot uncertainly.

"Maybe the guns have stopped because the Germans are preparing to retreat," Stasia said, trying to keep the note of desperation out of her voice. "And if that's the case, no one has to run anywhere." She glanced at the clock that ticked away the interminable minutes. It was just after one o'clock in the afternoon, though the thick smoke drifting over the city made it seem more like dusk.

"How long?" Helen asked tremulously. "How long to get there and back?"

"Thirty minutes. Maybe less."

"Promise me you'll stay here," Margot said to her mother. "That you and Minna will wait here for us to come back. Once we know more, then we can decide what to do next."

Slowly, Helen nodded.

"Let's go then," Stasia said to Margot.

Margot gave her mother a brief hug and then bent to embrace her little sister, kissing her on the top of her head. "We'll be back soon," she whispered.

Stasia looked away, already starting toward the door. Margot caught up with her at the bottom of the stairs. Both girls hesitated at the door leading out of the building and into the street.

"Maybe you should stay with your family," Stasia said.

"They're safe here for now." Margot pushed the door open with more force than she needed. It banged loudly against the brick wall, making Stasia jump.

"Besides, you're my family too." She gave Stasia a brave smile. "We'll look out for each other too."

Stasia nodded and stepped out into the street, knowing that if she didn't do so now, she might cower here indefinitely. Her heart was hammering in her chest, and her mouth was dry. Outside, the acrid smell of smoke hung heavy and thick, making her eyes burn and her throat itch. For the most part, the street was deserted, the occasional silhouette of a person rushing somewhere on foot or appearing like a specter on a bicycle only to vanish into the gloom again.

On the sidewalk, Margot reached for Stasia's hand and squeezed. "I'll follow you," she said.

Stasia squeezed back and then turned toward the port, breaking into a run. She looked neither left nor right, simply kept her eyes on the tip of Sint-Laurenskerk's elevated tower, which appeared and disappeared through the gaps in the buildings and the clouds of drifting smoke. By the time they crossed the Boezem canal, Stasia's breath was coming in ragged gasps, the choking air burning her lungs. But she dared not stop. The city was eerily still, as though it had been frozen in time, a sinister pall an almost palpable thing that hung around them. Occasionally, a muted thump followed by the roar of a flame echoed from somewhere across the river, and ghostly shouts ricocheted through the gloom.

She turned south, toward the wide river, straining to catch a glimpse of Noordereiland, wondering if the Germans had made it to the island in the center. The thought was terrifying, yet accompanying her fear seemed to be a bizarre sense of disbelief that she wasn't simply caught up in some nightmare from which she would suddenly wake, feeling both foolish and relieved. That the speculation that had swirled for months between citizens gathered on street corners, speaking in low, worried tones about the aggression of the Nazis, had now become reality.

"How much farther?" Margot asked from behind her.

"Not far." Just up ahead she could see the very crown of the Witte Huis. It had always been Stasia's favourite building in Rotterdam, and its glazed white brick and corner turrets beckoned like a pale, fairy-tale beacon amid the jumble of buildings from centuries past.

The last time she had heard from her father, he had been in the Maritime District. Even if she couldn't find him, surely someone there would know what was happening on the other side of the river. Surely someone this close to the water would be able to tell them something—

The scream of the air raid siren sliced through the pall and sent a shock of pure terror through Stasia, bringing her to a stumbling halt. Margot banged into her, clutching her sleeve as both girls remained motionless, trying to understand what was happening or where the threat might be coming from.

"What are those?" Margot coughed, out of breath and covering her mouth with her sleeve.

Across the river, somewhere in the south, a series of bright flares exploded in the sky, like shooting stars brought far too close to earth before being smothered by clouds of smoke. Stasia could only stare in confusion. She was looking for planes in the southern expanse, but it was almost impossible to see anything through the swirling, ashy haze. Somewhere close by, small artillery chattered, punctuated by sharp, booming cracks as larger caliber weapons fired. Who was shooting? The Dutch? The Germans? What were they shooting at? And then she heard them.

It was a faint noise at first, like a distant hum barely discernible over the siren. Like a swarm of hornets, a steady drone that built and turned Stasia's knees to water. Slowly, she turned away from the south, a sob catching in her chest as she saw the northeast sky filled with the black silhouettes of planes. There were maybe fifty or more—each plane's wings spread wide, its propellers a smudged blur on either side. Through the veil of smoke they kept coming, and it was impossible to count amid the paralyzing fear that had her feet rooted to the cobblestones.

Around Stasia, there were people in the street now, running in all directions, some shouting, some crying, and some utterly silent, their faces set into grotesque masks of terror. The throbbing howl of the oncoming planes had reduced the siren to an afterthought, and the white crosses on the undersides of the wings flashed in strips of daylight. And then the first bombs began to fall.

Stasia stood stupidly on the pavement, watching as each tumbled from the bowels of the planes like a deadly rain, whistling as they descended toward earth. The first one disappeared somewhere into the neighbourhood that they had just come from, and time seemed to stand still. Until the ground beneath her feet tremored, the explosion reverberated all around her, and the air compressed as if it too had nowhere to escape. A wall of fire erupted and the roar was deafening. Three more fell in rapid succession after it, each sending a shockwave through the ground.

"Stasia!" Someone was yanking on her sweater with a desperate strength, knocking her off-balance and finally forcing her legs to move. "We have to—" Margot didn't finish whatever she was going to say as another bomb detonated much closer to the river, knocking both girls sideways and sending a firestorm dancing hungrily into the sky.

A wave of intense heat washed over them, and Stasia put her hands up to shield her face and blindly turned away. She started running again, Margot at her side, tripping and sliding over a ground that refused to stay still. All around them, the world had disintegrated into a maelstrom of crumbling brick and buckling timbers, of sucking flames and debilitating heat. She headed for the river and the feeble promise of safety and the protection of the river walls.

Each step was an effort, like she was caught in a horrible dream in which her destination kept getting farther and farther away no matter how hard she ran. Burning bits of paper spun and eddied through the air from offices that no longer existed. To her right, just up the street, a building dissolved, its walls imploding and then vanishing into a curtain of ash, dust, and fire. Margot fell to her knees as glass and masonry rained down around them, and Stasia hauled her back up to her feet. Together they ran on. They were nearly at the water now, its normally placid surface a toxic mirror of red and orange, geysers erupting in places where explosives fell. Boats that had been tied up at the edges of the channels were rocking violently, many of them already engulfed in flames.

Stasia cried out as a woman suddenly stepped in front of them, her dress torn, her hair singed from one side of her head, and her entire face coated ghoulishly with dust and ash, save for the dark streaks of blood that ran from her temple. She was screaming something unintelligible and clawing at Stasia, pointing to a partially collapsed wall. Stasia tried to draw away but the woman would not relinquish her hold and with a startling strength, pulled Stasia closer to the ruined building, still babbling hysterically. She bent and started throwing broken bricks into the street, crying and begging Stasia and Margot to do the same.

"Her daughters." Stasia was finally able to understand. "They are under here."

"Then they're dead," Margot wheezed. "We can't stay here."

"We have to help her look."

"Are you insane?" Margo yanked at Stasia but she jerked away. "We're going to die if we stay here."

"I'm not leaving her. I have to help her." Stasia dropped to her knees, pulling aside chunks of stone and brick. "What if it were Minna?" Already her fingers were bleeding. She didn't care.

Margot swore and dropped beside Stasia, hauling aside rubble like a woman possessed. "Goddamn your goddamn goodness," she yelled angrily, flinging aside a broken board. "Goddamn your goddamn heart."

They worked frantically, nearly blind in the thick smoke roiling from every direction, bracing themselves against the sickening thumps as more and more bombs found their mark. A body pressed against Stasia's side, first one and then another, and suddenly there were a dozen hands working alongside hers, men all dressed in baggy, matching clothes with wide stripes. Prisoners, Stasia realized with a strange sense of detachment. Prisoners that had either escaped or been released from their cells were digging through the rubble beside them now.

One of them shouted, and they swarmed toward the man, clearing away a pile of shattered lathe and broken plaster. There was a hollow, under a flight of stairs that improbably still stood, rising to nowhere, and in that hollow, two small girls no more than four years old huddled, frightened and wide-eyed. The woman fell on them, sobbing hysterically, and gathered them in her arms, stumbling back over the ruins of the wall. Without even looking back, she vanished down the street into the wall of smoke and flames billowing from all sides.

The men who had been helping had scattered and now melted away into the inferno. Stasia grabbed Margot's hand and pulled her back in the direction of the water. If they could just get to the edge of—

The world went black for a moment, and a splitting pain lanced through her eardrums. She found herself weightless for a moment, before a crashing blow to her side knocked her almost senseless. Dazed, it took her a minute to understand that she was lying on her back against the side of a building, and that the dark, angular shape above her head was the trunk of a tree that had been ripped from its roots and tossed to the side like a toothpick. Farther out, the sky had gone a cataclysmic red and the branches of the remaining trees that had lined the street formed a blazing umbrella above her head. Her mouth was filled with the bitter taste of ash and earth, and she tried to spit, only to gag. Her ears were ringing and it was hard to breathe amid the heat and the embers and the flames. Stasia tried not to give in to panic. With effort, she rolled out from under the tree, gritting her teeth against the pain, and pushed herself to her hands and knees.

Margot lay beside her, coughing and retching, her left arm soaked in blood. The ground under Stasia's hands and knees shook and trembled. *Think*, she pleaded with herself. What should she do? Where should she go? How could she survive this? She blinked, trying to steady her vision as the wall beside her seemed to shift and sway, but the more she did, the worse it seemed to get. A tortured groan of metal tearing itself apart came from somewhere above her head, and with terrifying clarity, Stasia realized that there was nothing wrong with her vision and everything wrong with the building they were up against.

As the first chunks of masonry and brick began to fall, she grabbed Margot's shoulders with feverish desperation and hauled her friend toward her, shoving her beneath the thick tree trunk. She ignored Margot's cry of pain and pushed as hard as she could, crawling over her and shielding her as best she could.

"I don't want to die," Margot whimpered, and Stasia tried to answer, but a vibration started through every fiber of her being and knocked her teeth against each other. She clenched her jaw closed and squeezed her eyes shut as the tortured groan above her head turned into a shriek. More pieces of stone and wood and glass began to fall, and everywhere there was heat and fire and chaos. Stasia put her hands over her head and curled her body against Margot's.

And everything went dark.

CHAPTER

7

Nicolas

3 JULY 1940
MERS EL KÉBIR, ALGERIA

Everything was bright.

The sun was relentless here, bleaching the brown hills that surrounded the harbour, beating down on the stubborn, scrabbly vegetation that clung to them, and reflecting off the deep blue of the Alboran Sea with a blinding glare. On the western edge of the bowl that was this harbour, the town of Mers el Kébir also baked in the sun, the pale buildings dappled in places by orange-red roofs. To the northeast, the finger of land that jutted out from the hills narrowed into an unfinished seawall, snaking south across the mouth of the harbour and hemming in the French ships that had anchored in the still waters.

Nicolas leaned against the rail of the *Bretagne*, rubbing the back of his neck and staring into his coffee. He was exhausted. He had been up since long before dawn, fighting with a temperamental throttle valve that had continued to be belligerent and

bad-tempered. But then it seemed everybody was feeling belligerent and bad-tempered, so it was possible that the ship was
simply absorbing all the ill humour since France had surrendered
to the Germans a month ago.

That revelation had been met with furious, devastating shock
and disbelief. And humiliation. The humiliation had been the
worst. Twenty years ago, the French had held out for four years,
refusing to give in or give up. They had left over a million men
dead in the mud and the barbed wire and the trenches, and
countless more, like Nicolas's father, wishing they had died. But
in this new conflict, the French army had crumbled in barely
thirty days. Thirty days to surrender everything and stand by and
watch the Nazis goosestep their way past the Arc de Triomphe.
It was unconscionable.

Their officers had made their announcements, of course, and
Fontaine had managed to get his hands on a local newspaper
before they had left Bizerte. As far as Nicolas knew, Admiral
Gensoul had not surrendered the French fleet to anyone. But
while the Nazis took Paris and made themselves at home in
the French cities and countryside, the *Bretagne*, along with the
battleships *Provence*, *Strasbourg,* and *Dunkerque* and a collection
of destroyers, had sailed farther away from their beleaguered
country and cowered and broiled in the unremitting African
heat. For what purpose, Nicolas could only guess.

The French officers had been ridiculously tight-lipped.
Information was scarce though rumours were plentiful. The
Nazis were hunting what was left of the French fleet. The
Nazis had promised that they would leave the French fleet
alone. The Italians, in bed with the Nazis, wanted to get their
hands on the French fleet. The British wanted the French fleet
to repatriate into their own navy and flee to the Caribbean to

hide away until saner minds could resolve this war. The British wanted the French to scuttle their own ships to keep them out of German or Italian hands.

The latter seemed the most insane rumour of the bunch but Nicolas had no idea what to believe anymore. Every day seemed to bring a new round of speculation, yet every day in a month of preparatory exercises and drills had ended the same—with the French battleships continuing to sit at anchor, quiet and idle.

"You gonna drink that coffee or just admire it?" Oscar appeared beside Nicolas, a cigarette clamped between his lips and a dish towel slung over his shoulder.

"I haven't decided." Nicolas gave his friend a weary smile.

"Please drink it," the messman sniffed. "I have a reputation to uphold."

Nicolas took a deliberate sip of his cooling coffee. "Best coffee I've ever tasted."

Fontaine grunted. "Of course it is."

Nicolas shaded his eyes against the early evening sun. "You missed the latest round of excitement. The Brits already left the *Dunkerque* and ferried themselves back to their own fleet."

"Doesn't actually sound very exciting."

"It wasn't. Just more men standing and shuffling around, gawking and trying to guess what's going on."

"Sounds like a brothel," Oscar commented.

Nicolas snorted.

"You missed the mess line earlier. Will be another hour till we serve again."

"I was trying to figure something out in the engine room."

"And did you?"

"Not yet."

Oscar wiped the sweat from his brow with the shoulder of his uniform and gave him a knowing grin. "Finally forced you to come up here out of the caves down below to eat somethin' and see the sun, didn't they? You lot are probably all turning into vampires down there."

"Very funny." Nicolas rolled his shoulders, the muscles protesting.

"Well, I got a break now 'afore I need to get back to it." He flicked ash from the end of his cigarette toward the water far below. "Can I get you anything else?"

"An explanation why the British fleet continues to skulk about northwest of this harbour like we're the damn enemy?" Nicolas slapped his palm on the rail, making his coffee tin bounce. "Justification for why they sent their Swordfish to fly over our ships and drop mines across the mouth of the harbour after lunch? What, they don't want us to leave? Or they don't want anyone else to come in?"

"I was thinking more along the lines of toast or a biscuit." Oscar was eyeing him with concern. "I'm thinking they shoulda sent you up earlier, 'afore you got this tetchy." He dug into his apron pocket and withdrew a foil-wrapped bar. "Little melted, but maybe you should at least have some chocolate 'afore it's some officer whose head you take off next. They'll not be so forgiving, yes?"

Nicolas heaved a sigh and accepted the chocolate. "Sorry. Thank you. You're a good friend."

"I know." Oscar pinched off the end of his cigarette and tucked what remained behind his ear for later.

"We've trained for years to fight, and what do we do when the fight is put in front of us? We escort troops. We escort shipments of gold and planes. We search for German blockade-runners and commercial raiders, and when we fail at that, we come here. To do what?"

Oscar shrugged, smoothing his moustache that was still as thin as it had been two years ago. "Dunno."

Nicolas drained the dregs of his coffee and scrubbed at his eyes. "All this waiting is good for nothing."

"Not nothing. All this waiting means our mail could catch up with us." The comment came from behind him. A sailor stood there with a thick bundle of mail. "Been chasing us around."

Oscar rubbed his hands together with clear delight. "Pavel, my friend."

"I figured I'd find you peeling potatoes."

"They let us out of our cages from time to time to work on our tans up here. You got my newspapers?"

"Two from Paris. Both *Le Figaro*. And they are only a month and a half old." The sailor sorted through the pile. "Here." He extracted a bulky bundle tied with twine and held it out to Oscar. "Don't know why you bother. You'll probably just have to read about the invasion all over again."

"I like newspapers. A little piece of home, or whatever may be left of it." Oscar snatched the papers from the sailor's hand, digging into the deep pocket of his apron. "And God knows no one tells us much about nothin'." He produced a pack of Gitanes and handed them to the sailor.

"Always good doing business with you, Fontaine." The man's gaze transferred to Nicolas. "Name? Might have mail for you while I'm here."

"Navarre. Nicolas."

"Mmm." He rifled through the stack. "Two for you. Lucky man."

"Thank you." Nicolas took the proffered envelopes, the sight of the familiar slanted writing on the top one sending a rush of happiness through him.

"Oooeee, must be from your girl," Oscar said as the sailor moved on. He untied the knot that secured his papers. "Only time I see you blush like that."

"It's the sun."

Oscar barked out a laugh. He pulled the twine from the newspapers and smacked the end of it against Nicolas's letters. "You want to read me the naughty bits?"

"Don't you have a newspaper to read?"

Oscar laughed again and opened the first of his precious papers.

Nicolas ignored him, set his mug aside, and tore open the envelope, unwilling to wait. It had been months since he had heard from Stasia, and the mail that usually came regularly for the sailors had been interrupted and sporadic since the spring. He slid the uncharacteristically thin missive out and unfolded it.

9 May 1940

Dearest Nicolas,

Forgive the brevity of this letter but I am travelling back to Rotterdam as I write this. My father has asked me to leave Amsterdam, at least temporarily, fearing a German threat. I am certain that he is being alarmist and overprotective. However, I confess that I am not opposed to being close to family and home right now. I will write you again, hopefully soon, once the danger of war here has passed and I am able to resume my studies—

"Didn't you say your girl was from Rotterdam?" Oscar asked abruptly from behind his paper.

"Yes," Nicolas replied, frowning. What the hell was happening in Amsterdam that Stasia and her family felt the need to—

"They bombed it."

"What?"

"The boches bombed Rotterdam. On May fourteenth. It says here they think thirty thousand people died."

"What?" It came out as a croak.

"They didn't just invade, they destroyed the whole center of Rotterdam. And everything to the north of it. Forced the whole damn country to surrender. Jesus." He scowled at the paper. "You think they're gonna get the Brits next? Flatten London and bomb them right off their island?"

Nicolas barely heard him. The bottom of his stomach had dropped to his toes, and a horrible, smothering dread slithered through him.

I am travelling back to Rotterdam as I write this.

Had Stasia been in the city when it was bombed? Was she safe? She spoke often about their flat that was close to the ports in the city center near where her father worked, but had she been there?

"You all right?" Oscar's voice finally penetrated. "You look pale, even under all that grease and grime."

Nicolas looked at him helplessly, unable to even utter the unbearable thoughts that were clamouring in his mind. "What else does it say? Is there a list of the dead?" He finally found his voice.

"No. Doesn't say much." Oscar peered at him. "What's wrong?"

"Stasia . . ." He couldn't bring himself to say it.

"She's in Amsterdam, right? At doctor school? The boches didn't bomb that city. At least at the time this was printed. She'll be fine, I'm sure."

"She went home. To Rotterdam. Right before..."

"Shit." Oscar swallowed. "But that doesn't mean that anything happened to her, right? She's probably spittin' mad at what they did." He paused. "Weren't there two letters for you? Probably another one from her telling you not to worry."

"Right." Nicolas looked down at the letters he still held in his unfeeling hands. He pulled the second one from beneath Stasia's. The handwriting wasn't hers—it was heavy and deliberate and uniform. The postmark said *Rouen*, and the return address was one he did not recognize.

"Who's it from?" Oscar asked.

"I don't know."

"Well, maybe they have news. About your girl. About the war. Something. Anything."

"Yes," Nicolas replied faintly. He slid his finger under the lip of the envelope and tore it open. This, too, was a single sheet of paper, covered with neatly typed paragraphs, with a stamp at the top noting the name and address of a law office located in Rouen. It was dated at the beginning of June, more than a month after Stasia's letter. Fingers of ice slid through his body, making him shiver even under the relentless African sun. Nicolas lifted the page, realizing that his hand was shaking.

10 June 1940

Estate of the late M. P. Moreau & Mme. J. Moreau, Val-de-la-Haye, France / Account: 487001

Dear M. Nicolas Navarre,

We are writing to inform you of the final distribution to the named heirs to the estate of the late M. and Mme. Moreau, as per our clients' last will and testament. With the confirmed deaths of M. Michel Neimic and Mlle. Stasia Neimic on 14 May 1940, you are the sole remaining beneficiary of the current farm properties, assets of the estate—

Nicolas crumpled the letter in his fist and bent double, hands on his knees, gasping as if he had been punched. For a moment, he thought he might be sick.

Oscar was instantly beside him. The messman extracted the letter from his hand and smoothed it flat, squinting as he read. "I'm real sorry, Navarre," he said after a moment.

Nicolas couldn't answer.

"It says here that they got a notification from the company your girl's father worked for. Says they were killed on May fourteenth. Nothing left of either their home or place of work. No personal effects or records to forward."

Nicolas straightened and put a hand on the railing to steady himself. "She was worried for me. *Me*. Being in the navy. Worried that something would happen to me." A haze of grief was making it difficult to think or to put his thoughts into order. "I never even considered that she would be in danger. I'm a man on a goddamn battleship in the middle of a war, and somehow I'm safer than a girl who stayed at home to become a doctor." Fury and despair were expanding in his chest. "Fucking boches destroying everything they touch, and here we sit, hiding on ships that could blow Berlin to pieces." He sucked in a ragged breath. "I should have told her to stay in Rouen. I should have—"

"This wasn't your fault," Oscar said. "None of this. You didn't know this would happen. She didn't know this would happen. And if she had stayed in Rouen, who is to say she would have been any safer than—"

"I should have done something," Nicolas shouted.

A petty officer passing by paused to stare at Nicolas in disapproval. Nicolas ignored him.

"Like what?" Oscar asked gently. "There's nothing you could do. Nothing no one could do. Sometimes awful things just—"

A distant boom interrupted whatever he was going to say next. The officer that had stopped spun, squinting out toward the northwest. As he did so, a massive plume of water rose from behind the *Bretagne*. The sound of two more blasts roared, and another two columns of water erupted in the harbour.

"What the hell was that?" Oscar wheezed.

"They're firing at us," Nicolas said, stunned. "The goddamn Brits are firing at us."

"What? Why?" Oscar had gone white. "Why would they do that? We're on the same fucking side!"

Two ships north, Nicolas could see men swarming over the decks of the *Dunkerque* as the battleship started to pull away from the seawall, presumably in an attempt to escape the harbour. All around him, chaos had been unleashed. Officers were yelling, men were running, and still the sound of massive guns being fired thundered all around him. But not French guns. Aboard the battleships and cruisers and destroyers, nothing was answering the battery of the British assault.

"Goddammit, we're sitting here like dead ducks in a goddamn line—"

A crash of shells finding their targets reverberated, and Nicolas saw the *Dunkerque* shudder a second before a massive fireball rose into the air. The great battleship listed, crippled and drifting and burning. The screams of men filled the air, and Nicolas watched in horror as sailors flung themselves from the burning decks into the water. Smoke billowed in thick, black clouds, rising into the air and over the harbour as the *Dunkerque* continued to burn.

"Get to your posts!" An officer shoved by Nicolas and Oscar, his voice hoarse. "Now!"

Directly beside the *Bretagne*, the *Strasbourg* was now pulling away from the seawall, attempting its own desperate escape. Why wasn't the *Bretagne* moving? Why were they not firing back? What the hell were they waiting for—

The deck of the *Bretagne* abruptly rose and fell as an explosion rocked the ship. Nicolas was flung into the air and sent crashing into the rail as the ship bucked beneath him. A ball of fire shot into the sky, past the masthead, licking and curling as the flames fed on oxygen and accelerant. They'd hit one of the ship's magazines, Nicolas thought hazily. They'd gutted the *Bretagne* with its own munitions.

The heat kept him pinned to the deck where he lay crumpled as it crackled and roared above, blasting and assaulting him with the intensity of an open furnace. Nicolas put an arm up to cover his face, the heat biting and blistering exposed skin. Desperately, he rolled onto his hands and knees and crawled backward, away from the fire. He tried to scramble to his feet but the deck was tilting slowly, making it difficult. His surroundings blurred and faded, and Nicolas blinked hard, realizing that it wasn't the smoke but blood was dripping into his eye from a gash somewhere on his head. Frantically, he wiped it away with his sleeve, looking for Oscar. His friend was nowhere to be seen, the deck where he had been standing a mess of splinters and debris all shrouded in smoke.

"Oscar!" he yelled, coughing violently. "Oscar!" he shouted again once he caught his breath.

But there was no answer.

A corpsman staggered by awkwardly, stumbling to a stop when he saw Nicolas. His face was darkened with soot, and his eyes were a shocking shade of pale blue against the grime.

"You hurt?" he shouted, and it sounded like his voice was coming from a million miles away. Everything was muffled, Nicolas realized, whether from the effects of the blast or the unceasing roar of the fire that still licked heavenward.

"No." But where was Oscar?

"I need your help," the corpsman shouted. Without waiting for a reply, he strapped a canvas medical bag over Nicolas's shoulder, identical to the one he was wearing, and pushed Nicolas in the direction he'd been heading.

"I need to get to my post," Nicolas wheezed. "The engine room—"

"Engine room's gone," the corpsman yelled. "No power and no comms right now. I can use you here and now."

Nicolas stumbled forward. How could the engine room be gone? Jesus, what about the men with whom Nicolas had been talking less than a half hour ago? Had any of them survived? Where would they be?

The corpsman led Nicolas away from the worst of the flames, away from the choking black smoke still billowing, and toward the aft section of the ship. All around him, the sounds of men screaming were becoming audible now. Some were crawling and stumbling out of hatchways from below decks, some with burns too horrible to believe. A man, almost unidentifiable as one, his clothes burned away and his skin an agony of peeling black and red, reached for Nicolas before collapsing on the deck in an unmoving pile. Nicolas stopped, only to be hauled forward by the corpsman.

"Leave him. Nothing to do for him," he said with a grim expression.

"But—"

"Find the ones we can save. See to them."

Nicolas stared after him. He couldn't do this. His job was fixing valves and cylinders and pistons and crankshafts. Not fixing wounded and terrified and desperate men. He wasn't that person.

Stasia was that person.

Inexplicably, the thought seemed to calm him. He had a muddled notion that she was there, beside him, guiding him through whatever nightmare this was. He imagined what she would say, what she would do, how she would act in this hellish landscape. Her voice would be firm, her hands sure, her focus absolute. She had taught him basic first aid, and with it, she had taught him composure and control, how to assess and soothe. She had taught him everything he would need to get through whatever was coming next. He could do this. He would do this for her.

Nicolas stumbled after the corpsman, finding him bent over three sailors lying on the shattered deck. Two were motionless, and the third was covered in blood and rocking back and forth. He was clutching his arm to his chest, and Nicolas could see that above the bloody stump of his wrist, his hand was missing. Nicolas crouched, yanking a length of thick bandage from the medical kit with clumsy, shaking fingers.

One step at a time, he could almost hear Stasia telling him. *If you panic, your patient will panic. Act quickly but calmly.*

Nicolas managed to extract the bandage and wrapped it as

tightly as he could just above the man's elbow as a tourniquet then tied it in a knot. He wasn't sure if the sailor was even aware of his presence, his eyes wide and staring in shock, but at least the bleeding had slowed considerably.

"These two are dead." The corpsman glanced at Nicolas's work and jammed morphine into the man's thigh as Nicolas backed away. "Good job. You've done this before."

"Not really," Nicolas mumbled.

"Let's go."

"Should we take him with us?"

"Can't. We'll send a stretcher for him later. Hurry. There are more that we need to find."

Like Oscar. Where was his friend? Had he been knocked into the water by the blast? Was he alive somewhere? Dead? Or did he look like one of the horrible, blackened corpses that had once been men?

The corpsman said something that Nicolas didn't hear.

"What?"

"Goddamn traitors," he repeated, spitting in the direction of the British fleet. "We are not the goddamn enemy!"

Nicolas pushed forward, the deck of the *Bretagne* listing at a harder angle now. She was flooding from damage to her hull that Nicolas couldn't even begin to guess at, and the water, though possibly preventing more munitions below the waterline from igniting, was slowly dragging the ship down. Another seaman crawled toward him, dragging a leg that was a shredded, bloody mess.

"Wrap that, give him morphine for the pain, and move on," the corpsman shouted. "He might live."

Nicolas bent to do just that, grabbing the sailor by the shoulders and pushing him to the side. The man screamed and pummeled Nicolas, and, for a moment, he was transported to his childhood, his father shrieking at and punching Nicolas as he tried to help. "Be still," he said in the same voice he'd used with his father. "I'm going to fix you up."

Miraculously, the sailor stopped fighting him, his breathing a series of panicked gulps. "Don't leave me," he begged Nicolas. "Don't leave me here to die."

"You're not going die," Nicolas told him, knowing nothing of the sort. He administered morphine and used a bundle of gauze to awkwardly wrap the man's leg. He straightened.

"We're sinking," the sailor cried, grabbing the pant leg of Nicolas's uniform. "Get me off the ship."

"We're not sinking that fast," Nicolas said, having no idea if he was lying or not. "Plenty of time to get you and everyone else I can off."

"Don't leave me."

"You'll be fine," Nicolas told him, trying to pull away. "I'm going to help some others."

"I don't care about the others!" the sailor shrieked. "Get me off!"

Nicolas yanked himself away. "There's nowhere to go right now. Someone will be along shortly to—"

Another deafening explosion rocked the *Bretagne*, and once again, Nicolas found himself thrown to the deck. A new round of flames erupted somewhere in the vicinity of turret three, popping and crackling sounds of more ammunition being ignited echoing faintly beneath the roar. The sailor Nicolas had been treating was still lying nearby, his hands over his ears and his eyes tightly shut.

Nicolas hauled himself to his feet, the list even more pronounced now. He had lost his medical kit somewhere. More smoke billowed and enshrouded the decks, obscuring not only the ship, but the sky and the sea around them. He looked wildly for the corpsman but the young man with the bright blue eyes was nowhere to be found. Somewhere ahead of him, a sailor was screaming for help. Nicolas staggered forward but slipped and fell to his hands and knees before he could make it more than a few feet. With a peculiar detachment, he realized that he had slipped in a sheet of blood that was now sticking to his palms and soaking into his uniform.

In the distance, guns were still booming as the British continued to fire on the cluster of French ships. Death still whispered ever closer, from the air, from the water, from the very ship herself. Time had ceased to be measurable in any way or form. Nicolas pulled himself back up against the nearest bulkhead and wondered if perhaps he had simply died already and this was hell.

It could have been hours or seconds before the next explosion tore through the *Bretagne*, the once powerful battleship convulsing beneath his feet. The deck tilted wildly, and a shadow darkened the already obscure sky. With a mounting sense of disbelief, Nicolas realized that the shape looming over his head was one of the *Bretagne*'s massive towers as it bowed down toward the water. The battleship, a ship that he'd known to be impervious to capsizing, was doing just that. And she would take everyone with her unless they could get themselves free.

Nicolas scrambled toward the railing that was rising higher and higher in front of him. He managed to grasp it with hands still slick with blood, refusing to let go. The ship was rolling faster now, and Nicolas managed to swing a leg over the railing as seawater churned hungrily below him. Around him, sailors who were able were doing the same, trying desperately to avoid being crushed by the massive ship. Others were not so fortunate and slid or fell screaming toward the roiling sea, being sucked and spun beneath the carcass of the *Bretagne*.

With a monumental effort, Nicolas managed to get all the way over the railing as the ship continued to sink, getting closer to the water with the passing of each terrifying second. He clung to the railing for as long as he could, until he could feel the spray biting at his exposed skin as air and seawater were forced upward through the cratered blowholes of the broken ship. He took a deep breath and leapt as far out as he could, the water closing in over his head almost immediately. He found himself tumbling and cartwheeling underwater, and it took everything within him not to panic and fight an unwinnable battle.

Something heavy struck his arm above his wrist, and he recoiled, though the pain was strangely brief. His lungs began to burn as his body slowed, and he opened his eyes, fixating on the bubbles that were rising in front of him. He struck out, following them upward, swimming until his vision dimmed at the edges. Just when he was certain that he wouldn't ever see the surface again, his head broke clear of the water, and he sucked in great, choking lungfuls of air.

When he had slowed his breathing, he twisted, seeing that other men had made it into the water but they were pitifully few. Some were thrashing, others seemed to be treading water silently, too shocked or unsure of what had happened or what to do next. With a dawning sense of horror, he understood that the men in the water were what remained of the *Bretagne*'s crew. Only a shallow, jagged island that was the hull of the *Bretagne* was visible, like the carcass of a dead whale. A column of black smoke frothed from the edge where the ship yet burned from her wounds. The rest of the great battleship and her crew had vanished, marked only by a churning froth of bubbles and debris.

The *Strasbourg* was also gone, and through the smoke and madness, Nicolas couldn't be sure if that battleship had simply sunk or if it had escaped the harbour. Farther away, the *Dunkerque* continued to burn, bits of black and white ash swirling down around him like a ghoulish snowfall. In places, the water was on fire where oil had slicked the surface. Around him, chaos and destruction reigned.

He needed to get out of the water. But go where? The shore was too far. The seawall was the closest thing to him that was not burning or a target for the next round of devastation that would come from the British fleet. Nicolas struck out toward it, belatedly realizing that his left arm didn't seem to be working properly. He glanced down, fighting the spurt of terror as he saw the blood clouding the water around his wrist. Something had torn through the sleeve of his uniform, ripping away his identity tag that he wore around his wrist and leaving an ugly gash along the inside of his forearm. An unnatural bump suggested that the bone was broken as well, and as he assessed his wound, the pain that his terror had suppressed lanced through him.

"Shit," he muttered, forcing aside a new rush of fear. The irony that he might survive the destruction and capsizing of the *Bretagne* only to bleed out now was intolerable. Tucking his injured arm against his body, he gritted his teeth against the pain and slowly kicked in the direction of the seawall.

"Navarre." The sound of his name bounced across the water, garbled and desperate.

Nicolas spun, trying to pinpoint where the voice had come from.

"Navarre—" It came again but was abruptly cut off.

But this time, Nicolas saw the man who had uttered it, struggling in the water only a few yards away from him. "Fontaine," he yelled. He almost sobbed in relief. Amid the devastation, at least he hadn't lost Oscar too.

The messman's dark head disappeared momentarily before resurfacing, and Nicolas heard the man gasping and wheezing as he floundered.

"Can't . . . swim," he managed.

Nicolas turned back toward his friend. A piece of heavy, curved wood, perhaps part of what had once been a lifeboat or large barrel knocked against his shoulder, and with his good arm, Nicolas pushed it in the direction of Oscar. The messman grabbed it frantically and clung to the edge.

"I need you to stay still," Nicolas gasped as he reached Oscar. "Kick when I tell you but you can't panic. And don't let go."

Oscar nodded, his eyes squeezed tightly shut, his complexion sheet white.

It took an impossibly long period of time to reach what had seemed so close. When Nicolas finally touched the unfinished seawall with the tip of his fingers, his breath was coming in harsh gasps, and his vision had started to cloud with black spots. Along the edge of the jetty, heavy stones and rocks had been dumped as the foundation. Nicolas shoved Oscar forward. Weakly, Oscar fumbled at the shore for purchase, and Nicolas shoved him partially out of the water, until he was satisfied that his friend wouldn't slip back in. Then he pulled himself out, collapsing on his back as dizziness washed through him.

After a moment, he forced himself to sit up. His arm was still bleeding profusely.

"Use . . . my . . . apron." It was the first thing Oscar had said since Nicolas had started swimming.

"What?"

"That arm ... will kill ... you if you ... don't wrap it."

Nicolas started to refuse but stopped. His friend was right. With his good hand, he reached for the messman's apron and untied it from around Oscar's waist, dragging it away. With a shaking hand and his teeth, he wrapped it around his forearm, pulling it as tight as he was able. Twice he thought he might pass out. Twice he fought through the vertiginous haze, then finally collapsed back against the rough rock.

"Don't say ... I never saved your ... life."

Nicolas glanced over at the messman. His complexion was no longer pale but an ominous shade of grey. He lay slumped against the uneven rocks, his chest barely rising and falling.

"Never." Nicolas shifted closer to Oscar. "Where are you hurt?"

Oscar closed his eyes. "Chest ... doesn't feel so good. Hard ... to ... breathe."

Nicolas shoved up his shirt, but there was no outward bleeding. No holes, no lacerations, no shrapnel. Just angry, purple-red blotches beneath the skin along his entire left side that suggested damage far deeper and far more grievous than a simple hole.

Oscar coughed, a thin rivulet of blood brightening his lips.

Nicolas wiped it away, trying not to notice that his hand was shaking.

"That's not ... so good ... is it?" Oscar was staring at the crimson on Nicolas's fingers.

"You'll be fine," he lied. "We'll get picked up here, and the doctors will be able to patch you up."

"Mmm." Oscar closed his eyes. "Stay?" It was barely audible.

Stay. Nicolas had once uttered that request in an abandoned garden. And a girl from Rotterdam with cinnamon hair and whiskey eyes and a smile that had lit up the world around her had done just that.

And now she was gone. And now Oscar would follow, and Nicolas was helpless to stop any of it. A resurgence of grief and anguish and rage crashed through him and left him empty and raw and gasping, barely able to breathe. He wanted to scream and cry and hit something until everything he felt inside drained out and he didn't feel anything anymore.

"Navarre?" His name was a whisper. "Don't leave..."

Nicolas scrubbed furiously at his face with his good hand, trying to compose himself. "I'm not going anywhere," he said roughly. "I like it here. Good friends, a spectacular ocean view, time to work on my tan. Don't want me turning into a vampire, isn't that what you told me earlier?"

Oscar might have smiled, his lips bright red with his blood.

Nicolas settled back beside his friend. He looked up at the sky that seemed to dim and brighten in intervals, and he could no longer discern whether it was due to the burning ships and the curtains of smoke or if his eyes were starting to fail him. Where his good hand rested along his side, he could feel the hard lump of the lighter that Stasia had once given him, tucked deep in his pocket. His fingers closed tightly over the familiar shape. Distantly, he wondered if Stasia had looked up at the sky like this at the end and what she might have seen. Had she seen only fire and death around her, or had she not seen anything at all?

His head lolled to the side, the edge of a rock scraping painfully against his jaw. The burned skin on his face and arms stung like a thousand hornets had unleashed their wrath. His left arm throbbed with an agonizing intensity, marking each beat of his heart. If Stasia were here now, she would tell him a story to distract him—

"Shall I tell you a story?" he asked, turning his head to look at his friend. The world abruptly tilted and blurred before it righted itself.

Oscar's eyes were still closed, his face as still as death, but he nodded once, almost imperceptibly.

"Good." The sounds of the battle raging in the harbour seemed strangely distant now, which suited Nicolas just fine. "Then I will tell you the story of Little Briar Rose," he said. "It's my favourite."

CHAPTER

8

Stasia

There was a pink rose in a jar by her bed when Stasia opened her eyes.

Some days it was a single daisy or a tiny buttercup or a bright tulip, and in the winter months, a branch of cut pine often graced the table. It was something that one of the nurses had done in Rotterdam for all her patients, to remind those who teetered on the edge of darkness and hopelessness that color and hope still existed outside the walls. That new life could still be found amid loss. Margot and Stasia had not forgotten that, and when they had finally been well enough to leave that Rotterdam hospital, they had taken the practice with them.

After the bombing, Margot had recovered first, her burns and injuries not nearly as severe as Stasia's. Stasia had drifted in and out of consciousness for a fortnight, and it had been almost six weeks after that before she was physically able to get out of bed. Though there were many days that followed when Stasia found she couldn't muster the will to do so, and it was only the resilience and strength that Margot continually imposed upon Stasia that pushed her forward. Margot had simply refused to let Stasia succumb to the dark morass of pain and grief that threatened to do what the bombs had not.

It had been Margot who had sat at her bedside and told her that her father was gone. It had been Margot who had told her that Minna and her own parents had also been victims of the bombing that had taken so much from so many. And later, just when the wounds on Stasia's skin had healed and the wounds on her heart had just begun to do so, it had been Margot who had told her what had happened to the French navy in the Mediterranean. Had shown her the list of those who had perished aboard the *Bretagne* when Stasia had demanded to see for herself the name *Nicolas Navarre* in black-and-white newsprint among the dead.

And Margot had held her as her heart had shattered all over again.

"Get up, sleepyhead." The order drifted into the tiny bedroom that Stasia shared with Margot. "It's past seven. You're going to be late for your class."

Stasia rolled over, watching the morning sunlight create long lines where it streamed in through the windows. In the beginning, this routine had seemed wrong somehow. Wrong that waking, dressing, eating, and attending what classes remained at the university could still be happening, while her country had been overrun with roaches who dressed in grey and had left devastation in their wake. A legion of conquerors who had entrenched themselves in the facets of daily life and took pleasure in division and destruction, oppression and odium.

"Stasia." Margot was standing in the doorway now, already dressed in her coat. "Get up."

And Stasia obeyed because she was alive and there were so many others who were not.

There was a peculiar and unexpected mixture of guilt and duty that had come with that knowledge. Those sentiments were what had brought the girls back to Amsterdam when they were able to travel. It was what, initially, had made them leave the ruin of Rotterdam behind and return to their tiny flat and their studies. To honour their families, they had promised each other that they would not give up. They would not stop living because others no longer could. They would succeed because it was what those who had loved them most would have wanted. That had been two years ago.

That had been before twenty-five thousand of their country-men volunteered to serve the Waffen-SS. That had been before the Nationaal-Socialistische Beweging became the only legal political party in the Netherlands and embraced everything that the invading Nazis stood for. That was before angry Dutchmen—factory workers, public service employees, trans-portation operatives—had protested the oppression by striking, only to suffer crippling reprisals for their efforts. That was before the mass deportations of Jewish citizens had begun.

Their objectives had changed since then.

It was no longer about naively pursuing ambitions that had been products of a different time and a different world. Nicolas had once told her that being angry was far easier than being afraid. And most days he was right.

Most days.

"I'm sorry." Stasia sat on the edge of her bed and twisted the steel ring around her finger, the old ache of grief sharper and more cruel as of late, though she couldn't say why. "I didn't mean to oversleep."

Margot came into the room and sat down heavily beside her, making the springs creak. "Don't be sorry." She looked as tired as Stasia felt. Yet she was already up and dressed, a kettle whistling in the other room.

Impulsively, Stasia reached for the paper she had left on the tiny table next to her side of the bed. "Here." She gave the paper to Margot. "I drew this yesterday. I want you to have it."

Margot looked startled as she accepted the drawing. "Oh, Stasia. It's beautiful."

Stasia tucked her hands in her lap. She had drawn Margot and herself on the back of Pegasus. Margot sat astride the creature at the front, holding a gleaming shield as Pegasus's mane whipped wildly in the wind. Stasia had drawn herself tucked behind Margot, her arms wrapped tightly around her waist.

"I look quite fierce," Margot said, touching the outline of the winged horse.

"You are fierce. I drew you as Athena," Stasia told her. "Goddess of wisdom and war."

"And who are you supposed to be in this drawing, then?"

"Your sister."

"Which one?" Margot asked. "Maybe Artemis? Goddess of the hunt?"

Stasia shook her head, glancing at the pink, twisted scars on her legs that were just visible from under the edge of her robe. "Not a goddess of anything. Just your sister."

Margot reached for Stasia's hand and squeezed it. "I love it. Thank you."

"I wish I were as strong as you," Stasia said.

"What?" Margot turned.

"You are utterly indomitable."

"No," Margot told her, giving her hand another squeeze

before releasing it. "I'm not stronger than you at all. I think only that my rage burns hotter than yours."

"Then I wish I had that."

"No. You don't." She leaned closer to Stasia. "You don't want a rage that makes it hard to think. That sometimes clouds my judgement. That makes me wonder that if I let it go, set free the fury that is with me every waking minute of every waking day, I wouldn't simply be vanquished into nothing more than a shadow of ash, incinerated from within. Because then I have to remind myself that that would serve no one. Shadows cannot fight." She rested her head on Stasia's shoulder. "You are the single bright light left in my world," she said. "You still have the purest soul of anyone I've ever met. Please don't lose that."

"A pure soul doesn't fix this... horrible emptiness inside," Stasia mumbled. "My grandmother, she used to say that your soul is like a pail that can be filled up with anything you choose, kindness and happiness being the lightest."

"That's a good thing, Stasia."

"No, it's not. Because when your pail is light, it's easy for someone to kick it over. Again and again and again." She paused. "It makes you weak."

"Stasia—"

"If I don't fill the emptiness with anger, then the space inside me just fills with sorrow, and the anguish is intolerable."

"I am filled with sorrow too," Margot whispered. "All the time."

"But it doesn't cripple you. Some days I can barely breathe with grief. Not like you."

"No. I think you are simply more honest than I." Margot stood, staring down at the drawing in her hand. "And I think that I am just better at pretending." She retreated back into the kitchen, and Stasia listened as Margot took the kettle off the stove.

Margot wasn't pretending anything, Stasia thought. It was others who were pretending. Others around her who continued to go about their business, looking the other way as atrocities were carried out within the fabric of their society, pretending that the occupiers were a mere inconvenience. How long before they realized that they had mistaken war for inconvenience? Not the way war had come to Rotterdam, with planes and bombs and tanks, but a war cloaked behind orderly administration and polished police badges and neatly stitched Nazi insignias. Stasia stood, wincing as her feet touched the icy cold floor.

She had work to do.

★ ★ ★

The lists were always passed to Stasia by the pretty forger.

Stasia had met her at a students' association dinner not long after she had returned to Amsterdam and had first been charmed by Lotte's vivacious personality, quick smile, and infectious laugh. They discovered immediately that they had much in common—a love of fiction, a regret that they were only children, and most importantly, an abhorrence of the occupying Nazis. By the time Jewish citizens were forced to wear a yellow star, Stasia had discovered that Lotte had turned her considerable talent as a fine arts student to forging and altering personal identity cards. By the time those same citizens were indiscriminately taken from the streets and from their homes and deported east, Stasia had discovered that she could best help by becoming a thief.

What had continually hampered Lotte's forgery efforts was a

shortage of identity cards. Food stamps and ration cards were less challenging to copy—but when it came to *persoonsbewijs*, the real thing must be had if Lotte was to produce copies or alter them accurately to pass a central registry check. Resolutely, Stasia had offered to help because, after months and months of reading the illegal university papers and listening to the equally illegal radio stations championing resistance, it was time for her to stop merely listening and act.

The first time Stasia stole an identity card, she thought her heart might explode in her chest in terror of being caught. Two things kept her feet moving and her fingers deft and steady, the knowledge that what she was doing was necessary and would, if everything went well, possibly save a life, and the memory of Nicolas plucking a tobacco tin from the outside of a Rouen hospital with a cocky grin. She'd stolen two cards that first day, both from coat pockets that had been left unattended in the women's changeroom of the Stoops pool in Overveen. She'd strolled out as casually as she'd strolled in, and it wasn't until she was six blocks away that she'd sat down on a bench, shaky and out of breath, sweat running down her neck and sliding between her breasts, and shadows of guilt clinging to her conscience.

That had been almost a year ago. Since then, Stasia had perfected the art of liberating identity cards and any other documents she came across. She never stole from the same place twice in a month if it could be helped, for the last thing she wanted was for those privileged Dutch citizens not being hunted by the police and the SS and the Gestapo to be any less careless about where they kept their papers. She travelled from Amsterdam to Haarlem to Overveen regularly to remain unnoticed and unmemorable. She studied the newspapers for performance adverts because the cloakrooms at theaters and concert halls were easily accessible and were rich in opportunity and reward. She trolled the cafés and parks, sitting herself down next to discarded coats or open bags, smiling and studiously opening a large book across her lap, while beneath, her nimble fingers slipped into pockets and purses and took what she needed.

And whatever guilt she might have suffered in the beginning had long vanished.

I don't have the luxury of feeling bad, Nicolas had told her once in a French garden when she had asked how he felt about what he stole. Stasia hadn't really understood, not until now, what he had meant by that. That what he had done wasn't a choice, nor was it a matter of doing the wrong thing for the right reasons, or the right thing for the wrong reasons. It was simply a matter of survival. And every card Stasia stole meant another individual had a chance at survival. She took small comfort in the belief that Nicolas might be looking down on her, grinning his approval. And the empty space inside her soul was temporarily soothed.

A knock on Stasia's door interrupted her thoughts, and she opened it to find the forger standing outside her flat.

"Are you all right?" Lotte asked. "Has something happened? You look terribly sad."

"Not at all," Stasia lied as she closed the door behind the petite artist. "I'm perfectly fine."

Lotte gave her a long look. "If you say so." She transferred her bright blue gaze to her surroundings before flopping down on their little sofa. "Where's Margot?"

"Out." Stasia knew very well that Margot spent much of her day printing and distributing anti-Nazi pamphlets. Her efforts were like a small trickle of water against a firestorm of Nazi propaganda but no less important.

Stasia disappeared into the bedroom and crouched in the

corner nearest the wardrobe, where the noon sun glared across
the bare wooden floor. She ran her fingers along the edge of the
floorboard and pried it up, reaching in for the wrapped packet
that lay beneath.

Stasia returned to the living space. "Here."

"That was fast." Lotte reached for the packet with ink-stained
fingers, and it disappeared into the bodice of her voluminous
dress.

Stasia shrugged. "I got lucky at the Rembrandt yesterday."

Lotte gave her another long look. "If you say so," she murmured again. She tipped her head, her chestnut ponytail swinging
behind her. "Does Margot know what you're doing for me?"

"Of course."

Margot had been one of the first recipients of an altered
identity card that Stasia had stolen. They'd burned the one
Margot had been issued with the black *J* stamped on both sides,
and the forged papers provided far more safety and freedom to
move around the city.

"I need another card," Lotte said abruptly. "For a sixteen-year-
old girl. Anything up to age twenty I could make work."

"All right. Is this part of a new list?"

Lotte usually gave her a list denoting the gender and age of
cards required by the networks of people working to smuggle
Jews out of the country or move them somewhere safer. Lately,
Lotte's lists had become longer, with Stasia tasked with stealing
up to a dozen cards a week.

"No, just this one."

"Oh."

"I need it by this evening."

Stasia could feel her brows rise.

"It's an emergency. Can you do it?"

"Of course."

"All right then." Lotte stood. "Can you bring it to my place tonight? Before curfew?"

"Yes." Stasia studied the forger.

"How long, do you suppose?" Lotte asked, looking pensive.

Stasia considered where she might hunt. "I'll probably need to wait for the theaters to—"

"No, I mean how long do you think they'll let us keep going to school? How long before they shut down the universities or arrest all the students? Or at least the ones who don't sign an Aryan declaration like the professors did?"

"I don't know." The thought startled Stasia before a familiar, seething resentment reasserted itself at the reminder. "I will not sign anything. I refuse."

"Hmm." The forger sighed unhappily and then patted the front of her dress where the cards were concealed. "Well, thank you for these. I'll see you tonight."

"Yes." Stasia watched Lotte let herself out, unhappily musing over the artist's question. How long indeed?

★ ★ ★

In the end, Stasia curled her hair, put on her best dress and a slash of lipstick, and went to the cinema.

The Tuschinski Theatre was now named the Tivoli Theatre by the Nazis, who could not abide having such a building bear the name of its Polish-Jewish owner. They'd had the cinema seized and Abraham Tuschinski arrested and deported, yet the theater remained as Stasia remembered. Its cathedral-like Renaissance architecture rose toward the heavens above the recessed entrance, its twin towers on the façade's corners framing a masterpiece of ornately carved detail. The interior was just as impressive, with a Far Eastern influence that made Stasia feel like she had stepped into another world, which, she supposed, was the entire point. Judging by the crowd swelling around her as she made her way into the building, the lavish, opulent décor that had made the theater so popular with the locals made it just as popular with the occupiers.

The current patrons of the Tuschinski seemed neither to care about the fate of the theater's owner nor to imagine that such unfortunate circumstances could ever befall them, and it was for this reason that Stasia had chosen it. Nazi officers strolled arm in arm with pretty girls across the cinema's colorful, patterned carpets, and Dutch couples in fine clothes chatted as they made their way to their plush seats on the floor of the auditorium or up on one of the soaring, circular balconies above.

Stasia bought a ticket, not glancing at or caring about the film title. It would be Nazi propaganda, some sort of anti-Jewish film that nauseated Stasia but would serve its purpose in bringing together a wealth of individuals who possessed identity cards that allowed them to saunter unconcerned and unmolested through the streets of Amsterdam. She slipped out of the coat she was wearing and draped it casually over her arm as she navigated the sumptuous entrance, smiling pleasantly at those whom she passed, German and Dutch alike.

It was still too early for the cabaret dinner club in the theater to be open, and the tearoom wasn't big enough to attract as many patrons as the theater itself, so she ignored both of those and instead slid into the stream of cinemagoers who were drifting toward the elegant foyers, chatting and laughing as they checked their coats and hats with one of the theater's smartly uniformed staff. She deliberately picked the youngest checker, a boy who couldn't be much older than seventeen, waited to hand her coat to him, made sure to thank him profusely—enough to make him blush—and then tucked the numbered ticket she received in exchange into her sleeve. She retreated back into the crowd and entered the auditorium, choosing a seat at the very back of the theater on the main floor.

Stasia pretended great interest in the extravagant design of color and light on the ceiling above her until those lights dimmed and the curtain across the screen was swept to the side. The screen lit up with the opening credits of the film, and the sound boomed. Stasia did not pay any attention to the screen but instead focused on the watch around her wrist. After exactly five minutes, she rose and crept silently out of the auditorium.

She retraced her steps back to the foyer, the sounds of the film muffled. Sometimes at the smaller cinemas and theaters, she got lucky and once the film started, the staff temporarily abandoned their posts to watch or use the facilities or were called elsewhere, and Stasia could steal into the coatrooms undetected. But today, she could still see the youth who had taken her coat at his post. She fixed what she hoped was an apologetic and distressed expression on her face as she hurried toward the coat check.

"I'm so sorry," Stasia said before the young man could greet her. "But I fear when I gave you my coat, I left my spectacles in the pocket. I can't see a thing without them."

The checker blinked at her before smiling. "Of course. I remember you. If you give me your ticket, I will fetch your coat for you, and you may retrieve them."

"Oh, thank you," Stasia gushed, smiling back at him. "I feel so silly."

"It's quite all right," he reassured her, taking her ticket. He vanished into the cloakroom before reappearing a moment later with her coat. "Here you are."

Stasia shook her head. "I'm sorry, that's not my coat."

The young man frowned and peered at the tickets. "The numbers match."

Stasia bit her lip. "That's impossible. It's similar but that's not my coat. I've never seen it before." She let her voice rise an octave.

The employee was ineffectively checking the coat for spectacles that would not be there because they were tucked into a deep pocket sewn into Stasia's skirts.

"Did you lose my coat after I gave it to you?" Stasia asked. "Did someone else take it—"

"No, no, of course not," the checker interrupted her, glancing side to side as if worried someone might overhear. "Tell me what it looks like."

"It looks sort of like that one. Dark with pockets and a belt," she said, knowing she was describing at least half the women's coats hanging in that cloakroom. "But a little shorter, maybe." She wrung her hands. "What if my spectacles are gone? I can't see without them. I won't be able to work—"

"We'll find it." The youth visibly swallowed.

"How?" Stasia blinked rapidly as though she was fighting tears. "How can you find it by yourself? You don't even know what it looks like. Maybe I could help?"

"I'm not really supposed to let anyone back there."

"Oh. Well, maybe we should get your boss. Tell him what happened. That you mixed up the ticket. Maybe he could find it?"

"No, no." He looked alarmed. "No need for that. Just come back into the cloakroom. I'm sure it is just a simple mix-up."

"All right," she agreed tremulously. She allowed the young employee to lead her into the small room filled with rows of neatly hung coats and hats. Stasia glanced at him but he was still looking unhappily at the garment in his hands. She would have to work quickly, especially if the youth stayed in the cloakroom with her. "Goodness, so many coats, and they all look the same. No wonder it would be easy to get them confused," she told him. "I'm sure you're right, and there was just a mix-up."

Without waiting for him to reply, she quickly rifled through the women's coats closest to hers, making a show of looking for a coat she would never find and, at the same time, deftly feeling the pockets of each. The number of people who left items, especially personal documentation, unguarded in their coat pockets never ceased to astound Stasia. Though perhaps that was what happened when someone was in a position where they might be confident that they would not be dragged away should they fail to prove their identity quickly enough. Perhaps if Stasia had strolled in on the arm of a Nazi officer, she, too, would be just as confident and just as careless.

"Excuse me?" A man's voice echoed from out front. "Is anyone here?"

Stasia froze for a moment before she continued searching. The young employee hesitated, clearly torn between remaining in the cloakroom with Stasia and returning to the front.

"Please don't let me keep you from your job," Stasia assured him. "I'll keep looking, and I'll let you know when I find it. I just need my spectacles so I can see the film."

He nodded, set the coat aside, and then vanished, leaving Stasia alone. Stasia abandoned all pretense of looking for a coat and focused simply on the pockets, listening carefully to the sound of muted voices from the foyer. Within half a minute, she had found documentation for a middle-aged man and an older woman, both in an interior breast pocket. She left those untouched and continued on as quickly as she was able. The customer who was out front was still speaking to the employee. It sounded like he was asking directions to somewhere. She was grateful for the distraction but she still hadn't found what she needed.

Stasia forced herself to continue her search systematically, moving quickly through the rows and trying not to let desperation creep in as she got closer to the end. Just when she thought she would fail, she found what she was looking for. Alene Bakker, age eighteen, had been negligently kind enough to leave two colorful ration cards, one for meat and bread and one for textiles, and all of her personal documentation, including her identification card, in the right pocket of her finely tailored, fur-trimmed coat. With nimble fingers, Stasia slid only the identification card into the front of her dress, wedging it securely under the strap of her bra.

"Any luck yet?" The question came from behind her. "Have you found your coat and your spectacles?"

Stasia jumped, startled. Her pulse accelerated, and she cursed herself for not realizing that the conversation out front had ended.

In a fluid motion, her back still to the young man, Stasia slid the wire-framed spectacles with plain glass lenses from the pocket sewn into the pleats of her dress and turned, holding them up triumphantly. "Found them," she declared, sliding them on and pasting a wide smile across her face. "You were right. They were here all along. Thank you."

The young man looked relieved. "Of course."

Stasia brushed past him, heading toward the foyer in the direction of the auditorium entrance. A man was still standing near the coat check counter, and Stasia had a brief impression of a tall, lanky silhouette wearing a battered fedora. She thanked the stranger silently for the extra time he had unknowingly gifted her during her search as she hustled by.

"If I hurry, I'll have only missed the very beginning," she called to the young employee over her shoulder, turning slightly.

"What about the coat number—"

Stasia waved her hand but didn't slow. "I remember the number. I'll come back for it after the film is over. Thank you again."

The employee opened his mouth as if to respond but Stasia was already turning away, taking the colorful stairs up from the foyer two at a time. She slowed as she rounded the corner, her steps silent on the carpet and headed toward the auditorium. Except she bypassed the doors, the sounds of the film reverberating as she walked on, weaving her way down the corridors that eventually disgorged her out the rear of the theater.

She didn't look back.

★ ★ ★

Lotte opened the door to her flat almost immediately after Stasia knocked. She glanced behind Stasia before swinging it wide, letting her in. The curtains had been drawn, and Stasia blinked as her eyes adjusted to the dimness.

"I have—" Stasia started to speak but stopped short. "Margot?" Her friend was sitting at a tiny table, her feet tucked up under the spindle chair, her hands clasped in front of her, her face expressionless. "What are you doing here?"

Margot's eyes strayed from Stasia to somewhere over her shoulder.

Stasia spun. A man, tall and lanky and wearing a battered fedora, stepped out from against the wall into the center of the room.

The man from the Tuschinski. The one who had been asking questions out front when she had been in the cloakroom.

Her throat closed momentarily as fear surged through her and her mind raced. She had been discovered. She had been caught and followed. But there was still time to run.

She took an involuntary step back toward the door, her gaze darting to Lotte.

The man held up his hands. "I beg your pardon," he said, his voice rumbling. "I did not mean to alarm you. I mean no harm. I'm a friend."

"He's a friend," Lotte confirmed. "I promise." She gestured at Stasia. "Please. Come in. Hear what he has to say."

Stasia studied him warily. Beneath his fedora, he had dark hair peppered with grey. A craggy face with intense green eyes ringed with dark lashes. He was wearing a worn suit that looked too big for his slender frame, though neither of these things was uncommon anymore.

"My name is Frank," he said. He still had his hands up as though Stasia were holding him at gunpoint. "I work with Lotte."

Stasia glanced at the petite artist, and Lotte nodded.

"You were following me," Stasia said, her stomach dropping. She should have known that. She should have been more vigilant. Some thief she was.

"I was." He lowered his hands. "I am with the Council of Resistance," Frank continued. "And I wanted to meet both of you." He made a motion that encompassed both Margot and Stasia. "Because the council is always looking for more to join us. Especially those who already have accomplished much on their own. There is more strength in numbers."

Both women remained silent.

"I've seen the pamphlets you print and distribute," he said

to Margot. "Necessary and brave, given what the Germans are doing to anyone who dares to speak against them."

Margot sat back in her chair and crossed her arms over her chest but didn't answer.

Frank turned toward Stasia. "I am told that you have been critical to Lotte's efforts. That you are exceedingly clever."

Stasia shrugged, the corner of the stolen identification card still tucked under her bra scratching her skin with the action. "I get lucky from time to time."

The man made a dismissive sound. "One does not get lucky for that long. One gets skilled."

Stasia shrugged again. "Maybe."

"Tell me," he said. "How many cards did you take from that cloakroom?"

"Why are you asking? What difference does it make?"

Frank shrugged. "I like to know who I'm working with. How you think."

Stasia felt her brows rise. "Presumptuous, no?"

"Maybe." Frank seemed to take no offense. "How many cards did you take this afternoon?" he repeated.

Stasia walked over to the tiny table where Margot was sitting and sat down opposite her friend. "One," she said, not looking at him. "The one that Lotte asked for."

"Why only one? Surely there were more that you would have found? Why not take everything? Ration books? Coupons? Money? They would have been a big help to the Resistance." It sounded like he was accusing her of something.

"That many missing cards and ration books and money would be discovered immediately. The theft would be reported immediately. *I* would be reported. Because I was seen." Stasia pulled the single *persoonsbewijs* from inside the front of her dress

and placed it on the table. "The absence of a single document belonging to a teenage girl, when eventually discovered,
is unlikely to be reported and more likely to be attributed to
her own carelessness. Undoubtably, she misplaced it, given that
all her money and ration books were still there." Stasia slid the
identification card across the table toward Lotte. "And the hapless employee, if he values his job, will be equally as unlikely to
mention that he let a young woman into the cloakroom against
the rules who was only looking for her spectacles."

Frank glanced at Lotte, and Stasia tried to read his expression.

"See?" Lotte said, looking smug.

"Indeed." Frank sounded pleased. He turned his attention
back to Margot and Stasia and took his fedora from his head. "I
want you both to join the council. To come work for us."

"Doing what?" Margot spoke for the first time since Stasia
had arrived.

"We need couriers. People who can get information and
messages and documents across the city to those who need them.
Young women such as yourselves are ideal because, in our experience, the police and Nazis rarely suspect a pretty girl on a bicycle
of anything." He spun his hat in his hands. "It is my hope that
while you are assisting us, we may help you with resources from
time to time as well. We are stronger together either way."

Margot shoved her chair back and stood. "Yes."

"It isn't without risk—"

"I said yes."

Stasia stood beside her friend and put her hand on her arm.
"We will both do it." As if she would answer any differently.
Because this man was right.

They were stronger together.

CHAPTER

9

Isabelle

The plan had been to see the château together.

Yet there was still no sign of Emilie. Isabelle stood alone and seethed as she scanned the platform, watching people spill from the train. She'd been here yesterday as well, ready to pick up her sister, but the train had arrived, disgorged its passengers, and departed again, leaving Isabelle standing alone on the platform. Worried, she'd texted Emilie, only to receive a curt reply that something had come up and Emilie would catch the next train up from Paris tomorrow. No apology, no explanation.

And now Isabelle stood, yet again, waiting for her sister, wondering if she'd been stood up for the second day in a row. Wondering if she would need to go home and make more excuses to her parents, who were anxious to see their youngest daughter finally home. They'd both agreed that they would view the interior together, and now Isabelle was regretting that.

She pulled out her phone. No messages. The passengers disembarking had slowed to a trickle, and Isabelle tried to temper the irritation that was rapidly rising. A flash of crimson at the far end of the platform caught her eye, and Isabelle straightened.

Emilie was home.

It had been almost three years since she had last seen her sister, when Isabelle had been in Paris for a plaster workshop, but Emilie looked exactly as she remembered. While Isabelle's family often commented on her own resemblance to her great-gran, with her light brown eyes, freckles, and chestnut hair shot through with cinnamon, Emilie had generally been compared to other women of note by her family. Like Hedy Lamarr, or Marion Cotillard.

Or Cleopatra.

Isabelle watched as Emilie strolled across the platform, tiny suitcase in tow, gold-rimmed sunglasses perched in her glossy dark hair, crimson cashmere coat belted casually at the waist, a white silk scarf knotted at her throat and her designer heels rapping smartly against the concrete. She looked neither left nor right, ignoring the appreciative glances of a number of men who passed, and instead headed directly for the large station doors with a brisk efficiency.

In truth, Isabelle had been more than a little shocked at Emilie's quick agreement to travel from Paris to see the château when she had called her on that blustery November day to let her sister know that the château was for sale. Like always, Emilie had bypassed any small talk other than a perfunctory question about their parents' health and moved directly into an array of rapid-fire questions about the château. In the weeks that followed, via emails and phone conversations, they had drawn up a tentative budget and repair plan that addressed the exterior damage and some of the major restorations based on the photos that Luc had taken. They had started the process of investigating the requirements and limitations that revolved around the château's historic designation and researched the grants that may be available for such a property. They had reviewed the building's subsequent usage and sketched out tentative business plans for the château to be opened to the public in some capacity. Isabelle reflected that she had probably talked to Emilie more in these last five weeks than she had in the preceding five years.

Isabelle pushed herself away from the wall she had been leaning against, involuntarily brushing at the front of her thick canvas work coat and jeans before she caught herself. She dropped her hands with annoyance.

"Emilie," she called, waving her hand.

Her sister paused, her head turning toward Isabelle, her dark eyes widening first in surprise and then recognition.

Isabelle pushed through the dwindling crowd. "Your train was on time." She bit her lip. What a stupid thing to say to a sister she hadn't seen in three years.

"It was." Emilie seemed taken aback. "You didn't need to meet me. I told you I would take a cab."

"I wanted to pick you up." That was the truth, at least. "I thought we'd go right to the château while we still have the afternoon. The agent is there right now and is able to give us a walk-through." She'd had to call him yesterday and reschedule for today, and she was not about to do that again. The inspection of the interior would determine if this was really going to happen. If they would make an offer on the château and take on this project. Isabelle was going into the château today with or without her sister.

"Oh." Emilie pulled at the scarf around her neck. "I was going to stop at the hotel first."

"You're not staying at a hotel," Isabelle said patiently but firmly. They'd already had this argument over the phone. "Mom and Dad would be heartbroken. Mom's already made up your old room."

Emilie grimaced. "Fine. But I'm not doing yard chores."

"I take care of those," Isabelle said wearily. "And there aren't many to do. Just a half dozen hens left."

"What happened to the cows?"

"Mom sold them last year."

"What? She loved those stupid things."

"She couldn't manage them and look after Dad at the same time. It was just easier."

"Just as well. I never liked them."

Isabelle pressed her lips together in an effort to keep from snapping something churlish and headed out through the station. She would not allow Emilie to put a damper on her excitement. "I have the truck here. Do you want to borrow some boots? I've got an extra pair with me."

"I suppose." Her sister did not sound enthused. "Will they fit?"

"Unless your feet have suddenly grown in recent adulthood, then yes." When they were teenagers, they used to share everything. Clothes, shoes, books, secrets, wishes. Now it felt like she was walking beside a stranger.

She led them out to the street where she had left her truck and unlocked the doors. Emilie deposited her tiny suitcase in the back with another grimace and then slid into the front.

"How are things in Paris?" Isabelle asked as they pulled away.

"Fine." Emilie extracted her phone from the pocket of her coat.

"And Marcus? He's doing well?" Isabelle asked more out

of politeness than anything—she'd met Emilie's husband only twice. "Too bad he couldn't come today too." That also seemed like something suitably nice to say.

"He's a surgeon, Izz. He doesn't have time for field trips." She frowned at her phone.

"Right." Isabelle sighed and changed lanes. "Check the glove box."

"Why? What do you need?"

"I don't need anything. But I brought Great-Gran's last published story. The one with all the drawings of beautiful rooms in the enchanted château. I thought you might like to take a look and see how much we recognize once we get inside. Just for fun."

Emilie made no move to retrieve the book. "You were the one who was close to Great-Gran. Not me."

"That's not true." At least when they were younger.

"You're the family person. That's not really my thing."

"Not your th—" Isabelle clamped her mouth shut.

"There is no room in this venture for your excessive sentimentality, you know. The cost of interior restoration per square foot can be exorbitant. We might find out ten minutes in that this project is beyond us."

Isabelle focused on the road, her hands gripping the steering wheel with far more force than necessary. "Why did you agree to do this?" she asked.

"Do what?" Emilie's attention was back on her phone.

"Take this project on. Or at least consider it."

"It would look good in my portfolio," Emilie said, tapping at her screen.

"That's it?"

"I have an exhaustive selection of new builds but some of my wealthiest clients, many who buy from overseas and have purchased premier properties with historic buildings, like to see what I am able to do with the architecture in a listed home." Her tapping continued. "And I like the potential investment return. Just look at what Château de Jaques, Le Logis du Général, or Château de la Croix charges per week. And rightfully so. If we do this well, it has the potential for a better return than the global markets at the moment."

Isabelle didn't reply and instead wondered if she was making the biggest mistake of her life by ignoring the small voices in the back of her head. The ones that were telling her that no matter how much she missed her little sister and the bond they once shared, a building would never bring that back. The voices that whispered that the château was not really a thread that bound her to a great-grandmother whom she missed just as much, but simply a fanciful mirage.

That her heart and her imagination were no match for accounts and portfolios.

"I know we haven't really discussed it, but how much time would you spend here if we did this?" Isabelle ventured. "If we bought the château and opened it to the public?"

Emilie glanced up from her phone, her sculpted brow raised. "God, Izz, are you actually asking me if I'd consider leaving architecture to become some sort of provincial, glorified innkeeper?"

"Of course not. I was just—"

"I left this backwater for a reason. Perhaps if you had ever bothered to broaden your horizons, you too would understand how ridiculous a question that is." She smoothed her hair back over her shoulder. "One hires competent people for such jobs. They are simply part of the cost of doing business."

Isabelle felt a muscle in her jaw clench and made an effort to relax. She drove the rest of the way in silence, afraid she might regret what would come out of her mouth next. Her sister seemed fine with this arrangement, barely looking up from her phone, as if she had no interest in the city that gave way to frost-kissed trees and the silver-streaked river stretching beneath the pale winter sunshine. Emilie didn't look up from her phone until Isabelle turned down the château's drive and brought her truck to a stop beside a sleek black BMW.

Isabelle took a deep breath and doubled down on her determination not to let anything mar this moment. She hopped out of the truck. "Boots are in the back," she called over her shoulder, hefting a small tool bag from the box of the truck. Impulsively, she returned to the front passenger side and reached past Emilie, snapping open the glove box and retrieving the slim volume inside.

Emilie may not be interested in the place that this château had once held in Great-Gran's life, however imaginary, but Isabelle was. She slipped the book into her tool bag and started up the drive.

In the last weeks, Luc had done an extraordinary job of wrestling the grounds immediately in front of and surrounding the château into something that almost resembled groomed. Or at least tidy. The leafless, unkempt brush had been cleared, the overgrown grass clipped, and the shriveled weeds dug out from the drive. The château no longer looked abandoned but rather...enduring. As if it was simply waiting for the right set of hands to make it whole again.

The massive front doors stood open, and the sight sent a thrill sizzling through her. She took the stone steps two at a time and paused before knocking on the door.

"Hello?" she called.

A man appeared almost immediately, dressed in a long navy coat, his brown hair slicked back against his head, dark-rimmed glasses perched on his nose, and an earpiece set firmly into his left ear. His movements and bearing were quick and hurried, as though he were in a perpetual state of impatience.

"Good afternoon," Isabelle greeted. "Monsieur Carriere? Thank you so much for rescheduling."

"Mademoiselle Lange." The man stuck out his hand. "But of course. For a property as unique as this, it is no problem." His hand disappeared back into his coat pocket. "I must say I am an admirer of your work. My firm had the good fortune to acquire the Joubert House on rue de Bourgogne recently. One of your most spectacular Parisian designs and one of our favourites. Sold it with multiple bids."

Isabelle stared at him for a moment until she understood. "You have me confused with my sister. Emilie. She's the architect. I'm the contractor—Isabelle." She glanced back to discover that her sister had chosen to forgo the offered boots and was still wearing her heels, making her journey up the drive slow and perilous.

"Oh, yes, of course, of course." He pushed his glasses back up his nose. "A successful architect always needs someone to do the heavy lifting behind the scenes, no?"

Isabelle blinked. That was about the most accurate description of her entire relationship with Emilie she had ever heard. Dependable Isabelle who took care of everything behind the scenes.

"You and I spoke on the phone yesterday," the agent continued. "You indicated that you have substantial experience with properties such as this. Historic ones, that is. You're familiar with the things you can and can't do should you wish to undergo restoration and renovation?" He didn't wait for her to answer. "Good. So I'll not waste time explaining the permits and paperwork unless you have specific questions." He handed her a packet of paper clipped together at the top. "A list of the chattels that will be sold with the property. My client has already removed the bulk of the valued furniture, personal art, and any items that he wished to keep excluded from the sale. For the most part, everything that you see left inside comes as is. The outbuildings and their contents are also to be sold as you find them. While the family has paid to keep the château from falling into a state of disrepair over the years, I cannot say the same about the rest of the structures on the property."

"I understand. Thank you." Isabelle gripped the papers.

"I had your man remove one of the window boards on the northwest corner," he told her.

"My man?" Isabelle repeated, baffled.

"The groundskeeper. The person we hired to clean up this place. Whatever you want to call him." He waved his hand impatiently. "He said he knew you."

"Luc?"

"I didn't ask his name. He seemed competent with a tool belt." He glanced at his phone as it vibrated. "We thought you would like to get a better look at the damage today so we don't waste each other's time, no?"

"Thank you." She looked down at the papers in her hands. "And the blueprints for the château? Or whatever records exist of the design?"

Carriere snapped his fingers. "Your man has them. I'll send him in with them." His phone continued to vibrate.

Isabelle shrugged. "Sure."

"I'm sorry, I have a call I need to take. I've unlocked the château. Our own appraisers have been through, and save for the northwest rooms, the building is in remarkably good condition.

Please take what time you need to make your own inspection. I will be here if you require me for anything," he finished, already moving away.

Emilie had reached the steps and made her way up as the agent made his way down, talking into his phone. "Was that the agent?"

Isabelle refrained from commenting on Emilie's footwear. "Monsieur Carriere," she said, gesturing at the man who was now pacing back and forth up the drive. "And yes, this is his listing. A big fan of yours, by the way. Apparently sold a house you designed."

"Oh." Emilie was frowning as she glanced around. "Can we not go in?" she asked briskly. "Is there a problem?"

"We can go in whenever we like." Isabelle ignored Emilie's frown. She was too excited to let anything ruin this moment. She felt like she was six years old again, creeping downstairs to see what treasures might have been left for her on Christmas morning. She reached into her tool bag and withdrew two heavy-duty flashlights, passing one to her sister.

"Shall we do this together?" she asked.

Her sister nodded her agreement, and they stepped inside.

★ ★ ★

Someone—Monsieur Carriere presumably—had opened the interior shutters on two of the four tall, arched windows in the main hall. Bright January sunshine struggled in through the murky glass, bathing the hall in a filtered light that made Isabelle feel like she had stepped into a tinted daguerreotype photograph. She stood motionless, trying to absorb every detail. Beneath her feet, covered in a layer of dust thick enough to show footprints, a smooth, geometric arrangement of pale stone tile stretched away from the door.

Directly in front of her, on the far side of the hall, a wide, elegant staircase constructed of the same stone rose from the ground floor. It was bracketed by ornate wrought iron railings that swooped and curled gracefully as they climbed, and eventually flared to either side, providing access to each wing of the first floor. Above her head, a massive chandelier hung, its wrought iron arms crafted in the same intricate design as the stair railings and draped not in crystals, but in cobwebs.

Wooden wainscoting lined the lower half of the walls, with decorative and detailed carvings of flowers and vines bursting forth from each corner. The upper walls were papered in forest green, an addition likely made sometime in the later nineteenth century based on the pattern. Isabelle could see where the paper had faded and peeled from the wall near the ceiling and in the corners, and larger squares of darker green spaced at regular intervals betrayed where paintings or art had been removed more recently.

Isabelle closed her eyes and imagined what the hall might have looked like when it was first built, welcoming the family and their visitors into the château. She imagined bright plaster walls and wondered if she would find art painted on the surface beneath the paper. She imagined what the floor, buffed and shined, would look like under a dazzling blaze of summer sun pouring through clear, cut glass—

"I'm glad it's stone," Emilie remarked, knocking her heel against the floor. The sound echoed eerily around them. "Adds a more genuine feel. Almost medieval-ish. People will like it. And it adds a more diverse texture to the room. Especially with so much wood on the walls already."

Isabelle opened her eyes.

"The paper would need to go," Emilie continued. "Not only does it appear unsalvageable, it's terribly ugly. We'll be best to return the upper walls to their original plaster. A neutral color to showcase the stairs and decorative railings." She flicked on her flashlight. "The good news is, aside from the electrical and other mechanical considerations we've already discussed, it appears that the work required here seems almost exclusively cosmetic. Too bad the rest of the place won't look like this." She pivoted and headed toward the north wing, her shoes striking loudly across the stone floor.

"Where are you going in such a hurry?" Isabelle asked after her.

"To see the bad news."

Isabelle followed more slowly, wanting to savour this exploration. She passed under the arched doorway, admiring the detail in the tall, carved wooden doors that were pushed open. Neither showed any sign of warping or decay, encouraging Isabelle that moisture damage, at least on this floor, would be less of a concern. She trained her light on the ceiling looking for any other signs of water or rot but found none, which boded well for the integrity of the floors above. More good news that wasn't all cosmetic, she thought to herself.

Once through the doors, she found herself in a wide hallway where the floor, bare of any rugs, was crafted of the same stone that was in the main hall. The walls here were covered similarly, with a patterned paper on top and detailed wainscoting on the bottom. On either side, multiple gilded mirrors still hung on the walls, making the beam from her flashlight bounce and flash. One of the mirrors was badly cracked, and her image was reduced to a dizzying jumble. She paused in front of the broken mirror and lifted her hand to touch the tarnished surface. The webbing of cracked glass radiated out from a single small, round hole. It looked suspiciously like the mirror had been struck by a bullet.

Isabelle let her hand drop. Not the first bullet hole she'd come across in her restoration career, most of them documented on the outside of buildings where skirmishes had taken place in the streets throughout the years and wars that passed through them. She just hadn't expected to find one inside the château. She continued down the hallway.

On either side of Isabelle, more open doors beckoned into unseen, unlit rooms beyond, their windows still darkened by shutters. She paused at the entrance to the one nearest her, her flashlight roaming over the contents, and, without even realizing she was doing it, stepped inside. She'd seen this room before, or at least a version of it illustrated in Great-Gran's stories, and having it materialize before her eyes left her a little breathless. Like she had stepped into that magical imaginary world.

Isabelle advanced deeper into the room, spinning in a slow circle. The library was lined floor to ceiling with bookshelves, and most of the volumes were still where someone had left them last, untold years ago. A ladder was mounted to each wall on a rolling bracket so that one might access the upper shelves. In a few places, the dust had been disturbed and there were gaps in the collection, and Isabelle guessed that the more valuable editions or maybe personal journals or family records had been removed.

As she turned, her light caught the silhouette of a creature, its yellow eyes unblinking, and she stumbled back, swallowing the yelp of surprise that almost escaped. Isabelle put a hand to her chest, feeling ridiculous as she let her light play over her would-be attacker. Or attackers, as they were, carved in marble and rising from each side of the hearth that dominated the north wall. Twin painted sculptures of griffins, each nearly as tall as she was, stood sentry. Their amber raptors' eyes gleamed from crested hoods of feathers, and unfurled wings curled in golden arcs over tawny feline backs. A delicate chain with a single, perfectly carved rose encircled each of their necks.

A thrill of recognition ran through her. She'd seen these griffins more than once. She reached down and retrieved the slim volume still in her tool bag. Opening the book, she flipped through the story until she reached the third illustration. In the book, two griffins, identical to the ones on either side of the hearth, guarded not a fireplace but a mysterious cave full of treasure. Her great-gran had been here, in this room, at one time, standing perhaps where she was standing now, and Isabelle couldn't stop the delighted smile that she knew was creeping across her face. She could picture Great-Gran's pencil flying over the page, could hear the steady scratch, and if she closed her eyes and concentrated, she could even smell the sharp scent of the lead or charcoal.

As a child, she had watched her great-gran bring to life magical beasts and delicate fairies, whimsical unicorns and snarling dragons. Little drawings that she had produced at the drop of a hat, perhaps for a birthday or a special occasion, to brighten someone's day, or simply because a child had asked.

Isabelle slid the book back into the bag and returned her attention to the library itself. Whatever furniture or rugs or décor that might once have cluttered the room were gone, with only a single, sheeted shape in the very center of the space. She set her tool bag down and pulled at the sheet, and the fabric fell away to reveal a massive, gleaming desk, its ebony surface bare. She ran her fingers over the edge, speculating who might have done so last. Maybe even Great-Gran had sat at this desk under the watchful eyes of the griffins and written a story or two. She wondered when Gran had been inside the château. How old had she been? Why had she been here?

The sentimental part of Isabelle demanded that she buy the château then and there, if only for this extraordinary space. It was a room dedicated to the written word, a room full of imagination and wonder and learning and possibilities.

Idly, Isabelle pulled at the handle of the top drawer of the desk. It didn't budge. She crouched down, wondering if it was locked, but upon closer inspection, it looked as though it had been jammed shut, the wood at a top corner cracked. Unable to help herself, she reached for her lockout tool and small wedge that she most often used for timeworn, recalcitrant doors and windows. There was a trick to coaxing function back into damaged casings, and Isabelle rather prided herself on possessing a deft touch.

The drawer proved stubborn but eventually it yielded to Isabelle's expert efforts and slid open. She dropped her tools back into the bag with satisfaction and peered into the drawer. The cavity was wide and deep, and inside, she found a metal case about the size of a shoe box. It had a distinct military appearance, painted in grey, the initials O.F.D. engraved at the top left corner, and had a metal clasp. With care, she withdrew the box and placed it on the surface of the desk. Beneath that, at the bottom of the drawer, was a thick folder stuffed full of paper with edges that were curled and yellow where visible. She withdrew the folder, noting the same three initials punched into the thick paper beneath ominous double SS runes.

Isabelle set her flashlight on the surface of the desk and opened the folder. She squinted before picking up her light and aiming it at the pages. They were in German. With care, she rifled through the stack. They were all in the same language and appeared to be a collection of letters, memos, and tallies. Many had a Reichsadler stamp somewhere on them. Her German was not good enough to read through them but it was easy enough to pick out the dates noted on a handful—most seemed to be from 1944.

She set the documents aside and turned her attention to the metal box. The latch gave way easily beneath her fingers, and she opened it to find a haphazard collection of small, rectangular cards, each with a black-and-white photograph stapled to the corner. Unlike the documents, these cards were in French. *Carte de Combattant Volontaire de le Resistance* was printed across the top two that Isabelle could see. She lifted the cards from where they had been concealed. There were others here too, some that had *Carte d'Identité* printed above the photo and others still that simply had a photo and a list of names and dates written in ink beside the black-and-white likeness.

At the bottom were more photos, and these had nothing to do with identity cards. They were similar to the ones she had seen in documentaries and books, of civilians accused of working against the Reich. Almost all showed executed men and women tied to a post or stake, hands secured behind them, slumped in death. Two showed individuals who had been hanged, one no more than a boy. Crudely written signs had been secured around their necks, though from the angle the photos were taken it was impossible to read them.

Isabelle flinched even as the historian in her thrilled at the discovery. These documents had been left behind, probably untouched since the end of the occupation, and would no doubt tell a story. Isabelle would have to ensure that they, along with any others she might come across, were carefully preserved, especially the civilian photos. She had a contact at the Caen

Normandie Memorial Museum who would be interested in whatever she found related to the occupation—

"What the hell are you doing in here?"

Isabelle spun at her sister's question, squinting at the bright light being directed at her. "I found the library—"

"Who cares?" Emilie cut her off, the beam from her flashlight flitting across the shelves. "I thought we were going to look at the damaged rooms first."

"No, you were going to look at the damaged rooms first," Isabelle reminded her. "But I fixed the drawer in this desk. Come take a look at this. There is—"

"No. Look, we don't have time for whatever that is. We need to focus—*you* need to focus on the building. Not whatever trinkets and personal effects were left behind, because God knows this place is full of them." Emilie scowled. "We don't even own the château. Maybe you shouldn't be snooping through the drawers quite yet?"

Isabelle's lips compressed. She hated to admit it but her sister wasn't wrong. She had no business going through this desk. Or any others. Not yet at least.

"Hurry up. I need you and your contractor's opinion. It's a mess." She didn't wait for an answer but stalked away, and Isabelle wondered how she could have missed the clatter of her approach in the first place.

She sighed and closed the lid on the box and latched it once more. She shut the open folder and lifted it to replace it as she had found it, but as she did so, a slip of paper fluttered from the back. Isabelle picked it up, and her hand stopped in midair. She was holding a list of what looked like dates and times, followed by the names of what were clearly German military personnel. *Getötet / Verschwunden* was scrawled at the top, and Isabelle struggled to translate. Dead? Killed? Missing? She wasn't sure. But it was what was written along the bottom of the paper that made her freeze, unable to tear her eyes away. *Dornröschen* had been scribbled along the bottom of the paper and, in brackets next to it, the name *Briar Rose*.

Isabelle's mind raced. There was nothing else on the paper, no photo attached to it, no other description or information, nothing that indicated that the name was anything other than a seemingly random notation. But why was the name here? On German correspondence?

Perhaps she was holding in her hand the birth of the myth that had eventually become Briar Rose.

"Isabelle!" Her sister's voice echoed down the hallway. "We don't have all day!"

Isabelle closed her eyes briefly, and with a monumental effort, placed the slip of paper back in the folder. Part of her wanted to stuff the entire contents of the drawer into her tool bag to examine them later. But she could not bring herself to do so. It would make her nothing more than a thief, and her entire career was built on a reputation of principles and ethics that allowed her to work in and on historic properties and possessions of extraordinary value.

With deliberate intent, Isabelle tucked everything back into the drawer as she had found it. The contents had been there for the better part of a century. They would keep a little longer, at least until the château became theirs or at such time that Isabelle could contact the seller and arrange to acquire the documents. Properly. Not like a common criminal.

Isabelle replaced the protective sheet over the desk, retreated to the door, hefted her tool bag back onto her shoulder, and headed after her sister.

The air got progressively chillier as she neared the end of the hall, and a patch of daylight spilled from the wide doors that gaped open at the end. From somewhere beyond, Isabelle could still hear her sister's heels tapping unevenly across the floor, interspersed with the occasional curse.

She stepped into the room and stopped short. Over the years, Isabelle had been in many buildings that had sustained fire damage, and she'd thought she'd had an idea of what she would find here. She'd been wrong. This wasn't a room that had just burned. This was a room that had been demolished.

It had probably been a ballroom at one time, an imposing space at least twice the size of the library she had just come from. Though whoever had used it last, presumably the German military, had not been using it for dancing. Instead, strewn across the floor in uneven rows were towering heaps of what looked like mangled electronic equipment or machinery of some sort, melted and blackened and all covered in a thick layer of dust. The ornamental plaster ceiling, or what remained of it, gaped open in the center, exposing the beams above. There had once been a half dozen wrought iron chandeliers hanging in here too, Isabelle surmised, though they had been torn from their anchors and lay twisted and black amid the wreckage on the floor.

Close to Isabelle, the remnants of a pair of shattered desks, equally as charred and ruined, were identifiable only by the dull gleam of the drawer handles that ran up the sides of each. The skeletons of dozens of chair frames lay broken amid the destruction, their wooden seats reduced to ashy slivers. If there had been art or paper or curtains on the walls, they were long gone, swallowed by the flames that had left greedy, scorched streaks in their wake.

"How bad is this?" Emilie asked from somewhere across the room.

Isabelle gingerly picked her way in. The floor here was

patterned tile, remnants of faint reds and blues bleeding through the ash and debris where she walked. A number of the tiles had been fractured, fragments scattered to reveal the same stone that ran through the hall beneath. She was certainly not a fire or arson expert by any stretch of the imagination but she had seen and restored her fair share of buildings and structures damaged by fires, some recent and others centuries old. If she had to guess, this fire, contained to the room as it was, had burned hot and fast, but not for very long. The rest of the château would have gone up otherwise. It was miraculous that it had not.

She played her flashlight over the beams above her head. Isabelle would get an outside consultation, of course, before they proceeded with any restoration work, but on closer inspection, the thick timbers appeared to be undamaged, as if the fire had not touched them. However the fire must have burned, it had not burned through the ceiling, which likely explained how the château hadn't been reduced to a collection of broken stone walls and charred kindling. Isabelle wasn't immediately sure exactly how the plaster had sustained the damage it had, and though the destruction of the ornamental design was unfortunate, it could be replicated and repaired.

"Well?" Emilie demanded. "Can you fix this?"

"With enough money and time, I fixed a chapel with trees growing through the nave and the floor missing in the apse," Isabelle replied. She glanced over, her sister's coat a bright crimson spot like a drop of blood in a sea of grey and black.

"God, you'd never survive in the city," Emilie huffed impatiently. "That's not an answer. Can you fix this on a budget? *Our* budget? Yes or no?"

Isabelle tried not to bristle. "So long as the structure has retained its integrity, and my initial observations make me believe it has, at least for the most part, the rest is simply a fairly straightforward demolition and rebuild." Her gaze travelled over the stone floor. "Yes, I believe the repairs would be within our budget. But I'd like to know what is underneath the building here."

"Nothing." A voice from the doorway answered.

Isabelle turned. "Luc," she greeted warmly, a buzz of pleasure zipping through her. He was wearing his rough work jacket and a knit cap, his tool belt slung around his hips and his cheeks flushed from the cool air. He looked like an effortlessly handsome and capable advert for a workwear company.

"Monsieur Carriere asked me to stay to seal the window back up after you are done." He ventured into the room, looking around, a long roll of paper in his hand. "Wow. I thought it looked bad from the window. I think it looks worse from this angle."

"I think it looks worse than it is entirely," she murmured.

Luc held out the roll. "Carriere asked me to give these to you. The blueprints, or at least a copy of what existed in 1791. They were the only ones they could find, apparently."

Isabelle took them eagerly. "Thank you." She lowered her voice. "You won't believe what I—"

"Luc Legassé. It's been an age," Emilie interrupted as she stopped just in front of them. With great fanfare, she pecked the air at the side of both of Luc's cheeks. "Izz told me you were doing some work here. You're looking well."

"Thanks. You too." Luc shoved his hands in his pockets. "It's nice to see you home."

Emilie pursed her lips. "Well, it's not home, and don't get used to it. I need to return to Paris tomorrow."

"What?" Isabelle blinked at Emilie. "So soon? Why? Do Mom and Dad know?"

"They should. Oh, don't look so wounded," Emilie scoffed.

"My firm doesn't run by itself. I have employees and important clients counting on me. Unlike you, I can't just duck out whenever I need."

"I don't just—" Isabelle caught herself and held her tongue. Arguing with Emilie was a waste of time. Her sister would say what she would say. Instead she turned and bent, retrieving a twisted piece of wire from the floor.

"But this opportunity was just too good to pass up on," Emilie was telling Luc brightly. "Like I said to Izz, this château would be a marvelous addition to my portfolio. I have some fabulous ideas that I think even Isabelle will be able to manage. Who knows, maybe with this project, I can help get her little company some real exposure."

Luc cleared his throat. "I think her little company has all the exposure it can handle right now, don't you?"

"What do you mean?"

Luc turned. "You didn't tell your sister about your Heritage Award nomination? For the Desblanc Chapel project?" It was more thoughtful than accusatory.

"I mentioned it. The trees growing through the nave, anyway." Isabelle shrugged. "Do you think these were radios?" She deliberately steered the conversation away from herself.

There was a heartbeat of silence before Luc moved to join her. "Looks more like switchboards of some sort. Or telephone equipment. Hard to say. There's not much left. Someone in town with expertise with old electronics could probably tell you. I could ask around."

"That makes sense, I suppose. If Nazi officers were billeted here, then of course they would have had communication equipment installed." Isabelle considered the wire fragment in her hand. "Too bad they destroyed it all."

"Scorched earth, I'd say," Luc suggested. "If the Nazis had to abandon everything, they certainly weren't going to leave it behind for someone else to use." He craned his neck to view the far side of the room. "When they said this damage was unrepaired, they really meant *untouched*. It's like someone just closed the door and tried to forget this all existed."

"Probably not worth the expense if no one was living here afterward." Isabelle set the piece of charred wire down and tried to refocus. At the moment, the history behind the damage, however intriguing, was not as important as their ability to fix it. Just as the history sitting in that library drawer needed to take a backseat. She'd mention her discovery of the Briar Rose name to Luc later. "What were you saying about the floors earlier?"

"I took a look." Luc gestured at the rolled blueprints. "There is nothing beneath the château, save for solid foundations. At least that is what the drawings show. There is a cellar directly under the kitchens but a Château de Brézé it is not."

"Brézé?" Emilie asked. She sounded subdued. "What is that?"

"A medieval castle with an extensive network of tunnels and chambers beneath it. It's quite something," Isabelle told her. "And very popular with tourists."

"Oh. That's disappointing then," Emilie muttered.

"Ah, but you didn't let me finish," Luc said. "You may not have a castle beneath a castle to market, but there is a tunnel, added in 1791. An escape hatch, if you will, with hidden doors. Angry people bent on death and destruction seem to have left an impression."

"What?" Isabelle straightened. "Where?"

Luc grinned at her. "Let me show you."

CHAPTER

10

Stasia

22 MAY 1943
AMSTERDAM, THE NETHERLANDS

The pounding on the door brought Stasia out of her bed with a jerk. She stumbled awkwardly, the sheet still half-wrapped around her legs, and groped her way along the edge of her bed trying to find her balance. She blinked rapidly, the cobwebs clearing from her mind as the pounding came again. On the other side of the bed, Margot had also tumbled awake and was standing frozen, staring out into the small living space cloaked in shadows.

"Who do you think it is?" Stasia whispered, her voice hoarse with sleep and fright.

"I don't know." Margot smoothed her hair and reached for her robe, which lay across the foot of the bed.

"What are you doing?" Stasia hissed.

"Answering the door."

"Don't."

"We have to."

"What if it's the police?"

"What if it's someone who needs our help?"

Stasia stood, frozen with fear and indecision.

"If it's the police, they are coming in whether I answer it or not." Margot was hurriedly tying her robe around her waist. "It's best that we don't look like we have anything to hide."

Stasia wasn't so sure. Wrapping her arms tightly around herself, she tiptoed to the window and pulled back the curtain. Outside, the night was still, the street empty, the windows facing it dark and blank. "I don't see anyone." Which didn't mean that there weren't men waiting out of sight. Waiting to arrest them for the pamphlets or the meetings or the documents that Stasia had stolen for the forgers. "I don't like this," she said, but Margot was already out of the room, hastening through the dimness toward the door.

Stasia followed more slowly, the floor like ice beneath her bare feet. She reached for her own robe, a small comfort against the chill of the night and the dread enhancing it. A fist pounded on the door again, and Stasia flinched. She could hear her heart pounding in her ears and was aware that she was breathing hard. There was nothing in their tiny flat that would incriminate them—Stasia had made sure of that. But there was also nothing that might be used as a weapon to defend themselves.

"Who is it?" Margot asked through the door.

"Frank." The answer was muffled and terse.

Stasia took a step back, a small measure of relief flooding through her. Not the police then. But what was this man doing at this hour at their flat? Nothing good ever came from the darkness of night.

Margot made a small sound and unlocked the door, swinging it wide.

A figure swept into the small space, making it impossibly smaller, more cold air billowing in his wake.

Margot had her head out the door, peering down the street, and apparently satisfied that nothing was further amiss, she closed it firmly behind the man. Stasia had moved forward and reached for the small lamp on the corner, flooding the room in a muted glow. She checked to make sure the curtains were tightly closed before turning to greet their guest.

Only to find herself staring down the barrel of a pistol.

It took her mind a heartbeat to catch up with her senses, disbelief and confusion dulling her terror, at least for a moment. Her eyes travelled up the arm holding the weapon, noting the familiar grey coat, the neatly knotted tie, and the black hat tilted at a fashionable angle.

"I don't understand." The words came out as a wheeze.

"I know who you really are. And what you do." Frank took a step back and turned the gun in the direction of Margot, who was standing as still as death inside the door, one hand still on the latch. "Your neighbours will be of no help if you're thinking of running," he said. "I'm sure they're awake by now, and I'm just as sure that they will keep their lights off and their doors locked against traitors like you."

Stasia's confusion cleared, and the terror was unleashed in a nauseating wave, choking her and making it hard to breathe. Making it hard to think.

Frank jerked the gun to the side, motioning at Margot. "Join your friend."

Margot eyed him coldly, her expression betraying nothing, but she did as she was ordered and joined Stasia in the corner of the room. Hidden in the folds of their robes, Margot's hand found Stasia's and gripped her fingers tightly.

"You probably thought you were quite clever," Frank said conversationally, taking his hat from his head and setting it aside on the back of the sofa. The muzzle of the gun never wavered.

"Who are you really?" Margot demanded.

"Frank." Their friend who was not their friend at all smiled, though the gesture did not reach his eyes. He ran his free hand through his greying hair. "I work for the Gestapo," he continued. "And my only job is to find traitors to the German Empire. Those who would disobey and betray our great Führer."

Stasia forced herself to take a deep, steadying breath. "We are not traitors."

"You've been helping Jews," Frank said coldly. "But now, if you wish to live, you will help me."

Beside Stasia, Margot scoffed. "We can't help you."

Stasia did not look at her friend. This man Frank, who had tricked them all horribly, might be aware of what they had done, but he did not seem to be aware of who Margot really was.

"I need addresses," Frank barked, shoving the gun closer to Stasia's face. "Addresses where you are hiding them. Addresses of everyone else who is helping them."

Stasia picked a spot on the wall over Frank's shoulder and stared at it, imagining only that they were caught in a nightmare and that she would wake soon.

"I need names." Frank was almost shouting now. He rubbed his face, the stubble on his cheeks making a faint rasping sound in the ensuing silence. "We have ways of making weak women like you talk, you know," he said. "Ways that you can't even imagine in your worst dreams."

It was odd, Stasia thought dully, how her world seemed to have slowed. The rush of terror that had almost overwhelmed her had somehow made sounds louder and light brighter, while her body retreated into a peculiar numbness. The small clock on the table beside the lamp ticked and ticked, the only sound now filling up the space. The soft light from the lamp made the small hairs at Frank's collar glow, like a curious white lace.

"No." The answer came from Margot. "We know nothing."

"No?" Frank's voice rose unpleasantly. "Make the right choice here, young lady."

"No," Stasia repeated, surprised by how steady her voice sounded. "Like she said, we have no information."

Margot's fingers squeezed hers again.

"I will give you one more chance," Frank said, his lips curling into an unpleasant grimace, "because I have a soft spot for pretty girls." He transferred the aim of the gun toward Margot. "And then, if I am not satisfied, I will simply shoot her first."

Stasia didn't actually see Margot move, only registered the loss of her touch where their hands had once been linked. But she heard Frank grunt, and the gun swung wildly around, and Margot shrieked as she jammed her elbow into Frank's midsection.

He doubled over, and Margot launched herself onto his back, her hands wrapped around his neck. Jerked out of her shock, Stasia snatched the lamp from the table behind them and brought it crashing down on the top of Frank's head, the base glancing off his skull, the bulb shattering and sending the room back into blackness.

Frank had fallen to his knees, Margot still clinging to his back, and Stasia kicked at him with all her might, ignoring the pain that shot through her foot where she made contact. The sound of the gun clattering to the floor was overloud in the tiny room.

"Stop," Frank garbled. "Stop. Please." His hands were groping along the floor and came into contact with Stasia's foot. She kicked them away.

"It was a test," Frank gasped. "Just a . . . test." He gagged. "Testing you. To make sure. . . . to make sure we could . . . trust."

Stasia froze, her foot poised for another blow. It was impossible to see his face or his expression in the shadows. "Say that again."

Margot must have loosened her grip around his neck because his voice came out a little stronger. "I was testing you. Both of you. I'm not Gestapo."

"How do we know that?" Stasia demanded.

"The gun is empty. I was never going . . . to . . . shoot you. I just needed to know what you would do . . . if it happened. If you would . . . protect us."

"He's lying." Margot's voice cracked out of the darkness.

"I'm not," Frank panted. "Jesus wept, I'm not lying."

Stasia lowered her foot, pain creaking through her toes. It was possible she might have broken one but she ignored that for now and crouched, her hands searching along the floor for the gun. Her fingers came into contact with smooth metal, and she stood, holding the weapon.

It fit neatly in her hand and felt remarkably like her grandfather's old Webley. A thousand times she had loaded and unloaded and cleaned that weapon, and to check this one in the dark took but seconds.

"The gun is empty," she confirmed to no one in particular.

From somewhere below her, Frank groaned.

Stasia heard a rustle in the darkness and felt, rather than saw, Margot join her briefly before she moved off. In a moment, a faint light emanated from the bedroom, strengthening as Margot came out into the living space with their lantern.

Frank was sitting on the floor, holding the back of his head, propped up against the sofa.

Both Stasia and Margot watched him warily.

"It was a test." Frank withdrew his hand from the back of his head and winced at the smear of crimson that stained his fingers. His coat and suit were rumpled, and his tie was askew. He glanced up at them. "A test that you both passed brilliantly."

"How can we know that for certain? How can we know that you are not lying to us now?" Stasia was still as taut as a bowstring.

Frank heaved himself from the floor and onto the sofa, tipping his head from side to side and rubbing the base of his throat. "Because if I were Gestapo, I would not have come alone. I would not have come with an unloaded weapon." He choked out a humourless laugh. "Hell, I would not have come with a weapon that is more than forty years old."

Stasia glanced down at the gun she still held in her hands. In the light, it was easy to see that it was, in fact, a Webley. An old one, and in far worse condition than her grandfather's had been.

Abruptly, she sank to the sofa beside Frank, her legs giving way with no warning. She became aware that her hands were shaking, and she set the gun to the side, clenching her fingers into fists, her nails biting into her palms.

"I would have killed you," Margot said flatly.

Frank offered her a weak smile. "I wasn't expecting that."

Margot sniffed. "Clearly."

If her friend was as shaken as Stasia, she wasn't showing it. Stasia wished she was as brave. Right now she felt as weak as a kitten.

Frank was studying Stasia keenly. "You know how to handle a gun."

"Yes." Stasia left it at that, not trusting her voice to deliver further explanation without betraying her fragility.

"Hmm." Frank retrieved his hat from the back of the sofa and spun it in his hands, his fingers sliding along the brim as he considered first Stasia and then Margot with careful deliberation.

"Why are you here, really?" Margot demanded. "What do you want?"

"I want to ask you if this is still something you want to do. Now that I've shown you what the risks might look like."

"Yes." The swiftness of Stasia's answer startled her. It must have startled Frank too because a dark brow climbed in dubious question.

Margot met her eyes and gave her a nod of agreement and encouragement.

The hat stopped its rotation in Frank's hands. "Up until now, you have done the council a great service but the tasks that we've asked of you have been..." He seemed to be searching for a word. "Not small," he hedged, "because the importance of papers and vouchers and money cannot be understated. But stealing and distributing such are of lesser risk than what I may ask of you now."

"Then ask," Margot said coolly.

The hat resumed its rotation. "Escorting children to new families or hiding places."

"We could do that," Stasia said.

Frank held up his hand. "I'm not done." He paused. "Theft and transport of weapons and ammunition. Armed resistance."

"Yes," Margot answered with a vicious satisfaction, and Stasia knew very well that her friend was no doubt thinking of her own family, murdered by those who oppressed them now.

"Mmm." Frank seemed neither surprised nor doubtful of Margot's answer. His gaze swiveled to Stasia. "And you?"

Stasia swallowed, the cold settling into her bones. "Yes," she said, because there was no other answer that she would be able to live with. Frank's test had been for his own purposes, of course, but it had also served as a severe reminder that they were at war. People were dying all around her at the hands of the police and the SS and the SD—men and women and children who had done nothing wrong other than fail to escape this horrid onslaught of hate in time—and pitiful few seemed like they were trying to stop it.

"If you are caught and arrested, you will be sent to prison," Frank said harshly. "At which point in time, you will likely wish you had simply been shot. Which they might do anyway."

"I'll take that chance," Margot said.

Again, Frank's watchful gaze slid to Stasia, awaiting her answer.

"I understand," she said. She flattened her palms against the tops of her legs, the fabric of her robe smooth under her skin, and wondered at the fact that they were no longer shaking, given the turn this conversation had taken.

"Very well then." Frank put his hat back on his head before wincing and snatching it off again.

"Sorry for that," Stasia said.

"Don't be." Frank only inclined his head. "The council will be in touch." He moved to the door, his steps quiet. "I want you both to expect us to ask a lot of you."

Stasia stood, her legs as steady as her voice. "Good" was all she said.

CHAPTER
11

Nicolas

20 MAY 1943
BIZERTA, TUNISIA

I know I'm asking a lot of you, but the truth is that we need *les Anglais*. Even though I despise them as much as you."

"Unlikely, sir." It was the first thing Nicolas had said since Captain Lefevre had called him into the canvas field office, though Nicolas still wasn't sure what he was doing in here.

The captain leaned forward across a table littered with maps and documents and the tiny, stubby corpses of crushed cigarettes. "But," he said, "I despise the boches more. And so do you. And we both know it."

"My men and I do what is necessary when it is necessary with whom it is necessary. My personal feelings regarding the English are not important."

"I'm glad to hear that." Lefevre straightened and rubbed his bloodshot eyes. "Your men seem to adore you."

Nicolas tried to cover his confusion at the abrupt change in topic before he suppressed an undignified sneer. "My men adore killing boches," he said flatly. "And anyone else who fights with them. I merely point them in the right direction."

Captain Lefevre shook his head. "And the collection of medals that you've accumulated in the last two years is a result of you merely pointing men in the right direction?"

"I don't need baubles for doing my job. Shiny decorations do not interest me." Nicolas was getting impatient.

"No, they don't, do they? That makes you a rather unique, interesting sort." He ran his fingers over his moustache. "Brigadier-General Koenig made you a sergeant for a reason, Navarre."

"Koenig made me a sergeant because the one before me lost his head to a round from a Panzer."

Lefevre waved his hand as if this fact were irrelevant. "Yet you managed to keep yours. Your head, that is, literally and figuratively. Throughout the worst of everything, in fact." He appraised Nicolas. "Your efforts and actions at Bir Hakeim got you noticed."

The sneer Nicolas had suppressed threatened again. "The efforts and actions of every single man and woman in that fort got them noticed. One does not oppose and survive the combined efforts of the Luftwaffe and German and Italian artillery, tanks, and infantry as well as extreme heat and lack of water for as long as we did by wringing one's hands. Sir," he added at the end, as if that might blunt the edge of his tone that bordered on insolent.

Lefevre seemed not to notice Nicolas's rudeness. "You fought your way out of that fort in hand-to-hand combat," he mused.

"We all did."

"It was said that you were . . ."

Nicolas could feel his teeth grinding. "That I was what, sir?"

"Indomitable. Matchless. *Terrifying* was even a word I heard used, though it was followed by the adulating clarification by that particular individual that he would not still be breathing had it not been for you."

Was that a compliment? Criticism? Tribute? Accusation? It didn't matter, he supposed, what one wanted to call Lefevre's words, because they didn't change the truth. The truth that while many of his men had survived, there were many who had not. And it was those men whose faces and names kept him up at night. "Why am I here, Captain?" Nicolas asked, tired of these games. "If it's all the same to you, I still have—"

"Resourceful. Clever. Selfless."

"What?"

"More reports from the men who have served under you, those coming from your service during Operation Torch."

An unwelcome tribute of sorts, then. Nicolas looked away, uncomfortable with the assessment because he hadn't been any of those things for those who mattered most to him. Oscar. Stasia. His father. Had he been all of those things, had he said or done something different at some critical point in time, perhaps they would still be alive. Instead, he had not been resourceful enough to help Oscar. He had not been clever enough to warn Stasia. He had not been selfless enough to save his father.

"I don't need another goddamn medal, if this is what this is leading up to," he growled.

"No, no medals. No, this time you are being awarded with opportunity."

"Opportunity?" Nicolas was thoroughly confused.

Lefevre picked up a document and studied it for a long moment. "Tell me, Navarre, why you left the navy."

Nicolas started. He never spoke about the *Bretagne* or what had happened at Mers el Kébir. To anyone. Ever.

"Trust me when I say I understand your abhorrence of *les Anglais*." The captain gestured to the paper in his hand almost apologetically. "Your military record was forwarded to me."

"By whom?"

"It's not important at the moment. Answer the question, Sergeant."

Nicolas frowned but did as he was ordered. "I died."

"I beg your pardon?"

"The navy made an error. In the aftermath of that attack, I was listed as dead." His hands had flexed into fists, and he forced himself to relax them. "I was in the hospital for a time. Broken arm. Burns on my back and scalp." He rubbed the side of his head above his ear where the skin was puckered and hair no longer grew. "By the time they sorted it, most of the survivors had already been repatriated back to France. Back to Toulon."

"You did not wish to join them?"

"To sit on my hands and watch more French ships sink? Fuck no." He paused. "Sir."

Lefevre waved his hand again, dismissing his outburst. "You joined the Free French then."

"I stayed and joined those who were still here in the business of killing boches." That truth escaped easily, and a small voice in the back of his head wondered what his father would have made of that. What Stasia would have made of that.

What she would have made of him.

By joining the navy, he had told them both, he would be distant from the war, idiotically believing that he would be insulated from its horrors. What had he said to Stasia? That his father had been in the mud and the shit and the blood, and that things would be different for him? And yet here he was, by choice, having crawled through the dust and the shit and the blood, wondering alternately if death by thirst or Nazi guns would find him first, and, with a profound sense of macabre irony, if he would survive only to end up one day in an alley in Rouen, seeing the ghosts of the men dead at his hand, trying to drink his way past the memory of it all.

He remembered the naval officer on the docks of Toulon who had made fun of the men in the trenches running around with their weapons looking for something to shoot at while the men on the *Bretagne* controlled a weapon of unfathomable destruction. Yet it had been a weapon they had never used, and in the space of a quarter hour, that weapon, along with almost its entire crew, had been relegated to the bottom of the sea. While the men with their rifles in the trenches still fought.

"Hmm." Lefevre was considering him.

"Why am I here, Captain?" Nicolas asked again. "I have duties—"

"I've been asked by those in much more lofty ranks than I to identify officers who I believe have...specific potential."

"For killing Nazis?"

"Perhaps. I don't actually know but I must assume that is part of it."

"Part of what?" Impatience was rising again, faster and hotter than before.

Lefevre placed Nicolas's record on the table. "Rommel is done. Von Arnim and his filthy Nazi hordes have surrendered; Marshal Messe has surrendered whatever is left. We have Tunis and Bizerta. Our work in North Africa, while certainly not finished, has changed approach." He paused. "As such, individuals with distinguished service will be redeployed."

"What does that mean?"

"It means that I have submitted your name as one of my

officers who I believe fulfills the qualities that these particular generals and individuals are looking for. It means you will be departing North Africa."

"What? Why?" Nicolas was aghast. "We have a path forward right into the throat of Italy—"

"You will be leaving here shortly, at the end of the month," Lefevre cut him off. "So gather what things you have and be ready."

"I won't leave my men."

"Your men have already been reassigned to very capable individuals."

Nicolas kept his hands at his sides only by an extreme force of will. "You can't do this."

"That is correct. I can't. But generals can. And it's already been done."

Nicolas spun and paced to the tent door and back, certain if he did not move he might simply hit something. "And where am I going?"

"To England."

Nicolas stopped, frozen where he stood, every fiber in his body screaming with defiance. "No."

The captain leaned on the table again, his eyes hard, his face darkening even further beneath his sunburn and the dirt worn into every crease. "That was not a question, Navarre. That was an order." His voice was steely.

"I don't speak English."

"Irrelevant." He paused. "You already told me that your personal feelings regarding the English are not important. Was that a truth?"

Nicolas cursed softly under his breath. "I'll work with the Americans but I cannot work with *les Anglais*."

"This is not a negotiation, Sergeant," the captain barked. "Refuse and the consequences will be dire."

Nicolas closed his eyes before opening them again, marshalling his composure. "I'm going to England to do what?"

"Again, I do not know. Truthfully, I do not wish to know. The type of men who accompany such commands are not men to be trifled with, nor are they men to be disobeyed." Lefevre's expression softened. "I'm not asking you to like *les Anglais*," he said. "But I'm ordering you to work with them. For the good of France."

★ ★ ★

The rain seemed unending in London.

Nicolas had been told a dozen times that all it did was rain in London, so the grey, leaden skies and spiteful, unceasing drizzle had not come as a shock.

What had come as a shock was the utter destruction of the city that seemed to extend everywhere he looked. Rows of shattered buildings jutted upward defying the rain, like a mouthful of broken teeth. In some places, a home or structure seemed untouched and unscathed while only a pile of blackened timbers and scattered brick remained immediately next to it. Once grand architecture had been reduced to something that resembled ruined dollhouses, entire façades torn away to reveal splintered rooms full of splintered furniture that citizens had once called home. Parks that had, at one time, no doubt been planted with flowers and greenery and featured benches from which one might enjoy the view were now home to antiaircraft batteries, surrounded by towering walls of sandbags and manned by helmeted crews who smoked and waited for the next attack to come from above. Here and there, the carcasses of burned-out buses, or possibly trolleys, listed terribly, half-submerged beneath the wreckage of demolished dwellings.

Nicolas was no stranger to the destruction of war. He had borne witness to the systematic obliteration of harbours and depots and bases throughout North Africa. But the systematic obliteration of a city the size of London was different. Here, where he walked, there were no hangars or battleships or fortresses. Here, as he turned in a slow circle, the rain dripping slowly down his back, there were only civilian houses and shops and schools. Or what was left of them. And even more perplexing was the seemingly indifferent, stoic attitudes of those who still went about their business amid the destruction as though they didn't see it.

At the far end of the street, a passel of children were playing a game of football, as oblivious to the rain as they were to the flattened homes on either side. Women, many in uniform, some in civilian clothes, hustled along the edges of the streets, stepping deftly around or over the debris scattered in their way. Men, also dressed in a diverse collection of uniform and plain attire, took little note of their surroundings and instead tucked their newspapers under their arms or over their heads as they ducked in and out of the drizzle, sending aggrieved glances at the clouds as if rain were the most irritating thing that had fallen from the sky. The streets were jammed with command cars and military trucks, all in a rush, it seemed, to get somewhere while their petrol lasted.

"Do you think," murmured the quiet French lieutenant who had accompanied Nicolas on their roundabout journey from Tunisia to Scotland and finally to England, "that this is what Paris might have looked like had we not surrendered?"

Having never been to Paris, Nicolas refrained from answering either yes or no. But standing in the destruction of this English city was undermining his determination to continue to despise *les Anglais*.

"Doesn't matter," Nicolas said, heading north in search of the address that had been provided to them at the train station. "Let's keep on."

The two men skirted Grosvenor Square and found the building they had been directed to on Duke Street. Nicolas stopped in front of the rather nondescript structure and frowned. It was a boxy four stories of fawn-colored brick sandwiched in a row of similar buildings, the hue of brick differing down the line. Ordered rows of windows lined each floor, though here and there boards had been nailed over the openings where the glass had been shattered. A single, somewhat warped door set into an arched doorway seemed to be the only way in or out.

"This is it?" the lieutenant asked, sounding faintly incredulous. "This is the office of the General Directorate? Special operations of de Gaulle and the Free French?"

"At least it's still standing," Nicolas muttered. "That's something, I suppose."

Nicolas led the way as the two officers ducked through the door into the interior of the building, blinking at the relative dimness. The main floor, or at least the room that they could see, was a maze of desks, populated by both men and women working industriously at typewriters or thick files of paper and all faintly blurred by the blue-grey veil of cigarette smoke that seemed to hang from the ceiling.

"Gentlemen." They were greeted by a small man, bespectacled and wearing what Nicolas guessed was a French uniform with a dapper beret, though the apparel was different from anything he had seen in Africa. "Your names and reason of business here?"

"Sergeant Nicolas Navarre," Nicolas replied. "Reporting to Colonel Giroux."

"Lieutenant Charles Brunelle," his companion said. "Also similarly reporting."

"Ah, yes, very good, very good." The bespectacled man rubbed his hands together as if delighted by this revelation, though he seemed preoccupied. "We've been expecting you. Please, come in." He led them in the general direction of the main floor. "Can I get you something? I'd offer you coffee, but I can assure you that you do not wish to drink what is passing for coffee these days. There is perhaps tea from yesterday's leaves but—"

"I'm fine," Nicolas cut him off. Brunelle also refused.

"Very good, very good." The diminutive man stopped and opened a closed door, ushering Nicolas inside. "Sergeant Navarre, please wait here. An officer will be along shortly to debrief you and conduct your interview. Lieutenant, please follow me."

Nicolas wandered into the small room that may have been a bedroom or tiny sitting room once. Its walls were painted a faded rose, the bare oak floors worn and scarred. The room was devoid of furniture save for a wooden table, one of its legs resting on an empty tin to keep it level. On one side of the table was a single chair, on the other a row of four mismatched chairs. Heavy blackout curtains were drawn across the window, and Nicolas made no effort to peer outside.

"Sergeant Navarre. *Bien.*"

Nicolas turned to find a tall uniformed man striding through the door with vigour, puffs of white hair sticking out from the sides of his head like cotton balls. His face was deeply lined, with a bushy white moustache almost covering the entirety of his mouth and a pair of round spectacles clinging precariously to the end of his nose, and wearing the same preoccupied expression as the man who had greeted them. He had a file of papers in his hand, which he dumped on the table's surface. "Welcome to England, Sergeant. Please, have a seat." He gestured at the single chair on the far side of the table.

Nicolas did as he was bidden.

"*Bien, bien.* I am Colonel Maurice Giroux. I trust your journey down from Glasgow was uneventful?" A paper slid from the folder, and he lunged to stop it.

"Just rainy, sir."

"Ah, yes. Well, one does not ever quite get used to this incessant rain." He opened the file with quick, abrupt movements and peered at the printed pages that tumbled out. "Ah, *bien.* Testing in Scotland went very well, I see?"

Nicolas wasn't sure if that was a question or a statement, so he said nothing. He, along with a dozen other French officers, had been subjected to a barrage of psychological and physical testing that had been, at various times, demanding, baffling, challenging, or maddening, but always cryptic. Questions had been met with blank stares or one-word nonanswers. None of the men being put through their paces knew why they were doing it or what the end goal was. At the end of it all, Nicolas had simply been handed a set of orders that had brought him here.

"I see you served aboard the *Bretagne.*" The colonel made a rude sound. "Nasty business, that."

Again, Nicolas wasn't sure if there was a question in that statement, so he remained silent.

"You have all the reasons in the world to hate *les Anglais.* Yet you are here. In England."

This time, there was a clear question.

"I am doing what needs to be done for France," Nicolas repeated what he had told his captain. "As are you, sir," he added.

The colonel grunted and returned his attention to the file. "You were an engineer."

"Yes, sir."

"How capable?"

"Sir?"

"How capable an engineer?" He pinned Nicolas with a look over the top of his spectacles. "I will learn this later on but an honest answer will save time now."

"One of the best."

"Bien." The colonel frowned slightly. "But the size and type of engines you worked with on the *Bretagne* will not be what you may encounter where you are headed."

Nicolas sat forward, his ears pricking at the reference to the future, however vague. "I understand."

"You familiar with smaller engines? Trucks, cars, whatnot?"

"Yes."

"This is lucky then, this skill you have. Will be an advantage." He pulled a pen from the front pocket of his uniform and made a notation. "What about German? You speak it?"

"A little."

"Hmph. We'll remedy that." He jabbed the pen down the rest of the page as if violently checking off items on a grocery list. "You spent a long time in Africa. Saw a great deal of combat as a soldier. Lots of commendations." He looked up again. "Irregular, wouldn't you say, for a navy man?"

Nicolas shrugged. "It's where I landed after Mers el Kébir. Where I could contribute."

"Many would say that a soldier is a step down from a naval engineer. A waste of skill."

"I suppose some would say that, yes." Nicolas sat back and pushed his hands into his pockets, his fingers finding the familiar warmth and shape of the lighter. "But you have my record in front of you. You can determine for yourself if it was a waste or not."

The colonel considered him for a moment, the preoccupied, slightly scattered look he had worn now sharpening into focus. He eventually dropped his eyes and studied the file in front of him. From the room outside the door, the banging and clacking of typewriters continued, competing with the sound of voices and the clatter of feet hurrying back and forth. From the other side of the curtain covering the window came the insistent bleat of a vehicle horn.

"Jedburgh," the colonel finally said.

"I beg your pardon?"

"The code name for the operation you will be joining is Jedburgh. The other officers already recruited have taken to calling themselves Jeds." He closed the file and looked up at Nicolas. "This is a joint operation with the American OSS and the British SOE. You will be returning to Scotland for further training."

Nicolas did not point out that he had just arrived from Scotland. Instead, he asked, "Training for what, sir?"

"This operation will see teams with specialized training inserted behind enemy lines. Belgium. The Netherlands." He paused. "France."

Nicolas went still.

"You will be receiving instruction in parachuting, radio oper-ation, coding, explosives, small arms, sabotage, espionage skills, navigation, and weapons, among other things. Some language training but your French may very well make you a candidate for an assignment in France. Your ultimate goal is to assist advancing Allied forces by working with local partisan and Resistance factions and coordinating airdrops of weapons and supplies to these groups wherever possible. In short, your mission is to attack and destroy the Third Reich from within by any and all means necessary."

Nicolas took a moment to sort through that information. "Advancing Allied forces?"

"We will have boots back in occupied countries soon enough," the colonel said harshly. "I don't know exactly when and how, but soon. And when we do, the Jedburghs will already be there willing and able to assist."

"Understood." The chance that he might get home, that he might take the fight to French soil, was almost too fantastical to believe. After years of fighting in different corners of the earth against an enemy that seemed to have infested it all, he might very well be headed home.

The colonel's preoccupied look was back, as if he had said all he needed to say and was already thinking about another task. "*Bien*. There will be a panel of officers wishing to host a series of final interviews with you here before your return to Scotland." He glanced at the empty chairs beside him as if half expecting those men to magically materialize.

Nicolas wondered what another round of interviews could possibly accomplish but didn't ask and simply nodded.

"In the meantime, you will be elevated to the rank of captain."

"Sir?" Nicolas felt his jaw slacken.

"We need the rabble of Maquis forces to respect both you and the skills you possess, and the best way, in our experience, is to make sure you have a rank that gets their attention. Is that a problem?"

"No, sir."

"Excellent. Lastly, you'll need to get rid of your name. Nicolas Navarre cannot return to France, or anywhere else for that matter, as we wish there to be no discoverable connection to places or families or past service. You'll be given new papers and documents. You may provide us with a nom de guerre of your choosing or we can provide one for you. It matters not to me but you do need to reinvent yourself. Your current name will be erased from our records so that there is no chance of being discovered." He picked up his pen and paused with the tip poised over the paper. "Do you have something in mind, Captain?"

Nicolas blinked at the use of his new rank and started to shake his head. "I don't—"

He stopped. And remembered the last time that someone had called him by a name that was not his. By a girl who had walked with him all the way from Rouen into an abandoned garden, where she had sat beside him underneath a stone angel and taught him how to roll a cigarette from stolen tobacco. Even now, he could still see the blue-and-gold tin in his hand, could still remember that first taste of smoky, woody leaves in his mouth, could still feel the warmth of the sun on his face, and could still feel the soft sureness of her touch on his skin.

"Thomas," Nicolas said quietly. "Thomas Phillipe."

The colonel bent and made a notation on the paper, the pen scratching in the silence. "Very good, Captain Phillipe." He gathered the papers strewn across the table and stood. "You'll be heading north shortly. *Bonne chance.*"

CHAPTER

12

Stasia

Stasia pedalled northeast along the edge of the canal and prayed that luck would once again be on her side. She took deep breaths and kept her pace steady as she guided her bicycle through the streets. The weight of the pistols secured deep in the sewn pockets of her long, thick sweater felt like anchors where they touched her thighs every time her knees came up. The packet of forged identity cards she had tucked beneath the waistband of her trousers felt like a brick, and no matter how many times she did this, she still had the irrational notion that anyone who glanced at her would be able to tell that she was smuggling both as easily as if she had a sign hung around her neck.

But she still hadn't been challenged. Not by the police who loitered in the streets and watched her as she rode by, not by the aggressive Nazi drivers who leaned on their horns to clear the streets as their ugly black cars roared past, and not by the arrogant soldiers at the checkpoints who looked at her papers and then at her breasts, though not always in that order. And each of those times she hid her revulsion and hatred behind a vacuous expression or vacant smile to give the Nazis and those who sided with them no reason to ever look any closer than that.

On the far side of the canal, the spire of Westerkerk church rose in defiance of the gathering clouds that bunched together ominously above the rooftops. Stasia pedalled past, carefully noting the streets on her left. A minute farther and she turned her bicycle around a sharp corner, angling west, and leaned into the wind that now pushed against her. In the distance, thunder rumbled, long and low, declaring its intentions.

Here, the streets narrowed, the brick buildings creating four-story walls on either side of her, rows of windows staring blankly across at their neighbours'. Stasia glanced behind her, where Margot followed on her own bicycle. She, too, carried a pair of bulky pistols and a collection of forged documents destined for use by the Resistance hidden beneath her clothing. For all outward appearances, simply a pair of schoolgirls on their way home.

"I'm still here," Margot puffed, her cheeks pink from the wind and the ride.

They weren't far from their destination now, and if their luck held, they would avoid both any police and the rain. The two women pedalled on, weaving their way through pedestrians, many glancing anxiously at the darkening sky, others shuffling with haste behind their handcarts. Above their heads, windows in the upper floors of the buildings were being closed against the impending weather. Shopkeepers peered out from their door-ways, and mothers hustled their children along.

Stasia heard the engine and at first mistook it for a roll of thunder. But it didn't fade and only grew, and by the time Stasia realized her mistake, it was almost on top of her. She thought she heard Margot yell something before a hulking military truck roared past, nearly knocking her from her bicycle. She veered to the side, the tyres shuddering on the cobbles, narrowly missing a woman fleeing in the opposite direction, and came to an awkward, painful stop against a brick wall of a café. She staggered, half falling, half jumping off her bicycle, but managed to keep it upright. A second truck thundered by, belching exhaust.

Frantic, she turned back toward Margot. Her friend had been quicker than Stasia and was hurrying toward her, pushing her bicycle along the walk that hugged the shopfronts.

"Are you all right?" Margot panted, letting her bicycle rest against the café wall.

"Fine." Stasia rubbed her arm and winced. Her sweater hadn't torn but her elbow and forearm would be bruised by tonight. She rather thought she deserved the reminder because she knew she should have been paying better attention. Trucks like these brought police, and police brought danger, and Stasia's inattention was unforgivable. The first of the dark grey-green trucks had already disappeared from view farther up around a corner, but the second truck was coming to a stop amid a chorus of shrieking brakes in the middle of the narrow street just past the café, in front of a tall, red-brick apartment building.

Another raid, Stasia thought, her pulse pounding and helpless fury swelling. Another roundup of Jewish civilians by those they'd once called neighbours. Another mass transport of families to Drenthe, to be interned at Westerbork and then sent God knew where. The deportations were becoming so regular now that Stasia despaired. Entire families dragged out of their homes and thrown into trucks and buses to be shipped east and never seen again. The contents of those homes carried out with far more care, placed into trucks and vehicles and shipped south, never to be seen again.

It all made Stasia think that no matter how many terrified children she escorted and helped hide, or how many weapons she delivered, or how many forged documents she couriered, or how much ammunition she dispensed, she wasn't doing enough. Nothing that she was doing was enough.

All around her, the remaining civilians were now scattering, ducking through doors or hurrying away as fast as they were able in the opposite direction in expectation of a deluge of Dutch police that would bring nothing good.

"Traitorous bastards," Stasia hissed under her breath as the back of the truck clanged open on its hinges.

Except it wasn't the navy-coated police who emerged from within. The men who jumped down from the back of the truck, their black boots thumping on the ground with the finality of a gunshot, were dressed in Nazi grey, the runic SS slashes on their black collars easily visible, as was the rifle slung over the shoulder of each. An officer appeared from the other side of the truck, strolling casually and watching as each of his men marched past him, heading into the apartment building. He lit a cigarette and leaned against the corner of the truck as if he were waiting for a train that was late.

Fear edged Stasia's anger now, brittle, icy, and ominous. "What should we do?"

"We need to get inside," Margot hissed, pushing Stasia toward the café entrance. "Now."

"Maybe we should go back. Get farther away."

"There is nowhere that is far enough away." Margot had barely finished her words before the Nazi officer stepped out into the middle of the street, glancing first at the leaden skies and then at his watch as though considering how much time he might have before the rain started. He looked up and down the deserted street, and Stasia shoved Margot into the café before they could come under scrutiny.

There was no one inside save for an elderly woman with a dish towel draped over one stooped shoulder and a kerchief covering her white hair. An overturned chair and a foursome of abandoned cups on a little round table bore evidence of an exodus of patrons through a rear exit somewhere. Stasia tucked that detail in her memory. Both she and Margot stepped to the side, flattening themselves against a wall where they could watch out the window without being seen.

The woman, presumably the owner of the café, was muttering under her breath, a litany of indecipherable words that sounded like a cross between a prayer and a string of curses. She glanced fearfully between Stasia and the window framing the soldiers outside.

"Why are there soldiers here?" Stasia demanded. "What are they doing? Do you know?"

The old woman wrung her hands in her apron and shook her head, either unwilling or unable to answer. Instead, she simply scuttled away, vanishing somewhere in the back.

Stasia reached out and gripped Margot's arm.

"We have papers," Margot reminded her in a low voice. Neither woman knew who might yet remain in the rear of the café listening or what loyalties they might have. "Good ones. If the worst happens, you'll be fine. We'll be fine." She sounded abnormally calm.

Yet Stasia was already considering where they might ditch the guns and the forged documents should it look like the soldiers would raid the café and search its occupants. Because they would not be fine at all if they were caught with those. They would be arrested and imprisoned, probably along with the owner of the café they had been found in. They would be tortured until they gave up the names of those with whom they worked. Or until they died, whichever came first.

No, they would not be fine, and both she and Margot knew it. But one thing at a time.

Stasia simply nodded and settled back against the wall, at least until a scream, followed by a gunshot, made them both jump. Another shot, and somewhere, the sound of shattering glass followed by a chorus of wails and desperate shouts.

The Nazi officer on the street seemed unperturbed by this and only moved into the center of the deserted road, his hands wide as if in supplication. "Citizens of Amsterdam." His guttural voice carried through the window still open to the breeze. "I am here today to remind you that we are not your enemy. That we wish only a peaceful partnership with this country. Yet there are those of you who refuse to understand this. Who actively target the hardworking members of the Reich with violence and death." He dropped his hands. "And this, dear citizens, will never be tolerated."

He had barely finished speaking when the first soldier emerged, followed quickly by the rest, each one dragging a civilian with him. There were ten civilians, all male, and most were elderly and stooped with age, though the last three brought out were only boys, not more than thirteen or fourteen. Three of the men were arguing loudly, and one of the boys was weeping. The rest of the group wore expressions of resignation or defiant hatred.

"Generalkommisar für das Sicherheitswesen has made clear the penalty for an assault on a member of the Nazi Party," the officer in the street continued. "Yet the vile, unforgivable actions of your cowardly countrymen have left us no choice but to visit justice and retribution upon your own population. There can be no other response."

"No," Margot whispered, her voice raw.

Stasia watched as the soldiers shoved their prisoners up against the wall of the building and stepped back. A sickening horror enveloped Stasia, making her vision waver before it cleared again. These men, these *children*, were not going to be arrested or deported or imprisoned. They were not going to be hauled away in the truck that sat idling at the curb. She didn't want to watch. She couldn't look away.

The Nazi officer tossed his unfinished cigarette to the street and withdrew his pistol, turning it this way and that in his gloved hands as if admiring it. He said something to the men lined up against the wall, and the soldiers laughed. Somewhere a woman was wailing.

The prisoner on the end closest to the café suddenly bolted, running across the street in their direction. He couldn't have been more than fourteen, and even from where she stood, Stasia could see the desperate terror stamped across his features. The officer casually raised his pistol and fired at the fleeing youth. The boy crashed to the ground, arms flying to the side like a ragdoll's.

Margot jerked and turned away and sank to the floor, crying silently. Stasia did not turn away.

The soldier closest to the officer, with brassy, brilliantined hair slicked back and gleaming even under the dull light, wandered over to the boy, kicking his body over. The boy twitched, his hand reaching toward the Nazi, pleading perhaps for help or perhaps only mercy. The soldier seemed to find this funny. He crouched, as if to speak to the youth, his round faced flushed, his wide mouth drawing back into a sneer. He slid his rifle from his shoulder and, with the barrel, poked at the youth once, and then again, and then stood. He said something that Stasia couldn't hear but had his comrades laughing before he raised his rifle and shot the boy.

Stasia was shaking as she slipped a hand deep into the inside of her sweater, feeling the familiar smooth bulk of the pistol that rested there. Her fingers curled around the grip, and she pulled it free. Both the pistols she carried were older English Webley Mark IVs, battle-scarred and of the smaller caliber model. The same kind of pistol her grandfather had put in her hands as an adolescent. The same gun that she had handled with ease for a decade. The same weapon she now imagined silencing the Nazi laughter that rang through the empty street. Without thinking, she took a step toward the café door.

"Don't." Margot was on her knees, and she clawed at Stasia, catching Stasia's sleeve in her fist. "Whatever you think you can do, you can't."

"I have to do something." She yanked her sleeve away from Margot, her breath coming in ragged gasps as if she were winded.

Outside, the brassy-blond soldier had rejoined the others, and they had spread out in a line in front of the row of prisoners as the officer looked on. Each now had their own rifle drawn.

"I can't watch you die too," Margot hissed. "You can't stop it."

"I can kill at least three of them." Maybe four with the element of surprise and the six rounds in each pistol Stasia had loaded herself before they had departed.

"But not all of them. Not before they kill you." She stared beseechingly at Stasia.

"Perhaps it would be worth it."

"Don't say that." Margot's hands were on the pistol, pushing it down.

One of the elderly prisoners against the wall started singing the Dutch national anthem, the words of "Het Wilhelmus" rising rebelliously across the silence. Another prisoner joined him and then another. Stasia's grip tightened on the gun.

"Please don't do it. Don't die, Stasia. You are the only family I have left. Don't leave me too."

Deep down, Stasia knew Margot was right. There were a dozen Nazi soldiers who would riddle her body with bullets and watch her die, and then they would kill their prisoners and who knew how many more in retaliation. But she would make those first shots count—

A volley of muffled shots punctured the air, a series of pops and cracks that sent Stasia to her knees beside Margot. A scream of anguish and helplessness caught in her throat, and she squeezed her eyes shut. Her hand curled into a fist, and she pounded the floor beneath her, the pain a welcome beacon in the suffocating grief.

She became aware of hands at her shoulders, of Margot beside her.

"I'm sorry," Stasia choked. "I'm sorry. I'm sorry." Sorry that she couldn't stop the deaths of innocents. Sorry she couldn't stop the atrocities that happened no longer in the shadows or the dark but in broad daylight while the city looked on or looked away.

"Promise me you won't die," Margot whispered to Stasia. Her fingers threaded through Stasia's and held tight.

"Promise me the same," Stasia whispered back.

"I promise."

"What do we do?" Stasia sat back against the wall with a thump, curling in on herself. "What do we do now?" Her forehead rested on her knees.

"We go on," Margot said. Three simple words that were not simple at all. That felt impossible. "We finish what we started."

"I can't."

"You can. And we will."

"But the soldiers—"

"Are leaving."

Outside, on a street gone eerily silent, the truck's engine roared back to life from its muted idle, the sound fading as the truck departed, coughing and clanging up the street. Slowly, Stasia and Margot helped each other to their feet. Stasia slipped the pistol back into her pocket. Wordlessly, they stepped out of the café and fetched their bicycles, Stasia's hands shaking so badly that it took her two tries to pull her bicycle away from the wall.

The body of the boy lay alone in the middle of the street, his sightless eyes staring up at the roiling clouds. There were more cries now, thin, keening, and desolate. Stasia's head was pounding, her throat raw, and her chest tight but she forced herself to move. Forced herself to put one foot in front of the other and get back on her bicycle. She still had weapons to deliver. Weapons that might, one day, with enough hands, rise up so that what she just witnessed would never happen again.

She didn't look behind her to see if Margot was following. But she did look at the blood-streaked brick of the apartment building as she pedalled by. Viewed the crumpled, lifeless forms, the ones of the men flung sideways in a failed effort to protect the smaller corpses that lay beside them, pale limbs askew and edges of clothing fluttering in the wind like piles of rags. Committed it all to memory so that she would never forget what had been done here today. And then focused her eyes on the road ahead of her.

By the time Stasia reached the top of the street, she was gripping the handlebars viciously in an effort to quell the trembling in her hands that still hadn't abated. She reassured herself that it wasn't far now and pictured the house in her mind. Her destination was a squat structure that seemed to her like an architectural afterthought stuck on the far end of a sleek row of tall buildings. From the front, the roofline of the house swooped and curled with fanciful carved corbels tucked beneath, as if it could make up for lack of height with flair. Frank would be waiting in the back garden of that house, as always, a pipe clamped unlit between his teeth, as always, his hat pulled low over his brow and his coat a size too big, as always. He would take the weapons from them and hide them down in the cellar, where a deeper hole had been excavated and cleverly hidden, big enough for their contraband or the occasional person. Stasia concentrated on those known entities, things she could count on, things she could hold on to that would get her through until she had time to grieve for what she'd witnessed.

The temperature had dropped, the icy fingers ahead of the storm snaking through the street and against Stasia's skin. She shivered as a raindrop fell, hitting her cheek, cold and heavy. Thunder growled, closer this time, and Stasia picked up her pace as she careened around the last corner. And recoiled in horror.

The same truck was stopped on the north side of the road, between Stasia and the safe house at the far end of the street. Though this time the truck wasn't idling; it was simply parked, as though it planned to be there for some time. For a moment her feet froze in terrified indecision on the pedals. Stop? Go faster? Turn around? Each option ran through her head in a blurred disarray and by the time she shook herself free of her stunned indecision, she discovered that the decision had already been made for her as she coasted past the truck.

The same Nazi officer had lit another cigarette and leaned against the truck again as he had earlier. He flicked the ash from the end and watched it blow away on the wind like dandelion seeds. Of the soldiers, there was no sign, and the significance of that sent a new surge of fear through Stasia's veins. Because if they weren't in the truck or on the street—

A cry, followed by the sound of something splintering, was swallowed by thunder. More raindrops fell, stinging Stasia's exposed skin. The unmistakable report of a gunshot punctuated the air. The Nazis were here, hunting a new round of prey in the name of retribution, forcing their way into the homes of people whose only crime was humanity. A window above her head exploded, showering glass among the raindrops, a broken body landing with a sickening thud beneath.

Stasia pedalled frantically now, terror pumping through her veins, knowing just how exposed they were out on the street. The safe house was just ahead, its distinct roofline easily visible, though she wondered if there was anything safe about it any longer. The hidden space in the cellar might offer refuge, and perhaps she and Margot should hide there. Because if they were caught and searched out here in the street, every awful thing that they had been warned of would become their reality. Interrogation and torture. Deportation and prison, or perhaps simply execution. Death would arrive quickly or slowly, but it would be inevitable. In this moment, Stasia had seconds to decide what—

A scream split the air and made the hair on Stasia's arms rise. Through the doorway of the building beside their safe house, a young girl fled, only to be yanked off her feet as she was caught by her hair from behind. A grey uniform topped by the sheen of brilliantined brassy-blond hair emerged, a round, flushed face laughing as the soldier pushed the struggling girl face-first into the street. Stasia veered desperately, but her front tyre wedged against a raised cobblestone, and she was sent sprawling, landing hard, scraping her palms and wrists, and knocking the wind out of herself.

She was distantly aware of movement that passed her as she slowly struggled to her hands and knees, and it took a long moment before she understood that it was Margot who had flown by her on her bicycle. It was Margot who was pedalling furiously toward where the young girl lay in the middle of the street, where the Nazi soldier stood beside her, a boot on the back of her neck, the muzzle of his rifle drawing the terrified girl's dress up and over her backside.

Margot was fumbling in her pocket, and too late, Stasia understood what Margot intended to do. Too late, Stasia opened her mouth in a scream that didn't seem to come. Too late to do anything but watch as the ruddy-faced soldier looked up to see a furious woman on a bicycle, a shriek of rage tearing from her throat, bearing down on him with the wrath of a thousand Valkyries. His expression of surprise turned quickly to one of amusement, and in one fluid motion, he raised his rifle and pulled the trigger.

Stasia didn't hear the report, didn't hear anything over the deafening roar in her ears. All she saw was Margot crumple from the seat, toppling in an awkward heap on the side of the road while her bicycle tipped and crashed alongside. The soldier sneered and slung his rifle back over his shoulder, bent once more to wrap his hands around the young girl's hair, and dragged her out of the street and back into the building.

Stasia stumbled toward Margot, half crawling, half running until she reached her, the entire time feeling like she was caught in a strange stupor where time slowed and senses were smothered. With hands she could no longer feel, she grasped Margot's shoulders and rolled her over. Margot's beautiful sea-blue eyes were still open, eyes that no longer saw anything. Blood from a single bullet wound in her neck just under her jaw seeped blood, the crimson streaks pooling in her honey-blonde hair before they were washed pink by the rain.

"You promised me," Stasia gasped in a throat that had gone completely raw. "You promised me you wouldn't die." She hugged her friend against her chest and rocked, listening to someone babble and sob incoherently for a good minute before she realized that that somebody was her.

She rested her forehead against Margot's, trying hard to catch her breath. To regain control. The roaring in her ears abruptly subsided and sounds from her surroundings leached back through her consciousness. The ticking of a bicycle wheel where it still spun impotently. The patter of raindrops as they hammered a canvas awning. The gentle snick of a window shutter being latched.

And the emptiness inside her, the emptiness that Margot had tried to keep from filling with anger and hatred, was now flooding with a dark, crystalline rage that was breathtaking in its strength and intensity. It spilled over, racing through her veins, vanquishing the tatters of sorrow, and leaving in its wake a searing, potent focus. Sounds became louder, her surroundings became that much sharper. Slowly, Stasia lifted her head.

From the doorway of the house, a frenetic scream bounced through the rain, followed by the thin, reedy wail of a baby. The wail rose before it abruptly stopped, and the silence that followed was even more terrifying in its absoluteness. After a heartbeat, a different sort of scream reverberated, this one born less of terror and more of anguish.

With hands that seemed to be moving on their own accord, Stasia retrieved the guns from Margot's pockets and shoved them beneath her belt, covered by her sweater. The packet of documents Margot had been carrying joined Stasia's, making the front of her shirt bulge awkwardly. But that didn't matter anymore.

"I'll come back for you," she whispered to Margot, gently laying her back on the ground. "But right now I have to do something."

She stood and walked through the doorway where the soldier had dragged the young girl. A set of stairs rose directly in front of her, leading to the upper floors, but it was the harsh, hysterical sobs and gasps coming through the open doorway directly on her right that she followed. She pushed her way into the apartment and found herself in a long, narrow hallway. She continued forward until she reached what appeared to be a kitchen and peered around the corner.

Amongst a sea of broken pottery and overturned chairs, two bodies, a man and woman, lay across the floor near her feet. Both had been shot, and a pool of blood was slowly blooming across the worn floor beneath them, enveloping the broken detritus in a creeping dark crimson. The man's spectacles were still perched perfectly on his nose, though a lens had shattered into a translucent cobweb, and his legs were bent askew as if he had been running before he fell. The woman lay facedown, her skirt and apron twisted around her legs, her arms thrown wide.

The young girl with the long dark hair who had been dragged back into the house was still alive. She had been released and was now cowering in the corner near a wide stone hearth, crying uncontrollably. The brassy-blond soldier was standing with his back to Stasia, taunting the girl with something he held in his hands. It took Stasia a moment to comprehend what it was. A baby, no more than a month old, swung lifelessly, its tiny feet caught up in the soldier's hands. Its head was misshapen, blood dripping from its scalp. Across the whitewashed stone of the hearth, a violent spattering and smear of bright red told Stasia exactly what he had done.

Stasia stepped forward, over the bodies, her eyes fixed on the back of the soldier's head. From the corner, the girl looked up at her, her pale face like a blurry moon against a darkening sky. The soldier turned, the laughter sliding from his expression and replaced by confusion. Or perhaps disbelief. But then it didn't matter, because his head snapped back, and he sank slowly to the ground like a puppet with its strings cut. Stasia's gaze followed him, as did the barrel of the Webley she held in her hand. A hand that was no longer shaking. A hand that was steady and sure as she pulled back the hammer and shot the soldier a second time.

The girl's sobs had ceased. Stasia glanced around, noting the kettle hissing on the stove top and the basket of partially shelled peas strewn across the counter. Strange things to notice, Stasia thought, rather disjointedly. She moved over to the stove and lifted the kettle from the heat.

"Christ Jesus, what have you done?" The question came from the door.

Stasia glanced back. Improbably, Frank stood inside the kitchen. "It was boiling," she told him, turning off the stove. "What are you doing here?"

"These are my neighbours. I tried... I tried to help. But I was too late." He was staring at the dead soldier. "You killed him."

Stasia looked down at the Webley still held in her hand. Odd. She didn't remember taking it out of her pocket. Which made no sense because she definitely remembered using it to shoot the Nazi soldier. "Yes. He killed Margot."

Frank's face seemed to crumple for a moment before he recovered. "I know. I saw it happen. I'm sorry."

"And he killed a baby, Frank. A baby."

Frank looked like he was going to be ill. "No, no," he muttered under his breath, picking his way around the dead couple and crouching beside the Nazi. He pulled him over, the tiny corpse of the baby visible now. "Oh, Jesus." He turned away, his hand pressed to his mouth.

The girl in the corner had made herself into a diminutive, rocking ball, her weeping muffled. Frank stood and hurried over to the girl, making shushing sounds as he bent to her. "Come, Brigit. You need to get up now. There's not much time." He pulled the girl to her feet, keeping her head tucked against his jacket, as if to protect her from the carnage of the room.

Stasia looked away from his kindness, however pointless and belated it might be.

"Go to my house," he told her in rushed, clipped tones. "Esther will hide you, do you understand? They'll not find you there even if they come looking."

When they come looking, Stasia corrected silently.

He pulled back to look the young girl in the eye. "Do not leave until I come for you. Go out the back and through the yard. Do you understand me?" he asked again with urgency.

The girl he had called Brigit, her eyes swollen with tears, looked like she might collapse but she nodded.

"Good. Hurry."

Brigit ran.

"You knew this family." Stasia leaned against the counter near the peas, feeling strangely detached.

Frank's complexion was grey. "Since Brigit was two."

"I'm sorry."

"Do you have any idea what you've done?"

"What was necessary." The coppery tang of blood and gun powder hung thick and heavy in the air.

"The bastards are here for retribution," Frank said. "Usually they pick them from the prisons."

Stasia made a sound that might have been mistaken for laughter. "Does it matter where they pick them from, Frank?"

He had no answer.

She pushed herself away from the counter, handing the gun she still held to Frank. "Take it," she said. "It was supposed to be for you."

Without a word, Frank took the Webley and slid it into the inside of his coat. Stasia extracted the two weapons Margot had been carrying and held them out to Frank. Just as silently, those also disappeared, though Stasia did not miss the tremor in his hands.

Stasia stepped over the dead soldier and began to work on the buttons of his coat. "We need to hurry." Outside, the sounds of violence and chaos had not abated.

"What the hell are you doing?" Frank wheezed.

"Making sure they don't find another dead Nazi. At least not right away." She yanked the coat from his arms and tossed it beside the hearth. "Are you going to help me or not?"

Frank swore again before joining her, yanking the soldier's boots from his legs, followed by his trousers. The boots and trousers joined the coat in a pile, leaving the man in only his underwear and shirt.

Stasia dragged the bodies of the woman and man from where they had fallen, covering the soldier in a staged array of death. A perfunctory glance would reveal only three dead civilians. It wasn't perfect but they were out of time.

"Take his uniform. I have his rifle and knife," Stasia said.

"What? Why?" Frank sounded like he was about to come out of his skin.

"Because they will all be useful at some point." She slung the rifle over her shoulder and tucked the soldier's knife into her own waistband.

Muttering, Frank gathered the uniform into a hasty bundle and jammed it under his arm. He stopped to crouch beside the tiniest of the bodies, his lips moving in a silent prayer.

"We need to go. Now." Stasia did not wait for him.

Nor did she look back.

CHAPTER

13

Isabelle

I still cannot believe you didn't come back for those papers the next day." Luc pointed the end of his pencil accusingly in the direction of Isabelle before jamming it back behind his ear. "And I still can't believe you didn't tell me that you found a reference to Briar Rose with them."

Isabelle paused outside the library door, a cup of coffee in one hand and a framed drawing in the other. "Good morning to you too, Luc. And for the record, I did tell you."

"Not until later." He sounded properly put out.

"You would have broken in like a common thief to snatch away those papers had I told you. I saved you from you." She wandered into the library and waited for Luc to climb down from the scaffolding set against the tall windows. She breathed deeply, the scent of summer flowers and warmed earth wafting through the room from the open windows.

"You know nothing of the sort." Luc's voice drifted down.

"I most certainly do, because I almost did it myself. You would have talked me into it."

"Yep. And neither of us would have regretted anything."

"They weren't mine to take."

"It was only a matter of time."

She grinned up at him. "And are we going to have this argument every day for the rest of our lives?"

"It's not an argument. It's a grudge that I'm working hard to cultivate." His boots hit the floor with a thud, and he joined her in the middle of the room, accepting the steaming cup. "Thanks."

Isabelle squinted against the morning sun as it streamed into the library. Even though protective sheets had been draped over the massive desk and bookshelves, and the room was littered with tools and sawhorses and scaffolding, she rather fancied that Great-Gran would have approved. Even amid the organized chaos, or maybe because of it, the library now looked loved instead of abandoned. She glanced over to where the griffins stood watch by the hearth and imagined that they, too, were glad for the company after so many years of solitude.

Every single time Isabelle had turned in to the drive of Château de Montessaire these last months, the thrill never lessened. She had restored dozens and dozens of buildings in her life, some more spectacular, some far older, and some with a much more storied history, but as much as she loved her work, those buildings had been just that. Work. This château, after months of negotiations and mountains of paperwork and planning, was special because it was hers. Well, hers and Emilie's.

"Hey, I saved this for you." Luc interrupted her musing and dug a folded paper from the pocket of his jeans. He smoothed the creases out and handed it to her. "I saw it online and printed you a copy."

"What is it?" she asked.

"An advert looking for a contractor specializing in historic restorations."

She frowned. "This is for a castle in Scotland."

"The Isle of Skye," he agreed. "They're accepting tenders through to the end of the year. The restoration is being funded by the estate, Historic Scotland, and Highland Opportunity Ltd. I thought you would be perfect for it. Probably win another award by the time you're done with it."

"I can't." She handed the paper back.

"You didn't even read the details."

"It's in Scotland, Luc."

"So? You'd be done here before you started there. I think it would be an extraordinary chance for you—"

"I can't just leave here. Besides, that is a big, complex project."

"You've done far more complex projects. Trees growing through a nave, as I recall. They'd be lucky to have you."

"It would take at least a year. Probably two. I can't be away that long." There was no way her parents would manage the farm without her.

"So you won't even consider it—"

"Thank you for the thought but my answer is no," she said.

"Fine." Luc sighed, refolded the paper, and slid it back into his pocket. "What do you have there?" He pointed to the frame under Isabelle's arm, effectively changing the subject. Isabelle was relieved.

She turned the framed drawing in his direction. It was about a foot square, the drawing secured under the glass mounted on a mat of white. "I know we're a long way from decorating or hanging art on the walls but I wanted to see this in here."

"Are those the library griffins?" He sounded intrigued.

"Yes."

"Where did you get that?"

"This is Great-Gran's original drawing from one of her illustrated stories. I had it framed, and I want to hang it in here, over the fireplace." Isabelle gazed at the drawing. It was, by far, one of her favourites, two young girls each mounted on a griffin, long hair streaming behind them, wearing capes with bows slung over their shoulders and looking like the warrior princesses they were meant to be in the story. The griffins were soaring through the sky, wings spread, the single rose at each of their throats secured by a loop of chain and easily recognizable.

"Is that supposed to be you and Emilie? Taking on the world together?" He leaned forward to study the drawing. "Because the girl on the right looks an awful lot like you used to. It's uncanny."

"Yes. Great-Gran always drew us like this. As a team." Isabelle tilted the drawing. "She always told us how lucky we were to have each other." The distance between Isabelle and Emilie now would have made her unbearably sad if she were alive to see it.

Luc whistled. "She was quite the artist. It's like looking at a photograph."

"She was talented," Isabelle agreed.

"Speaking of your sister, where's Emilie?" Luc said. "Didn't she get in last night?" He slurped his coffee.

"She did, and she's on her way here. I think." Isabelle kept her answer neutral. She knew she should be pleased that Emilie was here as the restoration work on the château was under way in earnest but she was a little wary. That her sister had seemingly changed her mind and insisted on returning to Rouen, and then further insisted on staying for at least a week, had been as perplexing as it had been welcome. As much as she no longer understood the sister she had once been so close with, Isabelle could not deny that Emilie was quite brilliant when it came to restoration architecture. She had an impressive ability to find unique modern solutions that still showcased the original features while adhering to their permit strictures. Looking back, Isabelle wished that she had had Emilie's expertise on more than a few of her recent projects.

"She didn't get a ride out with you?"

"She's staying in Rouen." Which was maybe for the best. After the horribly awkward visit at home in January, which was marked by Emilie's impatience with everyone around her, Isabelle didn't argue when her sister insisted that a little more space between them was better for everyone. Isabelle picked her way over to the hearth, not interested in getting into another discussion about her talented, if mercurial, sister. She propped the drawing up on the mantel before turning her attention in the direction of the scaffolding. "The windows look fantastic. I'm impressed."

"Honestly, I didn't do much repair in here. Replaced some hardware and some rails and muntins. I have some sanding and painting left but the frames were in great shape for the most part. I'll move to the ballroom tomorrow. Most of those window frames, or what's left of them, need to be completely rebuilt or rejoined. I'll have them ready for the glass when it comes in."

"Thank you." Hiring Luc was turning out to be one of the best decisions she had ever made.

"No, thank you. I love this kind of work." He arched his brows. "And to be able to do it where the indomitable Briar Rose once operated is even better."

Isabelle rolled her eyes. "Where a paper with the name

Briar Rose written on it once dwelled," she corrected him. "But that reminds me. Yesterday, I received copies and the translations of all of those documents and photos I found in the library."

"The ones you gave away." Luc made a face over the rim of his cup.

"The ones I put in the trust of the Caen Normandie Memorial Museum, where they might be archived and preserved properly," she said. "As I will do with any other documents relevant to the occupation or war that we might stumble across." She made a face right back at Luc. "I haven't gone through any of it yet. I was going to start reading tonight, but I was wondering, just out of curiosity, and because—"

"Yes."

"Yes? You haven't heard the question."

"Yes, I would love to go through the documents with you. I thought you'd never ask." He gave her a winning smile.

"Thank you, Luc, for volunteering both your time and your mystical mind-reading powers."

"I aim to please."

"Well, in that case, would I be allowed to finish my sentence?"

He feigned exasperation. "If you must."

"Because you weren't wrong when you said that a well-researched history will help market this place when we're ready to open it to the public," Isabelle said. "I was hoping that this afternoon we could head over to the Briar Rose tavern in town to talk with Monsieur Dubois. I called him this morning, and he is game. I didn't mention the château or where we found the photos, just that I had some I wanted him to look at."

Luc was staring at her, a slow grin creeping across his face. "Are you going to ask him about Briar Rose?"

"I'm going to ask him about the people he remembers who fought with the Resistance."

"And?"

"And maybe I will ask about Briar Rose," she admitted.

"Maybe?" Luc hooted. "I think the words you're looking for are 'Luc, you were right all along, and Briar Rose might indeed be more than just a legend.'"

"Luc, you were right all along, and Briar Rose might indeed be more than just a legend," Isabelle repeated drily.

"Thank you."

"Though not likely."

"Killjoy."

"I will reserve judgement. Briar Rose aside, he probably knows more than anyone else about the local Maquis groups that fought in the area. And if he really did tag along with the Resistance during the war, I'd love to see if he recognizes any of the photos or names that were in that desk. Real people. The sort of history I can dig into and follow up on."

"See if who recognizes who?"

Isabelle turned to find Emilie standing just inside the library. Her usually sleek hair was pulled into a messy ponytail, her always flawless makeup was absent, and she had dark circles under her eyes.

"Good morning," Isabelle said. "Welcome back."

Emilie grunted something unintelligible in reply.

"All you all right?"

"What's that supposed to mean?" Emilie demanded.

Isabelle held up her hands. "Nothing."

"To see if who recognizes who?" she asked again.

"Monsieur Dubois. I don't know if you would remember him? We were going to ask him to look at some of the old photos we found in this desk. He might be able to tie the château to some members of the Resistance during the occupation. I'm sure it's an exercise in futility but I thought it might be worth a shot."

"And she's going to ask about Briar Rose," Luc added smugly.

Emilie straightened. "I meant to talk to you about that," she said.

"About what?"

"Using the local legend of Briar Rose to promote the château. Briar Rose would be a great draw to visitors interested in World War Two history."

Isabelle exchanged a look with Luc. "We've already discussed this."

"Who? You two?" Her sister sounded displeased.

"Yes, before we even bought the château." Isabelle shook her head. "I didn't want to perpetuate myths then, and I don't want to do it now. If visitors come here for the history, I'd like to paint an accurate picture."

"For pity's sake, Izz, could you be any more shortsighted?" Emilie put her hands on her hips and tapped her foot. "There would be absolutely nothing wrong with exploiting the legend. We could have a Briar Rose suite for people to stay in. The way that the Ritz hotel in Paris has a Coco Chanel suite."

"Coco Chanel was a collaborator," Isabelle replied.

"Depends on who you ask."

"No," Isabelle said flatly. "It doesn't."

"Well, whatever she was or wasn't, it doesn't matter." Emilie waved her hand. "People still pay an exorbitant amount of money to stay in that suite. They still pay an exorbitant amount of money to have her label on their clothes. No one cares what actually happened."

"I care," Isabelle said stubbornly, wishing that Luc weren't here to watch them argue. But as much as Isabelle usually just tried to smooth things over, this was something she was not backing down from.

Emilie's lips thinned. "The point I'm trying to make, Isabelle, is that we have to work with what we have. Put a disclaimer on the damn door if you feel you need to. But the legend of Briar Rose is one that should be manipulated to our advantage."

"I don't think we should exploit or manipulate anyone's story to our advantage. Any history we use should be as truthful and as verified as achievable."

Emilie rolled her eyes. "You're impossible."

"We're talking about real war, Emilie. Real people. Not fiction."

"So?"

Isabelle took a deep breath, trying to keep her voice even. "Let's just say Briar Rose really existed. Let's say, for a moment, that she was a real person, who fought and suffered and died beside other real people. Does she deserve to have a persona invented for her? Should we make up a history for her? Pretend to know what happened in her life to fit the narrative we wish to sell? Contrive a fate for her to suit our purposes?"

"If it helps pay the bills."

Isabelle marshalled her patience. "Do you not wonder, if Briar Rose was indeed real, why she never stepped forward to claim credit for her actions? There is no memoir, no record of awards, nothing."

"Like you said, maybe she died during the war."

"And maybe she didn't. Maybe she simply did not want to be Briar Rose when the war ended. Maybe in order to move on, she needed to leave the war behind her. Just think of Great-Gran. She never spoke about any of what she lived through. She never spoke about the war at all."

Emilie heaved an irritated sigh and looked away. "Whatever. We can discuss this more later."

And Isabelle's opinion still wouldn't change. But she didn't say that. "You should know we're ahead of schedule," she said instead, changing the topic to the château—something that the two of them could discuss in a constructive manner. "In fact, you should take a look at the ballroom," she told her. "I think you'll be pleased. The plaster work was completed this past week. The ceiling is as good as new. The debris has been cleared, and the tile floor marked for repairs." She paused. "It was switchboards, by the way. For telephones."

"What?" Emilie's attention seemed to be caught on the two griffins.

"The equipment that was destroyed in the ballroom. The curator who came out to collect the documents from the library took a look. She took a few pieces with her but she said that there was nothing left of value that wasn't damaged beyond salvage. But she did say that it suggested that the château had been used as a communication headquarters during the occupation. I thought you might be interested to know that."

Emilie didn't respond.

"Did you hear me?" Isabelle asked.

"Those things," Emilie said abruptly, gesturing at the carved griffins. "They don't fit the interior of this library. Or my design, really. I don't like them."

"They are not for you to like or dislike. They are part of de Montessaire. Part of this library. Literally built into the original hearth. They even appear in the de Cossé coat of arms."

Emilie crossed her arms. "I still don't like them. They look like they escaped a theme room in some medieval version of Disneyland."

"You liked them when you were a kid. In Great-Gran's stories." She gestured to the drawing propped up on the mantel. "Don't you remember this picture?"

"Not really. I'm not a kid anymore, Izz, and neither are you."

Isabelle bit her tongue. Again. She wasn't going to have one left by the time this château was finished.

"About the Briar Rose tavern?" Luc interjected tactfully. "What time were you thinking of going, Izz?"

"One," Isabelle told him, grateful for the distraction. "When Monsieur Dubois is having lunch. He invited us to join him. My treat."

"First coffee and now lunch. Won't argue with any of that. Meet you out front?"

"Yep."

"I'll get back to it, then." Luc toasted the sisters with his cup and hastily retreated back toward the windows and scaffolding.

Isabelle reflected that it was a wonder he hadn't fled earlier.

"Let me show you the ballroom," Isabelle said to her sister, threading her way back out of the library. "It will really be a fantastic multipurpose space once it's finished. It's already easy to envision wedding banquets or reunions or gatherings. And I'll have the lighting back up by the end of the week, paint the following, but you'll be able to see for yourself how—"

"Can I come?" Emilie asked, catching up with her in the wide hall.

"What?"

"Can I come? With you and Luc. To the tavern."

"Um." Isabelle stopped. "Why?" She couldn't help asking.

Emilie jammed her hands into the pockets of her jeans, looking even more tired in the shadows of the hall. "I don't know." She lifted a shoulder awkwardly. "I'd like to see what you found."

Isabelle blinked at Emilie and swallowed the urge to ask why again. Instead her gaze drifted back to the library, where she could still see the drawing of the two sisters commanding their enchanted steeds as they charged toward the unknown.

She thought of her great-gran and swallowed her refusal.

"Sure," she said.

★ ★ ★

In the end, it was two sisters who arrived at the Briar Rose, not on the backs of enchanted steeds but in the cab of Isabelle's truck. Luc had messaged her that he had been called away but would meet them at the tavern later. Which was too bad, Isabelle reflected as she parked her truck and began the walk toward the tavern. Luc was a nice buffer between them, and Isabelle struggled for things to say on the ride there that would lessen the awkwardness. Beyond a brief discussion about electricians, the ride had been mostly completed in silence.

The building that housed the Briar Rose hadn't changed much since it had been built a century ago, though compared to some of the half-timbered buildings on either side of the tavern dating back centuries earlier, the tavern was practically new construction. The ground floor was still an attractive framework of leaded glass windows set in neat rows, their small, diamond panes reflecting the sunshine in geometrical patterns. The thick columns and lower walls had been painted a rich burgundy color, offset by black accents. Up above the tavern, where a second story perched and where at least part of the

Dubois family still resided, the façade was graced with blocky, cream-colored stone. Window boxes spilled over with bright flowers and a profusion of trailing greenery. It was a pretty building and attracted as many locals as it did tourists travelling through.

"I don't suppose you remember this place from when we were younger, do you?" Isabelle asked as they approached the tavern. "Mom and Dad brought us here a couple of times when we were just little. We ate bowls of beef soup and had apple juice poured into wine glasses."

Emilie tucked her hands into her pockets. "How do you remember this stuff? From when we were kids?" She made it sound like a criticism.

"Don't know." Isabelle paused. "Do you remember Monsieur Dubois?"

"Not really," Emilie said again.

"Maybe once you're inside." Isabelle held the door open for her sister.

The inside of the tavern had been updated from when they had been kids, though the original features were still easy to pick out. Thick beams ran overhead, the long mahogany bar that stretched the length of the room on the far side still gleamed in front of its row of stools, and the wide-planked floor remained as worn as she remembered. The long trestle tables and benches that had been here in their youth had been swapped out for smaller, more intimate tables for diners, and it was at one of these tables in front of a wall of black-and-white photographs that Renaud Dubois was sitting.

Isabelle threaded her way through the lunch crowd, inhaling the enticing aromas of roasting meat and baking bread. She stopped to greet numerous people as she went, asking after family or work, replying to the same, and introducing Emilie.

"Seriously, do you know everyone in here?" Emilie asked, sounding irritable as they turned away from a table.

Isabelle shrugged. "No. Not everyone."

"Seems like it."

"Well, Val-de-la-Haye is a pretty tiny place. It comes with the territory, I suppose," Isabelle said. "It's certainly nothing like Paris, where you are only one of millions and millions. Perfectly anonymous."

"Perfectly alone," Emilie mumbled, and Isabelle looked at her sister sharply.

"Are you all right?" she asked for the second time that day.

Emilie opened her mouth as if to retort before she closed it again. After a heartbeat, she said, "It's just stuff at work. People being difficult."

"Oh." Isabelle wasn't sure if she should probe. She did anyway. "How so?"

"Two of my best architects are threatening to leave my firm."

"Why?"

"Because they want to be made partner. They want more recognition. More diverse projects. More influence. A bigger piece of everything." Emilie wouldn't meet her eye. "Serves me right for hiring talent and ambition."

"Is that . . . unreasonable?" Isabelle ventured carefully. "I mean, if they are as good as you have suggested, wasn't that the goal? If they have excelled under your guidance, why wouldn't you want to allow them to help grow your firm—"

"I started this firm. I made this firm into what it is now. It's my name on it. And it is doing just fine. I don't need anyone taking that away from me."

"It doesn't sound like they are trying to take anything away. On the contrary, it sounds like they are trying to help build on what you started—"

"Whose side are you on here?"

"Yours," Isabelle said. "Always yours. But maybe—"

"Never mind." Emilie cut her off. "It's nothing that I can't handle. I shouldn't have bothered you with stupid work stuff. It's not like you can do anything."

"You should always bother me with stupid work stuff. And any other stuff," Isabelle said. "I'm your sister. It's my job to be bothered." She tried to keep her voice light because Emilie suddenly looked like she was going to cry. Isabelle glanced around at the crowd, slightly panicked, wondering if perhaps she should steer her sister back out the way they had come. "Em—"

"He left."

Isabelle's gaze snapped back. "What? Who? Your architect?"

"Marcus. He left me. For a barista who is twenty-one and who can give him, and I quote, 'The sort of attention, appreciation, and time that he deserves.'"

Isabelle wanted to reach out and hug her sister, but from the way Emilie was holding herself, she was afraid that she might shatter beneath the gesture. "Oh, Emilie."

"Whatever." Her sister looked away.

"I'm so sorry," Isabelle clasped her hands together, uncertain what she should say.

"Am I supposed to believe that I am at a point in my life when I can no longer compete with a...a child who doesn't know the difference between *their*, *there*, and *they're*? She texted me, you know, to clear the air. And to ask me not to be difficult." Emilie made a disgusted face. "It was like reading the thoughts of a *toddler*."

"I'm so sorry," Isabelle said again. "When did you find this out?" she ventured.

"Last week. He didn't have much choice. I walked in on them with his barista's legs up around her ears and my husband plowing her balls deep. In my bed. On my goddamn pillow."

"Oh, Emilie."

Her sister cleared her throat. "He'd been telling me for months that he'd been picking up extra shifts at the hospital. I never even paid that much attention to how much he was gone, you know? I was trying to deal with everything at work, and it never occurred to me that he was lying. He wasn't even man enough to tell me the truth."

"I always thought he was an asshole," Isabelle said. "Any man scared of his mother-in-law's chickens is not really a man."

Emilie laughed, a half-choked, half-raw sound.

"Do you want to leave? We don't have to be here. We can—"

"Mademoiselle Lange! There you are! Good afternoon!" Isabelle was being hailed from the far side of the room.

"No." Emilie shook her head. "I don't want to leave. And I don't want to talk about it. Not right now."

"Okay."

Emilie scowled. "And stop looking at me like that. I don't need or want your pity. I shouldn't even have told you."

"Okay," Isabelle said again, knowing that there was nothing else she could say right now that would make anything better. "Follow me, then."

By the time they made it to the far side where Monsieur Dubois waited, he had risen and already pulled out one of the chairs.

Renaud Dubois, famous for his love of French wine and French folklore, had always reminded Isabelle of an indomitable woodland sprite. Two bright blue eyes peered out from beneath bushy white eyebrows set above a crooked nose that looked like it may have been broken more than once. He had a wide grin that had no doubt charmed as many in decades past as it did now and a shockingly thick mop of snow-white hair that had probably never been truly tamed. Isabelle knew him to be in his nineties, but save for a tremble that the years had instilled into his hands and a stoop into his wiry shoulders, it was unlikely that he would be pinned as a nonagenarian had a stranger been pressed to guess his age.

"Mademoiselle Lange." Dubois was smiling, taking her hand and bowing over it like she was a reigning princess returning to court. "What a pleasure. In the future, you must come to see an old man more than once a year."

"The pleasure is all ours. And I'll do my best, I promise." She turned. "You remember my sister, Emilie? She is visiting from Paris."

Emilie was deliberately avoiding her gaze.

"Of course I remember," Dubois said, shuffling forward to repeat the process with Emilie. "Age may have curbed my dancing and drinking but not my mind or my memory. Besides, one does not easily forget two lovely, talented girls who grew up into two beautiful, talented women." He gestured grandly at the table. "Please, sit."

He waited until Emilie and Isabelle were seated before taking his own chair. A young waitress appeared almost immediately and took their orders before vanishing as quickly as she had appeared. "What do you think?" He gestured at a wide panel of intricate antique stained glass that bridged the top of the tavern's center window and sent shards of colored light spilling across the floor.

Isabelle studied it with a critical eye. "It turned out beautifully."

"Your sister saved it, you know," Dubois said to Emilie.

"I hardly saved it," Isabelle replied, sitting back. "I merely found a craftsman who could."

"Like I said, she saved it. It survived two wars untouched only to be damaged two years ago by a drunken whelp who threw a bottle at his friend and missed."

"I'm just glad it could be repaired."

"Your sister is the best sort." Dubois was still talking to Emilie. "She has a gift for connecting people."

"She's certainly lived here long enough," Emilie murmured, though her tone lacked the condescension that Isabelle expected.

Dubois only nodded. "Yes, yes," he agreed. He moved what looked like an old cigar box to the side before he leaned forward, placing his hands on the table. "Now tell me about de Montessaire," he said without preamble. "I want to know all about it. What was inside. I presume that is what you alluded to when we spoke on the phone."

Out of the corner of her eye, she saw Emilie blink in surprise while Isabelle only grinned. "You heard we bought it."

"Psht." Dubois's brows came together and then parted. "Don't insult me. I heard you bought it before you bought it. All of Val-de-la-Haye knows you bought it. Everyone knows that you are restoring it. What no one knows is what was inside."

"Not much, in truth," Isabelle told him. "Most of the furniture and art and personal effects had already been removed."

"To pay to keep the roof on the place, I would think," Dubois muttered. "Or maybe just to line someone's pockets."

"Well, if it paid to keep the roof intact, I, for one, cannot argue with the benefits of that sacrifice. The library was reasonably untouched, though," Isabelle offered. "Most of the books and an ebony desk were left."

"The desk didn't fit through the doors, I heard."

Isabelle stared. "You heard?"

"The movers stopped here for lunch last summer. Before the château was put up for sale. One hears things."

"One hears quite a bit here, I imagine," Isabelle said.

"That is the whole point of owning a tavern, no?" Dubois sounded amused.

"What else does one hear?"

"That you recently had a visitor from the museum in Caen. An expert in the Second World War."

"She also stopped here for lunch." It wasn't really a guess.

"Of course she did. And she was quite interested in my photos." Dubois gestured to the wall covered in framed black-and-white pictures.

"I'm sure." Isabelle rose, leaving her bag on the floor by her chair, and approached the wall, studying the collection of framed photos. All were in black and white, some predating the Great War and some taken of local people and places in the years after. But most were photos taken during the Second World War. On the bottom corner of each frame, a name and a date were written. A few were of local Frenchmen in uniform, posed neatly, and the sort of memento you might leave with a family or sweetheart. Most of the photos, however, were not posed neatly and instead told a story of chaos and destruction and desperation. There were shots of women here too, some staring defiantly through clear hunger and exhaustion at the photographer, a rifle or pack slung over their shoulders. Frames of young men and women laying what looked like explosive charges in rail lines and groups standing together, holding what seemed to be woefully inadequate weaponry. Still more of the photographs depicted groups with children—families by blood or perhaps families made by circumstance.

"Tell me what you found that would warrant such a guest at de Montessaire," Dubois said from behind Isabelle. "Tell me what the boches left behind when they infested that château. Besides damage."

"Various identity cards and photos, collected by the Nazis," she told him, scanning the faces on the wall. She had looked at this collection on the wall before, in years past. But now she was looking for familiar faces that might match those that she had found in the ebony desk. "Belonging to people we presume were involved in the Resistance. We had hoped you might take a look at them. See if you recognize anyone."

"Did you bring them?" Dubois asked, rubbing his gnarled hands together.

"Copies," Isabelle said. "The museum has the originals." She left the wall of photos, unsure that she would be able to recognize anyone without the cards to compare them to. She slid back into her seat and reached for her bag, extracting the thick file. "We're putting together a comprehensive history of the château. We know it was appropriated by the Nazis during the occupation, and we know that the area had an active Maquis cell. Those documents we found in the château suggest a connection. Perhaps Resistance members who were actively hunted in the area, given that these photos and cards were clearly in possession of the Nazis."

Dubois leaned forward, fumbling in his shirt pocket for glasses. He slid them on as Isabelle began laying pages before him, four different cards copied on each.

"Weren't you a child during the occupation?" Emilie spoke up.

"Yes." Dubois was peering intently at each page. "I was seven when the boches invaded. Twelve when we finally chased them out for good."

"And you think you could remember a face?" She sounded

doubtful. "You were awfully young. And that was a long time ago."

Renaud Dubois set down the paper he was holding. "My brothers fled the Compulsory Labour Service law by hiding here, in these forests, along with others who would have rather died than be deported to work for Nazi Germany. I went with them. It is not something that one easily forgets."

"I wasn't suggesting that—"

"By 1943, that law had created ten thousand Resistance members in Normandy. Less than a quarter of us were combatants, of course, and we were scattered, and not very well organized at all. We were trophies for the Gestapo and whatever boot-licking Sicherheitsdienst officer who needed to prove his value to the Reich. We lived rough, hiding wherever we could with those we could trust. We were always hungry. And cold. That I remember well. We didn't have adequate weapons or strategy or communication or leadership. Not until she came."

"Until who came?" Emilie asked.

"Briar Rose. She was something else. Even a child understood that."

Isabelle clasped her hands together and tried to keep her expression neutral. As dismissive as she had been before, she could not put the document that she had found with the name Briar Rose out of her mind. Luc had not been wrong.

"And then the Jeds came," Dubois continued, "and all of a sudden, we had access to real weapons and information. We had hope. We had a purpose."

"Jeds?" Emilie asked.

"The Jedburgh teams dropped into Normandy ahead of and after D-Day," Isabelle clarified.

Monsieur Dubois pushed his glasses up onto his head. "There

were three of them on the team that I saw. I don't remember too much about two of them, other than that one was French and one was British, but I remember the American. He was the biggest man I had ever seen. I remember he let me look at his commando knife when they arrived at camp." He smiled at the memory. "To be honest, my brothers were older than me and kept me out and away from most of the dangerous parts. Certainly from the worst of the fighting and sabotage. Never talked about plans or missions in front of me. Sent me on ridiculous errands. Had me guard things in our camp that never needed guarding. At the time, I thought what I was doing was brave. Important."

"You were," Isabelle said. "Brave and important."

Dubois shrugged his slight shoulders. "I don't need to pretend to flatter myself. Once I became a father, I understood these things far better than I did then."

Isabelle unclasped her hands. "Do you recognize any of the people in the photos?"

Dubois slid his glasses back in place and slowly perused the photos. "Her." His finger landed on a photo of an unsmiling young woman, blonde hair cut short at her ears. "I knew her as Minon."

Isabelle and Emilie both leaned over the table to get a better look. The name on the card identified her as Eveline Stern from Amiens. Whether or not that was her real name was debatable.

"She was executed. With two others. Shot in the forest south of Rouen." He said it blandly, like he was stating the weather. "My oldest brother was sweet on her, I think. She had the loveliest voice when she sang." He pushed the paper aside and studied the next, and then two more. "Him." He tapped the photo. Michel Beavais from Le Havre. "He just disappeared. No one ever knew what happened to him. I only remember that because he was supposed to arrive with ammunition that we needed. He never made it, and no one heard from him again." He went through the remaining copies but recognized no more.

"Tell me about Briar Rose." Isabelle pulled the list of German names that had been headed with *Getötet / Verschwunden* from her bag. *Killed / Disappeared* had been translated neatly underneath. *Little Briar Rose* had been written beside *Dornröschen* at the bottom of the page.

Dubois took his glasses off and rubbed his eyes before meeting Isabelle's gaze. "She was real."

"Mmm." Isabelle made a noncommittal noise.

"I know most people think I'm making it up, but she really existed, though she was like a ghost. She allowed no one to take her photo, told no one her real name, wrote nothing down on paper. Ever. She appeared suddenly in the early spring of '44— I remember that because the forget-me-nots had just started blooming. No one knew where she came from. Or whether she was even French."

"Why would you think she wasn't French?"

"I heard her. Sometimes, at night, she would become restless in her sleep. Nightmares, I suppose, though no one paid much attention because we all had them. But when she talked in her sleep, she didn't speak in French."

"What then?" Isabelle asked.

Dubois shrugged his shoulders. "I can't say, exactly. I can barely string together a sentence in English. Whatever she spoke, I didn't understand any of it. I don't think anyone did. And when the war was over, when France had been liberated, she simply vanished, and no one ever had the chance to find out." He turned his glasses slowly in his fingers. "Though those of us who were left also scattered. I still hope that they all found their way home. And I hope she did too."

Emilie had been still, following the conversation, but now she was shaking her head. "So why would your group of fighters have trusted her? A woman who appeared from seemingly out of the blue, who wasn't anyone's friend, and who wasn't even French? She could even have been German. That makes no sense."

"She was really good at killing Nazis," he said in the same flat voice that he had used to describe Minon's execution. "And she was really good at teaching others how to do it."

Emilie's lips parted. "Oh."

Isabelle swallowed and set the sheet of names down in front of Dubois. "This was with the photos," she told him. "It's a list of German officers, noted as either dead or missing." She gestured at the bottom of the page. "*Dornröschen* is German for 'Little Briar Rose.'"

"And you think this is what? Some sort of list of Nazi officers dead at her hand?"

"I don't know what to think," Isabelle confessed.

"I hope it is," Dubois said with a cold, vicious satisfaction so at odds with his usual bonhomie that it sent a chill through Isabelle. He didn't bother looking at the list. "I hope she killed every last one of them."

"What did she look like?" Emilie put her elbows on the table, her brows furrowed.

Dubois leaned back, and for the first time since they had sat down, looked weary with his age. "Old enough to be my mother, perhaps," he said, his gaze fixed on some faraway place that only he could see. "Though it was hard to tell. War makes the young old very quickly." He paused. "She wore makeup, I remember. Not bright lipsticks, but the kind of makeup that a woman wears around her eyes that makes them seem darker. Her hair was dark too, almost black. She never smiled. Never laughed. She scared me, and she scared most of the maquisards too, even if they would never admit it."

"For a woman supposedly named after a fairy tale princess, she sounds like a monster," Emilie muttered.

"Not a monster. Not entirely." With slow movements, he drew in the cigar box he had brought to the table and opened it. "She was kind to me once. When Sascha was killed." He extracted a photo of three boys sitting on a front porch in the sunshine, the youngest perhaps five and the oldest perhaps sixteen. It was worn and creased with age. He passed it to Isabelle. "That was the three of us. Before the war. Me, Denis, and Sascha. The Three Musketeers, my ma used to call us."

Isabelle looked at the photo of the three grinning boys, feeling a profound sadness for a childhood and way of life that was about to be lost.

"Sascha died on D-Day," he said. "In June. He was captured and shot." His voice wobbled. "I was eleven and inconsolable. Later, after we had buried him, Briar Rose gave me this." From the cigar box, he withdrew a folded paper, softened and discolored with age and handling. "I've shown it to my family but no one else. Not until today. It was too . . . personal. Makes me remember a terrible time. But I want to share it with you now. Because of what you found."

"Thank you," Isabelle said with feeling.

"Mmm." He opened the paper to reveal a drawing executed in pencil. "Briar Rose told me to remember that I was strong and brave and that Sascha would always be proud of me, even though he was no longer with me." He smiled sadly. "It was those words that I remembered. That kindness that I recalled when I opened this tavern."

He lay the drawing on the table, and Isabelle felt the breath leave her lungs.

For rendered in exquisite detail was a twelve-year-old boy, a sword slung over his back, his expression as fierce as the creature upon which he rode. A magical, ethereal creature roaring its fury from under a crested hood of feathers while its unfurled wings spread wide over its feline haunches.

And around the griffin's neck, on a chain of delicate links, dangled a single, perfect rose.

CHAPTER

14

Stasia

4 JUNE 1943
HAARLEM, THE NETHERLANDS

Frank watched her from his chair, his knife moving in slow rhythmic motions, the pile of shavings growing as the block he whittled slowly turned into a deer. Or maybe it was a dog. Stasia wasn't about to ask, nor did she really care.

He'd been watching her like this for three days, in the confines of the farmhouse they had fled to outside the city. He watched her in the kitchen as she went about preparing their meager meals, in the yard as she chopped and stacked cords of wood or washed what few clothes they had in the tub out back. And she knew what he was watching for. What he was waiting for.

An outpouring of shock and grief. A deluge of distress. Something—anything—that would indicate remorse or guilt or regret. Yet Stasia couldn't give it to him. Because as she went about the numbing tedium of her daily chores, she felt none of those things. Just a steady, simmering rage that kept everything else at bay. A merciless sense of vengeance that she stoked regularly and a series of pitiless imaginings she tended carefully. All things considered, her lack of expected conscience was quite liberating. She was no longer chained to grief.

Stasia was cutting turnips in the kitchen when the knock came on the door.

She heard the chair creak as Frank rose, listened as the latch clicked and the hinges of the door protested. A low, masculine voice correctly asked if they needed any help in the garden, and Frank responded in kind that they had already finished for the day.

The door swung open, and Stasia turned her head slightly to watch Frank admit two men, both dressed as farm labourers. Her knife continued to rise and fall in a steady rhythm, slices of turnips rising into a haphazard pile.

"Join us, please." Frank's voice stilled her knife. He was standing in the doorway of the kitchen, the men he had admitted no longer visible, the expression of distracted deliberation that he had turned on her these last days now edged with something more urgent.

Stasia set down her knife and swept the turnips into a pot. "I'll just put these on to boil—"

"Leave them."

Stasia nodded and gently set the pot on the counter and wiped her hands on her apron. "All right." She obediently followed Frank into the sitting room.

The two men rose from where they had been perched on chairs, the taller of the two removing his cap. Stasia did not miss the way their eyes followed her, as if she were being silently evaluated for some quality she could not name.

"This is Jan," Frank said, pointing to the man with the hat. "And Paul." He gestured to his colleague. "They are also with the council."

It didn't escape Stasia's notice that he didn't introduce her by name, nor did she believe for a second that *Jan* and *Paul* were real names.

Stasia nodded her welcome.

"Please, sit." Frank gestured to the sofa behind her, and Stasia sat, the two men resuming their seats on their chairs.

The one called Jan leaned forward, folding his cap in his hands. His grey-blue eyes probed hers beneath a mop of prematurely silver hair. "Frank has told us that he believes you can be of great value to the council."

Stasia folded her hands in her lap but said nothing. She didn't look at Frank.

"He has indicated that you are very competent in your current role with the Resistance but he has brought it to our attention that you have greater potential."

Stasia held his gaze but still didn't reply, unsure what this entire charade was, or why these men were really here, or what any of it had to do with her.

A flicker of annoyance crossed Jan's face, and he glanced at Frank. "Is she simple?"

Frank's expression did not change. "No."

"She's very young."

"Yes."

"Why doesn't she answer me?" he demanded.

"Because you haven't yet asked me a question," Stasia said.

Jan's ruddy complexion reddened further but his companion chuckled. The man called Paul leaned back in his chair, crossing his booted feet and considering Stasia. He was younger than his partner, his hair inky black, his eyes almost as dark.

"Do you enjoy what you do for the Resistance?" he asked Stasia without preamble.

Stasia regarded him dully. "Sometimes."

"Why only sometimes?"

"Because it is not enough."

Paul's leg uncrossed, and his boot hit the ground with a thump. His amusement had vanished. "Why is it not enough?"

Because Margot is dead, she wanted to scream. *Margot, who would never again laugh, and little Minna, who would never grow up. The Kaufmanns, who had tried to run, and her father, who had tried to fight, and countless others who had been crushed beneath the heel of Nazi barbarism. All dead. All gone.*

And it wouldn't stop.

From above the mantel, a clock ticked, the sound loud in the utter silence of the house.

Jan made an exasperated noise.

Stasia ignored him. "Stealing documents and hiding people are only temporary treatments for the disease," she said quietly. "And while they may save a life, they do nothing to fix the rot within that will inevitably take more."

Paul leaned forward, his elbows on his knees, his round face expressionless. "And how would you fix the rot?"

"By cutting it out."

Paul sat back and exchanged a glance with Jan. "Those are brave words, and I have no doubt that you are a brave girl, but I am not sure you comprehend what you are asking for."

This time it was Stasia's turn to sit back. "Do not do that."

"Do what?"

"Speak to me like you know my mind."

"There is a big difference between smuggling weapons for the Resistance and using them." It was Jan who spoke, his tone flat.

Stasia's eyes snapped to the older man, something stirring within the black emptiness inside her. "Yes. There is."

Her answer seemed to surprise him.

Paul stood, withdrawing something from his waist. A pistol, Stasia realized. A Webley. Idly, she wondered if it had been one of the weapons from her pockets. Or maybe Margot's. She wondered if Frank had given it to him.

Paul held it out to her. "It's not loaded."

She took it without hesitation and checked to verify that it was indeed unloaded. It was. "What good is an unloaded weapon out there? Why carry it?" she asked. "Are you planning on throwing it at the Nazis?" She sounded angry, she realized. Which would never do. Emotion had no place here. "What do you want from me?"

Paul blinked. Jan had straightened, his attention riveted on the gun in her hands.

"Ah." That sensation of something stirring deep within grew. Ignited into a heat that was turning mere anger into fury. "You want to know if I would pull the trigger if I was asked to do so."

Their expressions gave her all the answer she needed.

"Why don't you ask Frank?" Stasia hissed. "Ask him if I pulled the trigger, since you seem incapable of asking me." She stood and tucked the Webley into the strings of her apron. "Now if you'll excuse me, I have dinner to prepare. I'll give you your answers once you start asking the right questions." She headed toward the kitchen.

"Tell me how you would keep the Nazis from exacting their reprisals for a liquidation." It was Paul again. "Ten citizens for every dead Nazi, three for a dead collaborator."

Stasia paused, her back still to the men. "The Pied Piper of Hamelin."

"I beg your pardon?"

"It's a fairy tale."

"I'm not familiar."

"The town of Hamelin, suffering the throes of a rat infestation, hired the Pied Piper to lead the rats out of the city. He played his magic pipe and lured the rats into the Weser River, where they all drowned." She turned slowly. "He did the same with the town's children when the mayor refused to pay him, of course, but the point is that neither the rats nor the children were ever seen again."

Both Paul and Jan seemed frozen where they stood.

"Your liquidations cannot be public. Kill a man publicly or leave him to be found and you make him a Nazi martyr." She shook her head. "Make them disappear. Vanish completely. Lure them away in such a manner that you might seed doubt. Create division among them."

Paul and Jan were still staring at her, motionless.

"It's not a guarantee, of course. But then, nothing is."

Frank spoke up for the first time. "If you do this, Stasia, what these men will ask of you, there is no going back," he told her, sounding almost like an anxious parent.

"I do not have a choice."

"There is always a choice," Jan said harshly.

Stasia's gaze swung back to him. "I have nowhere and nothing to go back to." And no one. Stasia twisted the ring on her finger, wondering what Nicolas would have made of this. What he would have made of her.

In the next second, she realized that it didn't matter. Nicolas was dead. And so, effectively, was Stasia. The girl from Rotterdam whom Nicolas had professed to love, and whom he had once accused of being kind and good, no longer existed. That girl had grown up and had her eyes opened to the reality of the world around her. The woman standing in this little farmhouse with a gun tucked into her apron strings only wished that her innocence had died sooner. Perhaps then, others might still be alive.

"The Pied Piper of Hamelin," Paul repeated thoughtfully.

"She's not wrong." It was Jan who spoke, his words almost inaudible.

Stasia stepped closer to him, pulling the Webley from her apron, letting it lay gently in the palms of her hands. She closed her eyes, seeing Margot's sightless, empty ones staring back at her.

"I will play a beautiful tune," she said. "If you let me."

★ ★ ★

The city forest became her preferred killing ground over the next months.

The Haarlemmerhout, with its winding paths, dense canopy, and thick undergrowth was the ideal place in which to make Nazis and their collaborators disappear. Over the summer months and into the fall, Stasia discovered that she had a knack for planning. For placing the right people with the right skills in the right place at the right time. For evaluating the information and whispers that were brought to her and selecting which of those tidings and targets were worth pursuing. Her team of liquidators perfected a system that had thus far eliminated almost a dozen Nazi officials. Men who, as far as anyone could determine, had viewed an evening film at a cinema, had dinner at a restaurant, or downed drinks at a bar and then simply vanished.

The targets were chosen with care—the council ignored

the clerks and the drivers and the foot soldiers—and formed a curated list of men who commanded those individuals. Men who, with the swipe of a pen, ordered the executions of many. Who, with a wave of a hand, commanded the torture of more. Or who, surrounded by aides and advisors, ordered the mass arrests and deportations of an entire people.

The killings the council carried out were never done in haste, nor were they ever done impulsively or attempted by a single individual. Occasionally, circumstance or fate prevented Stasia's team from achieving an assigned liquidation, and in the beginning, she had a hard time letting go of what she perceived as an abject failure. But she came to learn that there was always another name.

Like the one she was with.

Stasia stood and allowed SS Obersturmführer Ernst Kantschuster to help her with her coat. She smiled when his fingers brushed her bare arms and giggled when they drifted to the curve of her hip. In the mirror behind the bar, her gaze caught on her reflection. She didn't recognize the woman staring back through a mask of pressed powder, brow liner, lipstick, and mascara. She was no longer Stasia but Rose, the name plucked from the tale of Little Briar Rose that she had once loved for its happy-ever-after but now esteemed for its heartless queen mother. Unable to love and focused solely on vanquishing her enemies. That the queen had died in a nest of vipers of her own making was not something that bothered Stasia any longer. It was a risk that she was willing to take.

Kantschuster left her momentarily to settle his significant bill with the barkeep. Stasia wandered toward the door, her eyes meeting those of Jan, who sat alone in the corner, nursing a cup of something hot. He nodded, almost imperceptibly, and turned away, and Stasia lowered her eyes and adjusted the belt of her coat, which didn't need adjusting.

"*Moffenhoer.*" The slur was spat in a low voice as a narrow-faced man pushed roughly by her. He held a tray in his hand, his worn shirt open at the collar, and Stasia recognized him as one of the establishment's servers. "You are disgusting, spreading your legs for Nazi swine." He was gone before Stasia could respond, happy enough to accept the Germans' money but not the female company they kept.

It wasn't the first time she'd been called that, nor would it be the last. It didn't bother her at all—she certainly didn't need approval from strangers who were oblivious to the fact that the Nazi swine he had accused her of spreading her legs for now had his life measured in minutes. It didn't matter what strangers thought. Only her actions mattered. Only fighting mattered.

"Was he rude to you?" The obersturmführer had returned, and he sounded indignant, even through his thick accent. "What did he say? Shall I have him arrested?" He swayed slightly, before he steadied himself.

"Nothing of consequence." Stasia laughed gaily. "You are sweet to offer, but no. I am not so easily offended by men who do not matter. Especially when I am with one who does."

The SS lieutenant grinned widely, his flushed, fleshy cheeks stretching. "Such pretty words from a pretty girl."

"Shall we take a walk?" Stasia asked. "Just you and me? Somewhere a little more . . . private?"

"I'd like that." Kantschuster settled his black-brimmed cap firmly on his head. "Let me say goodbye to my comrades."

"Must you?" Stasia looped her arm through his and squeezed. She did not want anyone remembering who he might have left with.

The lieutenant frowned with displeasure.

"It's just that if you go over there, they'll buy you another drink, and you'll stay for another hour, and our chance at a little privacy will be lost." She went up on her tiptoes and brushed her lips against his jaw. "I like your friends. But I like you more," she whispered. "And I have something special planned for you."

"Since you put it that way." He pinched her backside with enthusiasm. "Lead the way."

The pair stepped out of the light and heat of the bar and into the crisp fall night. The usual foot traffic that one would have seen years ago was absent, no citizen in their right mind willing to risk being caught out after curfew, and only a watery moonlight prevented the darkness from being absolute.

"Let's take a walk through the forest," Stasia suggested, turning south. "The colors of the trees are quite spectacular this time of year." She wondered if he would point out that the colors would almost be impossible to see in the darkness.

He didn't.

Instead, Kantschuster staggered a bit as he followed her but quickly fell into step, and Stasia kept up a steady stream of inane conversation, skillfully dodging and occasionally tolerating the lieutenant's roving hands. *Moffenhoer*, indeed.

"Did you know," Stasia asked, as they reached the edge of the forest, "that the Spaniards burned this entire forest down in the fifteen hundreds during the siege of Haarlem?"

"Idiot Spanish," the lieutenant mumbled. "Still can't do anything right."

Stasia laughed and continued into the forest, walking more slowly now. Beneath the trees that still held on to their leaves, the shadows were deeper, the path more difficult to see.

"It was replanted, of course," she told him, "but it's why the road on the other side of the forest is called Spanjaardslaan."

"You know, I don't really care." Kantschuster abruptly stopped, yanking on her arm and making her stumble into him. "I didn't come here with you to hear about the Spanish." He kissed her sloppily, his hands clutching her shoulders.

"Not here," Stasia managed, slipping out and away from him. "Follow me. I have a better place where no one will disturb us." She didn't wait for him to agree, merely hurried forward, taking less care with her steps.

The SS officer grunted in irritation but followed her.

Stasia stopped in a narrow clearing hemmed in on either side by a thick, tangled mat of underbrush and vines. She waited for Kantschuster to join her.

He reached for her in the shadows, and Stasia stepped nimbly to the side. "Tsk," she said. "You Germans are so impatient. Anticipation makes everything that much sweeter."

"I don't like a tease," the officer growled.

"And neither do I," Stasia assured him. She tugged at the belt of her coat and was rewarded by a sound of approval. "Tell me," she said, "what it's like to have so much power."

"What?" The lieutenant sounded a little out of breath.

"The men you were with at the bar. Do you command them?" She already knew the answer but asked it anyway.

"Of course I do."

"And how do you decide?" she asked. "How to send those men into the cities to have the Jews removed? Sent away?"

"It's not a decision, it's a duty." He put a hand out to steady himself against the trunk of a thick tree.

"But what about the small children? Surely they pose no threat?"

"Jews are like a disease that will never be controlled unless you destroy it. All of it." Kantschuster was speaking slowly, as though he believed her too stupid to understand. "It will never disappear without removing them from our midst. Our Führer himself said that and has proven it many times over."

"Do you know, I agree with you," she said.

"What?"

"Disease will never disappear without it being removed from our midst."

The lieutenant stared at her in the shadows for long seconds as though trying to measure her sincerity. He shook his head and pushed himself away from the tree with an impatient grunt. "Enough talking. I'm tired of it. Now," he said, his fingers fumbling at the front waistband of his uniform trousers, "I want what I came for, and I want it now."

A breeze rattled through the leaves above their heads, and Stasia stepped to the side. "By all means," she murmured.

The shot, when it came, was unnaturally loud in the quiet.

But then it always was, the sound echoing and bouncing through the forest and sending a handful of roosting birds shrieking into the night. Stasia watched dispassionately as the SS obersturmführer sagged to the ground like a broken marionette. He landed face-first on the forest floor, his cap bouncing and rolling from his head. Stasia stopped it with the toe of her shoe.

The first time she had stared down at the lifeless form of a Nazi official whom she had lured into the forest, she had experienced an unwelcome twinge of conscience. A pricking around the very edge of her awareness that was faint but insistent. Yet as she had gazed down at the man's face, his expression frozen in confused surprise, blood oozing slowly from the back of his head into the collar of his uniform, his legs twisted awkwardly where he lay, she had been seized with the image of a helpless baby in his hands. An innocent, helpless child with a misshapen head who had died before it had had a chance to live.

And Stasia hadn't ever experienced an assault on her conscience again.

"I don't know why you insist on talking to them." Jan's voice drifted from the shadows before he appeared from behind the tree the officer had been leaning against. His silver hair was unnaturally bright in the darkness while the gun in his hand glinted only dully before it disappeared somewhere in his clothing.

"Every time they open their mouths, I am reminded of why I do this. And reminded that I cannot stop."

"You can't take on the entire Reich by yourself," Jan huffed, and bent, pushing the body over, and his hands worked quickly on the buttons of the officer's uniform. Uniforms were especially valuable to the council as the perfect disguise, and everything was taken.

From the shadows, two more silhouettes appeared, men dressed in nondescript clothes with caps pulled down over their foreheads, which made their faces impossible to see in the gloom. Without speaking a word, they assisted Jan in stripping the body, grasped the corpse by its hands and feet, and vanished into the forest as silently as they had appeared.

Stasia knew the men who came to collect the bodies only by first names, and those were names as fictitious as Rose. She did know, however, that they each carried their own weapon like she did, provided to them by the council. And though the manner in which she lured the German officers into the forests varied, and though the person who pulled the trigger was not always her, she knew that the men waiting had already dug a deep hole somewhere reasonably close by. And she knew that should someone come to investigate the sound of the shot, by the time they reached the approximate area where they believed that it might have come from, the body would be gone, the ground smoothed over with a new carpet of leaves and dead branches, and whoever might have been there had long since melted into the dark safety of the trees.

Jan bundled the uniform into a canvas bag and slung it over his back. He paused. "You all right?"

"I'm fine. I'm always fine." It was the truth. Her new truth, and one that she lived with every day.

"There is . . . " He stopped.

"There is what?" Stasia prompted impatiently.

"There is a rumour. That Generalkommissar Rauter has a man looking for you."

Stasia scoffed. "The generalkommissar should be the next to take a walk in the forest. I've said this for a long time."

"You need to be serious."

"When am I not?" Stasia said. "Besides, this rumour you speak of is nothing new. There are always men looking for all of us."

"Not men like this. This man is different. A specialist of sorts in a manner that should terrify you. It terrifies me."

"Gestapo? Police?"

"SS, I think. I don't have a name. I'll get one."

Stasia shrugged. "Doesn't matter. He will die too."

Jan exhaled heavily. "I worry about you."

"Don't."

"You are alone too much."

"I am perfectly fine."

"Stop saying you're fine," Jan repeated. "No one is fine."

Stasia looked away, silent.

"I worry that your need for revenge is consuming you."

"Revenge? You think what I do is simple revenge?"

"Yes. For Margot." He hesitated. "Is it not?"

Stasia examined that question before she spoke. "If it were merely revenge for Margot, then I would have been satisfied with the death of her killer. But revenge itself is not simple. It is a weapon—my weapon. Wielded on behalf of those who are no longer alive to do so themselves, like Margot, and plied on behalf of the innocents who will continue to die." Her lips curled. "So please do not worry on my account. Worry for those who truly need your concern."

Jan sighed loudly. He started to say something but then seemed to change his mind. "Get home safe" was all he said.

"I always do," Stasia replied, before she, too, melted back into the black oblivion of the darkness.

CHAPTER
15

Nicolas

5 JANUARY 1944
ARISAIG, SCOTLAND

There was someone in the darkness with him.

Nicolas opened one eye, making sure he kept his breathing even, every sense straining. The shadows in the room were broken only by a thin shaft of moonlight that pierced the far window and fell across the floor. An icy draft touched the skin on his face from where the window had been cracked open. The window that he had closed tightly before falling asleep.

The shadows in the corners were absolute, and it would be there that the intruder hovered. A small scratching noise reached his ears, as if something had been drawn across the surface of his tiny washstand on the other side of the bed. His fingers curled around the hilt of the knife under his pillow, and his entire body tensed.

The movement, when it came, back in the direction of the window, was fleet, and Nicolas exploded from the bed, hampered somewhat by the woolen blanket over his legs. But while the intruder was fast, he was faster. Nicolas got behind and wrapped an arm around the man's neck, yanking him nearly off his feet, and pressed the edge of his blade to the soft spot just beneath the intruder's jaw.

"Stop moving unless you'd like me to sever your jugular and watch you bleed out across this floor." Nicolas spoke in French, not knowing if the words would be understood but sure that his tone would.

"You'll be wanting to move your knife a bit forward for that, then" was the flat reply. The flat, very feminine reply.

Nicolas nearly loosened his grip before catching himself. He acknowledged what he should have taken note of earlier—the curve of her hip where it was pinned against his, the slight swell of her breast against the bottom of his elbow, though her entire body was strung as tight as a bow.

"What are you doing in my room?" he growled.

"Housekeeping." Her answer was still flat.

"I'll not ask again."

"And I'll not give you a real answer either way, so it would seem that we are at an impasse."

"Tell me what you took."

"Nothing."

The edge of his blade pressed a little harder against her skin. She stiffened.

"What did you take?" he asked again.

She moved and reached down.

"Slowly."

"Paranoid bastard."

"Yes. It is how we stay alive."

"I could have slit your throat while you slept." She was withdrawing something from her pocket with exaggerated movements. "I was all the way across the room before you knew I was even there."

She was right. He hadn't heard her come through the window, and that was unforgivable. "Show me what you have in your hand."

Almost leisurely, she lifted her hand. In her fingers, visible in the moonlight, was the unmistakable shape of his lighter. Anger ignited in him. "Give it—"

He never got to finish his sentence because he made his second unforgivable mistake in as many minutes. While he had been fixated on the hand that held the lighter, he had not been paying attention to her second hand. A hand that was now pressing the barrel of what felt undoubtably like a small caliber pistol into his lower ribs.

"Small firearms, even though they are called small, are loud," she said with regret. "And I generally prefer not to use them. I do hate the attention. Release me."

Nicolas held himself completely still. Who the hell was this woman? A Nazi spy? An assassin? Or another test? Another part of his Jed training?

"Shoot me, and I will still drag this blade across your neck," he said. "It might not kill you. Or it might. So it seems we are still at an impasse, no?"

"No, we are not." The barrel of her weapon dug in harder. "I know that you are aware of what a bullet does to a man's insides when fired into a chest cavity at close range, Captain Phillipe. So let's not pretend that you will do more damage than I. I'll take the chance with your inferior weapon. But I leave the choice up to you."

Nicolas barely heard the rest of what she said after she mentioned his name. "You know who I am."

Against him, her muscles were as tense as ever, yet she remained utterly still. "You have quite the knack for stating the obvious." Her voice was cold and steely. "So let me return the favour. Any advantage you had is lost. In three seconds, I will shoot you, and by the time that your friends stumble out of their beds to come to your aid, I will be gone out that window, and you will be dead."

"Fine." He was angry but not stupid. "I will release you but you will return my lighter to me first."

He heard her exhale in what sounded like surprise. "You wager your life against a piece of metal?"

"Toss it on the bed."

"Hmm." It seemed like she was considering his request. "Very well," she said, and flicked her wrist. The lighter landed on the bed with a barely audible thump, glinting silver in the shadows.

Nicolas loosened his arm.

With the speed of a coiled viper, the woman spun, flinging herself across the bed and rolling as she hit the floor, putting a barrier between them. She was three steps away from the door when Nicolas tackled her because, as she had moved, he had registered two things: The gun she held in her hand was not a gun at all but a pen, and the lighter that she had tossed onto the cover of the bed was no longer there.

He would rebuke himself later for every single error he had committed in the last few minutes, but right now, he was going to get some answers.

She fought well, and had Nicolas not fully anticipated her having the same sort of hand-to-hand combat skills that he had been taught, she would have easily triumphed. But Nicolas was just as fast and just as capable and just as ruthless, and fifty pounds heavier. He pinned her beneath him, her arms twisted and immobilized behind her back, his knees on either side of her, his weight on top of her. She struggled violently.

"Stop moving or I'll break your arm," he said harshly.

She went still.

"Good." With one hand, he felt in her trouser pockets and found his lighter. He slid it to the side, where she could not reach it.

Catching his breath, he studied her in the pale light. She appeared shorter than he, but not by much. She was dressed in trousers and a woolen sweater, her dark hair pulled back and secured at the back of her head. In the shadows, her face was pale, and dark eyes stared furiously at him as she twisted her head to look at him.

"Who the hell are you?" Nicolas demanded.

"Mireille Balin."

"Long way from a movie screen, don't you think? Try again."

"Doesn't matter, does it?" she sneered breathlessly. "I can give you any name I want, and you have no way to prove or disprove it."

"How did you know who I am?"

"Because only a fool would target a room on a mission without knowing who was in it first," she snarled before resting her forehead on the floor.

Nicolas scowled. None of this was making sense.

"There are no women in training with us here at this estate."

"No," she agreed, her answer muffled.

"Then where did you come from?"

"Paris."

"That's not what I meant."

"I know."

"Are you a spy?"

Beneath him, she tensed. "Not after tonight," she muttered.

A rap on his door made them both jump. "Captain? You all right in there?" It was muted through the door. "I heard a crash."

Nicolas glanced down to find the woman watching him intensely, a strange expression on her face that ranged somewhere between fury and fear. The fear was new. Not fear of him, he understood, because this was the first time he had seen it. It was fear of being discovered by someone other than him. Interesting. And potentially useful.

"I'm fine," he called. "Apologies. Got out of bed and knocked the washbasin over."

"Must have imbibed a little too much this evening, eh, Captain?" A faint laugh followed.

"Must have," Nicolas said. "Trying to sleep it off. Good night."

"Good night." He listened as the footsteps from the other side of the door retreated.

The woman beneath him scoffed. "Incompetent imbecile." The fear was gone, and the venom was back. "Hope he's not the man you'll be counting on to have your back in the field."

"Why?"

"You don't drink. At least, never, ever to the point where you would wake up drunk and walk into furniture."

Nicolas blinked, unsettled. "And how the hell would you know that?"

"Because I've watched you. Studied you." For the first time, a note of bitter defeat crept into her tone. "In the pubs on the evenings you go out." She banged her forehead on the floor softly. "*Merde*. And all for nothing."

"Explain."

"No."

"Then I'll yell and call my friend back, and you can explain to him and everyone else who will want to take a look at the woman who got caught breaking into my room."

"You're a bastard."

"I've been called worse. Much, much worse."

She rested her cheek on the floor and closed her eyes. "My mission was to steal something from a Jed's room—your room—and return undetected," she said wretchedly.

Nicolas didn't bother to ask where she would return to. He assumed it was close by.

"My instructors didn't think I could do it. And they were right." Her eyes opened. "I wanted to test myself against the best, you know? Against the daunting Captain Phillipe, whose reputation precedes him everywhere he goes. Because why sneak into the room of an American or a Brit who's drunk his way through four pubs too many and can't remember his own name? You could send a full company through their lodgings and they'd sleep right through it."

"Tell me what happens now."

She shrugged, a motion severely hampered by Nicolas's grip. "I've failed and will be evaluated as such. I will lose whatever opportunity I might have had to be dropped into France. To fight."

Nicolas adjusted his weight, considering. He'd heard that they were sending female agents behind enemy lines. He'd never met one. Until tonight. "You were right, you know. You could have killed me before I was aware you were here."

"My mission wasn't to kill the esteemed Captain Phillipe, so that's neither here nor there," she spat. "It doesn't change the fact that I've failed."

"You're very good."

"Not good enough."

"I'm not so sure."

"Says the man who has me pinned to the ground," she snapped. "Don't patronize me."

"I believed that the pen you had shoved into my ribs was a gun. You never lost your composure. I still don't know your name or where you're from. You managed to retrieve my lighter a second time. And I never saw you watching me in a pub. Not once."

Her lips thinned.

"I can help you."

She twisted roughly. "I don't want your charity."

For a wild moment, Nicolas was transported back to a château garden, where a bitter, angry boy had said the same thing. The effect was almost disorienting.

"It's not charity," he said with no little wonder, repeating the exact same words Stasia had said to him. Nicolas abruptly released the woman and stood. He swept his lighter from the ground. "You are too good not to have a chance at the real enemy. Too good to end up in some typing pool or sitting behind a desk listening to the enemy plan through a headset."

The agent had jumped to her feet, rubbing her arms, though she hadn't run. Instead, she was watching him, her chin raised defiantly.

"Of all the things you might easily have taken," he said, gesturing at the tiny desk by the window upon which rested his French-English dictionary, his fountain pen, and a postcard photo of Notre Dame that the lieutenant with whom he had first travelled to Scotland had given him, "why did you want this?" He held up his lighter.

"Because when you are out, you are never without it. Because it is in your pocket at all times, and when it isn't, it is in your hand. Like some type of good luck charm or talisman." She touched the side of her neck where his knife had pressed and winced. "Because even a half-wit watching you for a half hour could see that it was your most valued possession."

Nicolas looked down and turned the lighter over in his hands, the pads of his fingers tracing each groove, each scratch, each dent. "A girl gave this to me. Before I fell in love with her. Or maybe while I was falling in love with her." He flicked it open and watched the flame dance, a circle of gold warming the shaft of silver moonlight.

"Where is she now?"

"Dead."

The woman didn't reply, and for that, Nicolas was grateful.

"In case it gets too dark, and you need a light." He closed the lighter and the flame extinguished. "That's what she said when she gave it to me."

"You're lucky," she said bitterly.

Nicolas looked up. "I beg your pardon?"

"I have nothing left of my husband."

"That's not true."

Her expression hardened. "Are you calling me a liar?"

"No. I was just trying to help—"

"I don't need any more of your help."

I don't need any more of your help. He had once said that too, in an alley in Rouen. And he had never been more wrong.

Nicolas held out the lighter. "Take it."

The woman stared at him. "What are you doing?"

"Take it," he repeated.

"Is this some sort of trick?" She looked ready to bolt.

Nicolas took a small step toward her, and when she didn't move, took another. He reached for her hand and pressed the lighter against her palm. "I want you to have it. For when it gets too dark and you need a light," he said.

She hadn't moved, her face washed pale in the moonlight. "I can't take this."

"You can. Because you were wrong. It isn't my most valued possession. It is the memories I keep within me that I treasure above everything. And those can't be stolen. Not even by a French spy who nearly got the better of me with a pen."

A tear tracked down her cheek, and then another. "Why are you being so nice to me?" she whispered.

In his mind's eye, Nicolas could see Stasia laughing, her whiskey-eyes dancing with joy and wry humour. "I'm not being nice," he said, his voice catching as he repeated her words. "I'm being useful."

"What?"

He looked down at her. "France needs both of us. To fight." He was aware that their hands were still joined, the lighter held between them. "You had a mission. You've accomplished that mission. That's all anyone needs to know."

With her free hand, she sniffed and swiped at the moisture on her cheeks. "You are not who they say you are."

"I don't entirely know who I am yet. I don't know what kind of man emerges from a war like this." Though he knew what kind of man he wanted to be in this moment. The kind of man who would make Stasia proud, and that was something that he clung to.

The woman didn't speak for a long minute. "What is it like over there?" she finally whispered, and Nicolas didn't need to ask what she was referring to.

He thought for a long time before answering. "It's waiting," he said. "Waiting to be given orders, waiting for the enemy to attack, waiting to die, waiting to live. It's fear, the kind that twists your insides and rises up into your chest and throat and makes it impossible to breathe. It's moments when you become unrecognizable to yourself, when the waiting is over and the fear is gone and you are nothing more than a wild creature, a beast whose only need is to keep death at bay for one more second. For one more minute."

Nicolas stopped. "And then, much later, when you end up in a tavern or walking down a street, you'll think that all of that madness is written all over you, but no one seems to see it. The barkeep only asks if you want another, the neighbour you pass only nods and keeps sweeping. And you don't ever mention that madness because to acknowledge it, however temporarily, is to admit how fragile we really are." Nicolas curled her fingers around the lighter and let go of her hand.

The woman looked at the lighter in her hand gleaming softly in the moonlight. "Thank you," she said, "for the truth."

"What was his name?" Nicolas asked. "Your husband."

"Ephraim."

"In times when you are wondering how the world seems to go on as if nothing you did made a difference, hold that lighter in your hand and remember something good about Ephraim. Remember how he laughed, remember how he used to light up the room for you, and the waiting and the fear and the madness will diminish their hold."

The woman stared at him in the moonlight, and Nicolas couldn't begin to tell what she was thinking. Then without warning, she moved, sliding her hand around the back of his neck and pressing a soft, gentle kiss against his lips.

Nicolas closed his eyes.

"She was the lucky one," she whispered against his mouth. "Lucky to have been loved by you."

When he opened his eyes, she was gone.

CHAPTER
16

Stasia

3 FEBRUARY 1944
HAARLEM, THE NETHERLANDS

The propaganda films all started to look the same after a while.

They were a never-ending reel of handsome, determined gunners manning Panzers across burning fields, handsome, determined airmen hurling bombers into cloudless skies, handsome, determined seamen commanding U-boats through choppy seas, or handsome, determined soldiers marching victoriously through conquered cities. All set to buoyant, uplifting scores meant to assure the viewer that Nazi doctrine was both righteous and inescapable.

And while the images danced across the screen, Stasia watched with unseeing eyes, planning her own version of inescapable righteousness for the officer seated beside her.

He was an ordinary-looking man, as far as men went. Perhaps even less than ordinary if one was being critical. He had a narrow face accessorized by puffy shadows beneath his eyes, hair of a nondescript brown, a mouth that only rarely smiled, and a reedy build that made his uniform seem like it was a size too big. Had she met him on the street at a different time, in a different place, in a different world, and had he offered her a greeting accompanied by a compliment on her pretty eyes, she might merely have nodded her thanks and continued on her way and never given him another thought.

As it was, when Obersturmbannführer Wilhelm Faust had complimented her on her pretty eyes after she had deliberately stumbled into him in the middle of Grote Markt, she had smiled at him with all the warmth of a thousand suns. She had also blushed and apologized profusely in her stilted German for her clumsiness. She had been on her way to the Rembrandt Theater to watch the latest film, she explained, and in her excitement, she had not been watching where she was going. At which time he told her that he was on his way to the film as well...and would she like to join him? Stasia made a show of demure hesitation before accepting, because, she said with lowered eyes, it seemed wrong to decline such a happy coincidence.

Such a happy coincidence indeed.

Obersturmbannführer Faust, with his braided shoulder boards and embroidered SS runes, had held the door for her, insisted on paying for her ticket, helped her with her coat, and escorted her to her seat with all the gallantry and courtesy one might expect from a fairy tale prince. Idly, Stasia wondered if, as a former commander within his Einsatzgruppen unit, Faust had escorted the men, women, and children he had slaughtered to their mass graves with the same polite courtesy.

She had been told by the nameless men who collected information for her that Faust had been transferred from Poland to carry out special duties within the local SS. His reputation had preceded him, and it was said that even Generalkommisar für das Sicherheitswesen Rauter deferred to him on occasion. The rumours that had wound their way through their network from Poland were horrifying and nauseating, and Stasia tried not to imagine what special duties Wilhelm Faust might unleash on the Dutch population. If she did her job right, they would never have to find out.

In front of her, the film was drawing to its inevitable close—in this one, the handsome, determined Luftwaffe pilot had overcome his struggles, professed his great love for his country, and remembered just how much enjoyment one takes from bombing the enemy. Stasia watched dispassionately as he flew off with his mates to bomb England, all singing a rousing tune, happy to return to war.

"Did you enjoy the film?" Faust asked Stasia as the theater lighting brightened and they rose from their seats.

"Very much," she lied with what she hoped were bright eyes and an inviting smile. "Thank you. It was so exciting." She allowed him to help her don her coat, slipped her hand through his proffered arm, and ignored the way her skin crawled. "I wish that I could fly planes. I think that I would like to soar through the sky like a bird."

"And bomb your enemies?" Faust seemed to find her declaration amusing.

You have no idea, she thought viciously.

"And bomb my enemies to dust," she agreed, keeping a smile fixed firmly on her face.

"Bold and bloodthirsty, yes?" Faust steered them out of the warmth of the theater and into the wide expanse of Grote Markt. "You are lucky. I like that in a woman."

Stasia blinked in the late afternoon light. Already, the sun was starting to creep toward the western horizon, the days still short and the nights still much too long.

"Mmm." She squeezed his arm. "What else do you like in a woman?"

The lieutenant-colonel perused her slowly. "Many things," he said.

"Perhaps," she suggested, as the theatergoers brushed by them, "we might get a drink, and you could tell me more. It would be my treat. If, of course, you would like that."

The tavern she would take him to had already been selected, and Jan would already be waiting.

"I think I would like that."

"How lovely." And it was. Sometimes her targets were not nearly as agreeable. "Shall we go—"

"But I would like to see the church first."

"The church?"

"De Grote of St. Bavokerk." Faust gestured to the massive building almost directly across from the theater. "I have not yet been inside. I am told it is something that I would not wish to miss."

Stasia followed his gaze. It was a beautiful church with its Gothic architecture and rows of pointed, arched stained-glass windows interspersed with decorative pinnacles. The tracery on each window was impressive, and the alternating red-and-cream stonework on the exterior gave the church an arresting visual flair. The tower-like vaults reaching toward the sky, which Stasia had once imagined as the sort Rapunzel would have gazed out from, were framed by narrow, round turrets. The spire of the church rose to even greater heights from the center, making St. Bavokerk easy to find from a distance.

Stasia shivered slightly, trying not to frown at Faust's request.

It wasn't unreasonable, but it was unexpected and unplanned, and because of that, Stasia hesitated. Grote Markt was busy, and the foot traffic of civilians and uniformed men was steady. A handful of cars were parked along the sides in front of rows of buildings with fanciful balconies, ornate detail, or striking crenelated façades. But she saw nothing out of the ordinary. Nothing that would indicate that Obersturmbannführer Faust's request was based on anything other than curiosity.

"All right," Stasia agreed, unwilling to risk losing his company. The tavern would still be waiting when they were done with this little expedition. Jan would still be waiting. "Let's go see the church first." She would adapt. She always did.

"Excellent."

The lieutenant-colonel headed for the church's far entrance, and Stasia kept pace beside him. She tried to keep her muscles relaxed and the conversation light.

"The original church was built in the middle of the thirteenth century," she said slowly in German. "It was expanded in the sixteenth. And," she added, "the organ of St. Bavokerk has been played by both Handel and Mozart."

And maybe, she thought rather caustically, when the war was over and the Nazis had been either all expelled or all exterminated, she could become a tour guide of this city.

Faust nodded but didn't reply. They reached the entrance and stepped to the side as two other grey-clad SS soldiers exited. The officer once again held the door for her as they entered. It had been awhile since Stasia had been inside St. Bavokerk but it was as magnificent as she remembered.

The low sunlight streaming in through the colored glass gave the entire interior an otherworldly ambiance. Far above her head, the ceiling was ribbed in a geometrical pattern that Stasia had once sketched as stars bursting along the entire length of the nave. The pale walls made Stasia feel like she had stepped into a cloud, and along with the effects of the light and the stars, she was almost tempted to believe that she had stepped into a corner of heaven itself.

Stasia slipped her hand from the SS officer's arm and wandered ahead down the nave past rows of chairs that had been set up, not wanting to be touching this man in a place like this. At the far end, the extraordinary Baroque organ that the church was so famous for rose in richly gilded columns all the way to the ceiling. At the very top, two carved lions flanked the Haarlem coat of arms while a collection of sculpted figures kept watch over the church from their perches at the base and apex of the pedal towers.

She stopped in front of the western wall, gazing up at the organ. It was a wonder, she mused, that the Nazis had not managed to steal this as well. Disassemble and pack up the entire structure into wooden crates and ship it away on one of their trains, never to be seen again. Someone had once told her that there were over five thousand pipes. A number that, when it came to destruction, would give men like Faust no pause, whether they were speaking of instruments or people.

Someone coughed behind Stasia, and the sound echoed in the vast space. Reluctantly, she turned away from the beautiful organ. There were only three people scattered amongst the chairs set out in the nave, presumably praying, but Faust was nowhere to be seen. She cursed inwardly, unhappy with herself for her distraction. Her only job had been to keep the SS officer close, and she hadn't done that. No doubt he wasn't far, perhaps in the transept somewhere, but she didn't like her mistake.

Stasia started back down the nave. Something nagged at the edge of her consciousness, a disquieting feeling that she had missed something important. Her eyes swept the nearly empty church, trying to identify what it was, but she didn't see anything out of the ordinary—she stopped. Why was the church so empty? Where were the small groups of people who came here searching for answers to prayers that had thus far gone unanswered? Where were the clergymen offering comfort and guidance to the lost souls who found themselves here? The hair on the back of her neck rose.

The man sitting in the chair closest to her coughed again, a wretched, wracking sound. She turned her head in his direction and found herself staring into grey-blue eyes set beneath a mess of silver hair. It was only through a sheer power of will that she managed not to spin and bolt in a blind, terror-filled panic. Instead, she shoved her hands into her coat pockets and yanked out a glove, deliberately letting it fall to the ground. She bent slowly to retrieve it.

The man she knew as Jan, the man who had been her partner and conspirator for the last eight months, the man who was supposed to be waiting for her at this very moment in a Haarlem tavern, was sitting in this church. Sitting alone, hunched over as if in pain, his eyes bloodshot, the side of his face swollen and bruised.

From her knee, she looked back discreetly. The other two men who had been sitting in the nave had risen. Police, likely. Or maybe Gestapo, maybe SD or SS soldiers—she supposed it really didn't make a difference because, no matter who they were, they were here for her. Of that, she was sure. They had set a trap for her, and like a fool, she had walked right into it. Up ahead, out of sight, a door banged closed. She tried to keep her breathing steady but panic lanced through her, hot and caustic and paralyzing.

"What have you done?" she croaked, tucking her glove back into her coat pocket.

"I'm sorry, I'm sorry, I'm so sorry," Jan whimpered.

"What have you done?"

"They have my family." He was weeping now, and the sounds of booted feet behind her were getting louder. "He said he would kill them if I didn't tell him where you were."

"Fool," Stasia hissed. Her fingers found the Webley deep in her pocket. "Your family is already dead." And Jan would follow. As would she if she could not escape.

"I had no choice," he cried, and wept harder.

"There is always a choice." Her breath was coming in frantic gasps. "You told me that."

And what were hers? There were the doors on the western wall, under the organ, currently blocked by the two men who were approaching from that direction. There were the transverse doors, but without being able to see them, she had no idea who or what waited for her in front of or behind those options. There were doors at the eastern end of the church, and no doubt there were a dozen other, smaller exits connected by rooms and hallways and passages, but she was unfamiliar with the layout. All she knew was that she couldn't go up. She couldn't become trapped somewhere in the upper levels of the church. She needed to get out—

"Rose." The heavily accented Dutch voice came almost casually. "Or is it Briar Rose? So many different answers from so many different people. It was hard to know what to believe."

Stasia stood, lifting her chin.

A man stood at the intersection of the nave and transept.

He was tall, perhaps a hand width over six feet, with dark hair combed flat over his skull. He had an almost rectangular-shaped face with a full mouth, an aquiline nose, and close-set, hooded eyes that gave him the appearance of someone who was perpetually nearsighted. His uniform was grey, his boots polished to a mirror shine, and the braid at his shoulders and four embroidered dots next to the SS runes at his collar marked him as a major.

He took a step forward, and his eyes raked her where she still crouched. He frowned. "It's taken me a long time to find you. You've been more difficult than most."

Jan made a strangled noise. The men behind stopped a dozen paces away from her. Stasia ignored them all and stood, her hand still on her Webley deep in her pocket, and forced herself to acknowledge her real choices. The real choices that existed before her were not which door she might flee through but how many and which men she might kill before they killed her. The real choice she faced was whether she wished to die now, in this little corner of heaven, or if she wished to die days or weeks later, in some dark room, when her body finally surrendered to whatever torture they would inflict. Those were her choices.

The paralyzing terror that had made it difficult for her to breathe only a moment ago drained away, leaving her with a strange sense of calm. There was a sense of fatalistic freedom that came with the revelation that the enemy no longer lurked in the darkness, waiting to strike. The enemy was no longer a conceptual threat built of rumour and gossip that fueled debilitating fear, but a flesh-and-blood man. And he was here, standing in the light before her, and the choices now were hers to make.

She met the major's eyes without flinching.

He wasn't a lieutenant-colonel, and she couldn't be sure that he had commanded Einsatzgruppen units at one time, but it didn't really matter. If she was to die, today, in this church, then she promised herself that she would take this officer with her.

"You are the man the generalkommissar sent to find me," she said.

"Yes," he confirmed.

"And did he send you with an army?"

"I don't need an army."

"Mmm. Well," Stasia said, "I don't think I've been that difficult to find. Maybe you're not as good at your job as you think you are."

"For a woman in your current position, you're rather bold," the German officer commented.

"Obersturmbannführer Faust already accused me of the same," she told him in a bored voice. "You lot are nothing if not tedious."

A fleeting shadow of displeasure passed across his face. "You know, the obersturmbannführer almost didn't agree to steer you here," he said. "I don't think he truly appreciated just how very close he came to losing his life today."

"I could still remedy that."

The major smiled, though it came nowhere close to reaching his eyes. "I do believe you might just do that, given the opportunity. Unfortunately," he said, "your opportunities for such disagreeable tasks are over."

Stasia didn't reply because he didn't seem to expect one.

"Did you know not a single person I questioned could give me an accurate description of you? I couldn't even be sure that the girl who stumbled into Faust this afternoon in the square was you and not simply a clumsy whore in an absurd blue coat." He flicked a finger in the direction of Jan. "That was what he was here for. I needed him to recognize you."

Jan was still weeping, a soft, muffled sound.

Stasia's finger slid over the Webley's trigger guard and she considered her next words carefully. "Have you already killed his family?"

"I beg your pardon?"

"This man who betrayed me." She jerked her head in the direction of Jan. "He says you have his family. Have you already killed them?"

His full lips thinned. "I am not a complete barbarian."

She narrowed her eyes. "It's what I would have done."

"Bloodthirsty bitch," he said.

"Faust already accused me of that too. Like I said. Tedious."

This clearly angered the major. "Twenty-two," he snapped.

"Twenty-two?" Stasia repeated.

"Twenty-two of the Reich's finest men are dead at your hand."

Stasia smiled. "You missed three. Or maybe you're just bad at math. At the very least, you were a poor choice by the generalkommissar. And you never answered my question."

The major flushed. "Of course I killed his family," he snarled. "One cannot expect to inflict such grievous crimes on the Reich without suffering reprisals—"

Jan launched himself over the back of his chair with a roar of grief and rage. The attack, impossibly, seemed to surprise the major, and in the time it took for him to fumble for his sidearm, Stasia already had hers out of her pocket and was sprinting toward him. She slowed as she approached, trying to take aim, but Jan was in the way, and she didn't have a clear shot. The men who had been behind her were shouting now, and their boots pounded on the hard floor.

The report of a pistol ricocheted off the walls and reverberated off the ceilings. Jan stiffened and then slumped to the side, and

Stasia stumbled to a stop, found her target, and pulled the trigger. The major screamed, a terrible, gurgling noise, and staggered back before he crashed to his knees, his hands covering his face. She whirled and fired two more shots at the men closing in on her from behind, knowing that her aim was wild. But both of her pursuers twisted and dove to the side, affording her precious, precious seconds.

Stasia ran then, faster than she had ever run in her life, past the lifeless form of Jan and past the major, still on his knees. She had only the briefest of impressions of blood pulsing through the officer's fingers and splashing down onto the front of his uniform before she was by him, headed for the door at the north end of the transept that would disgorge her into the busy square. The possibility that she might yet escape dangled in front of her like a tiny, bright flame of hope. She reached the doors and fumbled to open them, the promise of freedom mere inches away.

Another shot crashed through the church, and Stasia was battered into the edge of the stone doorway. Her legs gave way beneath her, and she staggered to a knee, confused. Someone had punched her, or perhaps struck her with something heavy, yet there was no one near close enough to have reached her. Her body had gone numb and no longer seemed hers to control.

When she was twelve, she'd been kicked by her grandfather's gelding, a blow that she hadn't seen coming and one that had caught the side of her leg, close to her backside. She remembered lying in the dirt, stunned and frozen, while her grandfather yelled at her to get up unless she wanted to be stepped on or, worse, kicked again.

Her grandfather was yelling at her now. Or maybe it was her own voice that was pleading with her to get up. Numbness was quickly receding into a wave of pain, and a searing, white-hot agony that had started at the top of her left shoulder pierced down into her arm and chest. She thought she might vomit and turned her head to the side as she pulled herself back up with her right arm. She'd been shot, she registered dully. In the back of her shoulder. Or maybe her arm. It was hard to pinpoint the tide of pain.

Stasia had barely finished that thought when another shot rang out and a small shower of stone burst from the wall near her head. She fired her own weapon behind her desperately and yanked on the door, sending a new surge of agony crashing through her. She gasped and swayed, but the door opened, and she flung herself into the square, the Webley still clutched tightly in her hand. She braced herself, expecting to be tackled by waiting soldiers at any moment.

Except there were no soldiers. No police, no Gestapo, only startled pedestrians who stared at her with wary surprise, and if anything, moved out of her way with alacrity as she ran. Improbably, the major hadn't been lying. He had not come with an army to take her.

Each step was an exercise in pain unlike any she had felt before, but each step reminded her that she was still alive. She headed north across the eastern edge of the square, aiming for the relative safety of the narrow streets. There was too much empty space in the square. She would be too easy to see. Too easy to identify.

On the heels of that thought, Stasia yanked at the sleeve of her coat. She gritted her teeth against the sob of agony that escaped as she pulled her left arm through the sleeve. She tucked her revolver into the front of her dress. She had one bullet left, which would do nothing against the swarm of men who would no doubt descend on her shortly, but she couldn't leave it behind. What she did leave behind was the bright blue coat, letting it slide from her other arm and abandoning it on the street. They would be looking for a clumsy whore in an absurd blue coat. Not a woman in a charcoal dress. Maybe she could buy a few more precious seconds. There was a chance that she might survive this. There was a place where she might survive this. If only she could get there.

The winter air was cold against her skin, and her breath escaped in puffs. The light was also fading rapidly, gathering clouds rimmed by the sinking sun. Stasia forced herself to slow as she threaded her way northward away from the church along Smedestraat, even as the shouts she heard behind her in the square made her want to run. The street was narrow, the buildings on either side rising two or three floors, but there were fewer pedestrians here. She kept pace just behind a group of women carrying market bags, head down, doing her best to become invisible. A woman walking hurriedly would draw far less attention than one running hysterically. She tucked her left hand against her abdomen as spots danced before her eyes. She refused to faint. Blood was hot and sticky across her back, her dress no doubt soaked, but she was grateful for the dark color of the fabric that hopefully would make it less noticeable.

Stasia glanced behind her. There were police now, swarming across Grote Markt between the entrance to Smedestraat and the church, obviously summoned by the major, or if he was dead, his men. One of them held up her blue coat and shouted directions, sending officers scurrying in all directions. Four navy-coated men broke away from the pack and headed up the street toward her. Stasia turned away and increased her pace, pushing by the women with the shopping bags and ignoring their varied exclamations of annoyance and concern. She didn't look back, only kept her eyes focused ahead, searching for the right alley entrance. A commotion erupted behind her, men's voices urging haste and demanding information from the civilians they encountered. It would be only a matter of seconds before a finger was pointed in her direction.

She almost missed the alley, so focused was she on keeping her feet moving. She turned left and stumbled down the narrow passage. There were no pedestrians here she could blend in with. The peculiar, empty calm that she had felt in that church was long gone. She felt exposed and vulnerable, and she was terrified that the darkness crowding the edges of her vision was going to beat her to the building just ahead. She finally reached the door on the north corner of the building and pounded on it. The door opened a crack, a pale face peering out.

"Please," Stasia croaked, all of her efforts focused on breathing and not fainting. "I'm—"

The face blinked once, and then the door was yanked the rest of the way open, hands reaching to pull her inside. "I know who you are," the watchmaker said. "You are Lotte's friend. You delivered ration cards to us once."

"Yes." A stack of forged ration cards—more ration cards than a single Dutch family would ever need. Unless that family was hiding many extra mouths that required feeding.

Quick, sure hands steadied Stasia and examined the blood-soaked bodice of her dress. A soft voice issued a series of commands. A towel appeared and was pressed to her wound, and a bandage of some sort was wrapped tightly around her back and chest to keep it in place. An urgent, low discussion was conducted somewhere out of her line of sight. Stasia swayed and cursed herself for her weakness.

"I'm sorry," she whispered.

"Do not be sorry," the watchmaker told her. "You're in safe hands here. We will see to your wound but not yet. For now, you must come with me. And hurry."

Stasia nodded and followed the watchmaker through a door and up a set of tight, twisting stairs. Each step up became harder until Stasia found herself crawling up the last three. She staggered into a decidedly feminine bedroom that led directly off a tiny landing. It was small, with just enough room for a single bed and what looked like a tall, narrow linen cupboard. The stripes of delicate flowers printed on the papered walls swam before her eyes. It was quite possible that all of this would be for nothing. It was quite possible that she was going to die after all.

Downstairs, far below, someone else was pounding angrily on the door, a dull, ominous sound that echoed up through the house.

"I'm so sorry," Stasia said again, her entire being reduced to a world of hurt. It hurt to move, it hurt to breathe, and it hurt to think that she had brought wolves to the door of these people.

"Do not apologize," the watchmaker said. "Trust in God the way I do and know that everything will be all right. Now quickly. Let's get you hidden."

Stasia had no inclination to trust in anything or anyone other than the figure that had bent and was sliding the back panel out from under the bottom shelf of the cupboard.

"In you go. And whatever you hear, do not come out. Do not make a sound."

Stasia nodded and crawled forward, her left arm bound tightly against her ribs. She managed to wiggle through the opening that was barely bigger than her body, catching another sob in her throat as pain wracked every movement. The space she collapsed in, behind the cupboard and bedroom wall, was cramped and dark and stuffy.

And safe.

The watchmaker crouched, peering through the opening, and offered her a grim smile. "The Gestapo could search forever, and they will never find this. God is on our side."

Stasia nodded, unable to do anything else. She wondered if this extraordinary, devout, kind person would be hiding her if she'd confessed to being more than a ration card courier. Confessed who she really was. What she was being hunted for.

A hand reached through the small, square opening and gently squeezed Stasia's good arm. "You'll be all right. I promise."

Stasia looked into the pretty blue eyes of the pretty watchmaker. "Thank you," she whispered.

CHAPTER
17

Stasia

9 APRIL 1944
SOMEWHERE IN BELGIUM

Stasia leaned back against the stone wall, the surface rough and cool. In the absence of the sun, the night air was chilled, reminding her that summer was still distant. She drew deeply on her cigarette, the bright ember flaring and subsiding against the shroud of black surrounding her. High above, the waxing moon was partially obscured behind a curtain of broken cloud, and the handful of stars visible through that cloudy patchwork were only dull pinpoints against the velvet swath of sky, as if they had grown weary of battling the darkness. Or maybe that was just how they looked to Stasia. Maybe the stars were simply reflecting her own weariness. Her own hollowness.

Stasia tipped her head back. The clouds had now fully concealed the moon, plunging the garden into inky shadows. The air had gone still, as if holding its breath, the chalky scent of stone mingling with the earthy smell of vegetation pushing through the withered remnants of last year. The silence was absolute, and Stasia wasn't sure if she was relieved or resentful of that.

Heat bit at Stasia's fingers, and she dropped her spent cigarette. She shifted and ground the spark to nothingness beneath her heel, watching as it became no more than an unseen smear in the darkness. Fitting, she thought distantly. Everything that had once been bright ground to ash. Reduced to dust and forgotten as if it had never been—

She wasn't alone any longer.

Stasia remained still, listening to the soft crackle of leaves crushed beneath a heavy tread. The sound stopped, followed by a faint sigh of frustration and the unmistakable scratch of a lighter being struck. A spark jumped in the dark in front of her, only to extinguish immediately. It was struck twice more, and a flame sputtered and died, but the brief glow allowed Stasia to identify the individual who held it. It was the fair-haired man she had seen hidden in the shed behind the barn from her attic window two days ago, and again Stasia wasn't sure if she was relieved or resentful of his presence.

Relieved, she decided, after a moment. The silence had become deafening.

Stasia pushed herself away from the stone wall and winced as her shoulder protested. She slipped her own lighter from her pocket. With a flick of her fingers, a flame flared to life.

In the darkness, she heard the man stumble back, his feet tripping unevenly, followed by a muffled curse.

"May I?" she asked in French, unmoving. She was assaulted by the sudden memory of offering a different man, before he could even call himself such, the same courtesy in a sun-soaked garden.

Stasia recoiled. She'd thought she had banished those memories. Sealed all of those dreams and promises into the dark pit inside of her, never to be acknowledged again. Forgotten, they could not hurt her. Because despite the reassurances of many, time had never healed anything.

"Thank you." His voice was rough.

Stasia felt, rather than saw, his presence. His shape moved into the circle of light as he leaned forward to light his cigarette, looking up at her briefly as he did so.

He was painfully handsome and painfully young. Much younger than he had looked from her window. But beneath the fair hair that hung over his forehead, his eyes, pools of melted chocolate, were old. And tired. As old and as tired as she felt.

He inhaled, and the tip of his cigarette burned bright, and Stasia snapped her lighter closed. They were plunged back into darkness.

"I did not mean to startle you," she said.

"I thought I had the garden to myself." His French was precise but familiarly accented.

"I needed to see the sky again," she found herself telling him. "If only for a few moments."

"I understand."

Stasia could smell the acrid scent of the tobacco smoke. "I saw you when you first arrived. But I thought perhaps you had already gone."

"Another day, I'm told, before I can be moved again."

"It's dangerous right now. They're right to wait."

He seemed to consider that. "You are a...guest here as well as I," he said, and it wasn't really a question.

"Something like that." It wasn't really an answer. But it was the reason that she was still alive.

She had come close to dying in that tiny, hidden space behind a Haarlem wall. By the time the watchmaker and her family had felt it safe to come to fetch Stasia, she had lost a dangerous amount of blood. A doctor had been called, a nameless man who had worked silently and had asked no questions, and between them all, they had managed to save her life.

They had also arranged for her to flee Holland. Flee the Netherlands entirely, because to stay was too dangerous. A sketch of her was plastered all over Haarlem, they had told her days later, when she was able to sit up. The network of Resistance members that Stasia had operated within had been shattered, and eight of the ten cell members were either dead or arrested. She was, according to the police, wanted for forging and stealing ration cards, and there was a reward offered for anyone who might provide information that would lead to her capture. Exceptionally severe for a forger, they had mused, but then who could rationalize the motivations of the Nazis? The watchmaker's family were connected to people who in turn were connected to vast networks abroad who specialized in smuggling human lives, and while they had made the arrangements, they had never voiced the questions that she could see in their eyes. And Stasia had never told them.

She'd justified it to herself that her silence was for their own protection but that was a lie. The selfish and cowardly truth was that she couldn't bear to have these remarkable people, who had opened up their home and their hearts to help her, who possessed an extraordinary faith and goodness, learn who she really was. What she really was.

Stasia still wasn't sure that she had deserved any of their efforts and sacrifice.

"It's a beautiful night." The young man's voice floated out of the darkness. The tip of his cigarette flared, and she heard him exhale.

"Yes." She retreated back to the wall, lowering herself carefully to the ground.

"Not too cold."

"Yes."

"I—" He broke off with a barely audible curse, the glow of his cigarette jerking up and down as he fumbled with it in the darkness. "I'm terrible at rolling cigarettes, is what I am," he muttered to himself.

Another memory slithered out, and Stasia flinched. She looked up at the sky, wondering if perhaps the gods and the fates were executing their own brand of exquisite punishment by depositing this young man and the memories he incited in her path. If so, it was a punishment far more painful than any bullet.

The orange glow steadied, and he seemed to have fixed the cigarette's shortcomings.

The quiet stretched.

"I'll leave you to your peace," he said presently.

"Stay." The word was out before Stasia considered it. She closed her eyes. This was a mistake. She should tell him to retreat. Go and take with him all the painful memories that he seemed to provoke. Yet she remained silent.

Perhaps she was punishing herself.

"All right." There was a catch in his voice.

Somewhere above, the clouds parted, enough to create ghostly silhouettes. The young man moved and lowered himself beside her, his elbows braced on his legs as though he wasn't entirely comfortable.

Stasia studied his profile in the moonlight. "You're not with the Resistance."

"Depends how you look at it," he mumbled in Dutch. "The 167th seem to be under the impression we're resisting."

"I don't know what that is," she replied in Dutch.

His head snapped around to look at her. She could feel his gaze, and the weight of the questions behind it.

"Did I startle you again?" she asked.

"Yes."

"I apologize."

"Don't apologize." He looked away and took a long drag on his cigarette. "Where are you from?" he asked.

She hesitated.

"I'm sorry. I know I shouldn't ask—"

"Rotterdam." She found that she wanted to answer. Needed to answer. Why? Nothing good would come of this.

He was watching her again, as if considering his next question.

"Will you tell me what the 167th is?" she asked before he could ask the inevitable.

He leaned back against the wall, his shoulder brushing Stasia's. Out of habit, she started to shift. To move away, to keep her space and her distance. Yet something stopped her, and she stayed where she was, the heat from his body bleeding through the layers of their clothing to touch her skin.

"It's the Dutch RAF squadron," he said. "We bring down the buzz bombs launched by the fucking Nazi cowards." He seemed to catch himself. "Sorry."

"For what?"

"My language."

"I don't fucking care about your fucking language."

He made a muffled sound that might have been laughter. It was a strange, foreign sound—she couldn't honestly remember the last time she had heard anyone laugh.

"How?" she asked.

"How what?"

"How do you stop a pilotless bomb?"

"Shoot them out of the sky and try not to blow yourself up along with it. Tip them with your plane if you're out of ammunition or if the risk of detonation is too great."

"Tip them with your plane? What does that mean?"

She felt him shrug where his shoulder still touched hers. "Get your craft alongside and kiss the tip of the wing with yours. Do it right, and the bug veers off course and into a spiral. Every bug that goes down in an empty field or over the channel doesn't go down in the middle of London."

"And if you do it wrong?"

"You end up dead. Or hidden in a farm shed, sleeping on a cot, and relying on strangers to help you get back to England."

"How did you—" She stopped herself from asking the questions she knew he wouldn't want to answer. Probably shouldn't answer.

"Damaged plane, ditched in the channel. Fisherman pulled me out." His cigarette flared again. "Should've died," he mused on a cloud of smoke. He sounded desolate, as if that was a fact and not conjecture.

"But you didn't."

"I didn't," he agreed. "I'm sorry."

"For not dying?"

"For ruining your peaceful evening with such maudlin thoughts. I find myself in a moonlit yard with a beautiful woman. I should be charming you with clever, witty words."

"I'm not easily charmed. With words or otherwise. And stop apologizing."

He dropped his head, his pale hair falling over his forehead in strands of silver. "I hate it."

"You'll have to be more specific. There's a lot to hate right now."

"Every time I go up there, I'm tempting God, or fate, or whatever is left to believe in. Every time I'm back on the ground and crawling out of that cockpit, I don't feel relieved or satisfied. I feel..." He stopped, as if searching for the right word.

"Guilty," Stasia whispered.

"Yes." His head swiveled toward her.

Something stirred deep inside, something beneath the numb emptiness. It was as if under the cloak of darkness, anonymity, and the knowledge that this moment would be fleeting, the protective buffer of anger and hate she had so carefully cultivated was allowed to slip.

Stasia rested her head back against the stone. "You feel guilty that you continue to survive when others have not."

"Yes." The glowing tip of his cigarette dropped to the ground, extinguished immediately. "Why? Why do I continue to live and others—better men than me, men who are husbands and fathers—don't?" For the first time in the conversation, he sounded as young as he really was.

"I don't have an answer for you. No one will have an answer for you. Not a real one, anyway."

"But you know." He was still watching her, and Stasia wondered what he saw. "You know how it feels."

"Yes." She was seized by the sudden, inexplicable desire to reach out and touch him. "Every day, I wonder why I was allowed to live while better people than me died."

"There was a moment after I landed in the water when I—" He stopped abruptly.

"Wondered if it would hurt less to just give up?" Stasia asked quietly.

He drew in a sharp breath and dropped his head farther, pressing his forehead into his palms. "Admitting that makes me ashamed." He shook his head. "I don't know why I'm telling you all of this," he murmured. "I don't even know your name."

"That's why." Stasia did touch him then, the solid muscle of his forearm warm beneath her fingertips.

He went still.

"I should have died too," Stasia told him. "But people, better people than I, made sure I did not. And now I'm here, in this place, in this time, not because I think I deserve to live but because I cannot forsake their actions."

"So you will keep fighting."

"So I will keep fighting." Stasia withdrew her hand but he lifted his head and caught her fingers in his.

His hands were rough and calloused and gentle. "Where will you go?"

"Home."

"Rotterdam?"

"No." She would return to Normandy. Had insisted on it, to the consternation of those who asserted that England would be far safer. She didn't want safe. She wanted purpose.

"Tell me where you are from. Before you left to fly planes for the RAF," she said before he could ask any more questions.

"Dordrecht."

"Do you have family there still?"

His grip tightened. "No. They're gone." He took a ragged breath. "Yours?"

"Gone." She abhorred that word. "What about a sweetheart?"

He ducked his head and shook it, staring down at their inter-twined hands. "No."

"I thought pilots had women hanging off them like crystals on a chandelier." She nudged him with her shoulder.

His teeth flashed white in the gloom before disappearing

again. "My squadron likes to think so. I'm told I'm a crushing disappointment to them." He seemed to sober. "I just...could never enjoy the mess parties or the dances. I don't go. They feel like nothing more than a forced gathering of gaiety followed by a forced assembly of goodbyes."

She was assailed by the image of Nicolas kneeling before her, his heart on his sleeve and a ring in his fingers. The memory made her double over in a haze of grief and pain. "Not getting a chance to say goodbye is worse. Especially when—" She didn't trust her voice to go on.

"Especially when he was the love of your life," he finished for her.

Goddamn his perception. "Yes."

"I'm sorry."

Stasia shook her head, feeling perilously close to tears, which made her angry all over again. "I told you to stop apologizing," she said unevenly. "I loved him and lost him and nothing can ever change that. He's gone." That damn, unbearable word again.

"Does it make me selfish?" he asked quietly. "To want what you had? Even knowing that it too will be lost? That I will make promises that I won't be able to keep? That there will come a day when I don't come back?"

"Yes," she snapped. "It does." She scrubbed at her eyes furiously. "No one lives happily ever after. Do not make someone love you and then leave."

His fingers tightened around hers. "Then you regret it?"

"What?" Her breath hitched.

"I want to know if you regret it. Regret loving him."

It was a horrible question, one that she had avoided and one that came with a blinding crush of sorrow. Her initial impulse was to stand and retreat and leave this man and his awful question in the darkness. Instead, perversely, she compelled herself to consider it. She turned it over and over in her mind and forced herself to examine the unwavering agony of the what-ifs and the razor edges of what-might-have-beens. It was enough to leave whatever was left of her soul in bloody ribbons.

"I regret that I can no longer say what I should have said," she finally said into the night. "I regret that I can't say goodbye the way I should have." Something cracked inside her as the truth escaped. "But I will never, ever regret loving him."

The man beside her didn't say anything right away, merely slid his fingers over hers as if testing their strength. "I envy you that," he whispered at last.

A bitter sound caught in her throat. "I am not to be envied."

"But—"

"I am not to be envied," she repeated, her words cold and hard. "Because while I fell in love with a man who was real and imperfect and good, he fell in love with an illusion."

He started to shake his head. "You are—"

"Don't. Don't speak of what you don't know." It had been a mistake to stay here with this stranger, like this, in the quiet. It was all too much. Too much honesty, too much truth. Too many reminders of what had been lost. "You don't know who I am. What I am."

Stasia yanked her hand from his.

"Stay," he whispered. "Please."

"I can't. I have nothing left to offer you. Nothing good." She clambered to her feet and smoothed her palms over the rough fabric of her trousers. Her hands were shaking. She turned and edged away, hating herself for her cowardice.

"I should have."

She paused, her back to him. "Should have what?"

"Danced. Fallen in love with someone real and imperfect and good."

She heard him get to his feet.

"Dance with me," he said quietly.

Stasia closed her eyes, motionless. "You don't want to dance with me—"

"Don't." He cut her off, his voice rough. "Don't speak of what you don't know." He used her words. "Dance with me," he asked again.

Stasia opened her eyes and gazed up at the stars, still struggling to be seen against the darkness, and realized that she had been wrong. She did have something to offer this pilot who had lived a thousand lifetimes in the cockpit of a plane alone in the skies, and yet had not lived at all.

She turned slowly, looking up at him. His features were carved in silver and shadow.

Around them, the air swirled cool and heavy, the silence broken only by the sound of a lone owl calling in the distance. Slowly, Stasia put her hands on his chest, her palms flat against the thin fabric of his shirt. His chest rose and fell in shallow breaths beneath her touch.

One of his hands caught hers, another sliding over her back to draw her closer to him, strong and steady. He led, and she followed to the music of the breeze. She rested her cheek against his chest, listening to the steady beat of his heart. It was only after a minute that she realized she was crying silently, her tears soaking into his shirt, and no matter how much she fought it, she couldn't seem to stop. He didn't release her but kept her tucked tightly against him.

At some point, her tears subsided into an occasional hiccupping breath. At some point, they stopped moving and simply stood in the garden.

"He asked me to marry him," she whispered into his chest. "I thought we had time."

His heart kept beating beneath her ear, unbroken and constant.

"You remind me of him."

He didn't say anything.

Stasia looked up, suddenly and unbearably ashamed. This was something that she had thought to offer him. Something that she could give him, and yet she hadn't managed even that. Somehow this had become about her. "I'm sorry. That wasn't...I didn't mean to—"

He cut her words off with a kiss, a gesture so gentle and soft that her eyes burned anew, even as she gave herself over to his touch.

"I don't want you to apologize," he whispered against her lips. "I want you to be able to say goodbye."

Stasia stilled. He drew back, his eyes never leaving hers in the pale, silver light. She understood what he was offering her. What they were offering each other.

"Close your eyes," he said, and Stasia obeyed.

With a fluid motion, the pilot shifted and caught her up in his arms. She wrapped her hands around his neck, and he carried her through the garden, pushing open the door to the shed with his shoulder and laying her down on his cot.

And somewhere in the night, their bodies curled against each other, Stasia finally said goodbye to Nicolas.

CHAPTER

18

Nicolas

The flag was blue.

It fluttered lethargically near the base of the flagpole attached to the roof of the building across the street, attended by a single, helmeted man standing next to it. Nicolas had arrived at the designated building with his team at seven o'clock in the morning, and in the quarter hour they had been waiting in the briefing room on the top floor, the flag had yet to be raised. Instead, the helmeted man stood and stared alternately at the sky and the rope in his hand.

"Do you suppose he's simpleminded?" Major Lewis Franklin asked as he peered out the window at the man gawking at the blanket of clouds drifting across the brightening sky.

"What?" Nicolas tipped back in his chair.

Franklin gestured across the street at the man still standing motionless. "Grew up with a fella back in Minnesota who fell out of a tree when he was six and landed on his head. Wasn't ever right again after that. When he got older, folk would hire him to shovel snow but you had to go out to remind him from time to time to keep shovelling. Otherwise, you'd find him just leaning on his shovel staring into space. Like that."

The third man in the room, Lieutenant Thatcher, shuffled around Nicolas and elbowed Franklin out of the way. "He's an air raid warden, chief. He raises the blue flag when he sees a buzz bomb."

Franklin's thick brows disappeared beneath the waves of brown hair that flopped over his forehead. "Why?"

"As a warning to the neighbourhood." Roy Thatcher crossed his arms.

"Who the hell has time to watch a man standing on the roof? And by the time that warden sees a doodlebug buzzing in, it's too late to—"

The warden suddenly started hauling up the flag, and in the distance, Nicolas heard the faint puttering of a buzz bomb engine before it coughed and died, returning the skies to silence. A heartbeat later, a muted thump echoed from the distance, and over the roofs of the buildings, a faint haze of smoke and dust rose.

The warden began lowering the flag again with slow, mechanical movements.

"Jesus." Franklin moved closer to stare at the cloud of smoke. His massive shoulders blocked almost the entire window.

"I might suggest that a capable man might be better stationed," Nicolas said from his chair.

Thatcher sighed and wandered back to the table. He pulled out a chair and sat down next to Nicolas. "It's a directive from the Civil Defence Authority. For morale, you see? To convince Londoners that every precaution is being taken."

"Are you convinced?" Nicolas asked wryly.

"Quite."

"I heard the flyboys shoot them bombs out of the air," Franklin said, turning from the window.

"I doubt that," Thatcher said.

"It's true. Heard it's like hunting ducks from a plane."

"Ducks don't detonate," Nicolas said.

Thatcher seemed to find that amusing. He reached into his pocket and withdrew his cigarettes with his long, elegant fingers.

Nicolas still didn't much like *les Anglais* but he found that he very much liked the Englishman who held the position of radioman on their team. Roy Thatcher reminded Nicolas of the old-fashioned portraits he had seen in the rooms of Château de Montessaire—stern-looking men with aristocratic countenances and regal bearings. He'd asked the lieutenant once at dinner if he was a lord of something. Thatcher had only smiled an enigmatic smile and asked Nicolas to pass him the salt.

Franklin left the window and paced to the door. "The colonel is late."

Thatcher checked his watch, crossed his legs, and lit his cigarette. "Mmm."

"The colonel is only late if you're a general," Nicolas said, making himself comfortable again. He considered the maps of France that had been pinned to the wall opposite, wondering what purpose they served.

Franklin paced back to the window like a caged bull. "If we don't get our orders today, I'm going to join that man up there on the roof with something more effective than a flag to knock those damn bombs out of the sky—"

The door banged open, and Nicolas sprung to his feet. Thatcher uncrossed his legs and stood more leisurely.

Colonel Giroux hustled in, his cotton-ball white hair swaying around the sides of his head. He was carrying a scarred briefcase that he placed on the table with a loud thump and then retreated behind the table and waved the Jedburgh team in the direction of the chairs on the other side. Nicolas had a peculiar sense of déjà vu, only now the stakes were undoubtedly far higher than the first time he had met with the colonel in London.

He resumed his seat beside Thatcher while Franklin sat on the edge of the chair on the far side. The Englishman smoked, and the American drummed his fingers on the table. Through the window, behind the colonel, Nicolas could still see the blue flag and the air warden standing at attention.

"*Bien.*" Giroux fixed Franklin with a level stare over the rims of his small round spectacles. "Major Lewis Franklin, yes? Chief of the Hubert team?"

"Yes sir." Franklin inclined his head in the direction of the two men sitting beside him. "Lieutenant Roy Thatcher, radio operator, and Captain Thomas Phillipe, deputy chief."

Giroux contemplated Nicolas. "Yes, yes, the French naval engineer. I remember."

The blue flag caught Nicolas's eye as it began inching up the flagpole again.

Giroux opened the briefcase, and a landslide of maps and documents skated across the table. Nicolas stopped one with his finger before it slid into his lap.

The noisy puttering of a buzz bomb filtered through the window. Nicolas tensed.

"*Bien,*" said the colonel, retrieving the runaways like a mother hen collecting chicks. He seemed to be ignoring the sound of the approaching bomb. "You're anxious, I'm sure, for your orders," he said.

"Have been since the end of April. It's almost June." Franklin eyed the blue flag and rested his meaty hands on his knees.

The puttering stopped. Thatcher's cigarette paused midway to his lips.

"A week," the colonel said, oblivious. "You'll be dropped within a week, conditions allowing." His fountain pen appeared and he stabbed at a map in the pile of documents. "Normandy."

A thumping crash shook the building. A faint shower of dust drifted from the ceiling. The blue flag inched back down. Thatcher's cigarette resumed its travels. Franklin cleared his throat and focused on the map.

"Bien." The colonel continued blithely. "You understand this is a most dangerous drop?"

"We've been trained for nothing less," Franklin assured the colonel. "And our team is ready."

"Bien." The colonel shoved his spectacles up the bridge of his nose and peered at the Jeds. "Before we go further, I must pause to remind you that current practice by the Germans is to shoot any commando-type personnel on sight, whether or not you are in uniform, which of course is in direct violation of the Geneva Convention." He shrugged. "Not that the SS has ever adhered to that. They'll shoot you for fun. Once you are on the ground, your uniform will be good for impressing the maquisards and not much else, understood?"

"Understood." Nicolas answered for his teammates. This was nothing they did not already know.

Behind Giroux, the blue flag was once again jerking its way upward.

The colonel flipped through a small stack of documents and pulled one out with a flourish. "Our most current intelligence report for your target area." He frowned at the neatly typed lines. "Normandy is missing the cover that the south has. No mountains to hide in. Makes it very difficult for the maquisards here. Flat farmland."

Another droning putter was building, this one sounding much closer.

The end of the colonel's pen descended with a crack onto the tabletop. "But the area has forests. Lots of forest. Which is where many of the local maquisards who haven't already been arrested or shot can be found." He grimaced and consulted the document in his hand. "The report indicates that their networks are dis-organized, their leaders inexperienced and shambolic, and they have very limited resources. But they are willing to fight." He had to shout his last sentence over the puttering whine above.

The sound stopped.

The colonel opened his mouth as if to speak and then changed his mind and held up a finger.

Nicolas held his breath. He flinched anyway when the crash resounded. The building shook, and the glass in the window cracked but did not break. A new shower of plaster dust rained down on the room.

"Jesus." Franklin had stood.

The colonel peered at him over the top of his spectacles, and the American lowered himself back to his chair.

The blue flag slid back down the pole.

"Bien." The colonel dropped his hand. "Questions?" he asked the men.

Nicolas blinked.

"Is it always like this?" Franklin asked.

"Like this?" Giroux seemed confused.

"The bombs."

"Oh." The colonel shrugged. "Depends on the day, I suppose."

He waved his hand in a gesture of faint irritation. "Questions about your mission thus far?"

"This report," Nicolas asked, "how do we know it's accurate?"

"We had an operative on the ground in February who was able to provide an assessment."

"And you trust this person?" Franklin asked.

"Implicitly." He set the document aside and stood. "Your mission is divided into two objectives. The first is to make contact with the Resistance, take command, help them organize, and provide us with a detailed list of resources that you think you'll need for the weeks that follow. You will, of course, be dropped with a significant complement of weapons and explosives for use in your second, more immediate objective."

"And the second objective being?" Thatcher asked. A curl of smoke rose from his cigarette to vanish above his head.

"Sabotage of all major communication centers and infrastructure in the area to eliminate or reduce the ability of the German's wire transmission capabilities."

"You want to force them to use wireless transmissions." Nicolas understood immediately.

"I want them to not be able to communicate at all," Giroux spat, "but yes, when they do communicate, we'd like to make it difficult, and we'd like to force the use of wireless transmissions."

"That we can listen to."

"*Bien.* We are getting good at that, I am told by people here in London."

"What about bridges? Rail lines? Roads?" Franklin leaned forward.

"Not your priority. Not at first." He looked at Thatcher. "You will, of course, be in regular radio contact. You will be kept apprised of changes and will report your progress."

The team's radio operator nodded. "Of course."

"The Gestapo shot the leaders of the Maquis to the south of Rouen where we used to conduct our drops. There are no longer reception committees operating there." He moved toward the maps pinned to the wall and jabbed his pen at a spot near the center of the closest one. "You will be dropped here instead. West of Rouen. In this loop of the Seine."

Nicolas stared at the map where the pen tip had stuck, a shock of recognition travelling through him.

"Your team was selected for this mission because of Captain Phillipe." Giroux's pen was now stabbed in Nicolas's direction. "Specifically due to my understanding that he should be quite familiar with the geography of the area. All those early interviews we conducted were not for nothing, you know."

Nicolas ignored the speculative gazes of Franklin and Thatcher, his eyes still riveted on the map and the familiar terrain.

"There will be a reception committee waiting for you. The river is a bit of a hazard but makes a clear landmark for the pilots, and it is unlikely you'll find yourself dropped on top of a church spire." Giroux dragged his pen across the map. "After you land, you will head east and make contact with the Maquis that currently operates out of the forests here." The colonel glanced back. *"Bien?"*

"Bien," Nicolas replied faintly.

"Your primary target will be the communication headquarters southwest of Rouen currently used by the Wehrmacht." The tip of the pen slid south. "We want it inoperable, understood?"

"Inoperable?" Franklin asked.

"Inoperable." The colonel abandoned the map and returned to the table. He rifled through the stack of documents and yanked out a black-and-white photo. He slapped it on the table in front of Franklin. "This was taken by our operative in February. It is your target."

Behind Giroux, the blue flag was making another ascent up its pole.

"Fancy-looking place," the American commented. "Shame to destroy it."

The uneven buzz of another bomb became audible in the distance.

"Not a fancy-looking place, a dangerous-looking place," Giroux snapped. "It keeps every Nazi on the entire northeast coast of France and the interior connected to the decision makers in Paris and Berlin. It's heavily guarded for that reason. The communication hub is located in the lower northwest quadrant of the building. No photos or sketches though to tell us what that might look like inside. All indications suggest that some of the higher-ranking officers are billeted there. Elimination of any or all of these officers in the process is desirable. Chaos and destruction, yes?"

The droning noise became more insistent as the bomb coughed and choked its way nearer. The flag was at the top of the pole now, waving forlornly in the wind.

"Entrances will most likely have men posted to monitor any-one in and out. Expect additional men on the grounds. Billeting officers appear to be lodged on the first floor. If you're lucky, you'll find a local with some knowledge. It's possible the Maquis in the area may be able to help with that."

Franklin slid the photo to Thatcher, who studied it as he casually stubbed out his cigarette on the sole of his shoe. The bomb puttered above them.

"Destroy this Nazi communication center by any and all means. I don't care if you have to burn it to the ground but it cannot be operational forty-eight hours after you set foot in Normandy." Giroux's pen whacked the top of his briefcase. "Are we clear?"

"Crystal," said Roy Thatcher pleasantly.

He slid the photo along the table.

Nicolas picked up the black-and-white image.

The buzz and puttering outside above their heads stopped.

In the foreground of the photo, a dark-colored vehicle was parked, the small Nazi flag attached to the front fender easily visible. A handful of German soldiers stood casually on the grounds, rifles slung over the shoulders of their greatcoats. In the background, a château sprawled, neat rows of arched windows centered by a pair of tall wooden doors. Two bulky chimneys were easily visible on each end, and dormer windows jutted out from the slate roof.

The buzz bomb detonated then. The glass in the window shattered and fell in a tinkling cascade of shards. A crack appeared in the corner of the wall by the maps of France. The documents by the colonel's briefcase toppled to the floor in a flurry of white.

Franklin cursed, and Thatcher lit a new cigarette.

Outside, the blue flag descended again.

And Nicolas gently wiped the new layer of dust from the photo of Château de Montessaire.

CHAPTER

19

Isabelle

They had agreed to meet at the château.

Seeing the drawing by a woman known only as Briar Rose had been a shock. Not only because of its familiarity but because of the theories and possibilities that it had birthed. Implausible theories and questionable possibilities that Isabelle struggled to believe—yet the drawing was too real for her to dismiss. And so she had made some calls, starting with the woman who was still in possession of the original de Montessaire documents at the Caen Normandie Memorial Museum.

Lise had been curious when Isabelle had called her, asking after the legend of Briar Rose. Yes, the historian and curator had said, she was familiar with the legend. No, she confessed, she hadn't ever dug into the myth. Yes, she agreed, the list of apparent deceased and missing Nazi officers with *Dornröschen* written on the bottom was of interest. And yes, she insisted adamantly, it would be her pleasure to do a little research.

And now, a month later, Lise was back at the château to show Isabelle and Emilie what she had found.

"Sorry I'm late." Emilie was hurrying up the drive to join Isabelle on the front steps of the château.

"You're early, actually," Isabelle reassured her.

Emilie eyed the unfamiliar Fiat parked next to her truck in the drive. "Do you think your historian found anything?"

"I don't think she would have insisted on coming all the way to de Montessaire if she hadn't." Isabelle's stomach had been in a peculiar knot all day.

"I can't believe we're still thinking what we're thinking."

"I'm trying not to think anything until we speak to Lise," Isabelle replied.

"Right." Emilie stopped in front of the château's wide doors. "It's really nice of her to do this."

"It is." Isabelle nodded. "We've developed a good system over the years. I give her anything of historic significance that I come across during my projects, specifically anything related to either world wars, and she makes sure that it gets into the right hands for preservation, whether that is in Caen or Paris or farther afield. In return, she helps me with any historical queries. Even if they are . . ."

"Strange?"

"I was going to say insane, but either works." She paused. "But speaking of Paris, I was wondering if you and I could take a look at the garden before you go back? Come up with some ideas for it?"

Emilie fidgeted. "Actually," she said, "I was thinking that maybe I would stay here until the end of summer. That we could get a start on the garden together."

"Oh." Isabelle was pleasantly surprised. "I'd like that." She hesitated and then decided that there was no point avoiding the subject. "What about Marcus?" Emilie hadn't mentioned him again since she had made her abrupt confession in the middle of the tavern in Val-de-la-Haye.

"He's moved out. So there is no one waiting for me in my flat."

"Oh." Isabelle hesitated again. "I'm sorry."

"Don't be."

"How are you feeling?"

"I don't know. Humiliated. I was supposed to have the perfect life, you know? I had my perfect happy-ever-after all mapped out from the very beginning. Perfect job, perfect husband, perfect apartment. All the right circles, all the right parties, all the right connections."

"I don't think there is such a thing as a perfect life."

"You're probably right. I'm angry too. Disappointed. But maybe more with myself."

"At yourself?" Isabelle was indignant. "You can't blame yourself for his infidelity—"

"No, I'm not angry at myself for that. He waited until I left to slink off like a coward. That's on him, not me. No, I'm angry and disappointed in myself for not realizing sooner just how little I would actually miss him." She paused. "I don't know. Maybe it's because I've been so busy here. Maybe it's because we never really saw much of each other anyway." She made a face. "I'm angry at myself for wasting years."

Isabelle leaned against the heavy wood door. "I don't think they were wasted. A man doesn't define you or your accomplishments. And you've accomplished a lot."

"Thanks." Emilie looked almost embarrassed.

"What about your firm? Don't you need to be there?" Isabelle asked carefully.

Emilie played with the cuff of her sleeve. "I have two very talented and very ambitious architects who are running our firm in my absence."

"Our?"

"They've accepted my offer of partnership. Both have presented me with some very good ideas about where our firm could go. Some key areas we could expand into—" Emilie glanced at Isabelle. "Oh, don't look so smug. I'd rather keep them on my team than be forced to compete against them."

"Mmm. Right. Of course."

"It's a very competitive market," Emilie insisted.

"I'm sure it is. And I'm sure you are creating something amazing," Isabelle told her. "This is only the beginning. I know it."

"I am excited to see what they can do," Emilie admitted. "Though it's a little nerve-wracking. Giving up that control, I mean."

"Well, I'm glad to see you happy again. Embrace the journey, wherever it takes you. You have nothing to prove to anyone. Certainly not to a man like Marcus."

Emilie's smile slipped, and a crease appeared between her brows. "My husband accused me of loving my work more than him. I don't know that he was wrong."

Isabelle remained quiet.

"Maybe you had it right all along, Izz. To never get married. Remain a one-woman show."

"I didn't plan that. It just ... there was never the opportunity, I guess. It's not a complaint. And maybe it was for the best anyway." She shrugged. "I stayed. You left. You made opportunity for yourself. I didn't."

"You've made plenty of opportunity for yourself here. Everyone knows you. Respects you."

Isabelle shrugged again.

"I should have come home." Emilie was looking down at the toe of her work boot. "When Dad had his stroke."

"Yes. You should have."

"It's just, you fit in here. I never did."

"That's not true. That's just an excuse, I think."

"An excuse?" Emilie bristled.

"To not deal with hard things." Isabelle rested her head against the edge of the door. "Tell me I'm wrong."

"Maybe." Emilie looked away. "Or maybe you're just jealous."

"I am jealous," Isabelle told her honestly. "On some days. Some days I wish my job were my only responsibility. Some days I wish I had left too."

"You're not dead. You can still go, you know."

"And who looks after the farm? Who helps Mom and Dad—"

"Now who's using excuses?" Emilie asked. "You never once asked for help."

"I shouldn't need to."

"Maybe. Maybe I didn't step up when I needed to. But I can't read your mind either. I can't help if I don't know that you need it."

"Would you have come home?" Isabelle demanded. "If I had asked?"

Emilie shifted. "Yes. I would have." She glanced at Isabelle. "I probably would have been insufferable, but I would have come."

"I would have taken insufferable," Isabelle told her. "Insufferable would have been so much better than alone."

"Well, I'm here now."

But for how long? Isabelle wanted to ask but didn't. She suspected that she didn't really want to know the answer. Her fingers tightened on the door. "Shall we go in?" she asked instead.

Emilie nodded, and both women headed into the building.

The air in the château no longer had the scent of disuse but the intoxicating smell of cut wood and fresh plaster and new paint that Isabelle always associated with a successful project. The walls that she passed had been stripped and restored, and the spaces had gone from dark and worn to bright and welcoming. She could already imagine what it would look like once they started placing furniture.

"Izz."

Isabelle stopped in the hall and turned.

Emilie looked uncharacteristically uncomfortable. "Do you think Mom and Dad would be okay if I stayed with them? With you? While I'm here?"

Isabelle pursed her lips. "What's wrong with the hotel in Rouen?"

"Nothing. It's just . . . never mind." She made to push by Isabelle.

"Yes," Isabelle said. "They would like it very much if you stayed with them. They miss you."

"Oh. Good. Maybe I could help out some on the farm."

"That would be nice."

Emilie lifted her chin. "And you? Is it okay if I stay with you?"

Isabelle took a deep breath. "I'd like that."

★ ★ ★

Isabelle's favourite room was still the library, its windows now fully restored and repaired, the stone floor scoured and buffed, and the bookcases cleaned and polished. It was here that she found Lise and Luc, the historian already at the massive ebony desk and Luc pacing by the windows.

"Lise," Isabelle said warmly.

The petite woman holding court in de Montessaire's library was dressed in a brightly colored blouse, slim skirt, and plentiful jewelry, all with a bohemian flair. "I apologize," Lise looked up from her laptop, set in the center of a neatly organized blizzard of documents that covered the surface of the desk. "I'm early. Monsieur Legassé was kind enough to show me in. And give me a bit of a tour of the château. I hope you don't mind."

"Of course not. And please don't apologize. We are so grateful for both your expertise and your time. I haven't forgotten it's your day off."

Lise waved a hand, the silver bangles at her wrists catching the sunlight streaming through the library windows. "It's a gorgeous day for a drive. And I wanted to see what you've done with the château since the last time I saw it. It's extraordinary. And beautiful."

"It has the best working on it," Luc told her with a wink in Isabelle's direction.

"Which includes you," Isabelle told him.

Lise looked back and forth between them with a small smile. "Ah. Well, I knew it was in good hands. It does my heart good to see the history in this country curated with such care."

Emilie was eyeing the arrangement of documents on the desk. "What's all this?"

Lise's face lit up. "I'm glad you asked. Please, take a seat. Let me show you what I've found."

"So you found something about Briar Rose?" Luc asked.

She inclined her head. "Yes and no."

"Sounds intriguing," Isabelle said lightly. She fetched three stools from near the hearth.

Luc waved off her offer. "I can't sit for this," he said. "It's too exciting."

Lise laughed while Isabelle and Emilie both sat and watched
as Luc resumed his pacing by the windows.

"Let's start with the drawing you sent me. The one alleged
to have been drawn by Briar Rose." She slid a copy of Renaud
Dubois's drawing of his twelve-year-old self on the back of a
griffin. "It is exceptional. And I see what you were referring to
regarding this library and the sculptures in it." Lise looked at the
drawing and back up at the griffins watching the proceedings
silently from their perches on either side of the hearth.

"They're the same," Luc paused his pacing just long enough
to interject. "The griffins in the drawing are the same ones from
the library."

"I don't disagree." Lise adjusted her glasses and tucked a
strand of chestnut hair behind her ear. "It's not unreasonable to
think that whoever drew this sketch had seen those sculptures,
at least at some point in time. It does not, however, tell us who
actually drew it. There is no name, no date, nothing included
in this sketch that offers us anything more than assumptions and
guesses."

Isabelle and Emilie exchanged glances. They had agreed to
wait to show Lise the drawing from their great-grandmother
until they heard the historian out.

"Now, I'm certainly familiar with the local legend of Briar
Rose," Lise told them. "It's in the vein of the histories of Simone
Segouin, Lucie Aubrac, or Madeleine Truel. But the one thing
that those women have that your Briar Rose does not is proof.
Records. Photos. Some sort of documentation of their efforts,
where they came from, who they were, how they fought, and
what happened to them." She set the drawing down gently on
the desk. "More than a beautiful sketch."

"What about the word of Monsieur Dubois?"

"Not an unreasonable question," Lise acknowledged. "I have no doubt that a woman blessed a young boy with an act of kindness. Who she really was, though, is much harder to prove. She could have been anyone from anywhere. She would not have been the only displaced person in Europe during those tumultuous years."

"So that's it?" Luc asked from the windows. "Just another dead end?"

Lise peered over the top of her laptop. "Hardly."

Isabelle leaned forward. "What does hardly mean?"

"It means that I expanded my search and reached out to a few of my colleagues at different museums and universities." She picked up the list of dead and missing Nazi officers that Isabelle had shown to Dubois. "While there is no concrete proof to be found in France about a Resistance operative called Briar Rose, there is substantial documentation about a Dutch Resistance operative who went by the name Rose." She tapped her polished fingernail against the bottom of the page. "Or *Dornröschen*, as it is recorded in various German records."

"Dutch," Isabelle repeated faintly, wondering if she had heard that right.

"Yes," replied Lise, spinning her laptop so that Isabelle and Emilie could see the screen. "Ironically, she is referred to as a ghost in more than one document." On the screen was a collection of scanned documents that looked like reports of some kind. Some were typed, some were written in cramped handwriting, but all had the Reichsadler in their headers.

"These are a collection of reports generated from June 1943 to February 1944. All were written by or to Sturmbannführer Otto Ferdinand Diekmann, a major in the SS. It's the same handwriting and same initials that are on the bottom of this list." She gestured at the list of missing and dead officers still in her hand.

"The name is not familiar," Emilie said from her stool. "Was he important?"

"Not so much as the man he reported to." Lise tapped on a key, and the screen changed to reveal a black-and-white photo of a grey-clad, middle-aged, square-jawed man with a high forehead and receding hairline. "This was Diekmann's boss, generalkommisar für das Sicherheitswesen, Hanns Albin Rauter."

"Holy sh—" Luc stopped in his tracks.

Three sets of eyes turned to stare at him.

Luc cleared his throat. "Rauter was a convicted war criminal. Executed by a firing squad after the war. The location of his grave is still secret."

"Yes," agreed Lise, raising a shapely eyebrow. "I'm impressed."

"Sorry. Hobby of mine. And didn't mean to interrupt," he said.

"Good heavens, don't apologize," Lise said. "You're right. Rauter was the highest-ranking SS officer in the Netherlands during the occupation and reported directly to Himmler. During his tenure, Rauter had over three hundred thousand Dutchmen deported to forced labour camps and well over a hundred thousand Jews deported to concentration and extermination camps." She put an elbow on the edge of the desk. "The Netherlands had the highest number of Jewish victims in Western Europe. Three-quarters of the Dutch Jewish population was killed, and Rauter was a critical facilitator of that." She typed another key. A photo of the clear execution of four civilians by a German firing squad appeared. "As commander of the police, Rauter was also responsible for the repression, persecution, and retaliation of and against the Dutch Resistance."

"So what are you telling us?" Isabelle asked.

"That all of these reports—" the screen full of SS reports reappeared "—are a series of communications between Rauter and Diekmann regarding a Dutch Resistance fighter referred to sometimes as Rose and sometimes as Dornröschen, or, as you know, Little Briar Rose. Diekmann was handpicked by Rauter to hunt and exterminate this particular Resistance operative. There is correspondence here that registers the arrest and subsequent interrogation of Dutch individuals believed to be a part of her Resistance cell. And by interrogation, I mean torture. Everyone arrested died shortly after." She slid the list across the desk toward Isabelle. "This list is exactly what it appears to be. A list of Nazi officers in occupied Netherlands, almost all in Amsterdam and Haarlem, who went missing or were presumed dead and whose demise was attributed to this particular woman, whoever she was."

Isabelle swallowed. "Did you find a photo? Of this Resistance operative?" she asked, her voice sounding off even in her own ears. It was a piece of the puzzle that seemed, on the surface, to fit logistically, yet in so many other ways seemed entirely implausible.

Troubled, Isabelle tried to imagine her great-gran systematically killing Nazis. She tried to reconcile the gentle, soft-spoken woman she had known her entire life with the image of a cold, methodical killer and failed. But then, Isabelle reflected, she had not known her great-gran during the war.

"No," Lise answered her question. "Not one photo. Various descriptions, though none of them consistent. Whoever she was, she was clever. And careful."

"Was she ever caught?" Luc asked the next obvious question. "Or killed?"

Lise pushed her glasses up on her head. "There is no report

written by Diekmann that confirmed he had either caught or killed the Dutch fighter he referred to as Dornröschen. That said, she disappears from any written correspondence or records early in 1944."

"Wouldn't the capture or execution of a notorious Resistance fighter be splashed across all their propaganda?" Emilie asked.

Lise shrugged. "One would think so but it's possible that they simply made her disappear to avoid martyring her. It's also possible that those records were destroyed or I simply failed to find them." Lise tapped the keyboard twice more. An image of a new document appeared. "What I do know is that the hunt for Dornröschen appears to have conclusively ended by the spring of 1944. This is an order, dated May 1944 and signed by Rauter, ordering the transfer of Sturmbannführer Otto Diekmann to France."

Luc moved from the windows and studied the image on the screen. "Then she was here," he breathed. "And Sturmbann-führer Diekmann followed her."

Lise sat back, looking amused. "That's a bit of a stretch, I think. There would have been no shortage of work for a man like Diekmann in the months prior to D-Day. The Allies had all sorts of covert agents working in Normandy by then, many collaborating with Maquis groups. Assuming he was sent to hunt allied agents or Resistance cells in Normandy, he would have had a rich hunting ground. And he wouldn't have been the only one. The Gestapo were everywhere."

"What happened to Diekmann after he was sent to France?" Isabelle asked.

"Don't know. Presumably he was here at one point in time given the documents you found, or it's possible that his notes were simply forwarded on to someone else. I didn't find anything beyond this order." She gestured at the screen and image of the transfer order. "Which is not wholly unexpected. The Nazis were meticulous record keepers but they were also meticulous about destroying evidence and documentation of their actions when faced with the inevitability of a retreat. And Allied bombing of occupied cities destroyed not only infrastructure but records as well. From a historian's perspective, the documents left behind in this desk were a rare, happy oversight. Especially considering the deliberate destruction in other parts of the château."

"What about the Jeds?" Luc asked. "The officers that Monsieur Dubois remembered. The ones he said worked with Briar Rose."

"Now that was easier." Lise picked up a folder with a note paper clipped to the front. "There are definite records of a Jed team, dropped into Normandy near Rouen just ahead of D-Day. There were three in the team: An American, Major Lewis Franklin; a Brit, Lieutenant Roy Thatcher; and a Frenchman, Captain Thomas Phillipe. They were dropped with weapons, explosives, expertise in sabotage, and orders to collaborate with the local Maquis. I made a copy for you to take a look at later if you like. But nothing in these records mentions anything about a highly skilled Dutch-turned-French Resistance opera- tive, if that's what you're hoping. In fact, the details of their mission explicitly warn the Jed officers of the particularly poor organization and limited capabilities of the local Maquis."

"She was here," Luc insisted. "The Resistance fighter that was Dornröschen. I know she was."

"Except there is absolutely nothing here that proves that," Lise said gently.

"Show her," Luc said abruptly to Isabelle. "Show her the drawing."

Lise turned expectant eyes on Isabelle. "What drawing?"

Slowly, Isabelle rose from her stool and walked over to the hearth. She had taken her great-gran's drawing down from the mantel to compare it with the copy of the one Dubois had given them. She had left the framed art in its protective sleeve leaning against the foot of a griffin.

She brought the package over to the desk and slid the drawing out, placing it carefully on the surface of the desk in front of Lise.

The historian frowned. "What is this?"

"This is a drawing my great-gran did for me and Emilie when we were kids. She wrote and illustrated her own children's tales—fairy tales. It was a hobby for her, and they weren't widely published but she had copies made just for us."

Lise reached for Monsieur Dubois's drawing. She set them alongside each other. "I'm not an expert but they certainly look like they are in the hand of the same artist. The rose, the chain, the wings—I would hazard that they are too unique to come to any other conclusion."

"Yes," Isabelle agreed. "That's what we thought too."

Lise's eyes narrowed, and her forehead creased as she looked back and forth between the three of them. "I'm not sure where you're going with this," she said. "Your great-grandmother fought with the French Resistance?"

Isabelle shook her head. "I...I don't know."

"I do." Luc pointed to the two drawings. "Their great-gran was Briar Rose. That's what Renaud Dubois called her. The same Briar Rose that Otto Diekmann was hunting in the Netherlands. The same Briar Rose he followed to France."

Lise shook her head. "I appreciate your enthusiasm, but again, I think that is a stretch. A big one."

"She was Dutch." It was Emilie who spoke up. "Our great-gran."

"What?" Lise set the drawing down.

"Born and raised in Rotterdam," Isabelle added. "But as a kid, she spent summers at our farm that was then owned by her grandparents. Our great-grandparents times three."

"Are you saying you think your great-gran was Dornröschen?"

Isabelle winced. When she heard it stated out loud like that, it sounded even more far-fetched. "I don't know. Maybe?"

"Okay," Lise said slowly. "Do you have any proof that she was in Holland during the war?"

"No."

"Did she ever mention anything at all about Holland? Amsterdam? Haarlem?"

"No."

Lise grimaced.

"We have no idea where she was," Isabelle told her. "But I know she was in Rotterdam when it was bombed in 1940. She survived that. She never spoke of it in detail, but I saw the scars on her legs and back."

Lise was frowning. "And you think she came back to France after that?"

Isabelle held up her hands. "I don't know. I'd always assumed she came back to France after the war. She lived in Paris for some years then, which she did speak of. She met her husband there, I think. Our great-grandfather."

"And did he ever say anything about her past? Or the war? If he was French, he would have his own experiences."

"He never spoke of the war either." Isabelle glanced at Emilie, who only nodded her agreement. "Or of the past. Either of them. It was like both of their lives started in Paris sometime after the liberation."

"What did your great-gran say about Paris?"

"That it was beautiful, if a little crowded for her taste." Something Isabelle had always understood because she felt the same. "But maybe I assumed wrong. Maybe she was in Paris before the war ended? Maybe she was in Normandy before the war ended? Those years are mostly a giant blank. She never talked about them." She blew out a breath, the entire idea that they were attempting to rationalize seeming far too fantastical to believe. "I know this all sounds insane. I'm sorry."

"Not completely insane," Lise assured her. "There are certainly dots here that could be connected. Anyone else in your family have any more information?"

"No," Emilie answered. "We've asked, but Izz is right. The war was a topic that was off-limits and never discussed. If ever there was a time Great-Gran had said anything at all to anyone, it would have been to Izz. They were closest. Izz has the same kind heart she did."

Isabelle stared at Emilie, caught off guard by the unexpected compliment.

"It's true," her sister said, catching her stare.

Lise was absently tapping the side of her laptop. "I don't know what to tell you," she said. "I mean, it's all possible, I suppose, but it's pretty circumstantial. From an academic angle, there isn't enough real evidence to definitively connect those dots. Maybe your great-gran came back before the end of the war and fought with the maquisards in the area. Maybe she gave a drawing to a grief-stricken little boy. Maybe she even called herself Rose, or Briar Rose, after the infamous Dutch Resistance fighter." She looked around apologetically. "But as to the theory that the real Dornröschen, the one responsible for the systematic liquidation of Nazi officers in the

Netherlands, was here, fighting with the French Resistance—
there just isn't any hard proof."

★ ★ ★

The sun was starting to set when Isabelle found herself in
the garden.

She picked her way through the overgrown greenery bursting
from every corner with the colorful vigour of early summer. The
nocturnal creatures had yet to stir, though those that inhabited
the hours of sunshine had withdrawn and quieted. She brushed
her fingers over a riot of pale pink salvia, the delicate flowers
rimmed in gold where they caught the light of the sinking sun.
Bordered by the ancient stone wall and the thick forest beyond,
the garden was still a truly magical place. Isabelle felt like she
was twelve years old again, lost in a fairy tale world.

As busy as she had been with the interior of the château, she
hadn't been back in the garden since early spring, when everything had still been dormant and damp. She closed her eyes and
breathed deeply, letting the peace and tranquility of the space
settle over her.

A faint scraping sound made her open her eyes and turn. Curious, Isabelle wove her way through the narrow paths, following
the steady noise until she found herself at the edge of the small
clearing where the sculpted angel rose above the tall grass and
tangle of flora. Luc was crouched at the base of the stone pillar,
a pair of shears in his hands, methodically clearing the vines that
had begun their journey up the engraved column.

"Are you charging overtime for this?" Isabelle teased, stepping
into the clearing.

Luc shot to his feet with a yelp. The shears slipped from his hand and, despite his flailing attempt to catch them, tumbled to the ground.

Isabelle tried to suppress a snort of laughter and failed. "I'm sorry. I didn't mean to startle you."

"I think I'd believe that more if you weren't laughing." Luc bent to retrieve the shears.

More laughter escaped, and she couldn't stop it. "I do apologize. Honestly," she gasped.

"I can tell." He straightened.

"It's just you looked a little like a Muppet there for a moment." Isabelle waved her arms around, mimicking his movements.

"A Muppet," Luc repeated with a rueful shake of his head. "How very humbling."

Isabelle managed to control her giggles. "But a very handsome Muppet."

He pulled off his gloves and wiped his forehead with the back of his hand. He gazed at her with a gleam in his eye. "So you think I'm handsome?"

Isabelle felt herself flush. She had walked right into that one. "Yes, if you must know," she replied with as much bravado as she could muster. She deliberately avoided looking at the way his T-shirt hugged his broad shoulders and the way his jeans hugged his narrow hips. "What are you doing out here?" It was all she could do not to cringe at her graceless change of topic.

He gave her a look that told her she had fooled no one and gestured to the stone pillar. "I thought I'd tend the grave. This, at least, is a part of the château's history we can prove."

Isabelle wandered closer and pulled at the tendrils of vine still clinging to the stone. "I'm sorry we didn't get a better answer from Lise. One that proved you right about Briar Rose." The disappointment tugged at her. She, too, had wanted a better answer about the connection between her great-gran and Briar Rose. Yet the more they had learned, the more complicated and uncertain everything seemed to become. Though she wasn't willing to give up quite yet. She'd keep looking.

"Good Lord, Izz, don't be sorry," Luc said. "This was never about proving me right but about uncovering the truth, and history is rarely neat and tidy, packaged and delivered to fit nicely into our preferred narrative. I'd like to believe that a woman named Briar Rose fought here but that doesn't mean she did. I'd like to believe that your great-gran might have been that person but that doesn't mean she was." He stuffed his gloves into his back pocket. "Besides, she was your great-gran, not mine. It's not really my story to own anyway."

"No one owns a story. Except maybe their own." Isabelle pulled at the remaining leafy coils across the letters engraved into the stone, revealing the entirety of the inscription.

Simone Henriette Brodeur, Beloved Sister, 1856–1872
A Garden to Walk in and Immensity to Dream in—
What More Could She Ask?

"Do you know this one? This story?"

Luc contemplated the inscription. "Actually, I don't. Other than she died much too young." He paused. "That's a beautiful quote. She must have loved this garden as much as you."

"The quote is from Hugo's *Les Mis*, except the *he* in the original has been changed to a *she*." Isabelle ran her palm over the sun-warmed stone. "Emilie and I came across Simone's story when we were doing our research prior to purchasing the château," she told him. "Simone was the younger of two girls born to Richard and Huguette Brodeur, the last Comte and Comtesse de Cossé to have lived in the château. In 1860, Huguette died of diphtheria. In 1870, Richard left to fight in the Franco-Prussian War. He survived and returned in 1871 but withdrew from society and became an eccentric hermit of sorts. Dismissed the servants and the girls' tutors. Kept the windows shuttered and locked, even at the height of summer. Would not let guests inside the château with the exception of the town doctor, who diagnosed the comte with bouts of mania and melancholia. In 1872, Richard killed himself but not before he killed his younger daughter, Simone."

Luc stared at Isabelle. "That's horrible."

"The older daughter, Charlotte, had her beloved sister buried here, in the garden, where she could be close to her. Charlotte Brodeur was the last person to live in the château. She never had children, never married, and died in 1930 at the age of seventy-seven." Isabelle crouched, pushing aside the grass to the left of the stone pillar. She found the small, flat marker of the second grave almost immediately, with an inscription that read simply *Charlotte Marie, 1853–1930.* "In the documents she left behind, this was Charlotte's only request. To be buried in this garden next to her sister." Isabelle brushed the surface of the marker clear.

"I didn't even realize that there were two graves." Luc set the shears aside. "The comte brought his war home with him."

"I think so. Like so many others in so many wars." Isabelle looked up at the chipped and damaged wings of the angel. "I wonder how she did it."

"Who?"

Isabelle stood and jammed her thumbs into the pockets of her jeans. "Great-Gran. I wonder how she left her war behind her, however horrible it might have been, and embraced her future with as much joy and kindness and purpose as she did."

"Maybe she had someone to talk to. Someone who understood that there would be days when joy and kindness and purpose would be hard to come by."

"Maybe, but it sure wasn't us."

"Your great-grandfather? Perhaps a friend?"

"Maybe." Isabelle paused. "When I got older, I wondered if the fairy tales that she wrote about the château were therapeutic for her in some manner. A way to focus on happiness and hope. Maybe even give the château back some of its enchantment and wonder."

"Well, given the fact that her great-granddaughters are restoring it in a labour of love, I think she succeeded."

"Love and an eye to an architectural portfolio," Isabelle said drily.

"Is that entirely a bad thing?"

"No." Isabelle let her hands fall from her pockets and looked around. "Except Emilie is adamant that we return this garden back to its eighteenth-century origins with straight lines of flowers, manicured hedges, and wide paths that might accommodate a pair of panniers."

Luc winced. "That would ruin the magic."

"I agree. I'll keep working on her."

"When does she leave and head back to Paris?"

"She doesn't. At least not until the end of summer."

"Oh." Luc looked surprised but thankfully didn't ask why. "Have you ever wanted to go?" he asked suddenly.

"To Paris? I've visited three times. Once for a plaster workshop—"

"No, that's not what I meant." He shifted his weight, enough that their shoulders brushed. "Why did you never leave?"

Isabelle opened her mouth to answer while her earlier

conversation with Emilie around this very same topic echoed in her head.

"I'm sorry. You don't have to answer that—"

"Why did you?" she asked instead.

Luc tilted his head, shading his eyes with his hand against the last rays of the sun. His gaze was fixed somewhere in the distance, and it took him a long time to answer her. "I needed to figure out where I belonged, I think."

"There must be a lot of contenders. Most of the places with palm trees, I imagine." She did her best to keep her words light.

"No." He turned, his dark eyes holding hers. "Only one contender. And there are no palm trees. Though there is a garden."

A thrill of longing and desire flooded through her and lodged in her chest, making it impossible to breathe. Impossible to think.

He lifted his hand and slid his fingers down the side of her face, along the underside of her jaw, and then to the hollow at her throat, where she could feel her pulse pounding.

"But as it turns out," he said, "the garden isn't as important as you might think. Because where I belong is not a place at all."

Isabelle tried to speak and failed, the feel of his skin against hers electric.

Luc's fingers slipped around to her nape, and he brushed his lips against the column of her neck.

Isabelle's head tipped back, and her hands drifted around his waist. "Luc—"

Whatever words she was going to mumble were lost as he brought his mouth to hers. He kissed her thoroughly and unhurriedly, in a magical garden in the golden light of the setting sun, and for the first time in her life, Isabelle felt like a real fairy tale princess.

"I've wanted to do that for a long time," he murmured.

"Do what?" she mumbled inanely, trying to catch her breath and collect her wits.

"I wanted to know what it would feel like to belong to you." He lifted his head to look at her.

Isabelle closed her eyes and swallowed. For a wild moment, caught up in this magical fairy tale, she could almost believe that this perfect enchantment would never end, even when the clock inevitably struck midnight. But just as inevitably, reality returned, slinking back into her scattered thoughts. "Luc—"

"Don't." He took a half step back from her but caught her hand in his. "Don't say whatever it is you're going to say."

"You don't know what I'm going to say."

He gave her a sad smile. "I've known you since we were five, Izz. And I know that expression."

"What if you leave again?" she whispered.

"What if I don't?"

Isabelle shook her head. "I like . . . us, Luc. I like the way we are. We make a great team."

"We do," he agreed.

"If you go, I can't be left behind wondering if—"

"What if you leave?" he interrupted, a slight edge to his words.

"I won't."

"What if you leave and I come with you?" He was relentless. "What if I leave and you come with me? Our futures are all full of what-ifs and unknowns and opportunities that have no guarantees."

"I'm aware of that."

"Then what are you so afraid of?"

"I'm not afraid."

"Are you sure? Because it sounds like it." Luc let her hand drop, and Isabelle felt the loss of his touch all the way through her body.

"You're not listening," Isabelle said, frustration rising. "My place is here. This land has been in my family for generations. It's where my great-grandparents rebuilt after the war and raised their family. It's where my grandmother stayed to raise her family and where my mother did the same. I have responsibilities here. To my family and to the farm. I can't just turn my back on that."

"I'm not asking you to. I'm not asking you to do anything except embrace the same hope and happiness that you so admired in your great-gran. Live with the same joy and purpose, even if it's a little scary from time to time."

"You still don't understand."

"Let's go to Bora-Bora. Or Bali. I don't care. You pick."

"What?"

"You told me once that you wished you could see the places I've been. So let's start with one of those. Let me take you. For a week. Maybe two."

"Luc—"

"We could leave in a few days. Fly last minute. We could walk on the beaches, dive the reefs, hike the mountains. Get lost a few times. Maybe for a long time."

"I don't know how to dive."

"Learn."

"I can't."

"Why?"

"Because I . . ." Isabelle trailed off, angry that Luc was putting her in this position. Angry at herself that she couldn't give him the answer that he wanted. "I can't just leave. There are people who need me here. There's too much to do."

A muscle flexed in Luc's jaw. "Right."

"Maybe you should ask Emilie." Isabelle looked away. "She can jet off at the drop of a hat."

Luc didn't say anything, and his silence was damning.

"I'm sorry I'm not like my sister," she said.

"I'm not in love with your sister."

Isabelle's head snapped back around, and her heart missed a beat. "What?"

"You heard me." He pulled his gloves from his back pocket and wriggled his hands into them. "I have not lived a perfect life, and I certainly have some regrets, but not being honest with myself and the people closest to me, for better or for worse, is not one of them."

"I don't know what to say," Isabelle managed.

"Tell me you don't feel what I feel," Luc said quietly. "Tell me you feel nothing for me, or that there isn't a connection between us that goes far deeper than simply being a good team. Tell me all of that, and I will leave you be and never mention any of this conversation again."

"I can't." Isabelle couldn't bring herself to lie to him. But nor could she say anything else.

"Well, that's something, I suppose," Luc said.

"I'm sorry—"

"I'm not looking for an apology. Loving someone is terrifying, Izz. The most terrifying thing that I've ever done, and I've done quite a few questionable things in my life. But the regret I would be left with by never knowing what might have been, of not taking chances, of not truly living, is far worse than fear."

Isabelle could only stare at him.

"You have too much to offer the world to hide." Luc leaned toward her and kissed her softly on the cheek. "You are a brilliant, talented, beautiful, capable woman who is far braver than you give yourself credit for." He picked up the shears and with deliberate motions resumed a steady assault on the overgrown vines. "When you decide to start believing that, Isabelle Lange, I'll be waiting for you."

CHAPTER

20

Nicolas

The waiting reception committee had been skilled, quick, and competent.

The exact opposite of everything that the Hubert team had been told to expect when they'd been dropped west of Rouen. By the time Nicolas's boots had made contact with the ground, the canisters of equipment and supplies that had been dropped with them were already being collected by a small swarm of bodies that were barely visible in the dark. By the time he'd disengaged his parachute and stripped out of his jump smock, those same bulky canisters were already being concealed in the back of an oversized farm wagon. And by the time he'd reconnected with Franklin, who had landed a field over, and Thatcher, who had landed a half kilometer away in a quarry of some sort, the parachutes, the wagons, the horses, and the entire committee had vanished. The work had been done silently and swiftly, and the Jeds had been left looking at each other with a sense of immediate relief, albeit a wary one.

A single youth was left behind, presumably to be their guide. Nicolas had no idea how old he might be—perhaps fourteen, maybe fifteen—and he had an almost feral appearance. His face was thin, his cheeks more hollow than they ought to be. His hair was overlong, curling over the collar of his woolen jumper, which was visibly torn across one shoulder. He said nothing, only eyed Nicolas's uniform, adjusted his grip on the Sten gun he was carrying, and jerked his head in the direction of the river.

Nicolas watched the boy's grip on the Sten with some consternation. The Stens were notoriously hazardous in untrained hands. "Careful with that—"

"Quiet." The adolescent put a finger to his lips. "Too many Germans around, you understand?" he whispered. "They will have heard the plane. They know this field. We are already here too long."

Nicolas would have laughed at the absurdity of being reprimanded by a youth barely old enough to shave but the feeling of being exposed like this in the open gave his guts an unpleasant twist. The boy was right. They were standing in the center of a wide swath of farmland, broken only by the occasional hedgerow and crisscrossed by a series of roads. He had not survived all that he had survived only to be shot by the Gestapo because his ego had been too unwieldy to listen to a boy who knew this darkness better than he.

He had barely finished that thought when the distinct rumble of approaching vehicles cut through the stillness. To the north, a light appeared, sweeping back and forth across the empty fields.

"Jesus Christ." Franklin swore and unholstered his pistol.

"Hurry." The boy was already running toward the closest hedgerow.

Nicolas and his team wasted no time following, their gear and weapons banging against them as they went. They threw themselves into the low-lying scrub as three sets of headlights appeared over the ridge and roared down the rutted track in their direction.

Nicolas pressed himself to the ground. The carbine strapped across his chest poked uncomfortably into his shoulder. The vehicles slowed as they drew even on the far side of the field, and wild shadows danced around Nicolas as the search light was swung over their heads.

Keep driving, Nicolas whispered to himself. *Keep driving*—

The squeal of brakes assaulted his ears. Nicolas kept his head down. A car door slammed, and over the sound of his pulse banging in his ears, he could hear raised voices followed by the whine of dogs. His stomach dropped to his toes, and his heart lodged in his throat. They may be able to hide from men, but they would not be able to hide from dogs. This mission might very well be over before it even started. Very slowly, he reached down his body and unsheathed his knife.

The unmistakable sound of gunfire suddenly punched through the night, coming from the south, though the distance was difficult to pinpoint. The dogs were driven into a frenzy of barking. Nicolas heard the grinding of gears and the crunch of tyres spinning in the gravel and dirt. Within a handful of seconds, the vehicles were charging down the road in pursuit of the disturbance, and the roar of the engines receded. In their wake, only the sounds of crickets and the men's harsh breathing could be heard.

Franklin was muttering under his breath in English.

"Perhaps we might consider recommending a new drop location to London," Nicolas said with a calm he wasn't entirely feeling. "That was rather close."

"A capital idea," agreed Thatcher, who still sounded winded.

"The Germans come to find the containers." The boy's voice came out of the darkness. "They always come when there is a plane. They are fast." He sounded remarkably unshaken. "But now we are faster."

"Always with the dogs?" It was Thatcher who asked, and Nicolas could almost hear the shudder in his tone.

"The dogs are new." The boy had clambered back to his feet. "More of them have come. Milice. Gestapo. SS, too. They are thick like fleas in Rouen. And they are hunting us much harder now." This sounded like a point of pride.

And it was the second time the youth had used the word *now*.

"What is different now?" Nicolas asked.

"The Nazis fear us now," the boy said savagely. "They are reaping what they have sown."

Nicolas wasn't sure exactly what that meant, but before he could ask, Franklin interrupted.

"Where did the gunfire come from?" Franklin demanded. "Who was shooting who?" He was on his feet and checking his weapon.

The adolescent shrugged. "No one was shooting anyone. We have people scattered on drop nights to create distractions. Keep the boches chasing their tails all night long looking for ghosts."

Nicolas exchanged a look with the team chief. The assessment that these maquisards were disorganized, inexperienced, and shambolic was clearly not accurate. Nicolas wondered what else in their briefing had not been accurate.

"Follow me." The boy hefted his Sten gun and struck out east along the hedgerows. Every once in a while, he stopped, listening carefully before he struck out again. It was a slow, methodical process but Nicolas was in no hurry to run into a German trap.

They passed a tiny hamlet, giving the huddled houses a wide berth. Even so, a farm dog barked a warning, and they all froze, listening hard, but no voices were raised and no engines rumbled to life. They continued on.

Presently, Nicolas could detect the familiar, ripe scent of rotting vegetation and mud that was forever fixed in his memory. They were close to the river, he knew. A flash of silver glinted through the thick trees, and Nicolas stepped into a small clearing on the bank of the Seine. It was a bit surreal, he thought, looking at the wide, flat expanse of water that still flowed endlessly. All around him were sights and smells that remained the same, as if they had been waiting for him to return. As if trying to convince him that nothing had changed in the years he had been gone. Nothing could be further from the truth.

"This way." Their guide veered north along the river's edge, following a narrow, rutted track. He led them over a fence, through an empty pasture, and into a darkened farmyard. A farmhouse was now visible, a thick, two-storied box made of heavy stone with a steeply sloping thatched roof. There was no laundry on the line, no lights in the windows, no animals in the yard, no smoke curling from the chimney. A squat farm cart sat abandoned in the yard next to a dilapidated barn that had collapsed on one end.

Nicolas scrutinized the cart. It looked an awful lot like the one that had spirited their canisters away in the dark, but he couldn't be sure.

Without pausing, the boy hurried up the stone steps and knocked twice on the door.

Nicolas kept his hand on his pistol and examined the

farmyard. There was nothing to see, only a wall of impenetrable forest, shrouded in darkness, surrounding them. There
could be a hundred men in those trees, friend or foe, and he'd
not be able to see them. He wasn't sure if that reassured or
unnerved him.

"You will stay here tonight," their guide told them simply.

"I don't like this," said Franklin. He turned to the boy.
"Where are the men who met us at the drop? Where are our
containers?"

"And my radio equipment?" Thatcher added.

"I don't know. But they're safe."

"What do you mean you don't know?" Franklin demanded
impatiently.

"It means I don't know. I wasn't told anything. My job was
to bring you here. I'm just following orders."

"Not my orders," Franklin growled. "Those canisters were
collected and concealed before I even had my damn parachute off.
Before I could even make contact with anyone on the ground.
I need to know who took the containers or where they were
taken to."

The boy shrugged. "It's safer for us if you don't."

"What the hell does that mean?"

"It means," Nicolas answered for the boy who stood before
them, his hands resting easily on the Sten, and who remained
unflinching in the face of Franklin's irritation, "that the canisters
were collected first so that if we were caught by the Germans
after our drop, then the supplies would not be lost as well."

The youth was watching him without argument.

Nicolas considered the explosives and guns and ammunition
that had been in those containers and thought that the approach
was not only rather cunning but necessary.

"And," Nicolas continued, "it means that, if we're caught now, we can tell the Germans nothing."

"Jesus," Franklin muttered. "Is that true?" he asked the boy. "That your leader gave precedence to the supplies and not the personnel?"

The adolescent shrugged. "Said a container of guns in our hands kills a lot of Nazis," he said. "But we're not so sure what you lot can do yet."

Thatcher snorted. "I like this chap, whoever he is."

"I want to meet him. Whoever's in charge," Franklin said. "Immediately."

"You'll have your chance tonight sometime."

"When?"

"Don't know. Just said to tell you tonight."

The chief bristled. "I don't think you—"

The farmhouse door opened. An elderly woman, wrapped in a thick robe, her hair white against the shadows, stood in the doorway. "Do you wish to get us all shot, Monsieur?" she asked. "Because by all means, speak louder."

Franklin heaved an exasperated sigh.

"Get inside," she said, swinging the door wide.

The Jeds ducked through the door, Nicolas bringing up the rear. He turned to ensure the door closed after the boy, but their guide had vanished without a trace. Somehow, Nicolas was not surprised.

The old woman clutched her robe around her shoulders and led them through the darkened house without lighting a candle. Franklin cursed in the dark as his foot made contact with something immovable. She offered no apology, only continued until they reached a set of stairs. Slowly but surely, she led them up until they reached the second floor and a small room at the back corner of the house. Once they were all in, she lit a small lantern.

Nicolas blinked in the light. They were standing in a bedroom with a double bed pushed up against the far wall, a heavy curtain covering what Nicolas surmised was a window just above. The only other piece of furniture in the room was a sturdy dresser that stood near the door, and it was upon the top of that that the woman placed the lantern.

Their elderly hostess had turned to study the three men. Her white hair was long and secured in a braid that hung down over stooped shoulders. Deep lines were carved into a weathered face but her eyes were shrewd and her demeanor sharp. She dubiously examined their uniforms and then their Special Forces insignia in much the same way that the youth had.

"I hide agents in civilian clothes. Not..." She waved her hand at their appearance and the weapons that the three men were unstrapping to place in neat piles on the floor "...soldiers. I do not wish my home to become a garrison."

"Nor do we," Nicolas assured her.

"Hmph." She looked decidedly unimpressed. "I will wake you in the morning. Please don't leave the house, and stay away from the windows. The Germans rarely come here because I am careful not to give them a reason to, and I'd like to keep it that way."

"I'll need to get a message to London tomorrow, Madame," Thatcher said. "Provided I get my radio back."

"You'll get it back," she assured him.

"I'd like a look at the attic?"

The woman gestured back in the direction of the hall they had just come from. "Access door to the attic is at the end in the ceiling. Windows are covered, so you may use your torch."

Nicolas considered the woman, wondering just how many times she had done this.

"But you need to have a care," she went on. "The Nazis have trucks that can detect your radios when you're transmitting now. Watch for them. And limit your transmissions to less than five minutes."

There was the use of the word *now* again. Nicolas frowned.

"Mind the rats," she called after Thatcher as he ducked from the room.

"Why now?" Nicolas asked.

The old woman turned back to Nicolas and blinked at him owlishly. "I beg your pardon?"

"You said that the Nazis have trucks to detect radio transmissions now. The boy who brought us here said that they are hunted with dogs on drop nights now." Nicolas was aware that Franklin was watching him keenly. "What is different now?"

The woman didn't answer, only pulled her threadbare robe more tightly around herself.

"We are here to help," Nicolas said. "We are here to do whatever it takes to deliver France back to the French. This is my home too."

Still, she didn't answer.

"Please," Nicolas tried again. "If we are to do the job that we have been sent here to do, we need to know what we are walking into. We've been told that the Resistance here is ineffectual and inexperienced."

The woman seemed to come to a decision. "That was before Briar Rose," she said.

Nicolas started. The name sent fragments of memories slicing through him. Memories that started in an abandoned garden behind a forgotten château, the beginning of his journey that had taken him halfway around the world and had brought him home again, right back to the very same château that he had returned to destroy. The irony was breathtaking.

"And what, exactly, is a briar rose?" Franklin was asking.

The woman sniffed. "Not what, who. She is the leader of the Resistance here."

"Oh, Christ." Franklin rubbed his face with his hands. "That's all we need. A dame running around with a gun believing herself to be a general."

The old woman leveled a cold look in his direction. "Your man asked what was different now, so I'll tell you. Now, those who fight have a leader. Now, those who fight no longer squabble amongst themselves but work together. Those who have fled here after surviving cruelties at the hands of the Nazis are no longer reckless and rash. Disorganized has given way to dangerous."

Franklin's hand dropped. "And this woman, who is she? Is she an agent? SOE? OSS? Is she French? Where did she come from?"

The woman's expression shuttered. "Don't know. She is like a ghost."

"When did she come?" Nicolas asked quietly, thinking of their briefing report that had contained none of this intelligence.

"Maybe April. Who can say for sure?"

"Just grand." Franklin was pacing the room, his size making the space seem even smaller. "And this ghost, what does she do to inspire such allegiance?"

"She kills Nazis."

That brought Franklin up short. "What? How?"

Bony shoulders rose and fell beneath the robe. "I cannot say. I am only an old woman. I can only do my little part, yes?"

Nicolas didn't think that being responsible for hiding Allied agents was a little part at all. Nor did he believe for a second that she was as ignorant as she pretended to be.

"I am tired," the woman said abruptly. "You, too, should rest." She turned the lantern down so that the room was plunged back into shadows, the glow too feeble to reach the corners. "Good night."

She didn't give either man a chance to respond before she shuffled out of the room.

Franklin huffed. "This changes things, you know, Phillipe."

"To some degree, yes," agreed Nicolas. "That the Resistance is organized is a good thing but it will mean that the Germans will not be as complacent as we might have hoped. Our mission remains the same but—"

"But we'll have Nazis crawling up our asses," Franklin finished for him.

"Then let them crawl," Nicolas said. "We'll be ready." Franklin grunted and snatched the lantern from the dresser. "Going to go see what Thatcher is up to in the attic."

"Mind the rats." Nicolas grinned at his chief.

"Funny," Franklin muttered, and disappeared.

Nicolas sat down on the end of the bed and bent to loosen the laces on his boots, feeling his way by touch. He leaned back, the movement accompanied by a chorus of protesting springs beneath the sagging mattress. Exhaustion flooded through him. No, not exhaustion, he realized. Just an overwhelming sense of relief that he and his team hadn't died from the jump or the journey here. He laced his hands behind his head and stared up at the ceiling, his eyes wide open, his mind turning over what they were tasked with in the next forty-eight hours.

The destruction of Château de Montessaire still did not sit comfortably within him. The château had been his home more

than any other place, if only because it had been where he had
sought refuge when his father became violent or unmanageable.
It had been where he had taught himself the skills that had
become his life. It was where he had met Stasia. The first person
to believe in him. The first person who had made him want to
be better. It had been in that garden where he had heard his
first fairy tale and been made to believe that a happy-ever-after
could be his.

The door creaked on its hinges.

Nicolas twisted, expecting to see either Franklin or Thatcher,
but there was no one there. He could see only the faint outlines
of the doorway and the deeper shadows of the hallway beyond.
He sat up, listening intently. He heard nothing save for a faint,
muffled thud from above his head. He inhaled and froze.

Woodsmoke and damp wool. Those were the two distinct scents
he immediately identified. The third was sweat. Not the acrid scent
of fear but that of a warm body that had run a good distance.

"What do you want?" he asked into the darkness.

The air shifted in the room, an almost imperceptible disturbance and one he wouldn't have noticed had he not been alert.
A ghost indeed.

"An interesting first question," came the reply. The voice was
soft and unhurried. Not that of an old woman. "Most demand
to know who I am."

"Who you are is rather subjective. What you want is much
more precise." Nicolas hadn't moved.

"I agree."

She was closer now, somewhere near the top of the bed. "You
are the men sent by London."

"And you are responsible for our reception. Briar Rose."

"I am but one person. Your reception was conducted by many."

"And the weapons and equipment?"

"Recovered. The guns are welcome but the explosives even more so. I only wish there had been more."

"More? There were three canisters that held explosives."

"Ah." The voice sounded contemplative.

"*Ah*? What does that mean?"

"Two canisters were dropped off course and were lost in the river. We didn't know what was in them."

"Shit." He couldn't help the curse that slipped out under his breath.

The air stirred again, though he still couldn't see her. "Be grateful that it wasn't you who came down in the middle of the Seine with a parachute over your head."

Nicolas didn't reply. She was right but the loss of the explosives was troubling.

"Your radio operator will be pleased to know his radio suffered no damage during the drop. He will have it returned to him here, within the hour."

"Thank you." At least that was good news.

"I will send someone to collect you and your men just before dawn to take you to our camp. The rest of your belongings will be waiting for you. I apologize for the extra step but we cannot be too careful. With the roads full of Nazis looking for whoever and whatever was dropped from that plane, it's best to hide for the night. They will come to search the farms tomorrow. But you will be gone by then."

"Understood."

"I would ask that your radioman pass on our thanks to London. It is hard waiting for promised things that may or may not ever arrive. It's hard to fight effectively when you lack the tools to do so."

As Nicolas listened to her instructions, the feeling that there was something oddly familiar about the cadence of the voice nagged at him. The barest hint of an accent, perhaps, that suggested that whoever this woman was, she wasn't French.

"The boy who brought us here said that the Germans are hunting your men much harder as of late," he said. "That they have brought more men and dogs."

"They—" She stopped, as if reconsidering her words.

"They what?"

"They hunt me." She paused. "Something that you and your men should be aware of should you remain here."

Nicolas frowned.

"The war is not going well for the Germans. Anyone with a radio knows this," she continued before he could ask a question. "They grow increasingly cruel and increasingly desperate to maintain their control. You should know that too."

"I understand."

"Do you?" She didn't sound convinced.

"Yes. Because from what you've told me, even with limited resources, I think that you have been far more effective than you are suggesting."

"Perhaps."

"They hunt you because you have been targeting personnel," he guessed. "The officers." It was what he would have done.

"When one has only a handful of bullets at one's disposal, one does not aim at the tail of the viper, do they?"

She was SOE, Nicolas guessed. That was a Churchillian answer if he'd ever heard one and suggested training not unlike his own.

"You should rethink your uniforms," she said abruptly. "They will get you shot."

"They were meant to impress upon the partisans the military nature and urgency of this endeavor."

"A dead soldier will not impress many. A clever soldier, however, will earn respect."

"Is that what you are?" He couldn't help himself. "Clever?"

"Why have you come here with your men?" She ignored his question. "We were told to expect three agents and supplies. We were not told what they are for. The men, that is, not the supplies."

"There is a Nazi communication headquarters not far from here."

"Château de Montessaire."

"You know it?" Nicolas winced. That was a stupid question.

"Of course." She exhaled in the darkness. "You have come to destroy it." It was a statement, not a question, and devoid of any emotion.

"Yes."

"When?"

"Immediately."

"They are finally coming. The Allies." Again, it wasn't really a question.

"Yes."

"When?"

"I don't know. Soon."

"Yet too late. Too late for too many." She was quiet for a moment before she said, "You need our help for this."

"Yes."

"You will have it. Though I do not know if your leader will be happy about a dame running around with a gun pretending to be a general."

Nicolas winced again. "You heard that."

"Of course I did. I was listening. Information is power. One must collect it whenever possible. Unseen and unheard."

"Like a ghost."

"Ghosts are merely things people make up to keep others out of their business."

Nicolas went very still. An irrational notion lodged itself in his mind. A notion too implausible to really believe, yet the hair on the back of his neck rose.

"You waited until I was alone to have this conversation," he said. "Why?"

"Because I needed to have a conversation with a man who would speak with me and not at me. Because you said that this was your home. And because when you spoke, you reminded me of someone I used to know a long time ago."

Nicolas swallowed hard, though his mouth had gone dry. The notion that had planted itself into his mind sprouted, winding strands of preposterous possibility through his consciousness. He tried to tell himself that what he was considering was nothing short of temporary insanity and that it was merely a product of being back in France. Of being back in a place rich with cherished memories and gutting emotion and unrealized dreams.

But now that he allowed the notion light, he could not look away. He had to know.

"Who do I remind you of?" he asked unsteadily.

"Doesn't matter."

"I think it might."

"It doesn't." Her voice was cold and brittle. "He's dead. I should never have mentioned it."

Nicolas pushed himself off the bed, coming to his feet amid a new chorus of creaking springs. "I knew a girl before you who told me that ghosts are something people made up to keep others out of their business." He chose his words with care. "She told me that in the garden of the very château that I am here to destroy. After she told me the story of Briar Rose while she stitched a cut on my head."

The silence that followed was deafening. It stretched and stretched, and Nicolas was afraid to breathe. Afraid to move. Afraid that, if he blinked, he would discover that he really was in a dream and that he would wake up and all of this would be gone. She would be gone.

"Nicolas?" His name hovered in the space between them, barely a whisper.

He took a step forward on unfeeling legs. And then another.

He was close enough to her that he could hear her breathing. He could smell the woodsmoke caught in her hair and clothes. A manner of desperate joy was coursing through him and making it hard to think. Very slowly, he reached out, half-afraid that he would touch nothing and that he would discover he had merely become untethered from reality.

But his fingers touched the solid warmth of her arm. He ran his hand up to her shoulder, the wool of her jumper pilled and rough. He could feel the rapid rise and fall of her chest, could hear the soft sounds of her breathing that was not steady. She hadn't moved at all, as if she were frozen in place.

"How are you here?" she asked in a strangled voice. "I saw your name. On the list of dead from the *Bretagne*—"

"No, no, no." Nicolas closed whatever distance remained between them and brought both hands to cup her face. "Oh, God, Stasia. That was a mistake."

"A mistake?" she croaked. "You died, Nicolas. Died without giving me a chance to say goodbye." She was breathing hard, like she had just sprinted a mile.

"So did you." The skin beneath his hands was smooth and hot under his touch. He let his fingers explore, tracing the line of her jaw and the sharp angle of her cheek. He buried his fingers in her hair, the shorn edges brushing his wrists, and rested his forehead against hers. The feel of her was familiar and foreign all at once.

"What happened in Rotterdam?" he whispered.

She shook her head slightly, her skin against his.

"Where did you go?" His fingers curled against her scalp.

She didn't answer.

"Stasia?"

She made a small sound in the back of her throat. "No one has called me that in a long time."

There were a thousand questions pounding at him, demanding to understand how it was that she was here. That she was alive. But he ignored them all. Because they didn't matter. Not now. The only thing that mattered was that she was.

She still hadn't moved. Nicolas lifted his head, trying to see her face in the darkened room but there was only enough light to illuminate the gleam of her eyes as she looked up at him. He traced his thumb over her bottom lip and saw that gleam vanish as she closed her eyes.

"Stasia," he whispered again, but this time she flinched beneath his touch. His fingers stilled.

Her eyes opened again. "Don't."

She pulled away, and he let her go.

Cold air filled the places against his skin where her warmth had just been. "Stasia, I—"

"Don't call me that." She took another step back. "I'm not Stasia anymore."

Nicolas stood helplessly in the dark. He fought the urge to

reach for her and draw her back and crush her in his arms. To spirit her away from here, from this room, from this house, from this whole damn war and never look back. Just keep the greatest love he had ever known, the greatest love he had lost and now, somehow, found again, safe from the world around them. To never lose it again.

"I can't be here," she said. "I can't pretend to do this. I'm sorry." She had moved again, her voice coming from across the room now.

Far away from his reach.

"I don't understand," he said hoarsely. The desperate joy that had suffused him had been replaced by desperate despair. "Please stay. Don't go yet." He took a step forward and stumbled.

"Don't make this harder than it needs to be, Nicolas."

"Harder?" he choked. "Stasia, I thought you were dead. That was the hardest moment of my whole goddamn life. I thought I'd lost you."

"That's just it, Nicolas." She had moved farther away still. "You did."

CHAPTER

21

Stasia

6 JUNE 1944
NEAR ROUEN, FRANCE

They arrived in the camp just after the sun rose.

It was Sascha Dubois who guided the three Jedburghs from the farmhouse into the Maquis stronghold, and Stasia watched from her perch up on a ridge overlooking the camp where she sat silent and still in the thorny, tangled growth around her. She had chosen Sascha for the job because he was quick and clever and had been the one to deliver the Jeds to the farmhouse in the first place. A familiar face collecting a trio of wary soldiers before dawn would have made the journey smoother.

She watched as the three men walked into the camp. Their leader, the one they called Franklin, came first, followed by the radioman, Thatcher. The two were a study in contrasts— the American an unapologetic bull of a man while aristocratic refinement nearly dripped from the Englishman. Yet Stasia only had eyes for the third.

She thought she had prepared herself for this moment when,

in the daylight, she would no longer rely on her imagination to see Nicolas Navarre. Yet the sight of him still snatched the breath from her lungs. From where she watched, she could see that his face was cut into lines more severe than she remembered, as if whatever hardship he had experienced these last years had been permanently etched across his features. His blond hair was shorn close to his head, bright beneath his beret. He still moved with an easy grace, but his eyes were ever watchful, his posture that of a man who no longer took safety for granted. A bulky pack was strapped to his back, his carbine held easily in his hands.

Stasia closed her eyes briefly and shuddered, remembering what his hands had felt like on her skin last night. For one wild moment, she had been tempted to let the years fall away, to pretend that they had never happened and that she was back in a forgotten garden full of naïve dreams and blissful innocence. It was the perfect apex of a perfect fairy tale—a moment that, had she been writing a make-believe story, should have been one of extraordinary elation and uninhibited happiness. Yet all that engulfed her was a feeling of profound heartache and regret. Because it was just that—fiction. No one lived in a fairy tale. And no one could undo the past. The girl he had left no longer existed.

She couldn't go back in time any more than he.

"A capital spot up here."

Stasia started at the unfamiliar voice, so fixated on watching Nicolas that she hadn't heard anyone approach. She turned to find that Sascha had brought the radioman, Thatcher, up the slope. Both were standing a short distance from her, Thatcher peering up into the branches of the trees and Sascha watching him with wide eyes.

"What are you doing up here?" she asked, irritated at her own inattentiveness.

"The lieutenant is looking for a place to transmit," Sascha told her eagerly.

"Apologies if I disturbed you," the Englishman said. He didn't sound very apologetic.

Thatcher perused his surroundings on the ridge before he turned his attention back to the clearing below. Stasia followed his gaze. The men who lived in the camp had materialized from their shelters and, even though they were expecting the soldiers, were cautiously approaching Franklin and Nicolas like they were a pair of exotic animals. Renaud Dubois, Sascha's little brother, seemed to suffer no such restraint and scampered around Franklin like an overeager puppy, examining his uniform and weapons.

"Should I fetch Renaud back?" Sascha was also watching the commotion in the clearing, frowning in the direction of his brother who was now tugging on Franklin's arm.

"No." Stasia returned her attention to the radioman only to find that he was already scrutinizing her. She wasn't sure that she liked that. "Leave him be. If two grown Jeds can't handle a child, I don't hold much hope for them against the Germans."

Thatcher looked amused.

"What are my orders?" Sascha was looking between Stasia and Thatcher, fidgeting excitedly where he stood. His curly, nut-colored hair hadn't seen a comb in who knew how long and bounced around his head like a fuzzy halo. "Now that you Jeds are here. Now that we can fight for real. With proper guns and real explosives and—"

"Stop," Stasia said curtly. "You'll wait for a plan. Like always."

"Right." Sascha nodded, a furrow appearing between his

brows. "In the meantime, I could show you what I can do, sir."
He was speaking earnestly to the lieutenant now. "I cut telephone lines. Rather good at it, in fact. I'm fast. The fastest."

"Indeed," Thatcher replied.

"She showed me how, sir." He grinned at Stasia, and two
dimples appeared in his cheeks, making him look painfully
young.

Stasia shook her head. "You're not going up any poles or
cutting anything right now. Not after a drop last night. The
Germans will be looking for anything out of the ordinary."

"But that's good. If they're busy looking, I could finally get
the north road lines down—"

"No." Her voice was sharper than she intended but what he
was suggesting was far too dangerous. "You don't need to prove
anything to anyone, least of all these men."

Sascha looked crestfallen. "But I could—"

"Your little brother needs you. Do not do anything stupid."

"She's right," Thatcher said. "Don't fret. I'm sure you'll get
your chance."

The boy nodded unhappily.

"Go down and wait for orders," Stasia told him. "And save
your brother from himself while you're at it." Below them,
Franklin had given an enraptured Renaud his commando knife
to examine. She winced as the child brandished the blade in
erratic circles.

"Yes, Madame. Sir." Sascha shot one more wide-eyed look in
Thatcher's direction before he scrambled back down the slope.

A silence fell until it was broken by Thatcher.

"We've not been formally introduced. Rose, I presume? Or
is it Briar Rose?"

Stasia shrugged. "It matters not to me what you call me."

"No, I suppose it doesn't." He swung his gaze back to her, sharp green eyes evaluating. "Lieutenant Roy Thatcher. Your servant, Madame."

"Charmed." Stasia met the Englishman's cool perusal.

Again, Thatcher seemed to be faintly amused.

"Any problems on the way here?" she asked.

"No sign of any Germans, if that was what you were asking. Our guide was quite competent." He slid a crumpled pack of cigarettes from his pocket. "But then, you already knew that." He offered Stasia a cigarette.

Stasia stood and accepted, allowing him to light hers. "Thank you" was all she said.

"The boy who brought us here—what is his name?"

"Sascha," Stasia replied, not being able to think of a reason not to tell him. Below, the maquisards and the Jeds were making introductions, Nicolas doing a great deal of the talking when the French got too fast or perhaps too provincial for the American.

Sascha had reached the clearing and was extracting the large knife from Renaud's hand amid the boy's plaintive protests. He returned it to Franklin.

"You are fond of him. Our guide."

"No," she lied. "I pity him. His father was shipped east to a German work camp last year. His mother died shortly after. His older brother was shot at an abandoned farm nine months ago. These men are what family he and his brother have left."

"And they have you."

Stasia shook her head. "They do not need me."

"Mmm. He spoke of you, you know. On the way here. He seems to think you walk on water." Thatcher lit his own cigarette.

"He is a boy." Barely fifteen. "He doesn't know any better."

"Perhaps."

She could feel the Englishman still watching her.

"He told us that you are their leader. That you have made these men..." He seemed to be searching for a word. "...*combattants de la liberté*."

"I have made them nothing that they weren't already. Merely gave them...focus."

"Hmm." Long fingers slid his lighter back into his pocket, and he considered her again, unhurried. "Why are you up here?"

"I like the view."

"Let me rephrase. Why are you not down there with your men?"

"They are not my men. They are their own men, fighting for their country and their families and for each other. But this you will discover for yourself."

"I see." He exhaled a stream of smoke. "I confess that I regret missing your visit last night."

Stasia studied the glowing end of her cigarette.

"Captain Phillipe looked like he had seen a bloody ghost when we came down from that attic. About ready to come out of his skin, he was."

She tapped a bit of ash and watched it fall to the ground.

"He doesn't unsettle easily. Yet in the short time that you spent with him, you managed what every terrorizing commander I've seen him cross paths with could not."

She examined the ragged edge of her sleeve.

"You know, he told us very little about you. Other than your willingness to assist us in the coming days. To instruct your men—the ones who do not fight for you, of course—to assist us."

The ensuing quiet was broken only by the hum of voices from below.

"Have you nothing to say?"

Stasia lifted her head. "And interrupt your riveting narration of last night's events? I wouldn't dream of it. I'm waiting to hear the bit about the rats."

Thatcher grinned suddenly. "I can see why your men like you."

"Because I answer your pointless questions?" She ignored his reference to her men.

"Because you don't."

"Lieutenant Thatcher?"

Both Stasia and the radioman turned to find Nicolas standing behind them. He no longer had his gun in his hands but a rolled document of some sort. He avoided looking at Stasia.

"Major Franklin would like a word."

Stasia glanced back down at the clearing, where Franklin was now pinning a map to the trunk of a wide tree. Men were crowding around the base, pressing in for a better look.

"I see. Thank you, Captain Phillipe." Thatcher was languidly looking back and forth between Stasia and Nicolas. He offered Stasia a polite bow, as if he were excusing himself from court. "A pleasure, Rose," he said.

She nodded and watched the radioman pick his way back down to the clearing.

A silence fell. Somewhere over their head, a bird shrieked, a shrill, angry sound. Her heart was racing and sweat prickled on her skin.

"Stasia—"

"Rose." She crushed out her cigarette and let it drop to the ground. "If you must call me something. Call me Rose."

Nicolas stepped in front of Stasia, half guiding her back a

half dozen steps so that they were no longer visible to anyone from below. He lifted his hand, his fingers touching the ragged ends of her hair. She flinched, imagining what he saw when he looked at her. A woman who had lost too much weight, with dyed-black hair that had been cut short with the edge of a hunting knife, dressed in worn trousers and a salvaged sweater.

His hand dropped. "I didn't sleep last night. I was afraid that you might have been a dream. But you're not. You're real, and you're here. With me."

Stasia shook her head, her eyes fixed firmly on the toes of his jump boots. A part of her wanted to run. Just turn and flee and not look back. But she remained frozen, a strange, choking panic crowding into her chest. She motioned to the rolled document in his hand, grasping at the distraction.

"A map of the château?" Her words sounded stilted even to her but she forced herself to continue. "You'll want to do your own reconnaissance, I'm sure. The Germans haven't used anyone from the local populace to do menial labour for a long time so there is very little I can tell you about the inside. There are two men down there in that clearing who speak fluent German. I'll introduce you. You may need them. I think that we both know the way that the guards can be circumvented—"

"Stop."

Stasia flinched.

"What are you doing?"

"My job." The urge to run was almost overwhelming now.

"Your job?" He spoke so quietly, she had to strain to hear him. "I don't want to talk about your job right now. Or mine." He tossed the map of the château and the area aside. "These last four years I thought you were dead."

Stasia didn't look at him.

"I asked you last night what happened in Rotterdam."

"It doesn't matter."

Nicolas put a finger under her chin and forced her head up. She met his eyes, the icy grey of a Baltic storm. "There was a letter. That was forwarded from your grandparents' solicitor. That you and your father had both died when the city was bombed."

"My father died. I survived."

"That tells me nothing."

"That tells you all you need to know."

"I'm sorry about your father."

"I'm sorry about a lot of things." So many things.

His forehead creased. "Where did you go? What happened to you?"

Stasia tipped her chin away from his touch. "It doesn't matter."

Nicolas turned from her and paced to the edge of the ridge before returning. "It damn well matters to me."

"I don't know what you want me to tell you."

"The truth." He ran his hands through his short hair. "Just tell me the truth."

Stasia pressed her fingers to her eyes, making black spots dance behind her lids.

"How is it that you are with the Resistance?" he tried. "Here? In Normandy?"

"I had to . . . leave Holland." She was fumbling for words. "So I came here. I owed too many people too much to just hide. To give up. To surrender."

"You came back to the farm?"

"I tried. But it was gone. Burned to the ground before I arrived."

"By who?"

"The Gestapo. Some SS, I am told." She swallowed. "I didn't even know my grandparents were dead until I came back. That they'd been dead for years. Which, I suppose, was just as well. They weren't alive to see what became of their farm." She dropped her hands from her eyes and blinked away the fuzziness. "The Resistance had been using the empty house and barns. The Germans shot everyone they found. Four were children. They wished to make an example. So I chose to do the same. It is what I am good at, after all."

"What? What does that mean?"

"It means that I still fight Nazis. France, Holland, it matters not."

"Stasia—"

"I asked you to call me Rose."

"No."

She stared at him. "No?"

"Other men may call you Rose, or Briar Rose. But I will not. It's not your name."

"Says Captain Thomas Phillipe," she mocked.

A muscle in his jaw ticked. "I am Nicolas to you. I always will be. Just like you are Stasia to me. I never stopped loving you, not even when I thought you were gone. Do you understand that? The memory of your heart, your kindness, your . . . goodness is what got me through the days when there was only darkness. That will never change."

"Everything has changed. I've changed." Stasia shook her head. "Go back to your men, Captain Phillipe."

"Not without you. I came for you."

"You came for someone who doesn't exist," she hissed. "I am not the kind, good princess, trapped under a magical spell and waiting in the forest for her prince to save her from the evil dragon."

"I don't think that you are—"

"I am not the kind princess, I am the fucking dragon, Nicolas," she rasped. "The dragon that slayed its enemies and regretted only that it didn't kill more."

"Good." His eyes were burning furiously. "Because this world that we've found ourselves in needs dragons. Strong, terrifying, fierce dragons. I never wanted a princess. I only ever wanted you."

She shoved at his chest, and he stumbled back. "You're not listening to me. I've seen terrible things. I've done terrible things. I will do more terrible things."

"And you think you're the only one?" He regained his footing and stepped forward, and now it was Stasia who was forced back. "You think you're the only one who has seen terrible things and done terrible things?"

Her hip scraped against the rough bark of an oak, and she came up short, caught between his body and the tree. Her palms braced against the flat plane of his chest, as if that gesture would stop the charged emotion that was crackling between them like lightning.

"You want to run from me, that's fine," he snarled. "You want to believe that you are the only person who this war has changed, go right ahead. But know this." He put his hands on either side of her head against the bark, his face inches from hers. "I will not let you go a second time."

Stasia's fingers curled into the front of his uniform a second before her lips found his. She kissed him and clung to him with every ounce of anger and regret that was threatening to drown her. She kissed him with the urgency and desperation that she should have kissed him with six years ago, when everything had still been possible. She kissed him with the heartbreak and anguish that was squeezing her chest like a vise because she knew that this was the last time she would do so.

And then she pulled back from him, both of them breathing hard. In a graceless move, she ducked under Nicolas's arm, retreating a safe distance from him.

"Today, we will make plans for what must be done, and we will see those plans through together because I will not run from you or this fight," she said unevenly. She took another step away, farther down the slope.

Nicolas had turned to watch her but made no move to follow.

"And after that, if I still live, you will forget me. You will let me go. You will find yourself a kind girl who still has a heart to give away, and you will make her very happy." She steeled herself against the unwanted emotion that was threatening her control. "But that girl won't be me, Nicolas."

★ ★ ★

The Château de Montessaire had been infested.

That was the word that had stuck in Stasia's mind as she observed the grounds while hidden in the thick undergrowth of the forest that bordered the western edge of the property. A row of beetle-black cars scuttled up and down the long drive, disgorging their unsmiling passengers and accommodating new ones. Grey-clad men, visible through the tall windows, swarmed throughout the château, while a handful more, with helmets glinting under the sun like carapaces, skittered back and forth across the grounds.

"Damn lot of the bastards, isn't there?" It was Thatcher who spoke, his long body wedged awkwardly between two fallen

logs, his binoculars stuck to his face. "And they don't look happy.
We've kicked the hornet's nest to be sure."

The Allies were on the shores of France. Anyone who could
had listened to the BBC broadcast as the radios had crackled with
the news. Part of Stasia was still afraid that it was a false alarm,
that tomorrow they would wake to the news that the Allies were
not pressing inland from the beaches along the coast but still
besieged by bad weather, bad planning, bad luck, or all three.

But for now, she would believe that this was the start of the
end. The Jeds certainly believed it. The broadcast had mobilized
them into a sort of grim urgency that had pervaded the camp.
The maquisards had deferred to the Jeds immediately. Whether
it had been Franklin's decisive boldness, Thatcher's direct contact
with London, or Nicolas's quiet confidence as he spoke to the
men, it was impossible for Stasia to know.

Or maybe it had just been their uniforms.

Stasia shifted where she lay in the tangled brush, dampness
from the ground bleeding into her trousers and the elbows of her
sweater. The rich perfume of earth hung heavy around her. Above
her head, songbirds still sang as they flitted in and out of the leafy
canopy, though those sounds were layered on top of the steady
hum of an unseen engine somewhere in the rear of the château. A
generator, Stasia guessed, and one that Franklin and Sascha, posted
in the shadows on the opposite edge of the property, would be
able to see.

Beside her, Nicolas adjusted his own binoculars as another
black car roared up the driveway, its tyres splashing in the
remnants of puddles.

Stasia kept her eyes on the building, careful not to look at
him. Careful not to touch him.

"A half dozen officers have been in and out," Nicolas said.

"Hard to tell who might be billeted here. Perhaps a dozen men operating the exchange. Four more patrolling outside." He paused. "No way to know how many others are inside without watching for days, not hours. Cooks and clerks and such."

"We don't have days," Thatcher grumbled unhelpfully. "But you're right. Too much traffic for a daytime attempt."

Stasia stayed quiet and listened to the men speaking. They'd already had this conversation earlier in camp, and she had offered them the same opinion. That the activity in and out of the château, especially now, would make a daytime attempt nothing short of suicide.

Thatcher fiddled with the focus on his binoculars. "And this tunnel you spoke of, Phillipe, it exits in that garden?"

"Southeast corner. In a stone shed."

"And you think it's still accessible?"

Stasia heard Nicolas exhale.

"I think so, yes," he said. "Unless you know where to look, it's hidden well."

"And you've been inside this tunnel too?" Thatcher asked Stasia.

"Yes." She ignored the speculative look that the Englishman had fixed on her. "And the captain is right," she said. "Unless you know where to look, it would be difficult to find."

"Yet the both of you found it."

There was a question in that statement that Stasia chose not to answer.

Neither did Nicolas. "I don't see any dogs," he said instead. "That will make you happy, Thatcher." He checked his watch. "We need to go. Franklin will be waiting—"

"Wait." The radioman interrupted him and peered through his binoculars.

At the front of the château, the black car that had splashed up the drive had rolled to a stop. The driver frantically clambered out of the car to open the passenger-side door. He was too late. The German officer had already shoved the door open himself and stepped out, his movements angry and erratic.

"Now who is this delightful prince of a man?" Thatcher murmured. "He looks important. SS if I'm not mistaken." He passed the binoculars to Stasia. "Do you recognize him?"

Stasia put the glass to her eye, but she didn't have to. She already knew who the officer was. She had seen him well over a fortnight before, in Val-de-la-Haye, when she had gone into the town to collect messages. At the time, she had been dressed as a French countrywoman, wearing a bulky dress to hide her shape and a shawl over her head to help hide her face.

She had recognized him immediately even with the large patch he now wore over one eye and the red, half-healed scar that puckered the skin on his left cheek. It had been the first time she had seen him since she'd shot him, and the sight of him had shocked and jarred her so badly that she had fled back into the forest without the messages to collect her wits and calm her breathing.

When her faculties had steadied, she was left with only a profound regret that she hadn't killed him after all. He had survived. And now he was here.

And, she knew without a doubt, he was here for her.

"Sturmbannführer Otto Diekmann."

Both Nicolas and Thatcher twisted to look at her. She deliberately kept the binoculars set at her eyes. Two other grey-coated soldiers had stepped from the back of the vehicle and hurried around the rear of the château.

"You sound quite certain of his identity," Thatcher remarked.

"Yes."

"You've met him." That was from Nicolas.

"Yes," she confirmed.

"Where?"

"Church," she said.

"May I suggest that this might be an opportune time for you to answer us with more than single syllables?" Nicolas's words were flat and clipped.

"A church in Haarlem." Two men had exited the château to meet the irate sturmbannführer. Diekmann had a small canvas bag in his hand that he tossed at their feet with clear fury. He was shouting, making angry slashing gestures with his hands, though Stasia was too far away to hear what he was saying.

Thatcher reached for his binoculars and plucked them out of her hand. He squinted through them. "The men he is addressing are Gestapo," he mused. He lowered the glasses and fixed Stasia with a grim stare. "The Gestapo are not here to jump into the trenches to help defend their Nazi masters from whatever military wave is coming overland from the beaches."

"No. They are here for me. Diekmann certainly is."

"For you? That is a somewhat . . . bold assertion."

Stasia watched as another grey-coated officer came out of the château, his hands raised in a placating gesture. Stasia had no idea who the new German was but Diekmann paused his rant long enough to point in the general direction of the north. The two men seemed to fall into an argument of some sort.

"You didn't answer my question," Thatcher said.

"You offered me an opinion, not a question."

"Fair. Allow me to rephrase. Why would an SS sturmbann-führer be looking for you, specifically?" Thatcher's query was deceptively pleasant as he dropped his binoculars to look at her.

This was a version of the same question that Nicolas had tried to ask her earlier, when her emotions had been fragmented and treacherous and mercurial. At the time, she hadn't answered him, not how he had wanted. She hadn't been able to look him in the eye and irrecoverably destroy whatever illusion he might still be clinging to. But here she was not looking Nicolas in the eye. Here, she was looking at the enemy and reminded of the devastation that the black-and-grey uniforms left behind in their wake and in everything that they touched.

Here, her emotions were not treacherous and fragmented but unhampered and honed.

"He is here for me because I have liquidated thirty-six of his contemporaries," she told Thatcher in an equally pleasant voice. It was surprisingly easy to speak to this radioman whom she did not know and who did not know her. To say the things that she should have said to Nicolas earlier but had not. "Twenty-five in Holland. Eleven so far in Rouen."

Thatcher blinked.

"He hunted me in Holland. Tortured and killed members of the Resistance and their families to get to me. He almost succeeded. But he did not manage to kill me, nor did I manage to kill him. We both bear the scars of that altercation. Diekmann arrived in Rouen after I made seven German officers vanish. I cannot imagine that his arrival was a coincidence but perhaps you harbour a different opinion, since you have many." She pushed herself up on her elbows. "Is that enough syllables for you both?"

The Englishman cleared his throat. "Quite."

"You asked me earlier why I was not with my men," she said. "The more distance I put between myself and the men who have stayed to fight, the safer they stay and the safer I stay. I don't sit in camp and trade gossip about their families or futures. I don't want to know about their wives and their homes that they've left. I'm not their friend, and they are not mine." She took a deep breath. "I was betrayed once because I didn't understand that every man has his price. A weakness that can be exploited. I have been careful not to make the same mistake twice." She didn't look at Nicolas the entire time she'd been speaking, nor did she wait for him to say anything. Instead she wriggled backward through the thick undergrowth.

Similarly, she did not wait for the Jeds and instead retreated deeper into the wood, following ancient animal paths that zig-zagged into the heart of the forest that she had once traversed as a child. The air was cool, the temperature in the shade of the forest almost chilly. She wrapped her arms around herself and looked up at the crown of leaves above her head that blocked a grey and moody sky. She wondered where the men who were supposedly landing somewhere on the beaches of Normandy were right now. How far they might have made it. The Germans defending the shores of France would die, eventually, but they would die hard. And they would exact a price for that death.

Major Franklin was already waiting, sitting motionless on a fallen log at their rendezvous site. He caught sight of her and waved briefly, though his eyes continued to scan the forest and his bearing was still rigid. "It's about time." He didn't look happy. "Where are Thatcher and Phillipe?"

She shrugged. "Behind me."

"Yes, I see them now." He was looking in the direction she had come. He waited until Thatcher and Nicolas joined them. "You are all late. And time is not our friend at the moment." He scowled. "What did you see?"

Thatcher ignored the reprimand and launched into a recountal of their observations. He did not mention Diekmann. Franklin nodded as he spoke, though it was difficult to tell if he was pleased or displeased with the news.

"From what I saw on the other side, the telephone cables run into the château from the northwest corner where you have the ballroom marked," the major said. "I must assume that the terminal frames and switchboards are housed in the same space. Which would be a stroke of good fortune." He squinted at Nicolas. "Nothing underneath the ballroom, you are sure?"

Nicolas shrugged. "There is only a cellar underneath the kitchens."

"That you are aware of."

"That I am aware of."

Franklin grunted and swung his gaze to Stasia. "You've been inside. Do you agree with the captain that there isn't a basement or cellar under the ballroom? Where the terminal frames might be installed below the switchboards?"

"I've only been inside once." She didn't look at Nicolas. "But yes, the cellar under the kitchen is not large and does not extend very far. Certainly not to the ballroom. But that is all I can say."

"A mission built on goddamn guessing," Franklin groused. "And only enough explosives that we must rely on those guesses. I don't like it." He scowled, his thick fingers tapping against his thigh. "There is a generator at the back of the château, near the entrance to what looks like one of those fancy gardens kings and queens used to have. They've built a lean-to over the top of it to protect it from the weather and such. Diesel, from what I can see. Powers the entire telephone system, I must assume, and maybe the entire château. I can't say for certain. But I think both the communication equipment and the generator need to be destroyed. Don't want the damn boches to have everything back up and running again in a week. It must be irreparable."

"Do we have enough explosives to destroy the generator too?" Thatcher asked.

"Yes," Nicolas answered slowly. "But it means that every bit counts. It means that we will need to get inside that room. Get the explosives inside to the switchboards and terminals to do the most damage." He grimaced. "And that will be . . . challenging, even at night."

"Not if you're a German," Stasia said.

Three sets of eyes pinned her where she stood.

"We have many Nazi uniforms to choose from." She shrugged. "And perhaps if the generator was the first to go, and the power to the château was compromised, and it was dark and confusing, there would be a window of opportunity."

Franklin's face was a mask of incredulity. "What do you mean, you have uniforms to choose from?"

"Dead Nazi officers have no need of their uniforms. I collect the uniforms in the event that they might become useful. Such as now."

The major stared at her long and hard. Nicolas and Thatcher remained silent.

"How many uniforms?" Franklin finally asked.

"Eleven." Stasia crossed her arms.

"Eleven," Franklin repeated.

"More than enough for what you will need."

"And how do you know what we will need?" he demanded.

"You will not storm the Bastille with an army of partisans, no matter how loyal and enthusiastic they may be. Not for this. The Germans have the advantage of defence, numbers, and weaponry, and a blunt approach would simply turn the château into a fortress. They are already alert with the Allied landing. The only advantages you have, which are surprise and stealth, would be lost. Yes?"

"Yes," Franklin said grudgingly.

"The men in camp will create a diversion of your choosing in a place of your choosing at a time of your choosing. Enough to allow your team time to get in and out. Silent and quick and—" She stopped abruptly and frowned. "Where is Sascha?"

The young guide should have been with the major.

Franklin looked distracted. "Left. Said he had something to do while the boches were busy."

Stasia stood up. "What? When?"

"Probably a half hour ago. I've been waiting—"

"Where did he go?" she asked.

Franklin's expression darkened. "How the hell should I know? He comes and goes like a wraith. There one minute, gone the next."

"Did he have anything with him?"

Franklin's scowl only deepened. "A bag of some sort? Tools maybe?"

Stasia tried to keep the panic out of her voice. "Which way?" she repeated quietly. "Which way did he leave from here?"

Franklin gestured north. "That way."

Stasia was already running, tearing through the trees and the underbrush as fast as she could manage. Branches whipped at her face and snagged her sweater but she didn't slow. To the north lay the road that carved through the forest and led to the main road to Rouen. A road populated by telephone poles with cables that had never been cut because it was too close to

Rouen. Too close and too exposed to the regular traffic of the occupying Nazis.

Distantly, she was aware that there were booted feet running behind her but she didn't stop to ask why or who or how, only kept pushing until she saw the trees thin and the ribbon of brighter light of the cleared roadway ahead. She slowed as the shelter of trees gave way to scrub brush that had filled in the slope angling up toward the roadway.

"The wee fool did it, didn't he?" Thatcher said as he caught up with her. He sounded uncharacteristically distressed. "He tried to prove himself to us."

Stasia couldn't answer as she slid and scrambled up the slope. Nicolas had also caught up with her but she ignored him. All she could see in her mind was the bag that Sturmbannführer Diekmann had tossed angrily at the feet of the two Gestapo men at the château. Perhaps his fury was from the discovery that the cable had been cut. And that Sascha had escaped. Perhaps the boy had had to flee without his tools—

A hand grabbed her arm and yanked her back, and she found herself caught up against a strong chest. She was forced to her knees, and the arms around her were like a steel trap.

She struggled, unable to move. "Let me go—"

"No," Nicolas whispered in her ear.

"Oh, Christ," she heard Thatcher say. "Goddamn it all to hell."

Stasia shoved against Nicolas. "Get off of me," she snarled.

He let her go.

They'd hanged Sascha from a telephone pole. His hands had been tied behind his back, his feet tied together, and a thick coil of rope was wrapped around the upper cross braces of the pole and then looped around his neck. His pale shirt was spotted with dark, crimson stains where bullets had struck his slight body, though it was impossible to tell if he'd been shot or hanged first. His head was bowed at a crooked angle, his disheveled brown hair hiding his face.

There were two German soldiers who were on the far side of the road by the body. One had a camera, and Stasia watched as the other soldier lifted Sascha's head by his hair as a photo was snapped. He released Sascha's hair, and both of them laughed as his head lolled to the side. The soldier picked up a small, crudely written sign and hung it over the boy's head. It was written in French and German. The photographer took a dozen steps back and snapped another photo.

I am a partisan and helped Briar Rose.

Stasia bent double, her hands on her knees. Her chest burned, her eyes burned, her gut burned. Everything burned and twisted, and she retched into the bushes, her empty stomach heaving. When the worst had passed, she slid her knife from her belt.

Nicolas put a hand on her arm. "They have a man posted. My ten o'clock. A third of the way up."

Stasia found the soldier in a makeshift tree stand on the far side of the road exactly where Nicolas said he would be. The soldier, dressed in grey, had a rifle balanced in front of him. He was talking to one of the soldiers on the ground, gesturing with his free hand as they photographed the body.

"They would draw you out," Thatcher said, sounding subdued. He was crouched behind a thick stand of brush. "Draw us out. Any one of your men."

Stasia took deep breaths through her nose, trying to cool the helpless rage that was coursing through her. Nicolas and Thatcher were right, she knew. It was a crude trap, but an effective one.

"Is there more than one sniper?" Nicolas was asking the lieutenant.

"Can't say. Don't see another posted but that means nothing."

"We can't..." Nicolas trailed off, clearly struggling.

"We can't," Thatcher agreed. "Not now." He dropped his head. "Goddamn."

The two soldiers had finished with their photos and now lingered on the side of the road. The sound of an approaching car made them turn, and the same black vehicle that had roared up to the château now bounced down the road toward them. The same hapless driver brought it to a stop, and Otto Diekmann stepped from the passenger side and examined the soldier's handiwork. He put a hand up to the patch on the side of his face and said something to one of the soldiers. All three got into the car, and the engine sputtered back to life. The vehicle kicked up dirt as it sped off down the road, back in the direction of the château.

The sniper in the trees settled into his perch, becoming difficult to see.

"I'm sorry," Nicolas said quietly. "So sorry."

"Poor, foolish boy." Thatcher was pinching the bridge of his nose, his face pale.

Stasia barely heard them. She was trying not to picture Sascha's earnest face this morning. She was trying not to think about what she would tell his little brother. She was trying to find her way back to that empty cold center of her being that kept her safe and separated from the world and the hurt that it was filled with. She failed.

Nicolas moved to touch her shoulder, and she jerked away. "Don't."

If he touched her, if he drew her into his arms, if he even looked at her with pity or compassion or sympathy, she would splinter into pieces. She had never felt so fragile.

"Don't say anything to the men in camp. Not yet. Not until tomorrow, do you understand? And then I will tell them."

Nicolas's hands curled into fists. "St—Rose," he started, but she cut him off.

"Tonight, I will help you destroy the château and the Nazis within." She straightened, keeping low behind the bushes, keeping well out of sight of the gunman in the trees overlooking Sascha's body. "And then I will come back for Sascha. His brother needs to be able to say goodbye."

Both men nodded.

Stasia slid her knife back into its sheath at her waist. "And then, I will kill the rest of them."

CHAPTER

22

Nicolas

T hey slipped into the abandoned garden of the château two hours before dawn.

Late enough that perhaps even the most industrious of Germans would have stolen away to catch a few hours of sleep. Early enough that darkness might still cover the Jeds' retreat back into the safety of the forests. The clouds that had sat low and heavy these last days had parted enough to allow the waning moonlight to filter across the grounds. The wind that had tugged at the leaves and long grasses all day had settled, leaving a quiet stillness in its wake.

There were four of them—the three Jeds and Stasia. It had been Franklin's decision that Stasia accompany them. She had been in the château already, the major had again pointed out, which was surely an advantage, even if it had been only once. Franklin had, of course, said that after he had watched Stasia produce almost a dozen Nazi uniforms from a heavy wooden box buried somewhere close to the camp. After she had offered her regrets that one might be too bloodstained to use and that the weapons that had accompanied them had long ago been dispersed to Resistance members. And after she had outlined her plan for the Nazis occupying Château de Montessaire. It had been the first time that Nicolas had seen Franklin robbed of speech, reduced to simply nodding.

After that, Stasia had said very little when they had returned back to camp. She had remained silent as Franklin gave the maquisards their assignments and only listened when a few had voiced concerns or ideas. She had joined Thatcher and Nicolas in collecting the materials and working through the preparations, speaking only when spoken to. She had avoided the inevitable concern from the maquisards wondering where Sascha had got to, pleading ignorance. But most of all, she had avoided Renaud Dubois.

And if anyone in camp took notice that her face was paler, her expression harder, her manner rougher, no one said anything.

She crouched beside Nicolas now, in the overgrown web of vines near the west garden wall. If she was at all nervous or apprehensive about what they were about to do, she didn't show it. He resisted the urge to touch her, just briefly, just for a moment of reassurance. A moment of connection.

From here, he could see that the upper windows of the château were dark. On the ground floor on the far west side, where the ballroom was, bright light shone, casting long rectangles of radiance across the overgrown grounds between the château and the garden. Nicolas had to assume that there were still men at their switchboard posts. There were lights in the opposite end of the château as well, in the kitchen windows, though it was softer. They had seen only two soldiers on their approach, one at the front door and one guarding the rear, servants' entrance near the kitchens. The heavy guard that had been suggested in their briefing appeared to have been reassigned in the face of the invasion. Both Germans were slumped against the walls at their posts, appearing to be losing the fight with exhaustion.

Stasia rose from her crouch and slipped through the dark, moving quickly, her hand over the bulky leather satchel she wore across her body. The generator on the other side of the wall, closer to the château, continued to chug and rattle, covering any sounds that they might make. Nicolas followed her into the garden, staying close behind her, his own satchel solid against his hip. They wove through the overgrown pathways as silently as possible. Ahead, the dark shape of the angel rose up against the night sky, and he skirted the monument, trying to ignore the memories that rose up alongside it. In the moonlight, he could see that the angel's wings had been chipped and broken, brighter scars in the stone visible where the sculpture had been used for target practice. He looked away and kept going.

While the angel had been damaged, the ancient garden shed looked exactly as it had years ago, as if time and war and circumstance had simply passed it by. The pale stone still glowed in the moonlight, framed by the shadows of the trees on either side. Long grass and weeds grew tall in front of the door, suggesting to Nicolas that no one had been inside in some time. Nicolas listened hard, but aside from the distant hum of the generator, there was no sound of activity. He glanced at Stasia, who was waiting for him in the shadows beneath the slight overhang of the shed roof. She only nodded, her eyes impossible to see beneath the brim of the cap she wore.

Nicolas drew his commando knife, the one they had given him in Scotland during his training. If, for some reason, he needed a weapon, the discharge of a gun here and now would end the mission before it even started. Stasia was pulling the shed door open with effort, the hinges protesting after years of neglect. Nicolas winced at the sound but knew it was unlikely that anyone from the château would ever hear it.

Stasia slipped inside, and Nicolas followed with a peculiar sense that he was stepping back in time. In an instant, he was thirteen again, returning to his safe haven, a satchel full of stolen parts and pieces, hunger and cold hounding him. Except, he realized as the shed door closed behind him, he was no longer thirteen, this shed was far from safe, the contents of his satchel were not stolen, and he was sweating heavily under his uniform.

The shed was musty from years of neglect, the cloying scent of soil, mildew, and dust thick around him. He heard the rustle of fabric and a click, and the little shed was suddenly illuminated by Stasia's torch. She cupped a hand over the light to dim it and looked around. There were broken pottery bits strewn across the floor, and someone had removed the old garden tools that had once been propped in the corner. But on the far side, the cot that Nicolas had once slept on remained jammed against the wall, seemingly untouched though the canvas now hung ragged and gaping from the rusting frame.

Underneath, the door to the tunnel was undisturbed, a thick layer of dust and debris on top.

"They didn't find it." Nicolas kept his voice low. He sheathed his knife.

"No."

Nicolas lifted the cot out of the way and pulled the trap door open, turning his face away from the cloud of dust that rose. He pushed the door up against the shed wall. Stasia slipped by him, and the beam of her light bounced off the narrow stairs.

He caught her arm before she could descend. "Stasia."

She stopped.

Nicolas reached for her hand, the one that was not holding the torch. He took it gently in his. She didn't pull away, even when he turned it over. Very slowly, he ran his fingers over the steel band that still encircled her finger.

He heard her inhale.

Nicolas held on for a second longer and then released her. "I'll go first" was all he said.

He descended quietly, pausing every few steps to listen hard. But beneath his booted feet, the layer of dust on the ground remained undisturbed, and he left footprints as he advanced, Stasia's light behind him playing off the floor and guiding the way. It took them only moments to reach the château entrance. Nicolas listened at the door but heard only silence. This was the part of the plan where the first of many things could go terribly wrong. He might pull this door open to find that the occupying Germans had installed an immovable barricade against the wall like shelves or heavy crates. Or turned the cellar into a barrack for a dozen soldiers not possessing a rank high enough to earn them a bedroom upstairs.

Nicolas put his hand on the bolt, and Stasia extinguished her torch.

"Do it," she whispered.

As silently as possible, Nicolas slid the bolt back. He grasped the heavy iron handle of the door and pulled, opening it just wide enough to peer through. In the darkness, he couldn't see much. The air that whistled through the opening was cold and damp, which allayed his fears that he would open this door to face men bristling with weapons. His eyes slowly adjusted enough that he could see a faint line of light coming from the far side of the cellar, beneath the door that would lead up into the kitchens. The fact that light was visible meant that the Germans hadn't blocked the opening either.

Relief trickled through him.

He pulled the door open a little wider, his entire body tense. But there was no shout of alarm. There was nothing. They were alone in the cellar.

Stasia clicked the torch back on, careful to shield the light and keep it pointed at the ground. It was enough to see that the cellar was mostly empty save for wooden boxes of what looked like potatoes and turnips and heavier wooden crates filled with rows of wine bottles. Silently, Nicolas and Stasia stepped from the hidden door and closed it behind them. They crossed the cellar and climbed the stairs that would lead them into the kitchens. Under the kitchen door, a thin strip of soft light glowed. This was the point of no return, Nicolas knew. There was no going back once they stepped into the château.

"Ready?" he asked.

"Yes." She adjusted the cap on her head and the satchel across her shoulder and checked the weapons at her waist. She met his gaze with whiskey-colored eyes that burned only with unwavering resolve.

She turned off the torch once more, and he pushed open the door.

The kitchens were deserted. A light had been left burning on the far side of the wall, presumably for anyone who wandered into the space during the night. The pots and pans that Nicolas remembered hanging from above the large butcher block were still there, but the counters were now covered with bowls and utensils and tins and containers that suggested the kitchens would become a busy space when the sun rose. He had no plans to still be here when that happened.

Stasia had gone immediately to the windows facing south, toward the garden and the thick forests beyond that. She turned the torch on and off three times. Within seconds, an answering signal flickered from the darkness beyond.

She slipped the torch into her satchel and joined him. "One minute."

They moved away from the window and toward the hall entrance. Stasia checked the contents of her bag. Nicolas checked the weapons at his waist. Neither spoke. In one minute, everything would move very, very fast.

A clatter froze them in place, and with a sinking sensation, Nicolas watched as a German sentry stumbled into the kitchen, rubbing his face and blinking the sleep from his eyes. The rifle slung over his shoulder slid, and he caught it with clumsy movements before it could hit the floor. As he straightened, he caught sight of Nicolas and Stasia and straightened abruptly. Nicolas cursed inwardly. He stepped forward and pinned the sentry with an unforgiving stare.

The soldier opened his mouth to speak but then closed it as he took in Nicolas's uniform and the oak leaves on the badges at his collar. His eyes bulged.

"I am Standartenführer Karl Graf," Nicolas snapped in German. "I am here investigating threats to the Reich, some which we believe to be internal." His accent was probably not perfect, he knew, but he had practiced with Thatcher until the Englishman had been satisfied.

He waited for the soldier to demand to know why he was investigating in the middle of the night but the soldier was apparently as cowed by the uniform as Stasia had suggested he would be.

"Why are you not at your post?" Nicolas snapped.

Again the sentry opened his mouth to speak but was too flustered to answer.

"Return to your post immediately," Nicolas continued. "I will be making arrests shortly. If you interfere, I will arrest you too, understood?"

The soldier nodded frantically. "Yes, Standartenführer!" He scrambled out of the kitchen.

Nicolas looked out the window. All he could see was his reflection in the glass against the darkness beyond. Silently, he urged Franklin and Thatcher to hurry.

"Can I help you?" A new voice made Nicolas's head snap around. An officer stood in the kitchen entrance now, eyeing Nicolas and Stasia and appearing considerably less intimidated than the hapless sentry.

"Standartenführer Karl Graf," Nicolas repeated. "I am here investigating threats to the Reich, some which we believe to be internal."

The man standing in front of him took a step back but didn't leave. Nor did he reply.

Nicolas glanced at his watch. One minute was up. He deliberately did not look in the direction of the south-facing windows.

"I will be making arrests shortly," Nicolas said again. "If you interfere, I will arrest you too, understood?"

The man glanced at the SD diamond on Nicolas's sleeve. "Perhaps I should get Sturmbannführer Diekmann if you believe that the threat is imminent?" he suggested. "He is but upstairs just now. Perhaps he could help."

Beside him, he felt Stasia stiffen.

"No." Nicolas could feel an icy bead of perspiration slide down his back. His German was competent thanks to his training, but not good enough to fool a suspicious communications officer for long. He snapped his fingers at Stasia, her grey-and-black cap pulled low over her face, her uniform crisply pressed and brushed as befitting a standartenführer's aide. She obediently opened her satchel and withdrew a document that Nicolas snatched from her fingers and waved in front of the officer's face. It was an old document, taken from the same officer who had once worn the uniform and watch that Nicolas currently wore. It was, as far as they had been able to tell, a list of perceived political enemies scattered across Normandy prepared by the Gestapo in Rouen, but the official Reichsadler printed across the top was impossible to miss. "Do you recognize names?" he demanded.

The officer took it from his hands and started to read.

Nicolas glanced out the south windows, unable to help himself. Had something gone wrong? He didn't know how long this inane list would distract this officer.

The officer reading the list looked up, a deep crease in his brow. "This is months old," he said. His attention shifted to Stasia.

Nicolas stepped in front of her. "Do you recognize the names?" he demanded again. Jesus Christ, Franklin, he cursed silently. Where the hell are you? He was rapidly running out of options.

The officer was shaking his head. "Are you unaware of what has happened?" he said. "I should think that your attention would be better directed at the enemies that we can see on the shores of France right now. I will fetch Diekmann," he said. "And then—"

A deafening explosion ended his words. The south windows imploded, the building seemed to tremble, and all around Nicolas, everything went dark.

Dark except for a hellish glow that flickered through the

glassless windows as a red-orange fireball roiled and licked its way heavenward at the back of the château, somewhere near the garden wall.

Nicolas and Stasia ran then, past the stunned officer and into the darkened hallway. In the glow from the fire that filtered through the windows, he could make out the shapes of sentries running in all directions, shouting in panicked bursts. Nicolas and Stasia simply joined the panicked throng.

"We're under attack!" yelled Nicolas in German as loud as he could. "Get outside! The Resistance is attacking!" He had practiced that too. "Get outside! Follow them! Shoot them!"

Nicolas and Stasia ran across the great hall and into the west wing, heading for the ballroom. Both doors at the far end stood ajar, and they hurried through, coming to a stop just past the entrance.

The last time Nicolas had been in the ballroom, it had been eerily empty, with only the massive chandeliers that hung from the ceiling like giant wrought iron spider webs watching over the dusty, patterned floor. At the time, he had tried to imagine what it would have looked like if a thousand candles in those chandeliers were lit, the reflection of the candlelight bouncing off the glass in the windows and the long mirrors on either end. If the room had been crowded with people flushed with heat and drink and excitement, the women in brightly colored dresses, the men in severe black and white tailcoats as the perfect foil. If the strains of an orchestra had filled the air, loud enough to drown out the sound of laughter and chatter.

What he never could have imagined was what the ballroom looked like now.

The fire raging outside provided enough light to see that the patterned tile had been covered with long, narrow strips of carpeting running the length of the entire room. The chandeliers still hung but electric bulbs had been strung between them that, when lit, would illuminate the space in a harsh, artificial light. On the wall facing him, the ornamental mirrors had been removed and large blackboards mounted, with diagrams and schematics chalked out in careful detail. A pair of desks was situated near the doors, and behind them, two rows of long tables installed over the carpet ran the length of the room. An identical wooden chair with a metal frame was in place in front of each station, most tucked neatly under the tables but at least six had been pushed back in haste and two had toppled over altogether as their operators had fled. Towers of switchboards were secured to the tables, rows upon rows of jacks in each panel, and an array of cords and keys and receivers were mounted in front, waiting for their operators.

Mentally, Nicolas catalogued the number of switchboards even as his eyes skipped over the stations to the far northwest corner, where three tall racks stood near the back wall, a dizzying mess of colored wires weaving through each terminal frame. Franklin had guessed right. The terminal frames were here, with the switchboards.

But it would still be a lot of ground to cover. They would have to work fast.

There were only two men left in the room, both frantically jabbing cords into the female jacks. Their efforts were useless, Nicolas knew, for the source that powered the system had just gone up in a fireball thanks to an American and an Englishman.

"We're under attack!" Nicolas yelled again from where he stood. "Get outside! Get your weapons! The Resistance is attacking, get outside and shoot them!"

The men dropped what they were doing and stared in the direction of Nicolas for a brief moment before they, too, abandoned their stations and scrambled to follow orders.

Stasia was already hurrying toward the frames. Nicolas joined her, and she crouched before the first frame and opened her bag. Without speaking she started handing Nicolas the thin, narrow strips of plastic explosive they had prepared in camp. Nicolas wasted no time in molding the explosives throughout the frame. The sharp, acrid scent of almonds from the green plastic clung to his fingers. He had completed the first frame when Thatcher arrived, out of breath and sweating under his own SS uniform.

"Took your time, Lieutenant," Nicolas grunted as he secured the detonators and firing caps.

"Bit of a cock up out there," Thatcher panted. "Someone went and blew up a generator with a hundred liters of petrol stored next to it. There were two dozen Nazis who ran out of that château with their guns loaded in a mindless panic waiting for an officer to tell them what to do." He brushed at the braid on the shoulders of his grey uniform and grinned at Nicolas. "I was happy to oblige. Turns out three years of German studies at Oxford wasn't a complete waste after all." He examined Nicolas's progress and held out his hand to Stasia. "Fuses, my lady."

Stasia handed him the precut fuses.

The three of them worked quickly and silently throughout the room, planting and preparing the explosives as they had practiced in camp. Out in the hall, chaos still reigned as more men who had been woken clattered down the stairs to join the pursuit of the maquisards in the rear of the château. Outside, the sounds of gunfire could be heard, though it was farther away, in the forests behind the garden. The fire outside had abated somewhat, and with it, their light, and Stasia used her torch to help the men finish.

Nicolas unloaded his own satchel, which contained the thermite grenades that had been dropped with the Jeds. He placed them carefully throughout the frames next to the explosives. They would burn hot and fast once they were ignited.

"Will this take the walls down, do you think?" Nicolas asked.

"Don't rightly know." Thatcher finished twisting the bundle of fuses together. "These walls are stone and old and thick. Might just burn. Might burn the entire place down. Either way, I don't plan on sticking around to find out."

They were hidden by the long row of tables, near the slate boards on the wall where the mirrors had once hung. There was no good reason for anyone to come back into the ballroom because none of the equipment worked without power, but Nicolas wasn't taking any chances. Should a German stick his head into the ballroom, he wouldn't see the fuses. Not in time.

"Light it," said Thatcher.

Stasia produced a lighter and flipped it open, and the flame jumped. She bent and lit the fuse cords.

"Time to go," said Nicolas. They would have three minutes to get out and away.

Thatcher went first, crossing the room to the northwest windows. He fumbled with the latch and yanked the window open. He turned and urged Stasia forward. In a fluid motion, Stasia swung her legs over the sill and jumped, vanishing into the darkness beyond. Thatcher climbed up on the sill and peered down—

The shot came from behind them and shattered the window. Nicolas instinctively threw himself to the ground. Thatcher lost his balance and teetered on the edge of the window before he fell to safety on the other side.

Another shot, much closer this time, thumped into the sill.

Nicolas heard boots approaching, and he drew his weapon and fired blindly in the direction of the door. He had no idea if he'd hit anything but whoever had come into the ballroom after him could not come any farther without Nicolas risking them discovering the lit fuses. He closed his eyes and silently urged Stasia and Thatcher far away from this place.

"Surrender yourself and you will live." The lie was in French and heavily accented. "I wish to talk."

Nicolas would not live. At least, not for long. But he needed to live long enough to lead whoever had come into the ballroom back out in order to allow the fuses time to detonate.

He pushed himself to his feet and, running low, sprinted away from the windows and toward the ballroom doors. He fired a shot across his body as he ran.

The action seemed to surprise the German. Nicolas heard a shout of alarm, and two answering shots rang out, though they struck above his head. Good. He didn't bother to try to hide the noise that his boots made as he hurtled toward the doors. He heard pounding feet behind him and redoubled his efforts.

Get out of the ballroom, he chanted silently in his head. *Get out, get out.*

He burst through the doors unscathed and into the hallway. Another shot crashed from behind him, and the bullet shattered a mirror. A German soldier who had been hurrying through the great hall ahead slowed and looked in Nicolas's direction. He hesitated, confused no doubt by the dim light and the familiar uniform.

A torrent of furious German came from behind Nicolas,

and although he couldn't understand the words, the tone was unmistakable. The soldier at the end of the hall started toward Nicolas. Without pausing, Nicolas sprinted into the library, yanking the door closed behind him. There was no way to bar it, nor was the key in the lock. Nicolas swore and retreated toward the windows.

The library was unoccupied and only the carved griffins watched his flight in the soft glow of the old-fashioned sconce set near the door, candlelight dancing and creating shadows on the walls. Nicolas considered his options. If he jumped out the window now, it was possible that whoever was following him would abandon the chase and return to the ballroom to determine what he had been doing in there. At least, that's what Nicolas would have done. He tried to estimate how much time was left on the fuses. He guessed that less than a minute had passed since Stasia had lit them, though it felt like a lifetime.

He needed to keep them busy for two more lifetimes.

The door to the library crashed open.

A German officer stood in the entrance, the soldier from the great hall behind him. Both had their weapons drawn. Nicolas fired at the doorway in rapid succession and the soldier that had come from the hall dropped. The officer raised his own gun and fired. Nicolas dove behind the massive ebony desk sitting in the center of the room but not before a searing pain tore through the back of his right calf. He landed awkwardly on his shoulder and pushed himself up, ignoring the agony in his lower leg. He'd been hit, and he could feel hot stickiness sliding down his leg into his boot, but there wasn't time to examine his wound.

He lifted his revolver. Two shots left.

"I want to talk only," the German said again loudly in his choppy French. "But you are making this very difficult, yes?"

Nicolas looked at his watch. It was like time had slowed, the hands barely moving.

"You are not one of us." The German had moved farther into the room. "Yet you wear our uniform. I wish to ask about this."

Nicolas tried moving his leg and hissed at the pain. He wondered if the bullet had hit the bone.

"I come to France to find a person." The German was talking again, the sound of his boot heels subtle on the stone floor. "A person I know once in Holland. Who made our comrades disappear. I think for a time that this person is maybe dead. But then I hear news about Rouen. How more of those loyal to the Reich disappear again."

Nicolas leaned his head back against the desk. He just needed to give Thatcher and Stasia time to get far away. Time for Franklin and the rest of the maquisards to do their jobs.

"I think you must know this person." The officer sounded impatient. "This person who lures men to the forests. Always the forests." The footsteps paused. "Tonight I am woken by a . . . how do you say . . . loud fire. I look outside my window and see this fire and see so many German soldiers running after so few maquisards. I think, How do Germans get outside so quickly? These Germans are yelling for men to chase and shoot the maquisards, yet no one is shooting." His impatience was giving way to anger. "And then I see more Germans, real Germans, coming out of the château. These real Germans do not know the trap that they are running to. I cannot stop them in time. They run into the forests, following men in stolen uniforms. They will not come back. This I know because I know Briar Rose. She waits for them in the forests."

Nicolas slowly raised his revolver. His leg was on fire, his boot had filled with blood, and he was beginning to feel a little lightheaded. He shifted closer to the edge of the desk, trying to see around without exposing himself.

"I ask a boy today about this person. A stupid, stupid boy. He tells me nothing, not even after I take his fingernails and teeth. So he died."

Nicolas flinched, the memory of Sascha hanging lifelessly from the telephone pole flashing before his eyes. A rush of fury surged through his veins.

The officer sniffed. "Now I find you. Hiding behind my desk, yes? You don't have to die. Just tell me what I want to know. Where is Briar Rose?"

Nicolas lunged around the side of the desk and squeezed two shots at the shape that moved in the shadows. He retreated behind the safety of the heavy wood and opened the revolver, the casings spilling out. Quickly, he dug in his pocket for ammunition to reload. He wasn't quick enough.

"Leave your gun, yes?" The German officer was standing over him, his weapon aimed at Nicolas's head. "Or I shoot you now."

Nicolas recognized him easily from the afternoon prior. A wide black patch covered one eye, and beneath the skin was scarred and pulled tight. Sturmbannführer Diekmann. The Nazi who had hunted Stasia across a continent. With no little irony, Nicolas realized that Diekmann's obsession with Stasia was probably the only reason that he was still alive at this moment. Diekmann might not shoot him now, but he would likely shoot him in a matter of minutes when Nicolas refused to answer his questions about the Resistance fighter called Briar Rose. And by then, it would no longer matter. Whatever happened to him, he had done what he came to do.

"Get up." The gun jerked in his face.

With effort, Nicolas pulled himself to his feet, leaning heavily on the desk.

"Who are you?" the German demanded.

Nicolas didn't answer.

"You think you are brave by not answering. Noble, perhaps." Diekmann was studying him with his one good eye. He wasn't wearing a cap and his uniform was rumpled. His hair was mussed, and his cheeks were flushed with anger.

Nicolas remained silent.

"Open that drawer." The sturmbannführer motioned with his gun to the uppermost drawer along the side of the desk. "Go on."

Nicolas did as he was asked.

"Now take that box out. And open it."

Again, Nicolas did as he was ordered, glancing inconspicuously at his watch as he did so. Not so very long now.

The box was about the size of a small shoebox. In it was a collection of black-and-white photos, and an assortment of what looked like identity cards.

"Do you know who those people are?" the Nazi asked. "They are other people who thought that they were brave too. Like you, yes?" he said without waiting for an answer. "People who fought the Reich."

Nicolas's gaze had caught on a photo at the top, still glossy with recent developing. A young boy who had been hanged from a telephone pole with a crudely written sign around his neck.

"Ah, yes, you like that one?" Diekmann was watching him. "The stupid boy. I wonder how many in that box you know. They are all dead, yes? For their bravery." He spat the last word.

"You don't have to die though, yes? Just answer my questions. Where did you get this uniform?"

Nicolas looked away, his gaze settling on the griffins. *Once upon a time,* he thought to himself, *there was a boy from Rouen who believed that he could help win a war.*

Perhaps Stasia would one day write one more story. Their story.

"Answer me," Diekmann demanded.

Nicolas said nothing, only closed the box with deliberate motions and let it fall back into the open drawer. He slammed the drawer shut with enough force that he heard the wood crack and splinter.

This seemed to enrage the officer. He put the muzzle of his gun on Nicolas's forehead. "Tell me."

"I'll tell you that your men should know better than to run into a forest," Nicolas said. "Forests are dangerous. Ever changing and unknowable. Full of wolves. Every childhood tale tells of this."

Diekmann whipped the butt of his pistol across the side of Nicolas's head, and he staggered but didn't fall. The edges of his vision became blurred and the muzzle of the gun once again bit into the skin on his temple, pushing his head to the side.

"I have heard these stories. You forget what happens to the wolf in the end. The hunter always kills the wolf." His lips pulled back into what might have been a smile. "Tell me where to find Briar Rose."

A motion at the door caught his attention. Another Nazi officer stood, one with short dark hair that just barely curled under the cap pulled low. The officer had a gun held loosely by his side and was stalking into the room with purpose, though Nicolas wasn't sure if it was an illusion or reality. Everything was swimming in a sickening fog before his eyes.

"The story was changed," Nicolas managed. "To soften the truth that—"

"Tell me where to find Briar Rose," the German barked.

"—the wolf eats the unwary."

The sturmbannführer lowered the muzzle of his gun and shot Nicolas through the thigh. Nicolas went down in a daze of shock and pain.

"You will die but I can make it easier than this, yes?" Diekmann snarled, bending closer to him. "I have many bullets. All you have to do is tell me—"

His words ended with the sharp report of a Webley. The sturmbannführer crumpled unceremoniously to the floor beside Nicolas, his face slack, his one good eye wide and blank. There had been no clever words, no drawn-out declaration of vengeance, just an abrupt execution of justice.

"Get up, Navarre." Her voice seemed to come from a distance.

Nicolas tried to lever himself away from the body, but everything seemed so much harder, and his muscles didn't seem to want to work properly.

Hands grasped him under his arms and hauled him back toward the windows.

"You can't be here," he mumbled. "You need to get out."

Stasia ignored him.

There were explosives sent to detonate. Soon. Now. "Stasia—"

"Shut up," she snapped.

"Get out," he repeated. "Go away."

"No." Stasia levered him up against the wall. "Now help me."

Numbly, Nicolas managed to get his good leg underneath him, leaning weakly against the wall. Stasia unlatched the windows and hauled them open and then shoved Nicolas forward so he was half-draped over the sill, his head hanging out the window.

A man who faded in and out of focus and who looked remarkably like Franklin was standing underneath.

Stasia grasped his legs, and Nicolas lost his breath as pain washed through him. Without hesitating, she toppled him over the sill, and Nicolas crashed toward the ground outside, his fall broken by strong arms and accompanied by a string of curses. Stasia joined them, rolling as she hit the ground. Nicolas found himself heaved upside down over a broad shoulder as the American ran for the cover of the forest that edged the west side of the drive.

And in the next breath, the explosives detonated.

CHAPTER
23

Stasia

5 JULY 1944
ROUEN, FRANCE

S tasia found Renaud Dubois in the barn.
A barn cat had had kittens, and the boy was sitting alone in the corner with four tiny, squirming felines on his lap. He didn't look up when she sat down on a broken crate across from him. He just stroked the ginger tabby that wrapped herself around him while keeping a watchful eye on her babies.

"You shouldn't be in here," Stasia said.

Renaud shrugged.

"The barn is as likely to fall down on your head as it is to stand another day." The dilapidated barn had completely collapsed at one end and probably didn't have much time left before the elements completed the job.

"Doesn't matter." A kitten tumbled off his knee, and he scooped it back up.

"Your brother would think it matters." It would have broken Sascha's heart to see his little brother so withdrawn and despondent.

"My brother is dead." The boy swiped at his eyes, not meeting hers. "Both of them."

"Yes." The guilt that clung to the knowledge still stole her breath. It didn't make any difference that the men responsible for that were also dead. "But I don't think they would want you to die also. At least not yet. You still have much to do."

"Like what?" Renaud buried his face in the fur of the kitten.

"What do you want to do?" Stasia asked.

He finally looked up at her, his face tearstained. "I don't know."

"Sure you do. Tell me one thing that makes you happy."

He looked away into the shadows of the derelict barn. "I like making soup. With Madame."

Stasia tipped her head. "Then you should do that. Maybe you could learn to make more things to eat besides soup."

"It's dumb."

"It's not dumb. Everyone needs to eat. Food brings people together."

"I miss him," he said suddenly. "Sascha."

"I know. I'm sorry." She would never be able to tell him how much. She pulled out a piece of paper from the deep pocket of her trousers. "I made this for you." She stepped toward him and handed him the drawing.

Renaud looked at it, wiping at his nose. "That's me," he said, blinking.

"Yes. To remind you that you are still here. And that you are brave and strong like your brothers."

"I am riding a dragon."

"A griffin," Stasia corrected. "A griffin is more powerful and more majestic, and it guards the most priceless of all treasures."

"Oh." He ran his grubby finger over the sword she had drawn in his hand. "I look like a prince."

"You look like anything you want to be," she said. "And your brothers will always be proud of you, even though they are not here anymore."

The sound of Renaud's name being called across the yard had them both turning their heads.

"Madame needs you," Stasia said. "There is firewood that needs splitting."

Renaud got to his feet, kittens spilling gently to the ground. He eyed Stasia warily. "Thank you for the picture."

"You're welcome." She held herself stiffly. "Now see to your chores."

Renaud nodded and ran off, past the old farm wagon in the yard and toward the stone farmhouse.

She dropped her head and rubbed her face, feeling emotionally spent.

"That was kind of you."

Stasia jumped, stumbling back. Nicolas was standing in the bright summer sunlight, leaning on his crutches, watching her. He had shaved since she had seen him last, and someone, probably Madame, had trimmed his hair. The lines of fatigue and pain around his eyes had lessened.

She took a step away from him. "You were spying on me?" she accused.

"I'm not much of a spy these days." He lifted a crutch. "I'm not much of anything right now. There is a twelve-year-old boy doing the chores that I should be doing."

"It's good for Renaud to stay busy." She paused. "You shouldn't be out here. You might be seen."

"By who? The only other soul here besides Madame is Renaud. And I'm careful not to let him see me."

"You should still be careful."

"You came back." The statement was abrupt. "I wasn't sure you would."

Stasia hadn't been sure that she would either.

"It's been weeks since you were here last." Nicolas was watching her.

"It was better for everyone that I stayed away. Safer." She couldn't meet his eyes.

"Where have you been?"

She scuffed the toe of her boot in the dirt. "Rouen. What's left of it. The Allies are bombing the city into oblivion. At this rate there will be nothing left for the Germans to defend."

"Why?"

"To damage the German supply lines and bridges—"

"No. That's not what I meant. Why were you there?"

"So that when the Allies come to take the city, they have whatever information they need to avoid walking into an ambush."

"Are you safe?"

Stasia scoffed. "Is anyone?"

"The men you led—"

"I never led men."

Nicolas's lips thinned. "The men you . . . helped, then. Where are they?"

"Some are still here. Watching. Sabotaging when the opportunity presents itself in and around the city. But most went with Franklin and Thatcher to Caen." She paused. "Perhaps I should have gone with them."

"Why didn't you?"

"I didn't want to leave Renaud until I knew he would be all right."

"Ah." He looked like he was going to say more but mercifully fell silent.

"How does your leg feel?" she asked, having no desire to justify anything she did. Or didn't do.

"Much better, thank you." He was wearing trousers scavenged from somewhere, baggy enough to hide the bandages wrapped around his calf and thigh.

She wrapped her arms around herself. "You should have your leg up. You should be resting."

He made a face. "If I stare at the ceiling in that cellar for another moment, I will lose my mind."

"I don't really care. At least you won't lose your leg." She put her hands on her hips. "Let me see."

He shrugged and hobbled over to the remnants of a low stone wall that bordered the edge of the barn. Stasia bent and rolled the hem of his loose trousers up past both wounds. Someone had done a neat job of wrapping each with clean gauze. She made a sound of approval.

"Madame is particular," he told her. "I think she is a little scared of you and your instructions."

"Madame is not scared of anyone or anything." The white-haired woman who'd hidden the Jeds in her farmhouse had nerves of steel. Stasia knew that she had done a lot more over the years to defy the Nazi occupiers than hide men and look after a wounded Allied soldier.

Stasia unrolled the gauze on his calf and peered at the wound. The bullet had missed the bone but the damage to the muscle here was greater than to the one on his upper thigh, and she wasn't entirely sure that Nicolas would walk without a limp even when it was fully healed. But there was no unnatural redness or discoloration. Which was a relief. Those first two weeks, when Nicolas had lain weakened and exhausted, she'd been terrified that she might have missed something when she had cleaned his wounds. But there had been no debilitating fever, no dangerous infection. She checked the injury on his thigh and was equally satisfied that it was healing from the inside out.

"You were lucky." She rewrapped the gauze.

"Says every man with bullet holes in him."

"You were lucky that you have healed as well as you have." She rolled the leg of his trousers back down with care, overly conscious of how close she was to him.

"I had a good doctor." He caught her hand. "A very good doctor."

"I'm not a doctor."

"Not yet."

Stasia stilled.

"What are you going to do now, Stasia?" he asked quietly.

"Check in on Madame and get her to radio the German positions, or what's left of them, back to—"

"That's not what I meant, and you know it."

Stasia looked away.

"What do you want to do?"

Stasia pulled her hand from his.

"It's what you asked Renaud," he pressed. "And it is a good question. Probably the only question that really matters."

"I don't know."

"Yes, you do."

She laughed bitterly. "Can I tell you I want to make soup?"

"If that's what you want." A silence fell between them. From somewhere near the farmhouse, the steady thunk of wood being split drifted across the yard. "I think I'd like to fix things."

"What?"

"When this war is over. I'd like to open a shop or a garage and fix broken things. Spend the rest of my life making things whole again." Nicolas winced and shifted his weight on the stone wall and considered his crutches.

"I don't know that this war will ever be over."

"They say that the Brits and Canadians are close to taking Caen, and the Americans are closing in on Saint-Lô. It will not be long before the Allies liberate Rouen, and the rest of France. This will end, Stasia. I promise."

"You shouldn't promise things like that."

"Do you still write stories?" he asked suddenly. "Fairy tales?"

"No."

"Why?"

"Why?" she repeated incredulously. "Because they are useless. What good does a fairy tale do anyone anymore?"

"You told me that fairy tales were written to remind us of our humanity and principles and morality."

Stasia drew a shaky breath. "I don't think I have any of those things left."

"I'm not so sure." He tugged gently on her hand and she sat with an inelegant thump on the stone wall beside him. "I just watched you give away a drawing to make a scared, sad little boy feel better."

"To make myself feel better."

"Ah. And that was what you were doing when you drew a picture for me, then? When I was bruised and bleeding and scared and sad? You were making yourself feel better?"

"That wasn't the same."

"Wasn't it?"

Stasia stared down at their entwined fingers. "The day you arrived in camp, I told you I wasn't a princess but the dragon," she said. "But that was a lie. A dragon is a dragon from the time it is small. It doesn't pretend to be anything other than a dragon."

"Stasia—"

"You speak of principles and morality. Well, I'm not the dragon in this story, Nicolas. And I'm not Briar Rose, either. I am the queen mother who deceived those she pretended to love. Pretended to be one thing while hiding the fact that she was an ogre. An ogre capable of terrible things who has made her peace with meeting her fate in a pit of vipers of her own making."

"I see." Nicolas tipped his face up to the sun and closed his eyes.

"No, I really don't think you do—"

"The day the *Bretagne* sank," Nicolas said, cutting her off, "a thousand of my mates died, most within minutes, some a little longer." He opened his eyes and looked at her. "There wasn't time to do much besides survive. I tried to help those I could, I did, but they all died anyway. That I tried to help did not make me feel better."

Stasia saw a shadow of pain pass across his features.

"Oscar died that day. The one who I wrote to you about. Do you remember him?"

"The messman who liked newspapers and Gitanes and never met a deal he couldn't finesse or a meal he could refuse."

His lips curled sadly. "Yes. That was Oscar. I was with him when he died. It was slow and painful, and there was nothing I could do except watch it happen."

"I'm sorry," Stasia whispered.

"I told him a story at the end. When he was scared. The

story of Briar Rose because it was the only thing I could think to do so that he wasn't so afraid." He reached out and tucked a strand of her hair behind her ear. "You know what he said to me when I had finished telling him the story? He said that perhaps the prince should have been honest with his mother from the very start. And that the ogre's only sin was loving too much." He made a choked sound. "Well, that and she should never have trusted another cook with her sauces."

Stasia sniffed, her vision suddenly blurry.

Nicolas rubbed his fingers over the ring on her right hand. "Why do you still wear this?"

Stasia couldn't answer, emotions making her thoughts muddled and uncertain.

"If you want to run, I won't chase you." He looked up at her, his face grave. "Can't chase you at the moment, in fact."

She swallowed, her throat tight.

"Just tell me that you no longer love me."

"I can't." The words slipped out.

"I never stopped loving you, Stasia. You. The person you were, the person you are, the person you will become." His voice was hoarse.

"I don't think I know how."

"How to what?"

"How to become this person you think you will still love."

"Just . . . be."

"Be?" She stood again in sudden agitation, unable to stay still. "What the hell kind of answer is that? Is that what you are going to do? Just be? Pretend none of these last years ever happened? Forget it all?"

"I'm not going to forget anything. All of this will happen again if no one remembers." Nicolas lunged to his feet, balancing awkwardly without his crutches. "I can't change the past. I can't undo a war I never wanted, I can't unsee those who died while I lived."

He swayed slightly, and Stasia steadied him, his body heavy and warm against hers. His hands slid around her and pulled her to him like he was drowning.

Maybe they both were.

"Do you remember what you told me about your grandmother the day I met you? That she believed a person's soul is like an empty pail and that they can choose what to fill it with? That happiness and kindness are light and anger and sadness are heavy?"

"I remember," Stasia said. "You told me that was the stupidest thing you'd ever heard."

"I've learned a few things since then."

Stasia leaned her head against his shoulder.

"My pail is really fucking heavy right now, Stasia," he whispered raggedly against her ear. "And I think yours is too." He took a shaky breath, his chest rising against her cheek.

She tightened her arms around him, listening to the thump of his heart under her ear.

"I can't carry it by myself."

Neither could she.

"But I thought maybe," he said, "if I carry yours when you need me to and you carry mine when I need you to, that over time, if we keep looking forward and not back, they may not stay so heavy."

Stasia nodded against his chest, unable to trust her voice.

They remained like that for a long time, the sun beating down on them, songbirds bickering in the rafters of the decaying barn the only sound.

"Madame told me that it didn't burn," Nicolas said presently.

"What?"

"The château. It didn't burn down."

"I know."

"It doesn't sound like the ballroom will be ready for dancers anytime soon but the building survived. It's empty now. A blank canvas again for your imagination."

"Nicolas—"

"You should write a new story about the château. Or the garden. Imagine it again, not how we saw it last, but how you want it to be. I could help."

"Maybe."

"Maybe it would help us figure out how we can leave behind a better world than the one we were given."

"Maybe."

His arms tightened around her.

"What happens now?" Stasia asked after a time.

"We finish this war," he said. "We finish our fight."

"And then?"

"I heard there is a good medical school at the Université de Paris."

Stasia looked up at him. "Do you think it will still be standing by the time this is over?"

"We could find out."

"And if it isn't?"

"There is a farm not too far from here. Waiting to be rebuilt."

Stasia clung to him, unable to utter anything, her words trapped and teetering precariously on the edge of a terrifying cliff that felt like hope.

"Maybe we could do both," he mused. "If you wanted."

She still couldn't find the right words.

"I just...I want you to stay. With me."

Stasia finally found the right word. "Yes," she said.

"Yes?" Nicolas looked at her quizzically.

"I'll stay," she whispered.

The boy from Rouen held out his hand.

And the girl from Rotterdam took it.

CHAPTER
24

Isabelle

12 SEPTEMBER 2022
ROUEN, FRANCE

The garden, in the waning summer, was just as wild and overgrown as the last time Isabelle had been here. It was still painted in a stunning palette of colour—rich emeralds and jade interspersed with brilliant bursts of amethyst, ruby, citrine, and pearl. Birds sang all around them, butterflies danced across blooms, and bees went about their business with single-minded determination. No matter how old Isabelle grew, this place would always retain its enchanted fairy tale aura.

"It does seem a shame to restore this garden to its original state."

Isabelle turned in surprise at Emilie's comment. That was an abrupt departure from her insistence on paring the gardens back to what they would have looked like when the château was built.

"Really? You'll surrender your eighteenth-century vision of sheared hedges, sparse flowers, and austere paths?"

"That's a little dramatic." Emilie turned in a slow circle,

shifting the tablet she'd been using for notes and photos. "It would be historically accurate to restore this space to a Versailles-like layout, though on a much smaller scale." Her sister made a face. "Formal gardens with an army of full-time gardeners to keep it manicured and ordered."

"They would certainly need to be manicured," Isabelle agreed. "Forever and ever and ever and ev—"

"Point made." Emilie rolled her eyes and then paused. "What if we took your idea and left the gardens as they are? But tidied up a bit? Cleaned up the pathways, trimmed back some of the overgrown vines and undergrowth, repaired the stone benches and cleared the plot around the angel and the graves? Left everything the way it appears in Great-Gran's books?"

Isabelle looked up at the stone angel with her damaged wings and scarred silhouette. The angel was still beautiful despite the damage. Perhaps even more so because she still stood, imperfect and flawed. "I think it would be perfect. And very romantic."

"You don't think people would find it too creepy? With the graves and all?"

"No. The graves and the angel are part of the château's history. This is one of the beautiful spaces here to come and pay respect to both that history and the sisters who loved this garden as much as they did each other." On impulse, Isabelle lowered herself to the long grass and sat cross-legged beneath the angel, tipping her face to the sun and breathing in the rich perfume of her surroundings. "Truly, this garden is just the sort of place anyone might fall in love." She tried not to think of Luc as she said that.

Because she still hadn't managed to admit to anyone that she herself was in love. Most shamefully, she hadn't managed to tell Luc how she really felt. She'd worked beside him all summer, trying to muster the courage he seemed to believe that she had, while he had been nothing but courteous and wonderful and polite, giving her all the time and space that she didn't really want but took anyway.

Emilie joined her sister on the grass, their shoulders touching. "Maybe we could open the secret entrance up too for visitors to use during the day in the summer? It adds to the romanticism a bit, I think."

"I like it." Isabelle considered her sister, grateful for the distraction. "What made you change your mind about the gardens?"

"I was reading all of Great-Gran's stories again." Emilie slid a slim volume from beneath her tablet. "And I was thinking that the reason that we loved this place so much was partly due to her and the way she imagined it." She shoved a flyaway strand of dark hair from her eyes. "She would have been happy with what we've done with the château, I think."

"I think she would have loved it," Isabelle said. "But I think she would have loved the fact that we did it together more."

Emilie opened the book to the page illustrated with two defiant warrior princesses mounted on two identical griffins. "She always drew us like this, didn't she? Together."

"Yes." Isabelle pulled out a long blade of grass. "I missed that. Having you on my team."

"Me too." Emilie glanced in the direction of the château, the roof just visible over the garden wall. "We did a really good job on this, didn't we?"

"We did." Isabelle turned her head. The work on the château was nearly complete, the gardens and grounds the last major project left to tackle. "Are you disappointed that you didn't get your Briar Rose suite?"

"No, I'm not." Emilie smoothed her hand over the pages of

the story book. "Are you disappointed that we couldn't prove that Great-Gran was a Resistance legend?"

"No." Isabelle twirled the blade between her fingers.

She had spent months looking for more evidence that tied her great-gran to the legend of Briar Rose but had come up empty-handed. Even the information that Lise had provided on the Jedburghs who had landed in Normandy hadn't been helpful. Both the American and the British officers had records indicating that they had gone on to further service within the American and British armed forces, respectively. Both veterans had since passed away, and nothing they had left behind in any formal records made a reference to a Briar Rose. The French officer, Captain Thomas Phillipe, was recorded only as having been wounded in action, and his trail seemed to vanish after that.

All Isabelle had to tie her great-gran to a fierce Resistance legend, who may have started her fight in Holland and had ended her struggle in Normandy, was a drawing of a mythical warrior.

"Whoever Briar Rose was," Isabelle said slowly, "whether she really was Great-Gran or someone else, it was her choice, and her choice only, to leave her war behind her. To look forward and not back. I hope, whoever she was, that she was able to find happiness."

"I hope so too."

"Do you remember what Great-Gran and Great-Grandpa used to tell us when we were little? Whenever we fought?"

"The souls and pails thing?" Emilie laughed. "Happiness and kindness are light and sadness and anger are heavy?"

"Yes. And then they would always say that we were lucky to have each other. That if our pails ever got too heavy, that we should help each other carry them."

Emilie drew her knees up. "I remember Great-Grandpa saying that to me. Out in his shop, covered in grease, his head stuck under the hood of an old Renault. 'No one can carry everything alone, Emilie.'" She rested her chin on her knees. "He must have told me that a hundred times."

"I think that maybe that is good advice." Isabelle let the grass fall to the ground.

"You know, I think he would have been happy too. That we fixed something that was broken. Made it whole again."

Isabelle nodded and leaned back, watching the wisps of clouds drifting across the cerulean expanse of sky. "We should do this more often," she said.

"Sit in a garden?" Emilie sounded amused.

"Work together."

"Actually, I was going to ask you about that."

Isabelle looked over at her sister. "About what?"

"Since I've made my senior architects partners, I now have time to focus more on restoration architecture, and I've been asked to consult on a potential project. A small, eighteenth-century manor. The client would like to both preserve and make it a livable space, much as we've done here. They gain possession in early spring."

"Something else to add to your portfolio?"

Emilie's lips twisted wryly. "Yes, in fact." She played with the corner of the storybook page. "The client also requires a contractor with substantial experience in such restorations."

"And you suggested me?"

"Actually, the client suggested you. My contract is contingent on your agreement to take on this project."

Isabelle felt her jaw go slack. "You're serious."

"You're more famous than you think."

"Where is it?"

"Brussels. Just outside the city, actually."

Isabelle sat back with a thump. "Oh."

"You'll need to travel."

A dozen reasons why she couldn't sprung to mind. "I—"

"Don't say no. Just think about it." Emilie was watching her. "Luc has agreed to help out Mom and Dad if they need it in the time that we'd be gone. He also seemed pretty keen for the opportunity to run the château without either of us meddling. Something about installing tiki huts and umbrella bars in the back."

"What?"

"He was joking."

"No, that's not what I meant—"

"I asked him for help, Izz. He was happy to." Emilie paused. "Also, for the record, he thinks you should go to Brussels."

"Why does he get a say in where I should or shouldn't go?"

"Because he thinks that you are very good at what you do. And also, I'm pretty sure he's in love with you."

"I am." The words were out before she could reconsider.

Emilie blinked. "You're sure he's in love with you?"

"No. Yes." Isabelle took a deep breath. "He already told me that."

Her sister's jaw dropped. "What? When?"

Isabelle waved her hand impatiently. "It doesn't matter—"

"It doesn't matter?" Emilie shrieked. "Have you lost your damn mind—"

"That's not what I'm trying to tell you. What I'm trying to tell you is that I'm in love with Luc." The confession spilled out, and with it, an effervescent joy that made Isabelle laugh with a giddy abandon. "I'm in love with Luc Legassé," she repeated.

Emilie's mouth snapped shut. Then opened. Then shut again.

Without warning, she hugged Isabelle. "I'm so happy for you. For both of you." Her eyes were shining. "My God, he's good at keeping secrets. He said nothing all summer."

"Umm." Isabelle cleared her throat. "I haven't actually told him that I'm in love with him. You're the first person I've told."

"Well, I thank you for your confidence," she said. "But what the hell are you waiting for?"

"I think I need to pack," Isabelle said slowly.

"What?"

"He asked me to go to Bora-Bora. Or Bali."

"What?" Emilie screeched. "And you didn't say yes? Again, have you lost your damn mind?"

Isabelle shook her head. "No. I think I've finally found it. It's just...taken awhile."

"Then go." Emilie waved her tablet at Isabelle. "Go and tell him. What are you still doing in this garden with me?" She grinned. "And you should ask him out to dinner. Immediately. The Briar Rose would be my suggestion. The two of you could talk history and mortar and legends and wainscoting all night long. Well, maybe not all night. I would definitely recommend at least an hour or two of no talking—"

"Stop." Isabelle could feel the heat in her cheeks as keenly as she felt the butterflies in her chest. "I will tell him. When I'm done talking with my sister."

"So are you saying yes?"

"To which part? Your arrangement of my career or your arrangement of my love life?"

"Both."

Isabelle laughed, happiness fizzing through her. "Yes," she said, "to the first part. I would love to work on another project with my sister."

"Good." Emilie looked smug.

"And yes to the second part."

"Good," Emilie said again. "You deserve a happy-ever-after."

"So do you."

"I think I had my chance."

Isabelle reached for the book in Emilie's lap and put it in her own. She smoothed her hand over the drawing of the two warrior princesses on their griffins. "There are lots of happy-ever-afters," she said. "Not all of them require a handsome prince. Sometimes they require only a best friend."

"Like a sister?"

"Like a sister." Isabelle looked up. "And nowhere in any story does it say that happy-ever-after won't have a few hardships along the way." She closed the book. "Perhaps we can dedicate the garden to Great-Gran. It was she who brought us here after all. It was her stories that made this place come alive and made us a team again. It was she who made us believe in happy-ever-afters in the first place."

"Do you think that she truly found hers?" Emilie nudged the edge of the book. "Even after the war?"

"I'd like to think so. She had a family she adored. She had an extraordinary career. And she had her art and her writing." Isabelle ran her fingers first over the title embossed on the cover, *The Garden of Lost Secrets*, and then her name, *Dr. Stasia Navarre*. "She survived, and despite what the war might have cost her, she gave us our future."

Emilie got to her feet and held out her hand. "Shall we go find out what that might yet be?" she asked.

Isabelle smiled and reached for her sister's hand. "Yes."

ACKNOWLEDGEMENTS

First and foremost, I would like to thank everyone who has chosen one of my books to read. Without readers, no story can come to life, and I am grateful for all the support and opportunity.

A heartfelt thanks to my family, who have always been my biggest cheerleaders.

My sincere thanks to my editor, Alex Logan, who unerringly finds the missing pieces in each story and makes the editorial process incredibly rewarding. Every author should be so fortunate. And to the entire team at Forever who work tirelessly on my behalf, each book is a team effort, and I am thankful for all you do.

To my agent, Stefanie Lieberman, who has believed in me from the first—thank you for your continued and invaluable advice, honesty, and support.

ABOUT THE AUTHOR

Award-winning author **Kelly Bowen** grew up in Manitoba, Canada, and attended the University of Manitoba, where she earned bachelor of science and master of science degrees in veterinary studies. She worked as a research scientist before realizing her dream to be a writer of historical fiction. When she is not writing, she seizes every opportunity to explore ruins and battlefields. Currently, Kelly lives in Winnipeg with her husband and two sons.

Learn more at:
www.KellyBowen.net
Twitter @KellyBowen09
Facebook.com/AuthorKellyBowen

READING GROUP GUIDE

 YOUR BOOK CLUB RESOURCE

AUTHOR'S NOTE

When I sit down to write a story set during a war, one of the most important things that I focus on is finding and researching the real stories of those who lived through it. Those who faced tragedy and hardship with courage and resilience, survived, and emerged on the other side as heroes, whether they wished to be recognized as that or not.

And it is so very important that these heroes' stories are not forgotten, including the unspeakable cruelties and unimaginable brutalities that should never be repeated. As an author, it is often tempting to gloss over or soften the trauma and devastating details of their experiences because evil on such a scale is often difficult to understand, much less write about. Yet, as I read memoirs and listened to interviews by these real-life heroes and heroines who possessed the courage to relive and recount their terrible experiences in an effort to preserve history, I felt that to be any less accurate as an author would do them a great disservice.

Acts of inhumane cruelty committed against babies, children, men, and women, whether at the hands of an Einsatzgruppen unit or a single Nazi soldier, have been carefully documented. In this novel, I included some of them, as told by those women whose lives inspired this story in the first place. Truus Oversteegen's account of the murder of a small baby in her memoirs is real, and the tragedy had a profound, lasting impact on her, as did witnessing the execution of civilian hostages in retaliation for the death of a Nazi inspector.

George Santayana is credited with saying, "Those who cannot remember the past are condemned to repeat it." These words have been paraphrased and reiterated by many, yet they remain no less veracious and relevant as time marches on—perhaps even more so. It is my belief that history cannot be divided and sorted into palatable and unpalatable columns for selective consumption by modern audiences but must be presented as a whole. In this novel, I have endeavored to represent the entirety of history.

DISCUSSION QUESTIONS

1. Female friendship is an important theme in *The Garden of Lost Secrets*. We see the friendship between Stasia and Margot in the historical time period and sisters Isabelle and Emilie in the current day. How does each friendship grow and change over the course of events? Is a friendship between sisters easier or more difficult because they are family?

2. Over the course of the story, Stasia transforms into Briar Rose. What do you consider the major events of the war that cause this change? The young Stasia who we see before the war is very different from the older Stasia seen through Nicolas's eyes in 1944. How and when did you see the young Stasia begin to change? What was the catalyst of those changes?

3. The Château de Montessaire also transforms during the course of the story, from the glamour of the comte and his family before the Franco-Prussian War, to abandonment and neglect while Nicolas is staying in the garden shed, to the bleak reality of the Nazi occupation, and finally to the restoration

of its former glory by Stasia's great-granddaughters. During which of these periods was the appearance of the château most vivid in your mind? What features of the château did you imagine as being the most beautiful?

4. Reading about the atrocities of war can be difficult. Was there one event from WWII that you found more harrowing than the others? Why do you think the author chose to include it? What do you think the author hoped her readers would take away from this reading experience? Do you think that the way modern media often reports on recurring violence shields audiences or overexposes us to the reality?

5. The sinking of the battleship *Bretagne* is based on real-life events. Did you already know this history or did you learn about it here? There are many impactful events from WWII. Did you learn of any others for the first time in this book?

6. The château has a sad history. Isabelle discovers that the Comte de Cossé returned from the Franco-Prussian War and killed his daughter in a murder-suicide. Both Stasia and Nicolas have mental as well as physical wounds from WWII, and both had family members who struggled with the same from WWI. How do they help each other heal? How is PTSD handled in their time as compared to now?

7. Throughout the book, Stasia finds many ways to support the Resistance. Discuss the different actions she took. Which of them did you find to be most useful? Most touching? Most shocking?

8. Nicolas takes a more traditional path to fighting the Nazis. Were you surprised when he joined the navy? Do you think that he contributes more to the war effort than Stasia?

9. What makes Briar Rose so successful as a Resistance fighter? Discuss the different actions she took throughout the story. Which did you find most useful? Most touching? Most shocking? Would you be a successful Resistance fighter? What useful skills do you possess?

10. The château's garden inspires Stasia's stories and illustrations. How are you inspired by nature? Do you prefer a formal, manicured garden or a more natural, overgrown garden?

11. Stasia's stories help Isabelle and Emilie to continue to feel close to their great-grandmother after she is gone. How do you think you would react if you found out a beloved family member was both a murderer and a war hero?

12. Stasia believes that Nicolas has died. And Nicolas believes that Stasia has died. In the moment that they reunite, how intense were the emotions that you felt? Was it the most emotional moment in the book for you? If not, what was?

13. Isabelle's relationship with Luc is complicated. Was there ever a time when you didn't agree with a choice she made with regard to Luc? When and why?

14. If you had to come up with a lesson or moral to each

character's story—Stasia, Nicolas, Isabelle, Emilie, and Luc—
what would it be and why?

15. Did you cry while reading this book? Which scene moved
   you the most? Which character's fate would you say was the
   most tragic? What will you remember the most about *The
   Garden of Lost Secrets*?

HISTORICAL NOTE

The Garden of Lost Secrets is a work of fiction and purely a product of my imagination. However, it is framed around real events and inspired by real people. The initial inspiration for this novel and the character of Stasia developed after I read Sophie Poldermans's nonfiction biographical account of Jannetje Johanna (Hannie) Schaft and Truus and Freddie Oversteegen, all of whom were Dutch Resistance fighters during the occupation of the Netherlands. Poldermans's book, titled *Seducing and Killing Nazis*, details exactly that—and the horrifying events that shaped these women's lives and turned them into lethal Resistance fighters. Learning all that they faced and endured during the occupation was humbling and stayed with me long after I finished the last page.

Many of the fictional events that my character of Stasia encounters were directly inspired by the shocking, all-too-real experiences of Hannie Schaft and the Oversteegen sisters. Their stories, like those of so many others who fought so bravely during the occupation, left me with questions: How does one rebuild a life and continue on when the war is over? How does one move past the cruelty and atrocities and retain hope for the future? The only thing that I am certain of is that there is no single answer to these questions.

When one references the occupation in the Netherlands, it is often connected with the well-known story of Anne Frank, whose diary was first published in 1947. Anne and her family had fled Germany for Amsterdam in 1934, hoping to find safety. Unfortunately, Anne's tragic fate at Bergen-Belsen was all too common—of the 140,000 Jewish people living in the Netherlands prior to WWII, approximately 107,000 were deported to the eastern Nazi camps. Of those, 102,000 were either murdered outright or worked to death. This was the highest mortality rate for Jewish populations of all the occupied Western European countries.

Among the Dutch citizens who resisted the Nazi occupiers by hiding Jewish people was the ten Boom family, Caspar and his two daughters, Corrie and Betsie. The ten Booms ran a watchmaking business (Corrie became the first licenced female watchmaker in Holland), and they lived above their shop at Barteljorisstraat 19, near Grote Markt in Haarlem. In 1941, the ten Boom family's home became part of the underground for Jewish refugees fleeing the war. By 1943, the family was secretly sheltering Jewish people in their home, which they had renovated to include a secret hiding space behind a false wall in Corrie's bedroom, capable of concealing up to six people. It is this space to which Stasia flees in my story, and she finds the kindness and help that Corrie ten Boom believed in wholeheartedly. On 28 February 1944, the entire ten Boom family was arrested by the Gestapo. Caspar died ten days later in prison, and Corrie and Betsie were transferred to Ravensbrück. Betsie died in the camp but Corrie survived and was released. The ten Boom house and its history have been preserved, along with its hiding place, and can be visited today.

The fall of the Netherlands to Germany was marked by the

bombing of Rotterdam on 14 May 1940, often referred to as the Rotterdam Blitz. Initial reported casualty records estimated that 30,000 people had been killed—that number was later revised to approximately 900, with 85,000 left homeless. At the time of the bombing, the Dutch and the German commanders were in negotiations for the surrender of the city, and the Luftwaffe had been ordered to remain on standby pending further talks. However, the message was not passed on to the pilots, and two groups of Luftwaffe bombers initiated their flight toward the city—one from the south and one from the northeast. In the German-occupied south part of the city, the Wehrmacht fired red flares, aborting the bombing mission for those planes coming from the south. In the north, where the Wehrmacht had not been able to gain a foothold, no flares were fired. Just over 1,300 bombs were dropped by the Luftwaffe, and the residential area of Kralingen and almost the entire medieval city center of Rotterdam were destroyed. The fires started by the bombs spread uncontrollably over the next days, destroying 642 acres of the city center, almost 25,000 homes, and over 3,000 structures including stores, schools, churches, and warehouses. The Germans threatened to bomb the city of Utrecht next, and without significant means to combat the Nazi forces, the Dutch command surrendered.

The attack of the French fleet by the British Navy on 3 July 1940, as part of Operation Catapult, in what was formerly French Algeria, is a real piece of history that is still contentiously debated today. The British, afraid that the French fleet at Mers-el-Kébir would fall into Axis hands, issued an ultimatum to French Admiral Gensoul: Either sail under British command; sail with reduced crews to a British port; sail with a reduced crew to a French port in the West Indies or the United States, where the ships would be demilitarized; or face destruction by whatever force necessary to prevent the ships from falling into German hands.

British Admiral James Somerville was ordered to present this ultimatum to Admiral Gensoul. However, it was British Captain Cedric Holland, who spoke fluent French, who delivered the message to the French admiral. Gensoul was insulted that such a negotiation was being delivered by a mere captain and sent his own lieutenant to parley. This led to a great deal of confusion and delay, and ultimately the French Navy Minister, Admiral Darlan, never received the entirety of the British ultimatum, including the option of removing the fleet to the West Indies. When it became clear that negotiations were going nowhere, the British opened fire.

The attack resulted in the deaths of 1,297 French servicemen, 977 of those aboard the *Bretagne*, which capsized and sank. The battleships *Provence* and *Dunkerque* were damaged and run aground while the *Strasbourg* escaped the harbour with four destroyers. The salvaged *Dunkerque* and *Strasbourg* were later scuttled by the French in November of 1942 when the Germans attempted to capture what remained of the French fleet in Toulon, leading many to maintain that the destruction of the fleet by the British in Algeria had been unnecessary. Other historians maintain that it demonstrated the ruthless resolve of the British to fight the Nazi forces by any and all means, especially to the Americans who, despite Churchill's entreaties, had thus far refused to enter the war. Ironically, it was the destruction of the American fleet at Pearl Harbor that would tip the scales and finally engage the US.

Following the destruction of the French fleet in my story, Nicolas joins the Free French forces and remains in Africa, fighting under the command of real-life Brigadier General Marie-Pierre

Koenig. This was a diverse assembly of troops, including French Marines, Foreign Legionnaires (including many refugees from occupied European countries), and troops from Senegal, Madagascar, and what is now Central Africa. These men and women defended the old fortress at Bir Hakeim against overwhelming odds from the combined Italian and German forces commanded by Nazi General Erwin Rommel.

Though the fortress eventually fell to the Germans, the Allies achieved a vital, strategic victory in delaying the advancing German troops. When it became clear that the fall of the fort was imminent, the French forces retreated, fighting their way out in hand-to-hand combat. Incredibly, the majority of the surviving garrison made it to safety, and General Koenig was driven out of the fortress by Susan Travers, an English ambulance driver. The British, given valuable time to prepare their defences, would later defeat Rommel and turn the tide of the war in Africa.

The Jedburgh teams that Nicolas becomes a part of were also real. Operation Jedburgh saw teams of three men, including SOE, OSS, and Dutch, Belgian, and French officers, dropped into France, Belgium, and the Netherlands. Each Jed team generally consisted of a chief (or commander), an executive officer, and a radio operator. They all received elite commando and subterfuge training. The female agent that Nicolas unexpectedly meets in his room in Scotland was, in part, inspired by the real experience of William B. Dreux (OSS), who chronicles a similar experience in his biographical military history, *No Bridges Blown*.

The Jeds' key objectives were to assist local Resistance operations and carry out varied military missions. France was one of the most important objectives, with ninety-three different Jed teams inserted into the country from the night of 5–6 June 1944 through September 1944.

The telephone and communication hub that I describe in a château just outside Rouen is completely fictional but modelled on any number of real military communication centers. Both the Axis and Allied militaries used varied wired and non-wired (radio) communication modes throughout the war. The requirement for communication between homelands and distant front lines spurred the need for improved long-range overseas communication systems. Research and development of all communication technology increased dramatically, including that of the high-capacity telephone switchboards needed to coordinate the movements of highly mobile field units.

FURTHER READING

Colbert, David. *Ten Days: Anne Frank*. (Simon & Schuster, 2008).

Dreux, William. *No Bridges Blown: The OSS Jedburghs in Nazi-Occupied France*. (University of Notre Dame Press, 1971).

Gies, Miep and Alison Leslie Gold. *Anne Frank Remembered: The Story of the Woman Who Helped Hide the Frank Family*. (Simon & Schuster, 2009).

Irwin, Will. *The Jedburghs: The Secret History of the Allied Special Forces, France 1944*. (Perseus Book Groups, 2005).

Jones, Benjamin. *Eisenhower's Guerrillas: The Jedburghs, the Maquis, and the Liberation of France*. (Oxford University Press, 2016).

Lornier, Dominique. *Mers-el-Kebir, Juillet 1940*. (Calmann–Levy Press, 2007).

Melton, George. *From Versailles to Mers-el-Kebir: The Promise of Anglo-French Naval Cooperation, 1919–1940*. (Naval Institute Press, 2015).

Menger, Truus. *Not Then, Not Now, Not Ever*. 8th ed. (Netherlaad Tolerantin, 1998).

Moore, Bob. *Victims & Survivors: The Nazi Persecution of the Jews in the Netherlands 1940–1945*. (St. Martin's Press, 1997).

Poldermans, Sophie. *Seducing and Killing Nazis: Hannie, Truus, and Freddie: Dutch Resistance Heroines of WWII*. (SWW Press, 2019).

Sommerville, Donald. *World War II: Day by Day*. (Bison Books, 1989).

Wouters, Nico. *Mayoral Collaboration Under Nazi Occupation in Belgium, the Netherlands, and France*. (Palgrave Macmillan, 2016).

YOUR
BOOK
CLUB
RESOURCE

VISIT
GCPClubCar.com

to sign up for the **GCP Club Car** newsletter, featuring exclusive promotions, info on other **Club Car** titles, and more.

 @grandcentralpub

 @grandcentralpub

 @grandcentralpub